BLEED THE STARS

Book Three of Devour the Stars

R Coots

Arts Eklektos

CAMBRIDGE, MN

R Coots

Arts Eklektos
PO Box 70
Cambridge, MN 55008
www.artseklektos.com

Book Layout © 2017 BookDesignTemplates.com

Bleed the Stars/ R Coots. -- 1st ed.
978-1-7336359-6-7

To those at the store, for all their encouragement

Contents

> What Came Before

TO RECAP

Since there's been a bit of time between *Devour the Stars*, *Star Roads*, and this book, both in real life and in the story, I thought a refresher was in order. If you'd like to skip this, of course, you are perfectly free to do so.

First, where are we? Somewhere far, far from Earth. Travel between solar systems happens via a system of interconnected space gates known as Barbicans. The destinations of each gate are locked and limited in number.

The Navlad Empire controls a significant number of these Barbicans. Hundreds of solar systems, thousands of planets and space stations. But about three hundred years ago, the Empire started crumbling from the inside out.

Why? Well, Jossalyn and Delfi, a pair of soul-bonded ESPs (or sai) fled the Imperial harem. The sousi (or soul-sib) couple found safe passage on board a merchanter ship called the *Skatasi op Essie*. Eventually, they married the captain and navigator, respectively.

But the Emperor wanted them back, so he hounded the ship and its crew across the Empire and beyond its borders, abandoning most of his duties in the process. In a last-ditch effort to lose their pursuers, the crew of the *Skatasi* came up with a plan. They found an abandoned solar system, cobbled together a pair of cryo caskets, and left Jossa and Delfi asleep while the ship tried to draw off the hunters.

What none of them knew was that the system where the two women were hidden had been emptied on purpose so it and its

Barbican could serve as tripwires in the network that would eventually be known as Hadra's Net.

The network wasn't put in place for show, or even on the off chance that any of the systems beyond the Imperial borders would decide to attack. It was meant to defend against a very specific enemy, one the Empire had been watching advance on its borders for over a hundred years. And for over a hundred years, nothing had been able to stop it. It swallowed up system after system, locking Barbican after Barbican so only its ships could use them. The enemy came from all directions, splitting up as paths diverged through the Barbicans, homing in on the network's original gates in the center of the Empire. To the Imperials, they are the Svis Konanuog, or Star Eaters.

The oncoming enemy calls itself the Kuchen Fleet, or simply, the Fleet. It is ruled only by those strong and smart enough to stay in control. Roughly four years ago, its principal armada came under Syrus's leadership after he infiltrated the flagship and beat the former warlord to death.

Syrus is what's known as a nehkeh, or Savage, in the Empire. Born in the gutter and seen as less than human, he is one of the rarest of rare: a *man* with sai abilities. This brought him to the attention of the local nobility, who took him in as a guard for their sai daughter, Rissa, and *her* sousi, Onika.

Once their daughter was old enough that keeping Syrus around became a risk to her virtue, the family sold him to the Karukap, the Imperial military. After a number of years in service, he managed to escape, retrieve Rissa from her husband, and make his way past the borders. Rissa's husband eventually caught up with them and managed to take Rissa back, just in time for the Fleet to arrive in his system. By the time Syrus got there, the planned rescue turned into vengeance on the Fleet warlord who killed her. In the aftermath, Syrus found himself made warlord and driven to hide everything that made him unique lest his newfound underlings lynch him instead of obeying orders.

This brings us, almost, to the present. Just over a year ago, the Fleet entered the system where Jossa and Delfi were hidden. Finding only one energy signal in the whole place, Syrus took a team down to investigate. He wound up returning to the Fleet with two unconscious women as cargo. The arrival of a second branch of the Fleet cut short any further investigation.

The second warlord, Kizen, was distinctly *unhappy* to find an Imperial in charge of the main armada. Spurred on by politics, Syrus declared a faster-than-usual attack on the next solar system, and the two foundling women were left in his private infirmary to wake up in their own time. Meanwhile, Syrus discovered that touching their bare skin set off alarm bells in the nanites present in both his bodies and theirs. On top of being a man with sai, he is also a descendant of the last legitimate emperor.

The list of things Syrus had to hide just kept growing.

But he had more immediate problems. The latest target of the combined Fleet offered more resistance than expected. Worse, it was a dead end in the Barbican network. Suspicions aroused and not entirely sure where they were in relation to the Imperial border, Syrus sent out scouts and grilled Jossa after she woke up. He also got her to tell him how to turn off the light show her nanites performed every time he touched her. Delfi remained asleep for the time being.

The discovery of a hidden Barbican and a base guarding it coincided with the disastrous consequences of Syrus inducting Jossa into the harem for real, a formal banquet, and Delfi's awakening. By the time the metaphorical dust settled, Syrus was on his way to the shadow base in an Imperial ship, planning to use his old military credentials to gain access to the keys that would allow the Fleet to pass through the hidden Barbican before the Karukap could scramble its own ships or implode the gateway. He brought Jossa and Delfi along to solidify his cover.

The plan went as well as could be expected for the end of a book. Back on the Fleet, Kizen staged a coup, set out after Syrus, and stormed the base just as the trio stepped off the ship into the landing bay. What followed involved an empty room, a group of cannon-fodder Fleet soldiers, and a small eternity of physical and mental torture.

Delfi lost control of Jossa's emotions.

Jossa, unable to rein in her abilities, lost herself to anger and despair, driving everyone in the room mad.

Only when she was on the verge of collapse could Syrus scrape enough sanity together to remember how to fake a sai bond, having learned from the pair he guarded in childhood. He broke free of his restraints, pulled the last living Fleet soldiers off of Delfi, and finally managed to calm Jossa enough to get her to stop emanating despair.

Once everyone was gathered up, they got out of there. They found Kizen in the infirmary, which had been shielded against Jossa's sai. Syrus took care of the other warlord, they put Delfi in a medunit to heal her injuries, and Jossa snuck off. She took a scrap of cloth covered in Syrus's blood with her.

Syrus tracked her down. She told him that she and Delfi would die before they'd go back to being toys in his harem. With his blood, she could open any Barbican in the Empire.

Syrus decided that, given how spectacularly fubar things had gone since Kizen's branch of the Fleet showed up, he was less than enthused about going back himself. It was only a matter of time before someone figured out he had sai. If that didn't get him killed, his second-in-command would lock him up, so there'd be someone to legitimize a claim to the Imperial throne in the eyes of the populace. Taking all that into consideration, Syrus decided to go with the girls. He got the keys to the Barbican, handed them over to his second as promised, and got out of there.

Jossa was less than happy that he'd hijacked her escape, but they managed to strike a deal: He guides the girls across the Empire, helping them acclimate to three hundred years of cultural drift. They crew for him, don't try to kill him. And at the end, he'll leave them in the Gatekeepers' solar system. With only two Barbicans that touch the

Empire, they're the only people Syrus could think of with even a hope of holding out against the Fleet.

That was just over a year ago. Now, finally, they have arrived in the last solar system between the Empire and the Gatekeepers. Safety is just a step away. So long as they can take that step.

If, at the end, you decide you want more, feel free to join my mailing list: https://www.artseklektos.com/ml-landingpage/
There'll you'll find the occasional short story to expand on the world, art, bits of world building, and odd rant about the math of space travel (math, ew).

PROLOGUE -- DELFI

*Who bonds with whom is out of our control. What we can
do is help the bondmates grow together. Above all things,
they must be in balance. Catastrophe is a mild word for
what happens if they aren't.*
   - Karukap Mistress of Sai to aides

Delfi sat on the bed, the cool metal of the wall at her back doing little
to counteract the fire running through her veins. She'd snarled her
fingers in the tassels along her blanket on purpose, trapping her
traitorous limbs in some semblance of obedience. It didn't help much.
She was too aware of what Jossa was doing with Syrus in his bunk. It
wasn't just Jossa's lust bleeding into the soul bond between her and her
sister. It was siphoning both, bouncing the emotions off each other in
a feverish crescendo that reverberated through her brain until she had
almost nothing left to combat its effects.

   It took most of her willpower to keep up the siphon on the bond. It
took everything *else* to keep from shifting her legs together. She should
keep them apart. Keep them still. But that way lay screaming fear and
too much in the way of memories.

   She couldn't afford to let the terror win. If she did, if she let her
emotions backwash into the soul bond, then they could all die. For all
it would be a blessing to cut short what Jossa was feeling right now,

her sister's reaction to the terror would be beyond dangerous. As close as Syrus was with Jossa, he'd pick up on it immediately. Once he Felt the great gnawing monster that lurked around the edges of Delfi's heart, things would be all over.

Desire gone. Lust unslaked. Beckoning heat vanishing into acid pain. Soft petals melting as the piercing agony of thorns drove ever deeper.

Only the fact that they were floating in space, three million miles from anyone, would save lives. Well, lives other than their own. She didn't like the odds of them surviving the results of a nehkeh and a projective Feel being overcome with fear. Especially since the nehkeh was a Feel himself. And being nehkeh, he reacted to almost any overwhelming emotion by getting immediately, furiously angry.

Delfi couldn't afford to simply suck Jossa dry either. Not the way she had that day over three hundred years ago, just before Rui and Denz put them in the cryo coffins. If she did, she might put Syrus into a catatonia the same way she could Jossa. Who knew when, or if, they'd recover—or how Syrus would react when he realized what she could do to him via Jossa?

Over in his bunk, he dragged demanding fingers from Jossa's collarbone to hip, squeezing when he reached his goal, snugging her pelvis closer to his. Jossa arched into him. Heat ricocheted down the bond, carrying the sensations—*all* of them—straight to Delfi. She gasped, then whimpered as she curled in on herself, clutching tighter to the blanket.

No. No, don't do it. This is your purpose in life. You failed her once already, getting distracted and losing control. She nearly killed all of you because of it. You have to be the strong one. The anchor to reality that drags them both back.

Focusing on the pattern of rivets in the ceiling above her, Delfi hauled on the lust, bracing herself against the sensation of rose petals and thorns that teased and tore at her mind as they ripped through the bond. Down, down, down, she carried them. To the bottomless hole in the core of her being that swallowed emotions the same way Barbicans swallowed ships.

Except a ship exited a Barbican, emerging somewhere else in space. As far as Delfi knew, the feelings she drew from Jossa, and sometimes Syrus, went nowhere. They simply vanished into the vast emptiness rooted in her soul.

A tear trickled down her cheek. She gulped down a sob and built another wall around her insecurities. Another barrier, keeping the paralyzing memories from crossing over in the backwash of the siphon. She would not poison her sister's heart. She *wouldn't*.

Jossa thought she was helping. She'd gotten it in her head that Syrus had designs on Delfi, and nothing would convince her otherwise. Delfi had tried. So many times. Her sister, beloved and unable to control her sai without help, would not listen. No matter how Delfi railed, ranted, or begged.

She'd given up trying to convince Syrus to quit bending Jossa over any available surface. Leaving a note on his screen, where he couldn't ignore it, was a nonstarter. Trying to force actual sentences from her mind to her fingers on the keys tripped some alarm in the language center of her brain. She spent more time trying to unravel the garbled mess of He'la words in phonetic Navlad than she did actually typing.

Using a stylus for handwriting was out as well. Her scribbles ended up pure He'la glyphs, not a trace of her birth tongue to be found. By the time she hit on the idea of using computer code as a sort of back door to the words—because, for whatever Ancestors-blessed reason, she could actually work the alphanumeric coding language—she was so frustrated that she botched the message anyways. The final message amounted to little more than 'Stop mounting my sister!' in such a mess of High and low Navlad that she was amazed any of it was legible at all.

It wasn't remotely convincing and said nothing at all about her struggles to control them as they self-combusted with lust, but she'd hit the send key before she thought about that part.

Syrus showed it to her when he found it, humor crinkling the corners of his eyes, and told her that from now on, one of her jobs as crew involved monitoring the ship's computers for fissures in the code. Two sets of eyes, two heads, and so on. Not a word about the content of the message.

Vocal speech was even worse than written. Delfi couldn't back up and delete the sounds coming out of her mouth. Ancestors, she couldn't even make her tongue shape Navlad words. The one time she was able to make him understand what she said, he reminded her that she'd get them all caught or killed if she used the language of the Foreseers where others could hear. Then, while she sputtered at the truth of it, he told her that if she hadn't been sneaking into his bunk at night, he wouldn't have had to carry her back to her own bed and get caught by Jossa.

He was right. She hated acknowledging the truth of what he said. She was the cause of her own pain. From her failure to control Jossa's emotions on the shadow base to her botched attempts at getting past his internal shields.

If she hadn't been looking for proof that he'd betray them... If she hadn't been digging through his dreams, looking for the truth of his memories of two women, one living and one dead, tangled in a heap on a blood-soaked mattress, she wouldn't have ended up here. If she hadn't tried to make it easier to penetrate his shields by sneaking into his bunk while he slept, he wouldn't have felt her and woken up. She wouldn't have plastered herself to him in a desperate attempt to burrow through his defenses. And Jossa wouldn't have had any evidence for her assumptions as to his intentions.

Even now, months later, Delfi wanted to hang him by his own entrails. To top things off, she'd never gotten so much as a *hint* as to why the mystery women were so important. Not even Jossa blowing his brains, and his mental shields, up via orgasms morning, noon, and night yielded any results. Keeping control of herself and of *them* took too much concentration.

In the other bunk, her sister's nonsensical chanting turned to a hiss of frustration, dragging Delfi back to the present. Jossa's nails dug into Syrus's skin. His answering surge of arousal and amusement gave only the barest of warnings. Focus, girl!

Phantom teeth bit into Delfi's shoulder. She nearly cried. Nearly wept at the remembered pain.

Another man. Not the one between Jossa's legs, but real enough in memory. The guttering rasp of his curses in another language as he pounded into her, tearing, bruising, breaking.

Jossa clawed at Syrus, near mindless and blind now with lust. Delfi tore her hands free of the blanket, biting her knuckles as she rolled to her side and curled into a ball. She wouldn't go for the toy in her nightstand. It didn't help anyway. She'd tried. Once. The failure was compounded by Syrus's reaction when she chucked the thing into the hall and nearly hit him in the head. He'd laughed under his breath before giving it back.

He knew. He knew what she'd tried to do. He knew her function as the stable half of her pairing with Jossa. And he'd *laughed*.

Forget gutting him. She wanted to skin him alive and shove him out into space itself.

Mouths on skin, firm suction on her breast—but not *her* breast. Delfi found herself once again yanked back to the current reality, which was more lust-filled horror than she ever wanted to live through again.

She whimpered, trying to muffle the sob with her hand. *This* was happening *now*. It wasn't a memory. She couldn't hide from it. No matter what she did during the day. No matter what flamboyant costume she wore outside this ship; she was as trapped here and now as she'd been that day on the shadow base.

Slip, slide. Grind. Pants and gasps and growls. Hands on breasts and teeth on the neck. Tabs and slots lining up. Slick heat and frictionless penetration. A single unit, lost in the moment. Delfi felt Jossa and Syrus's internal shields disintegrate, the last vestiges of whatever control they had over themselves lost to the stars. Keening aloud, she grabbed with both mental hands and dragged the excess emotion through the bond, stuffing it down, down, down into the emptiness at her core. Into the nothingness of her soul.

It was her duty.

She would not fail again.

One--Jossa

We had to separate the empaths. They were creating feedback loops of emotion. We barely got to the last pair before they self-destructed.
   - observations, Professor Rusithe, New Hopks College of Medicine

Jossa clawed her way free of the sheets in a semi-coordinated thrash of arms, legs, and snarled hair. Grumbling to herself about the inconsiderate *achek* who liked to wrap her up like a street vendor's roll, she finally managed to kick her feet free and swing her legs over the edge of the mattress.

She froze and ran the sequence of events through her head. Thrashing with no resistance or complaints from her bed partner. Being able to get straight out of bed instead of having to swim over half the mattress. No huge hands dragging her back.

Relief and frustration churned through her in equal measure. Syrus was already awake, gone long enough for her to have worked her way over to his side of the mattress as she slept. Safe for now then, thank the Ancestors. She could get up, ready herself for the day, and not find herself back in the throes of a sex-charged fever dream. A dream that was all too real.

She still wished he'd woken her when he'd gotten up. Rare was the morning he didn't claim his half of the deal from her. Which meant that they'd finally, *finally* gotten clearance to dock at the Kallura lis Kerute, the last base available before a ship smacked into the Gatekeepers' Barbican. She would rather be awake and prepared by the time the tug finished bringing them in than be caught half naked and filthy by a customs inspector.

Jossa shuddered, worked her arms out of their cocoon, and stood. With a hop and a shimmy of her hips, she won free of the sheets. She wrinkled her nose. Time to do laundry again. Three days of use, and the stench of sweat and dried body fluids was too much to bear. The pheromones alone would be enough to knock an aethermoose flat into rut.

How exactly had she managed to get herself into a situation where she was doing laundry every three days for the express purpose of keeping a mattress covered?

::You offered.:: Delfi's mental voice was sullen.

Jossa opened her mouth to snap back, entirely on reflex, then thought better of it. Delfi was right, curse it.

Delfi harrumphed and gave her a mental nudge, emotionless and dry. Jossa hid her wince at the lack. Time was, Delfi'd let Jossa know everything she felt. Now she closed herself off more often than not, her thoughts and feelings both opaque.

If Jossa could bring the men who'd raped Delfi back to life and kill them again, slowly, she'd do it and dance for joy.

::I'd dance with you.:: Delfi flashed mental teeth. ::But wishes aren't stardust, and the laundry won't get done any faster for you standing there letting his come dry on your legs.::

::Delfi!:: Jossa snatched for the sheets, tripped over a pillow, and landed back on the mattress. ::That's crude.::

::It's also true. You stink. Even the Savage is better about cleaning up before starting the day.:: And then Delfi was gone, the mind bond closed down to the narrowest possible thread as she went back to whatever she was doing before Jossa had woken. She did it gently, but the pain still reverberated through Jossa's skull.

After taking a couple breaths to adjust to the change, Jossa looked down at her bare legs and sighed. She hated how often Delfi was right.

>>><<<

She showered, sent a prayer to the Ancestors for proper baths on the other side of the Gatekeepers' Barbican, and went about her chores. Only to discover that the laundry cycle wouldn't start until she'd confirmed the water levels in the tanks. Jossa scraped her wet hair back into a ponytail and headed to the lower deck.

Muffled cursing and a series of dull thuds pulled her attention to the starboard side of the cargo hold. Frowning, Jossa wove her way through the stacks of crates and piles of assorted junk. A crate by her head rocked as she neared the location of the mutters. She jumped back, bracing herself against the stack opposite the moving pile.

The metal box, evidently not so heavy as it looked, dropped back down to level and then slid away. Jossa shook her head and walked around to the other side of the stack. "A little warning would be nice," she said.

Syrus grunted at her as he lowered the crate to a sled hovering near his knees and turned back to the pile. He looked like he might explode into violence the minute someone sneezed at him. Jossa hoped he wouldn't crack the screen he'd picked up. It was the only one they had set up to handle the manifests.

She couldn't feel it, of course. He kept up nigh-impenetrable internal shields. As strong or stronger than the external ones Delfi held over Jossa's mind. He might slip them here and there to provoke a reaction, but rarely did he drop them unless he needed to. That was good, all things considered. Syrus lived in a state of near-constant rage. If Jossa had to Feel it day in and day out, she'd go mad, even with Delfi's help.

::Or unless you blow his brains out with an orgasm,:: Delfi put in helpfully.

Jossa felt her face go hot. Syrus stopped scanning the next crate and raised an eyebrow at her in question, which did nothing to mitigate the murderous scowl on his face.

She turned away. ::Delfi! Please *stop* rubbing my nose in it. I can't help it. He can't help it. I do my best to keep it from getting...:: She trailed off, unsure of how to explain herself. So instead, she shoved frustration and anger down the bond. ::Besides, if you're going to lock me out of your head, you should let me think to myself without an Ancestors-cursed audience.::

Delfi sent the impression of munching on crispy fried snacks at a festival as she propped her boots up on the table.

Jossa growled.

"Move," Syrus snarled. Jossa yelped and jumped, coming down to face him, hands reaching for weapons she hadn't yet clipped to her belt.

White teeth flashed against dark tan skin. Syrus took her by the shoulders and shifted her to the side.

More munching of crispy snacks, complete with crunching noises, came down the mind bond. But Delfi also siphoned off the worst of the panic and frustration.

"What are you doing?" Jossa asked once she'd gotten hold of her reactions.

"Sorting," he replied.

Jossa managed not to roll her eyes or cross her arms or tap her foot while she waited for him to quit playing around and answer her in truth.

Three more crates thudded onto the sled. Two found homes in other stacks.

"Got an updated set of orders from customs." Syrus scanned the last crate with the intake port of the screen, then picked it up. "Half this shit ain't legal on the base."

"Oh. We're worried about legal now?" Three quarters of their cargo as free merchants wasn't legal to start with. The rest, well. Manifests might say one thing. What was actually in the crates could be something else entirely.

He gave her a flat look and took hold of the sled's handle. "Out of the way."

She stepped aside. He stalked past her, dragging the sled behind him. "So why the last-minute changes?" she asked as she followed him down the aisle towards the aft cargo hold.

He lifted one shoulder in a shrug, answering without looking back at her. "Probably to put us off kilter. Not give us a chance to get everything hidden. Either so they can confiscate it or fine us out of a ship." Hard amusement trailed through the air behind him.

It wouldn't work. He'd told her once that before he crossed paths with the Fleet, or Svis Konanuog as they were called in the Empire, he'd run a small merchanter vessel through the Edgeworlds, a region even more vicious than the Empire had become. He knew all the Customs tricks and how to avoid them. Far better than Rui would've.

The *Skatasi op Essi*, the ship she'd lived on before Syrus found her and Delfi frozen in cryo caskets, had been a freighter. Its captain, her husband, had taken illegal cargo on occasion. And turned a blind eye to a good number of mislabeled crates as well. But the world she and Delfi had left behind wasn't nearly so blatant about the cutthroat practices of corrupt base officials. At least, not at the quasi-legal level the crew were operating at when she and her sister first came aboard.

By the end, before the Emperor's hunters caught up with them, things were very different.

Jossa set those memories aside and turned her attention back to the present. "There's no way all of that will fit under the deck plates or in the walls. What will we do when the inspector comes?"

Syrus snorted and threw a black look at her over his shoulder. "Already done." He waved a hand at the stacks of cargo around them. "Most of that is done already. This..." He nodded at the sled and its load. "This is the bribe."

"What!?" Jossa ran to catch up with the sled. "This is our cargo, not yours!"

"Look closer," he growled, though he didn't stop moving.

Jossa trotted up the length of the sled, checking the slips of silplat on the crates. Relief blew through her, followed by a pang of embarrassment.

Humor, wry and twisted, tapped her on the head and vanished. Jossa glared at Syrus, who kept grinning. Stubborn man. He couldn't just answer honestly. Had to tease and play mind games until she was thoroughly wound up. "All right, fine," she said, throwing her hands in the air. "Half of it's yours. Are you sure it will work? They won't go looking for more?"

"Might," he said. He slipped through the open door of the smaller cargo hold. The dark that ruled the tiny room swallowed him completely. Jossa followed in time to hear Syrus say, "All that shit up in your old bunk too. That should—"

Jossa clutched at the door frame. Ancestors preserve her, she was used to it by now. No. It was the fact that she'd completely forgotten she had over a billion credits worth of unmarked goods stacked in her bunk.

Stupid, stupid, stupid, she chanted to herself, spinning on one heel. How could you have forgotten all the trade goods?

Delfi's hand ghosted over Jossa's shoulder in a phantom pat. ::I got it,:: she said. ::While he was moving the big stuff. There's a little bit in there, so they can find *something*.:: Here she gave Jossa an image of her old bunk; stacks of rough wooden crates full of fiber packing material lined the walls, the occasional bit of merchandise showing through the slats. ::Couldn't do much about the boxes. We'll have to leave them there.::

Jossa sagged against a nearby crate. Oh, thank the Ancestors.

::Thank *me*,:: Delfi groused.

::Thank you.:: Jossa reached a mental hand to lace her fingers with Delfi's, then dropped the contact. Her sister was doing something with the control panel on the bridge. Best not to distract her too much.

::I love you too,:: Delfi said. ::We'll be fine.::

Easy for her to say, Jossa thought. But she kept the words to her side of the bond.

"You want something in particular?" Syrus asked as he came up behind her.

Jossa turned to look at him and nearly rammed her nose into his chest. Ok. He was still messing with her.

He caught her as she backed away, one huge hand wrapping around her arm to pull her in closer. Jossa swallowed, trying to shove down the surge of lust that rippled through her body.

Not fast enough. The corner of his mouth quirked up. "Guess that answers that," he said, fitting her hips to his.

The desire rose, crested, and flowed down the mind bond to Delfi before Jossa could do more than drop a hand to his belt. Cold clarity welled up in its place, hard edged as a spacer's knife and twice as sharp.

Jossa jerked away, gasping for breath as hormones fought reason. Syrus followed her for a second, then let go of her arm. He growled deep in his chest. Jossa looked at him and, somehow, managed to arch an eyebrow.

She must have mimicked his expression well enough because the growl cut off, transmuted into a rough laugh. She did *not* blow out the breath she'd been holding. Showing weakness was a good way to find herself pinned up against the crates with his teeth at her neck and—

::You are hopeless,:: Delfi snapped as she tightened the shields around Jossa's mind. ::I take my mind off you for a *second* and you and Mister Morning Wood over there are at it again.::

::Mister Morning *Wood?*::

Jossa wasn't sure if the epithet was a reference to his current randiness or Delfi's way of reminding her that they weren't dealing with someone who obeyed the normal rules of civilized behavior. Although Jossa doubted he'd ever try to take her without her conscious consent again. He'd made that mistake once, just once, the first week or so she'd slept in his bunk. Her traitor body, thinking it was Rui waking her in the best way possible, had responded perfectly. She, half-waking as she shivered over the edge of orgasm, had simultaneously panicked and wailed in grief when she realized the man moving inside her was *not* her husband.

Delfi'd had to drain her down to the dregs before either Jossa or Syrus came out of the death spiral of emotions. Jossa'd threatened to remove his dick and balls *both* if he ever pulled a stunt like that again, deal or no deal. She'd made the threat stick by using a spacers knife to open a wound in his leg the size of her palm.

But she'd returned to his bunk that night. And the next. And the next. He kept his *usik* to himself while she slept. She never gave him ammunition to retaliate, doing her best to hold herself away whenever *his* dreams woke her to a lustful haze. And somehow they managed to find equilibrium.

"I'll ask you again," Syrus said. "What do you need down here?"

"Water tank," Jossa answered, trying to scrub the memory of that horrific morning from her mind.

"The fuck for?"

"Laundry."

"What, now?" Syrus swung her around to face him. "We're fine. Got enough clean clothes and shit to last us into the Gatekeepers." He narrowed his eyes at her. Jossa was reminded of the baby dragonets she'd had to tend while still in service to the Emperor. Except Syrus was a full-grown adult, not a tiny lizard more likely to kill her with the stench of its breath than its tiny claws.

"One of you bleeding again?"

Jossa's brain rebounded off the image of Syrus as a dragonet and finally registered his question. "No!"

Although she was due. Any day now.

Syrus dropped his eyes to look at her crotch, then raised an eyebrow. Lust rippled through the air again. Jossa felt gooseflesh rise on her arms in response.

Delfi's mental slap almost knocked Jossa off balance. She stumbled against Syrus. ::Get your head back between the nav beacons,:: her sousi snapped before subsiding back into watchful silence.

"Sheets," Jossa blurted as she pulled away. He kept hold of her arm, but not tightly. "Need clean sheets. Or *new* sheets, now that I think of it. Your bunk smells like a whorehouse."

That was definitely humor. Syrus's eyes lit. He opened his mouth.

Jossa yanked free and fled for the water tanks. It was a bad move. Syrus followed. In fact, he all but boxed her into the tiny space full of gauges and dials, a predator with his prey. Jossa tried not to stiffen or drop a hand to her belt knife, but it was a near thing. She succeeded, but only because she remembered that she'd left her knives on a desk in Syrus's bunk. Luckily, she had a distraction from the mountain of muscle looming behind her. "We're going to need water."

Syrus muttered a curse. "Fees are going to bite us in the ass."

Jossa leaned over and opened another panel. "Either that or fresh sanitizer solution for the gray water."

Syrus looked at the floating gauges on the two tanks, then opened the last panel. Black water, filthy and unusable, filled the gauge.

Jossa winced. Syrus cursed again. "Fucking Base Ops and their fucking runaround docking protocols."

She agreed. They'd filled the tanks at the last base. Apparently, they should have gotten extra tanks. Nearly two weeks floating in locked orbit around the base had dug deep into their reserves.

"Can we do it? Afford it, I mean. With what we're paying these people who're..." Jossa frowned. "Are they smuggling us? Is there a point to resupply if we're going to end up shoved in boxes with holes for ventilation and shipped through like cargo?"

Delfi brayed with laughter, audible all the way down the stairs. Syrus leaned back, raising both eyebrows this time. "The fuck, woman?"

Jossa stuck her chin out. "Is it worth resupplying on this base?"

"Yeah." Syrus turned, heading for the engine room. "Once we meet the transport, we can't leave this ship till we're through the Barb. I'll need whatever's left once I drop you off with the Gatekeepers."

Jossa stuttered to a halt behind him, clinging to the open doorframe between hall and engine room. "What now?"

"Me, dropping you off. The fucking deal, remember?"

She remembered. Their original bargain. He'd agreed to teach her and Delfi how best to survive this new and terrible version of the Empire she'd once loved. Passage. Work for their keep. Safety from the Fleet as it chewed its way through the Empire's defenses, swallowing system after system in its ever-hungry maw.

Until this moment, she hadn't registered how very close they were to actually making it. Months, they'd been running. She and Delfi had settled in. Gotten used to life on board a merchant ship again.

They never should have let that happen. Safety was a lie. She'd learned that lesson long ago.

"Joss?" Syrus asked, letting her feel the curiosity in his voice.

"Don't call me that," she told him automatically.

He chuckled and started typing on one of the wall-mounted screens.

"What are you doing?" she asked him, trying to distract herself from the realization that soon she'd have to pack up more than just the day's cargo.

"Locking everything down," he told her. "This system's always been about the worst place for trying to force a link from the base to the ship." He laid his palm on the lockpad next to the screen he was working on, waited a moment, and went back to adjusting dials and settings. "We'll have maybe three days before the automated systems start putting real effort into getting through the firewalls. Not"—he looked up at her, flashing his teeth in an animal snarl—"that I plan to be attached to this floating hunk of metal in three days. But if they get through, I'm overriding life support and power so they need to come in and hook them to the base by hand. Or else get the local rard to authorize a total system wipe."

Jossa stared at him. "The local *rard?* "

He looked at her, frowning. "Yeah. Asshole lives on base. Doesn't like taking his eyes off the Barb." Syrus snorted and turned back to the screen. "Don't blame him. It's a fucking bomb ready to go off. Easier to keep a lid on things when he doesn't have to depend on reports filtered through seventeen layers of bureaucrats on the take, all edited to make it look like there's not a riot or who the hell knows what else happening. Means the laws actually get enforced, including what's allowed on base."

"Riots," Jossa said. "You aren't kidding."

"Think, woman. Everyone in the fucking Empire is either running to the Core or for the Borders, trying to get away. This Barbican is one of *two* that lead into the Gatekeepers. The Imperials aren't the ones who decide when the damn thing opens."

"You know," Jossa said, suddenly wanting to bash him over the head, "You could have explained what we were getting into. We've had almost a year. Or at the least said something during the last two fikekoj *weeks* we spent floating around waiting for them to let us hook on."

"You had a fucking year to do your *own* research." Syrus set his palm on the lock pad again in a careful gesture that was completely at odds with the tension in his shoulders and the muscles working in his jaw.

Jossa felt her face go red. Awkward silence reigned for a few minutes, even in her head. Bless Delfi for not rubbing her nose in her nearsightedness.

After a little while, she tried again, groping for a line of the conversation that wouldn't give the man too many opportunities to make her look a fool. "What are the chances they'll get access to our systems before the three days are up?"

"Ask your sister." Syrus jerked his chin at the ceiling. "She's adding a couple layers of code to what I've already got in there.

Jossa swallowed. Delfi was not a Crack, one of the sai who could read and generate code faster than most people could think. But she'd spent the better part of ten years married to one, helping to pilot the *Skatasi op Essie* back and forth across the Empire. Ancestors allow, somehow what she'd learned from Denz had stuck through cryo and their captivity. But would it be enough?

::Worry more about three hundred years of coding drift,:: Delfi told her. ::Although that may work in our favor, if they're looking for modern patterns.::

::Are you sure it's changed that much?::

::Yes,:: Delfi replied. ::Brace yourself.::

"Wha?" Jossa asked aloud.

Then it hit her. A vast weight, coming at her from all sides. Like an airlock pressurizing. Only it didn't just pop her ears. It compressed her mind, her very soul.

An entire space base's worth of people. Their sorrow, their joy. Their anger and frustration and hope. It had been explained to her once, long ago, that no matter how great her teachers. No matter how grounded her knowledge of *how* her abilities worked, nothing would make up for the shields she was supposed to build inside her mind. And they warned her, before removing the crown from her skull, that the only way she could learn to hold her interior shields without artificial aid would be to practice.

She'd lasted ten minutes before her whole reality became a raw, screaming nightmare. Three days before she'd been sedated. Over twenty years before Delfi managed to pull a working mind from the wreckage they'd stored in long-term cryo.

Delfi caught her before she finished crumpling to her knees. Little by little, the pressure faded. Drew back. And finally, all but vanished.

Alone in her head again, Jossa stayed in her crouch and pressed her forehead to the cool metal of the door frame. ::Bless you,:: she thought at Delfi. ::Ancestors behind and Progeny ahead, I couldn't live without you.::

Delfi set a phantom hand gently on her sousi's head in reply.

"Hey." A real hand landed on Jossa's shoulder, far rougher. She looked up into Syrus's brown eyes. "You good?" he asked.

He had no one to bolster him. He wouldn't feel the base for at least another hour, but it would hit him much harder. "Brace yourself," she told him. "We're almost there."

Two--Jossa

As detestable as it may be, necessity dictates we allow gutter trash to know our most valuable secrets, lest we sink to their level in the course of undertaking work vital to the safety of the Empire.
    - memo to Isloste Fielu, from Vamalkute Utten, in charge of Uvlaku ranks

Jossa wasn't around to see how the emotional load of the base affected Syrus. While Delfi interfaced with the automatic tug bringing them in to their assigned dock and the nehkeh man finished rearranging the cargo hold, Jossa took care of the other pre-docking chores.

Snatch breakfast, start laundry. Inventory came last. Water wasn't the only thing running low. They needed food too. Protein mainly, along with anything that carried natural vitamins. She shuddered to think of what fresh fruit might cost out here. Maybe supplements would be cheaper? She doubted it.

::Another sponge disintegrated on me,:: Delfi put in as Jossa looked at the list on her screen. ::And we're almost out of the cleaning solution.::

Of course. Because the minute they ran out of menstrual sponges and the assorted paraphernalia needed to clean them properly, one of them was bound to start bleeding. Ancestors, but she hated that they were both so irregular. Commoner women ran like chronos, but there was something about being highborn that sent endocrine systems off the nav beacons, and neither of them could risk finding a temple and a priest to get the meds needed to regulate. That, at least, wasn't new. It was the price they paid for running from the Churus lis Kuchruis to start with.

Jossa sighed and added the items to the list. ::Anything else?:: she asked her sister.

Something hovered in the mind bond, as if Delfi were about to choose a thought for Jossa to hear. Then it vanished behind the wall of her sister's shields. ::No, that should do it. Brace.::

Jossa stuck a foot under the lower edge of the galley counter and braced her hands on the lip of the sink opposite. A muffled *thud* reverberated through the ship as it made contact with the base. A series of smaller noises followed as docking clamps took hold of the hull and the airlocks rotated and shifted to match seals.

::We never would've noticed if it were Denz flying this thing,:: Delfi growled.

Jossa swallowed the lump in her throat and blinked back the tears threatening her eyes. ::Rui never would have allowed a tug near the ship at all.::

Delfi leaned into the bond for a moment, then went back to what she was doing. Jossa sniffed, grabbed her screen before it tipped off the edge of the counter, and headed for the lower deck.

She wasn't racing the base chrono, she was racing his.

Syrus met her at the bottom of the stairs and raised an eyebrow. "You sure about that?"

Jossa stopped with one foot halfway to the next step, frowning. "What?"

He gave a one-shouldered shrug and moved back so she could come all the way down to the deck. "The outfit for one. The hair for another."

"What are you, a fashion critic?"

He bared his teeth at her and headed for the bay doors, where an alert flashed on the lockpad. "Maybe."

Before she could sputter out a reply or demand an explanation, he tapped in an acknowledgement for the alert, then placed his palm on the sensor. The airlock parted with a tiny explosion of air, then slid back into the walls. The large screen inlaid on the outer doors flashed its own message: the "Open up, Official Business" alert of Customs officials the Empire over. As Syrus went to open the second lock, Jossa gave her shopping list one last look. Maybe she could get him to take the food, at least.

A blast of sound from outside the ship all but deafened her. Jossa nearly dropped the screen. ::Del,:: she said. ::What in the name of Ancestors is going on out there?::

::How should I know?:: Delfi snapped back, letting Jossa feel her irritation in full force. ::I'm up here in a metal box with no way to— Oh.:: She dissolved into a storm of curses.

::Oh, what?:: Jossa asked as she took a firmer grip on her screen and watched Syrus lead a rail-thin man wearing the uniform of a Customs official into the cargo bay. If she hadn't known what to look for, she wouldn't have seen the tension in Syrus's shoulders. Or the set of his jaw. Or the way one hand drifted to the hilt of the spacer's knife clipped to his belt. But she did, and she saw. If he killed the Customs man before their cargo got the official stamp of approval, they'd never make it off the base.

::Delfi,:: Jossa said as she straightened her spine and went to join the men. ::What. Is. It?::

Delfi shoved a mental image down the mind bond. Stylized sperm set around equally stylized ova. Tiny baby boys with the glyphs for "natural" and "miracle" emblazoned on their foreheads.

First Natural Son Day. Ancestors preserve.

Jossa clamped her mouth shut on a few curses of her own as the Customs man turned to look at her. Curiosity and contempt oozed off him in equal measure as he raked his eyes up her too-skinny legs, nonexistent hips, and equally diminutive breasts. He stopped for a moment at her face before turning back to Syrus. "Your wife?" he asked. His voice was a dry rasp, devoid of the emotions currently setting Jossa's teeth on edge.

Syrus tipped his head, the very image of a close-mouthed trader captain. When he held out a hand, Jossa stepped forward to slip in under his arm. She wished she dared elbow him in the side or, better, slam the edge of her screen into his nose. But beggars couldn't be choosers, and she *was* wearing a maruste with the marriage glyph in it, so she was more or less stuck. He might be the next thing to a change-lizard when it came to assuming new personalities at need. She, on the other hand, needed a lot more practice; it still felt like a betrayal of Rui's memory.

Just a little while longer. Soon, very soon, she and Delfi would be free of this man forever.

Syrus snugged her in closer and let a ripple of humor escape his shields. The Customs man didn't seem to notice the display, having glued his nose to the screen in his hand. "Hm," he said. "Coming from Ikklesab, I see. What cargo?"

"Bits and pieces," Syrus said in a voice as falsely amiable as his smile. "Broke with the Freighters Guild a while back. Couldn't afford the fees to cross sectors. Small merchant seems to be working ok."

True so far as it went. The fact that eighteen people had died so the three of them could travel under new identities needn't be mentioned. Jossa just hoped he'd put away his skin-print equipment and the stash of blood bags as well as he claimed to have hidden their cargo, or they'd end up in more trouble than anything smugglers ever landed in.

"Honey," Jossa said in her sweetest voice, once it looked like the Customs man was going to stand there and go over every item on his checklist letter by letter. "If we're to eat tonight, I needs must go to the markets."

Syrus eased his arm off her shoulders and gave her a gentle shove towards the stairs. "Go then. I'll catch up."

The Customs man coughed. "Missus Oropan," he said, his dry voice rasping over the honorific and her assumed name. "It is advisable that you wait until your husband can escort you." He looked her up and down again, one eyebrow raised. "And change clothes as well."

That ripple of humor again, although Syrus kept his face straight. Jossa gave him a flat look, then frowned at the official. "And how long until you are done with him, if you please?"

Irritation rolled across her skin in a wave of barbed pinpricks, although she couldn't pinpoint exactly why the Customs man might feel that way. He was possibly one of the least emotional people she'd ever met, and that was saying something. So, she watched him closely as he consulted his screen and looked around the cargo hold. "Several hours at minimum, *ma'am*."

Ah. There it was. She'd left the honorific out. Well, he could breathe vacuum for all she cared. It had taken her weeks to feel comfortable going out in the markets and ports. Weeks before she'd been able to convince Syrus that she could manage without getting robbed, cheated, or lured into an alley and caught by slavers.

Only Delfi knew how many times she'd dealt with unwanted propositions or assumptions in the markets, spaceports, and bases. Only Delfi had the barest inkling as to how grateful Jossa was to her sister for siphoning all the myriad emotions, enabling the ignoring, rebuttal, and sometimes violent negation of all those overtures.

Syrus's screen beeped at him before she could think of an answer unlikely to prompt the official to confiscate *all* their cargo, instead of skimming what he wanted. Syrus frowned and checked the alert, then raised an eyebrow at her. "Buyer set a time."

::Delfi, what time is it on base?:: Jossa asked through the mind bond.

::Almost fifteen hundred,:: Delfi replied. ::Syrus is thinking very hard at me about having to be somewhere at twenty-thirty.::

Five hours to push and shove through a base full of people celebrating a high holiday. All the while praying that Delfi could siphon off enough excess emotion to keep Jossa from losing her mind and infecting the entire base.

Not enough, especially not as she sat around waiting for this bureaucrat to crawl his way through the checks and run down the clock.

Right. No.

Jossa gave the Customs man a half bow, doing her best to keep it sloppy and on the uneducated side of formal. "I appreciate your concern, sir," she said, slurring the honorific on purpose. "But if I'm to make dinner tonight and my husband to have clean clothes, I must go now. I'm sure neither of you need *me* in order to finish checking the cargo."

"Wait," the man said.

Jossa stopped halfway through her turn. Alarm and frustration beat at her, carrying with them a rapid staccato of imagery she couldn't parse.

She gave him a lifted eyebrow. Behind him, Syrus had a hand over the lower half of his face, probably to hide a grin. But *his* emotions were still shielded.

"If you insist on going off the ship by yourself, you must accept the rules of the base." The official held up his screen. "If harm comes to you, nobody but yourself will be liable."

Delfi's end of the bond flared white-hot rage. Jossa gritted her teeth and did *not* give in to the temptation to ram the man's screen down his throat. She couldn't jeopardize things this close to the end. But oh, she wanted to see the look on his face when she cracked the thing across his nose.

He went beet red. "Ma'am," he said in a harsh voice. "Your acknowledgement, or possible fines and incarceration. Which?"

Behind him, Syrus growled deep in his throat.

First she'd gut him like a fish and let him watch that precious list of rules get covered in blood and half-digested food while his intestines tried to crawl back into his body. Second, she'd break his screen and shove the shards in his eyes and may his Progeny scream at the sight of him. Then she'd—

::Odavek!:: Delfi's curse cut through Jossa's train of thought with all the fanfare of a block of ice dropped in hot oil. The mind bond gave a huge convulsing jerk, and suddenly Jossa could breathe again. Reason returned in a cold rush, rocking her where she stood, knife hand raised. Less than a foot away, the Customs man struggled frantically against the arm Syrus had wrapped around his throat, fear and rage all but pouring off him.

::Double odavek,:: Delfi snapped. ::Joss!::

::Yes!:: Jossa gathered up the sudden clarity Delfi'd given her and threw it out like a net. Peace. Calm. No anger here. No rage. Please, she prayed. Peace.

The Customs man quieted first, sagging back against Syrus. The nehkeh—Savage to the core as he was—kept his hold tight, teeth still bared. Finally, just when Jossa thought he'd actually lost it, Syrus growled. "You go after my wife again, you won't get a warning." Then he let go of the man's neck, caught the screen before it fell from limp fingers, and looked at the data on its surface. "My dear?"

Ancestors bless his quick thinking. He had legions of faults, but he wasn't dim. Jossa took a breath, smoothed her hands down her skirt, and stepped forward to look.

"If-If you would, ma'am." The man motioned at her screen. "I can transfer them."

"No," Syrus said before Jossa could reply. "We're not opening a data link." Syrus turned the screen so Jossa could read better. She glanced up at him as his fingers brushed hers. He was still as angry as she was, but the contact was too brief to tell if he'd gone back to his default state of being or if something in the list of rules had set him off again.

She took the screen and listened with half an ear as he backed the Customs official against stack of crates and kept him there despite all the man's babblings about "explaining" and "make sure she understands completely."

::Well,:: Delfi said as Jossa read it all for a third time. ::I guess the real question here is would you be half so mad if they were trying to shackle you to Rui instead of Syrus?::

Tukovoj skat. Jossa locked the thought away. Too slow. She felt Delfi's flinch as a physical thing and nearly fumbled the screen. Immediately, Jossa sent a wave of apology through the bond. It bounced off Delfi's shields and washed back to her.

::Del,:: she said. ::Del, I'm sorry.::

A slight crack opened in the wall between them. ::You know I'm right.::

"Everything ok, my dear?" asked Syrus.

Translation: Just sign the thing already.

Jossa took a deep breath and looked up. "Sorry. I just wanted to be sure I understood *everything*." She dropped enough acid in the word to eat through the hull of the ship. Meeting the Customs man's eyes, she placed her thumb on the icon in the corner of the screen and said, "I understand that if I go off this ship alone, merchants will demand to see my marriage glyph and possibly even validate it. I agree to stay in the markets designated for these docks while unescorted. I understand that even if I do *not* stray from this section of the base, without my husband around to *guard* me, I might still get kidnapped, raped, killed, or any number of unpleasant things." She let her face settle into what Syrus called her "try-me" expression. "I'm doing it anyway."

She shoved the screen back into his hands and spun on her heel, very pointedly *not* stomping up the stairs. After a couple seconds of quiet, she heard Syrus start up the routine bargaining for the lowest possible bribe needed to clear customs.

::You'll have to change shirts,:: Delfi said as Jossa mounted the second half-flight.

::I know.:: Something with a mesh back, not a warm shipside shirt that covered her entirely. It was a good thing she'd already refreshed the false skin on her hands. Pulling that out, using it, and getting it hidden again with the official on board would just be begging for trouble. ::I want you to stay on the ship.::

::Excuse me?:: Delfi's head popped out of the bridge as Jossa reached the top of the stairs. She glared at her sister and opened her mouth to continue out loud.

Jossa covered the two steps between them and clamped a hand over Delfi's face. ::Not where he can hear.::

Delfi stuck her tongue out and licked her sister's hand.

Jossa flinched away. "You're disgusting."

::We could go out together. We'd be safe. I'm bored, cooped up in here every time you two get to run around.::

::Leaving the ship on planet is one thing,:: Jossa said. ::The minute you open your mouth, half the base will know what you are.::

Delfi crossed her arms, stuck out her tongue, and stomped back onto the bridge. When Jossa tried to follow her, the closing door nearly took her hand off.

Sighing, she rested her forehead on the cool metal. ::I just want you safe, Del. Don't you understand?::

Nothing.

Jossa stayed there for another heartbeat, waiting for the wall on the other end of the mind bond to open. When it didn't, she shook her head and headed down the hall to her bunk. She'd need most of her weapons if the base was as bad as the Customs man said.

THREE--JOSSA

Rusithe is going to have to scrap the entire breeding program if he keeps ignoring the glaring, mental health-shaped hole in his team.
-private notes of Professor Tolst, New Hopks College of Medicine

Jossa winced as she laid her hand on the scanner, but not because the needles hurt. She felt them, of course, but only barely.

Barely was enough. The layer of synthetic skin mixed with microscopic pockets of a dead woman's blood should have held up for nearly a week, given normal use. Longer, if they'd been floating out in space without stopping at a base or planetside port. She'd just reapplied the disgusting sludge this morning, another one of the chores that went with traveling alongside a former Uvlaku operative who'd survived who knew how long running from literally everyone in existence. Just like tucking herself under his arm and pretending to be a good little wife, she'd learned not to argue about the more revolting aspects of their life on the run.

If it weren't for the years she and Delfi had spent running, she would have thought the lengths Syrus went to in order to keep them all safe ridiculous. And too disgusting to contemplate. But she'd tried all the alternatives. Bribing everyone from border guards to Karukap, or military, personnel to priests, synthskin over their maruste, Denz pushing his sai to the limits to keep ahead of scans just like this. Three hundred years ago, true. But her crew, her *family*, hadn't had access to the sort of tech Syrus carried around in that battered duffel. Eventually they'd simply run out of tricks. Out of places to run.

Out of time itself.

Ancestors bless the Karukap and its pet scientists. Bless it twice for being so stupid as to give Syrus an opening to escape his forced service in the Uvlaku and take all his toys with him. But those toys weren't perfect. As evidenced by the slight rippling around the edges of the synthskin and distinct flakiness near the joints.

That didn't mean she wasn't nervous about the efficacy of some of the measures taken. Like this one.

She glanced up as the little machine chirped and beeped its way through the digital walls separating her blood and nanite scan from the false accounts Syrus'd set up to pay for supplies. Across the counter from her, the shop owner's wife watched her husband with anxious eyes while he glared at the reflection of Jossa's bare back in the mirrors mounted to the ceiling.

Jossa ducked her head before the man noticed her watching him and started an interrogation. She didn't need to turn the volume up on his irritation and suspicion if she could help it. Delfi already had enough to do taking care of the dull roar that was the base as a whole.

Besides, Jossa knew a good part of the annoyance prickling the back of her spine originated with herself. The store was chilly, and her shirt had no back. Useful in the general sense, since nine of ten shopkeepers she'd met today had demanded they check her back to make sure Denz maruste matched the scanners. Not useful because it did nothing to keep her warm.

Not to mention this was taking forever. She would've been back at the ship ages ago if she could've just used credit slips to pay, like she'd planned. But no. She'd nearly gotten law enforcement called on her at the first store, trying to speed things up like that. Because apparently the whores carried cash, and the rest of the female population weren't even listed on their men's credit accounts.

Syrus'd had a field day with that shop owner when the idiot called the ship to confirm Jossa's right to purchase so much as a hairbrush.

Three hundred years ago, not even the strictest social sticklers on the Capitol planet had been this unbending about a woman's place. Sometimes she wished she'd agreed to die alongside Rui rather than go into that casket.

The scanner beeped again. The shopkeeper's wife murmured something inaudible and looked at her husband. He scowled at Jossa. She flinched before she could catch herself. Had the machine picked up the wrong information? Ancestors please, don't let this be what ruins everything.

In the back of her head, Delfi stirred from whatever she'd been doing and pulled a little harder on the emotional siphon running through their mind bond. It was just enough to keep Jossa from stiffening in indignation when the man in front of her made a turning motion with one finger. "Lemme see it," he barked.

She turned, waiting to grind her teeth until she faced completely away from him. She couldn't tell what was going on in his head, not like Delfi could Hear thoughts, but the rise of emotion told her enough. A few flashes of the glyph for whores, a surge of disappointment, and the shopkeeper told her to turn back around. His wife pushed the bag with Jossa's purchases in it almost off the counter in her haste. The shopkeeper scowled as he told her that the charges would show in her husband's accounts by end of day, and Jossa decided now was an excellent time to call it a day. Anything she'd missed could wait.

Turning on her heel, she ignored the alternating hostile and wary gazes aimed at her back and waved a hand at the sensor for the phasewall guarding the entrance to the shop. She hopped through as it flickered out of existence, stepping out into the small plaza that housed this shop and its neighbors.

While it wasn't really quiet near the store, what with all the vehicles and their occupants dropping from and rising to the ceiling and the guide-tracks that lined it, it wasn't overwhelming either.

Music thrummed through the air, filling the halls and corridors of the space base with a steady undertone. Laid over top of the various songs, lyrics, and the occasional boom of bass was the chatter of a night market in full swing. Someone called out an order of food to a vendor. A cluster of people spilled out of a shop, talking amongst themselves.

Above, flits flowed along the ceiling, setting the colored lights hanging from it swaying with the air currents. Decorations for the holiday were sparse here compared to the common areas of the business clusters. Stalls and booths lined the corridor, with the occasional gap for a store or restaurant set into the walls. The odd cluster of ova attached to a post by grav tether, a few stylized sperm cells floating in encapsulated air fountains—pink, of course. Tiny curled-up babies, all boys. The figures and their carriers were made of every substance imaginable, all depending on the whim of the person decorating and often the goods they sold.

Jossa made a face at an infant molded of pulled sucrose candy, disturbingly lifelike in color, and kept going. Everything else she'd bought was already on its way to the ship via the various delivery services, but she wanted to get Delfi's necessities put away and pick up her sister before the meet. If she kept moving and didn't let anyone stop her, they should be able to get to the meeting in time. Rest with Delfi for a few minutes. Breathe without who knew how many thousands of people touching her.

The step-father's blessing of the crush was that there were so many people that, unless a large number of them felt the same thing at once, and strongly, none of it was clear enough to distract her for long. Fear was ever-present, but not the immediate panic she associated with a base about to be under siege. A flash of anticipation. A whisper of sadness. Sun-bright afterimages floated past her mind's eye as she was jostled, pushed, and moved along with the flow of traffic. She did her best to let them come and go through her mind, relying on Delfi to siphon them off as needed.

She dodged a woman and a man wearing the badge of a local chaperone service marching through the throng like they were on a mission, nearly rebounded off an elderly man with a bubbling water pipe hanging out of his mouth, and then ducked to avoid the waving arms of a man arguing with his companion.

"... telling you, I saw her!" he all but shouted.

"So drunk off your ass you can't remember a woman with wings would die in vacuum, you..."

Jossa rolled her eyes as she lost the thread of their conversation. That spacer's tale was old before she was born. It was so common, and so patently impossible, that Rui'd named his ship for the mythical beings just so he could listen to port control twist themselves in knots during official communications.

The spacers moved on while Jossa was still trying to swallow down her heartache. In that moment, she couldn't find the wherewithal to take another step. A few people cursed her absently. A few more buffeted her on the shoulders and elbows, leaving the imprints of frustration, anxiety, and fear laid across her mind.

Gently, Delfi reached through the bond and pulled the feelings away, leaving her sousi clearheaded enough to push through the crowd. She followed the flow of traffic, even though she didn't need anything from the other shops. It was easier than fending off the hard looks and harder emotions than trying to move counter the slow clockwise spin of people.

On top of that, this way she didn't stand out from the crowd as she pushed her way through. At least so long as she didn't stay put long enough for anyone to realize she didn't have an escort. That was fairly easy to do. Outside the shops, everyone moved just as quickly as she. Nobody lingered. Nobody stopped to chat. They paused in front of a booth or a shop, chose what they needed, and kept going. Here and there a cop stood, watching with wary eyes.

A street merchant waved a handful of slippery purple tentacles and declared a bargain price to anyone who came in earshot. Jossa ducked under the man's moving arm, nearly got slapped in the face by a dripping tentacle, and kept moving before he could mistake her wiping at her eyes for interest. He did shout at her a bit, but she was free to escape the stench of day-old fish once he locked on to a new target.

Was he *trying* to kill someone with that smell?

Hot fat sizzled over a large convex dish as the next food vendor waved a squeeze bottle over the surface. Liquid squirted, hit, spat and hissed, making the man's audience jump back as it bubbled up into solid form. The smell of spices and sugar bloomed in the air. Jossa's stomach growled.

Anticipation and fear blossomed near her hip. More fingers, tugging lightly at her belt pouch. It wouldn't open. The thief tried again before Jossa could dodge past the couple in front of her trying to comfort their crying child. Not giving up this time.

She snapped a hand down and found herself blocked by the meaty elbow of a man as he turned and nearly plowed into her. The pouch slipped free. Cut.

She ducked around the man and lunged for the thief. Barely hip high, long ratty hair over a threadbare shirt. The child slid between two pedestrians as they stepped away from a stall.

Jossa snagged the back of the child's shirt and yanked, then grabbed again higher as the old fabric tore. She got hair this time. The child shrieked in alarm.

Wrapping her hand in the greasy hair, the color of which she was afraid to wonder about—too late; was that dirt, or natural?—Jossa hauled the thief closer, grabbing for the child's fist and the pouch it clutched. He, for it was a he, fought her, refusing to loosen his grip. Fear laced with determination punched up her arm, then drained.

Bless Delfi forever.

"You'll give it back," Jossa said, putting as much steel in her voice as she could manage. She'd spent the last year running around known space with a nehkeh who'd spent the previous three years flattening solar systems for fun. She could manage quite a bit of steel.

The boy stared at her, eyes wide. But he didn't speak. And he didn't let go of her purse.

Jossa dug her thumbnail into the tendons of his wrist. He held out longer than she'd expected, but eventually the little boy squawked. His grip on the pouch loosened. Jossa snatched it before he could recover. "Now go away," she told him. "And don't send your pack after me or they'll find out what other tricks I know."

He might have a pack. He might not. From the sullen burn of anger and the glower he gave her, she guessed he did.

No matter. By the grace of her Ancestors, she was an adult who could feel them coming. Unless they swarmed her, unlikely in this crush, she should manage. Slipping past the boy, she started off again, this time keeping an eye open for a spot out of the crush where she could stop and hide the pouch elsewhere on her person. Just before she was out of earshot, the boy muttered, "Fucking bitch."

Ah. That explained things. Including why he hadn't spoken when she threatened him. A street Savage. Nehkeh, or the next thing to. If she were still a good citizen of the Empire, she'd go back there, catch him again, and drag him before the authorities and a marus-priest so they could check the nanites in his blood and make sure the glyph for his caste showed on his back.

She wasn't a good citizen anymore. The Empire as she knew it was gone, crumbled to bickering factions and near civil war in the three hundred years since she'd last known it. The fact that it was under siege was the only thing that kept it from falling apart entirely. Which was why she was here, on this overstuffed chunk of pressurized metal, instead of out in the vastness of space where the entirety of their emotions couldn't batter her brain to bits.

Speaking of. She reached along the mind bond that linked her to Delfi, sending out a wordless call for attention that shouldn't jar the younger woman much if she were in the middle of something.

Used to be, she'd just speak directly through the bond and Delfi would answer right back. Somehow, in the time since their escape from the Svis Konanuog, that had changed. Jossa wasn't sure how or why, although she suspected it had something to do with the twin blows of realizing their husbands were dead and then Delfi's rape at the hands of Svis Konanuog soldiers. Their arguments over whether to pry into Syrus's secrets hadn't helped.

Either way, Jossa had taken to calling first. And learned to accept that sometimes, Delfi wasn't going to answer.

::I'm always listening though,:: Delfi said. Her voice felt slightly cool, the words absentminded.

Jossa snorted, both aloud and in her mind. ::Yes, but that's because you're always storing up ammunition for some sort of prank. Or argument. Or—::

::Ha, ha.:: Delfi managed to give the impression of rolling her eyes without conveying the visual.

Jossa glanced around, looking for signage. ::I think I'm about halfway to the ship. What time is it?:: If she stopped to check her little rented screen, she'd probably have yet another pickpocket on her hands.

Vermin, all of them.

::You don't have enough,:: Delfi replied after a moment. Her mental voice drifted, then sharpened. ::There's some sort of clog between you and the docks. Besides, I'm not on the ship.::

::What?::

::Watch coming in through the bar. The guard'll need proof you're allowed in back. But if you come in the side entrance::—she sent an image of a small doorframe set into a niche in the walls—::the guard will think you're here to bet on the fights.::

::Wait.:: Jossa stopped. No fewer than three people collided with her. They shouted various curses on her and her Ancestors and kept going. Jossa scrambled for balance as their emotions blinded her with a wash of confused imagery. Finally she found her footing, but not before another knot of people nearly ran her over. Moving perpendicular to the traffic, she worked her way over to the space between two booths, checked to make sure nobody was going to jump her out of the alcove behind her, and tried to get a grip on the news. ::Wait,:: she said again. ::Where are you?::

Delfi hummed slightly. Jossa got the impression of swaying movement and sparkling lights. ::I'm at the meet. Well. At the place where the people will come get us for the meet.::

Jossa pinched the bridge of her nose and blew out a breath as she fought the frustration rising in her gut. Delfi was still doing her job, siphoning off the base's worth of outside emotion. Jossa wouldn't make things harder by loading her *own* feelings on her sousi. ::Why?:: she asked once she was reasonably sure she could keep her words calm.

::Because I get bored on the ship,:: Delfi answered in the same distracted voice. ::And because I'd rather know what's going on firsthand than try to watch through your eyes. Or worse, assume you and the man will tell me everything right away.::

Sometimes Jossa wished her soul sister had stuck to hiding on board the ship while Syrus and later Jossa herself had ventured out to find them work and cargo. Once Delfi decided to conquer her newly acquired fear of people in general and men in specific, she'd done so with a vengeance.

That she'd transferred those terrors over to Jossa was something the older woman had been careful to hide from her sister in the months since Delfi's butterfly-like transformation. What if she were attacked? What if a man liked what he saw and wouldn't take no for an answer? What if someone snatched her right off the street? On reflex, Jossa sent her sai out in a wide pool, checking to be sure nobody could get her either. What if, what if, what if? So many possibilities.

While Delfi had refused to leave the ship, she'd been safe. Jossa had only needed to worry about what might happen if Syrus took an interest in her. Which he hadn't. At least, not at first. She wasn't sure when he'd flipped that switch, but it happened. Next thing Jossa knew, Delfi got rid of all the clothes Jossa had bought for her, found new, and started strutting around in things that made their costumes as former concubines to a dead Emperor seem downright chaste by comparison.

At which point, Jossa had stepped in and demanded he leave Delfi alone. Not go near her. Not talk to her unless absolutely necessary for the duration of their travels together. He'd listened about as well as could be expected, given he was an adult nehkeh man who'd survived everything the Empire and Fleet could throw at him. Which was to say, he didn't listen at all. She was convinced he did it out of sheer spite. And probably as part of his long-term plan to get back inside her. Which, Ancestors curse it all, had worked.

::I'm not a child,:: Delfi snapped, forcing the words through the bond in needles of angry frustration. Jossa gasped and clutched at her head.

::I am an adult,:: Delfi continued. ::A widow, even! When will you treat me like I can think for myself?::

Sorrow, fought off once today, won the second round. It choked Jossa with memories. Of Rui. Of Denz, Delfi's husband. Of the family they'd lost three hundred years ago, although it was barely a year since she and Delfi had learned of it.

Sighing, Delfi siphoned it off before Jossa lost control and infected the people around her with the emotion. But she didn't apologize.

No, Delfi didn't do apologies.

::You keep using the widow thing,:: Jossa muttered, swallowing down tears, ::like it's a valid argument. I'm a widow too. Do you see *me* painting my body in silicon and wandering around in public?::

::I don't *paint* myself,:: Delfi grumbled. But she'd gone distant again, attention no longer on the disagreement. Jossa pushed, carefully, and saw Syrus stomping his way through a mass of shouting people. Glee and anticipation in equal measure, so not an angry mob.

Someone jostled her from the side and kept going, leaving fear and urgency burning down her arm as distant stars exploded behind her eyes. Jossa froze, fighting to keep still. Get away get away get away, a voice inside her cried. It's too late, time to get away. This wasn't the low-grade worry she'd been dealing with since she came in range of the base. This was bright. Fresh. The next thing to lizard-brain terror.

::Delfi,:: she called, sucking frantic gulps of air into her lungs.

Delfi didn't answer, but the urgency faded, the fear dimming to the smallest awareness of those around her. Not gone. There were too many people in the vicinity still muttering and shooting furtive looks over their shoulders. But enough. Enough that Jossa could think clearly again.

Frowning, she slid back into the crowd, shoring up her shields such as they were and opening the bond wider to facilitate flow over to Delfi. Some saw her coming and moved. Others didn't. They stood clustered around a single point. The flow of traffic dammed against them, compressed, and tried to continue on. For every person who kept going, another two stopped to see what was happening. Soon the whole street would be blocked.

Catching sight of a uniformed officer out of the corner of her eye, Jossa realized he wouldn't break up the snarl in time. Either this was a common occurrence in this section of corridor or he didn't know what had everyone so curious.

She watched as he tilted his head in the subconscious gesture of anyone new to their jaw implant.

Her musing was interrupted as his face went from attentive to slack.

To horrified.

Then he pulled the tase-billet he carried on one hip and started prodding the people around him. "All right," he called. "Enough. Move along. Move along!"

Most obeyed. Some needed a harder shove or a stronger threat from the club before tearing their attention from the object of fascination. Another officer appeared down the street. He shouldered his way past the remnants of the crowd and banged on the door of the shop, demanding to be let in.

Jossa stepped back, feeling her shields crumble as the attitudes of the two men stoked the people's emotions from low coals to a fire. Trickles of fear ran through the crowd as the people who'd been gathered in front of the shop dispersed, carrying their news with them. Jossa sucked in a breath, shored up her sad defenses as much as she was able, and clawed along the mind bond for Delfi as she turned on her heel and pushed back into the moving river of people.

If they were about to riot, she didn't want to be there. Couldn't be there. Ancestors behind, even being on this base was dangerous.

::Don't stop,:: Delfi said. ::Don't ask. Get here fast.:: She wrapped herself around Jossa's mind, thickening the external shields. Jossa's sense of the surrounding people dimmed, suppressed so deeply that she could hardly tell they existed with the sai alone.

Jossa didn't question her sister when she used that tone of voice. Delfi had minor sai of Hearing. If she'd picked up on whatever it was and decided it was too dangerous for Jossa to Feel for herself, it was dangerous indeed. She couldn't shield like this forever, either. Not against the entire base. Not even against the people only on this level of it.

The meeting spot was down a small side corridor, then down an even smaller branch hall. Jossa escaped the crush of people on the main thoroughfare, but she couldn't escape her own rising emotions as whatever news she'd missed traveled from one person to another. The noise of the corridor behind her changed from the usual chatter of business to a buzz of alarm long before she was out of earshot.

Jossa trotted faster, slipping one hand under the edge of her shirt and pulling out the hilt of a spacer's knife. Those in the side hall were intent on their business. Few spared her more than a look. Curiosity brushed against her, faint through the shields Delfi held for her, but that was it.

Once or twice she almost reached for the small screen on her belt, but decided against it. None of them carried anything that could let the data feeds of the bases they visited link the ship. Instead, they bought disposable units in each port of call and resold them before leaving. The tactic kept cartel Cracks from feeding malware into the ship via their screen subsystems, and it kept the base administrators from killing their accounts with data charges.

It also made things tricky when the equivalent of a system-wide alert hit everyone's feed at once, because the rentals weren't hooked into the feeds the way personal ones would be. The practice had kept them safe, so far. Jossa hoped it wouldn't prove a liability today.

The dread grew as she trotted down the corridor. Here and there she caught a glimpse of a screen, but they didn't hold images. Just words too small to read.

The side hall that housed the bar was more crowded than the one she'd just come out of. Dredging up her mental map of the base, she realized that most of the customers arriving here weren't coming from the direction she had. This hall opened directly into another large corridor, which mainly held residences and local offices for official business. She wanted to say Customs lay in that direction? She wasn't sure. The local guild halls for the Freighters and the Merchants were that way for sure, so it made sense that Customs would be there too.

A tiny voice snagged her attention as she rounded the last corner. Did she just hear? Svis Konanuog? A flare of alarm punched through Delfi's shields, freezing Jossa in place for half a moment. Shaking herself free, she followed the sound.

A man leaned against the wall, just past the outflow of customers from a restaurant. He held a screen in both hands, tipped dangerously close to falling. His face was aimed at it, but his eyes were glassy. Jossa reached out and steadied the screen, bracing herself against the gut-wrenching feeling of terror as she came closer to the man. "Sir?" she asked. "Sir, your screen."

He started and blinked at her. A white scar stretched from jaw to ear on the left side of his face. Deep pockmarks decorated his temple. Pulse bolt blowback.

"Sir," Jossa tried again. "Sir, what is it?" If all else fails, play the meek mouse. Most people didn't get scared of timid women. Sometimes it even calmed them down.

The roil of emotions building inside the man didn't quiet, but his eyes focused. He tilted the slate to show her. "They're coming," he whispered in a hoarse voice.

Jossa leaned over to look. A man in a stiff formal coat clasped his hands together on a desk, knuckles white. His eyes were huge. "... just heard that Avesab has gone dark. Rumors put a large armada there, sustained by the Karukap and supported by the local Rard—"

The vid feed cut out. Rotating on the screen, the emblem of the local House replaced the visuals while a crisp voice announced that the news feed was currently experiencing some technical difficulties.

The man lurched away from the wall, taking the screen with him. Jossa jumped back, then cringed as his emotions went from a low boil to a full-blown explosion. Unasked, Delfi reached through the bond and siphoned off the excess, re-buffering Jossa's crumbling shield in the process. By the time Jossa was aware of her surroundings again, the man was gone.

::Del,:: she asked along the mind bond. ::Did you see that?:: Silly question. She had—why else have Jossa move so fast, or put up shields this strong?

::They're coming,:: her sister said, her mental voice strained. ::It was inevitable.::

::Can he really get us to safety in time?:: If he couldn't, if this deal of his fell through, what then? Travel halfway across the Empire, *again*, to try the only other Barbican into the Seps Coalition? Did they even have time given how close the Fleet was?

No. It was this or nothing. The Navlad name for the Fleet fit well. Star Eaters chewed through solar systems too quickly for a different escape route to be remotely viable. The whole past year could end up as a futile exercise, one more attempt to run in a lifetime of failed attempts.

::Well, we don't know if he can, do we?:: Delfi's voice shook, but she shoved each word at Jossa like a stab in the gut. ::No news feeds here. Get in so we can get out.::

Rubbing her stomach, Jossa clutched her market bag tighter and headed down the hall. Her sister was right. The sooner they got this meeting over with, the sooner they could get off this base, out of this system, out of the Empire, and away from the threat of the Svis Konanuog.

Four--Syrus

There's a whole shadow society full of folks who deserted the military. Everyone knows it. The Karukap leaves them alone because they have bigger problems than one or two runaways here or there. But mark my words. A day's coming when those running won't have anywhere to run anymore. And won't we have a job in front of us, rounding them all up?
   - officer of Metachesab law enforcement, speaking to a trainee

Syrus wasn't sure if the pounding in his ears came from his heart or the music in the bar out front. Frankly, he didn't care. What mattered right now were the bared teeth and hard fists of his opponent.

What mattered even more was the need to keep himself on a leash. To avoid cutting loose and beating the other man into so much red pulp. The monster that lived under his skin practically screamed to be let loose. To hurt and maim until the bastard in front of them begged for mercy. Then stopped begging forever.

Oh, how he wanted to. To get rid of this asshole flailing around with clumsy fists. To move on to the crowd jeering and catcalling around them. And then to the bar. And the—

One of those clumsy fists caught Syrus alongside the jaw. He fought for balance, turned the fall into a lunge, and came up under the other man's guard. An elbow just under the sternum, grab for a handful of the kicker's shirt, pull him back in for a punch to the throat.

The man staggered back, clutching at his neck. Syrus followed one step, two, before he got himself under control. The crowd roared its gleeful frustration. Syrus swung around to glare at them. It'd be so easy. Half were drunk out of their minds. Half drugged with the favorite local brain killer. Two thirds of them had decided to try both at the same time.

So easy. Kill them all. Keep going. Silence everyone he could reach. Get them out of his head, out of his skin.

Yes, but then someone would silence you, and all that killing would be wasted.

He couldn't hear Rissa's disembodied voice in his head. He'd buried her too deep, too far out of reach. But he knew what she'd say. She'd said it to him a thousand times as she'd hauled him, growling and snarling, from a thousand other rings just like this.

The memory was enough to abort his attack on the bystanders before wish turned to action. It almost wasn't enough to save the ref's life when the man popped up in front of him. But Syrus managed to stop the punch and look where the ref pointed.

The other fighter lay on the ground, hands still clutching his throat, face purple. Under the pulsing throb of the crowd's emotions, Syrus could feel the acid burn of panic.

No way they'd get him to a medunit in time. Stupid fuck.

Syrus waited just long enough for the ref to make the win official, then headed out of the ring. His monster wanted more. He didn't have time to give it any. He used the four steps between himself and the crowd to shove the animal rage back into the pit where he kept it most of the time. He barely, *barely* managed to get the metaphorical lid in place and locked down tight before the first person reached out to clap him on the shoulder.

At least he'd taken his knives off his belt for the fight. Otherwise, the struggle to keep himself under control would've been infinitely harder.

Behind him, a new challenger stepped into the ring, shouting insults and calling for an opponent. Bets flew thick and fast through the air as the crowd shuffled credit slips from hand to hand, jeered, and encouraged whoever wanted a fresh coat of bruises to step on up. Their anticipation hummed against his skin. But not enough. Never enough.

He tripped the last man who stood between him and freedom, helping the stranger to the floor with an elbow to the back of the head. The man lashed out blindly as he went down. Syrus sidestepped the attack and kept going. He was out of reach by the time the man clambered to his feet, mounting the steps from the fighting space and into the makeshift gallery that ringed the room. There was an audience up here too, mostly women waiting for their men to find a little sanity and detach from the human amoeba down near the ring. Guards stood at each end of the walkway, marking the boundaries of where violence was allowed.

A ripple of amusement, rough with the coarse sand of chiding, washed over him, real as an actual wave. He looked up at Delfi. She stood on the table in the center of the booth he'd claimed, hands braced on the upper bar of the struts that framed the space. A few strands of light cord dangled around her, blinking feebly here and there as the old units tried to draw a last gasp of energy from whatever power cell fed this part of the room.

It made her look like she stood among stars, an ancient being of sex, violence, and chaos. Most of the people in here probably assumed she was drunk. Why else would she be standing on the fucking table, swaying to a beat most of them could barely hear over the noise they made? Syrus knew better. Up there, she could watch the crowd and keep an eye on the doors much better than if she were sitting on one of the benches. She wasn't vulnerable either. Couldn't get trapped if a random stranger decided to try for a taste of her. Because, off limits or not, she wasn't afraid to flaunt what she had.

Ropey red curls fell over her shoulders, held away from her face by a pair of scarves wrapped around her head. An abbreviated green shirt that did sweet fuck all to cover her admittedly impressive rack. Her pair of pants looked like they'd been painted on. A dress of double weave mesh over the lot was her only nod to modesty, and a pitiful one at that. It sheathed her like a second skin, barely hitting the tops of her thighs, and since it was backless from neck to rounded hip, the only thing holding the top half in place was a thin chain around her neck. At least her boots were sensible.

Syrus never asked her how she managed to move without ripping half her seams open. He figured she dressed to draw the eye—and obliged by keeping watch over her whenever she wandered past. At first, it'd been a good way to rile Jossa and get her naked. It still was. But he also kept an eye on Delfi because one day that careful armor of hers was going to shatter, and the resulting mess would probably only be manageable if there was someone right there to do damage control. It'd better be him, because leaving that to Jossa would get all three of them tossed in a cell, there to wait until Quinn rolled the Fleet right over whatever system they got stuck in.

No thank you.

Delfi growled and tried to boot him in the face. He dodged, slapping her leg as a warning. Anger, frustration, and... he didn't catch that last one... burned his hand from the brief contact. He glared up at her. She sneered back. Then she rolled her hips, taunting more than inviting, and jerked her chin at the shouting mass of people around the ring.

"Yeah, yeah," he said, not needing to be told again. "I'll keep my thoughts to myself when you stop listening."

She wasn't as good at covering her emotions as suppressing Jossa. Syrus shook off the skittering jolts of alarm, reaching past her into the booth to detach the magbag from the bottom of the table.

Too much fun, that was the trouble. He'd had too much fun. The kind anyone of his background and breeding couldn't get enough of. The kind that landed his people in Uvlaku black-ops teams when they couldn't control themselves. He'd had three years to beat, shoot, and kill as many people as got in his way. Three years in which his biggest worry was how long he could stay alive to keep it up. He was born addicted to it, and the Fleet let him wallow in that addiction till he was nearly mindless with it.

He'd left it behind. On purpose.

All because he'd pulled two women out of long-term cryo on a planet no one knew existed. Because of Delfi and her sister and the part of him they'd resurrected. Because of Rissa, the reason he'd ended up with the Fleet to start with. He'd buried her memory the day she died. Locked her out of his thoughts and gotten on with life. Then he'd had to bury her all over again when Delfi turned nosy and snuck into his room one too many times while he was sleeping, looking for his secrets in his subconscious.

Although in the long run, the tradeoff wasn't so bad. The deal he'd made with Jossa, totally unnecessary as it was, came down as a win in his book. That, coupled with the occasional underground fight set up by and for his people, helped keep the edge off. Mostly. Sex and blood. His two worst vices.

He just had to hold out a little longer. A few more days. A week or so at most. Then he could pass through the last of the Barbicans between here and freedom. Disappear from the Navlad Empire for good. Make a new life out of reach of the military and the Kuchen Fleet both. Ride out the inevitable in a place where neither could reach.

Leaning against the table, Syrus turned his attention back to the current fight, ignoring the coughing, hissing cat noises Delfi made in place of a normal language. She understood things fine, but she hadn't made any progress with relearning her birth tongue. She probably refused to practice out of spite towards him. Or maybe spite towards everyone, if the anger and frustration she aimed at anyone who came in spitting distance were anything to judge by.

For his part, he'd learned as much as he could of He'la, the language the young woman spoke instead of Navlad. One of these days, she'd yowl at him and he'd answer back in the words of the prophets, and then he'd have himself the best laugh of the last few years watching her try to cope with the shock.

Delfi growled again, high in the throat, and bumped him with her knee. Surprise buzzed through his shoulder and up his neck in an offbeat staccato. Syrus jerked around, wondering if he'd dropped his interior shields without realizing. Had she picked up on his thoughts?

No. She still had her hands wrapped around the horizontal strut the light cords were dangling from, but her weight hung loose. Her eyes were glazed, her lower lip caught between her teeth. Carefully, Syrus leaned back until he had just the lightest contact with her leg. It gave him a great view of her chest. It also gave him a clearer read of her emotions.

What she was feeling had nothing to do with anything in this room. Fear brushed his mind with acid fingers before vanishing, sucked into the girl herself. How she did it, he had no idea. The ways of soul-bonded sai were a mystery. Nobody asked how they balanced each other, Unstable and Stable halves of a pair. They were sacred.

And sacred things should remain a mystery.

Syrus snorted to himself, broke contact with Delfi's leg, and went back to watching the crowd. The pair who'd replaced him in the ring came staggering out, one with blood pouring from his nose and the other cradling a limp arm. That one's shoulder looked malformed, possibly dislocated. As the money started changing hands again, Syrus noticed that all the congratulations were aimed at the one with the busted shoulder. Well, there were worse ways to win a fight. He'd won plenty of his own that hadn't looked like victories to anyone outside the situation.

Which was a good way to sum up how he'd landed here, as a matter of fact. That and the whole fucking religion built around sousi and everything associated with them. Just by existing, he tainted it. His birth, his background. They were unforgivable. Anathema to good Navlad society. And wouldn't they just shit themselves if he used that word in their hearing and proved that street Savages had brains as well as an overabundance of physical attributes?

Delfi kneed him again. Syrus turned to growl at her. Mental funk or faking, she needed to cut the shit. If she'd decided she could go back to digging through his brain for loose thoughts just because they were almost done traveling together, he'd teach her a hard lesson. And fuck the deal with Jossa.

Her eyes weren't glassed over anymore, although she looked more *through* him than *at* him as she scowled and tried to pull her weight up by her hands. No, not pull her weight up, position her leg so she could lean it against his shoulder. On purpose.

Acid washed down his arm where she made contact, coating his hand and ribs in searing pain. Fear. Not hers. *Everyone's.* Everyone on the base. What'd been a dull throb in the back of his head, brought on by too many people, bloomed to a pounding headache.

Syrus grabbed her ankle, all unthinking, and barely caught himself before he dumped her on the floor. For one, the guards were eyeing him from the other end of the walkway. For another, it wasn't her fault.

Jossa. Headed this way, acting as an amplifier for every panicked person between here and the docks. Syrus couldn't tell what she'd seen or heard or even done. That wasn't his talent. If Delfi knew, she was too focused on keeping her sister from broadcasting that fear right back to the people. She didn't have time to explain to him.

The young woman's hands slipped on the strut, fingers tangling with the light cords. Whatever she was looking at, it wasn't in this room. Syrus tucked his shoulder in under her ribs as she fell. She draped over him slowly, boneless, sighing something as she came to rest. It sounded faintly like "She'o gatsyruks." He didn't know the first word, but if he had the translation right, the second was "come."

Come? Who came? Their hosts? Local authorities? Maybe. It could be the military. That particular execution order'd been out for so long, they'd given him up for dead. He didn't know if the kemvate in charge of the shadow base had gotten a chance to update the files before Kizen and the Fleet rolled over them.

No matter who it was, Delfi wasn't in any state to tell him. Grumbling to himself about Foreseers who couldn't speak Common and went off into their minds instead of giving an actual warning, he reached up to detangle the light cords.

Delfi groaned and pressed her face into his back, right between his shoulder blades.

Heat blistered his skin. All the warning he had of incoming trouble.

"What in the name of Ancestors do you think you're *doing?*"

Well, shit.

Syrus threw up more shields to shore up the ones eroded by Delfi's outburst and craned his head around to see Jossa standing just down the walkway, lean and tall. Her skin, darker than his, flushed a deep red brown. Eyes so dark they looked black snapped at him from behind a haphazard curtain of dark hair. A silplat shopping bag swung from one wrist as she propped her hands on her hips.

What the fuck was she pissed off for? Whatever she and Delfi'd been talking about through their mind bond?

"Get your hands off her, you fikekoj achek."

Syrus raised his eyebrows, then looked up at Delfi's fingers still tangled in the cords. He caught a glimpse of her ass out of the corner of his eye. Her very firm ass, right next to his face.

Whether she was responding to the direction his thoughts took right then or to Jossa's indignation, or if she'd just decided to return to the land of the self-aware, Delfi came alive. She tried to get her hands around to brace herself as she straightened her back, but she drew up short when the cords ran out of slack. The support frame clattered and jangled. Delfi yelped and tried again, this time folding herself back down over his shoulder as she tugged at her trapped hands. Fresh panic cut a jagged trail down Syrus's torso, front and back. His shoulder felt like someone'd stuck a knife in the joint and tried to debone him.

The frame jangled as Delfi pulled again, harder. One end popped loose of its connection with the upright. Syrus caught it before it landed across Delfi's back, snarling under his breath. His hosts were going to make him pay through the nose to replace an ancient light curtain and a couple bars of rusty metal. Perfect.

The monster rammed itself at the lid he kept on its hole, trying to see if the seal had weakened. It took monumental effort, but he kept the rage tucked down, down, down. Away from the freedom to rip and maim.

Stuck, Delfi made angry kitten noises against his shirt and bit him almost in the ass.

Better and better.

"You're what now?" Jossa hissed at Delfi.

"Hey," Syrus barked. "Public place."

She refocused on him. "And *you*. Did you let her get drunk? She wasn't even supposed to leave the ship!"

Syrus snorted to himself, then realized he was waiting for the snippy voice of his conscience to chime in with an opinion.

"Well," Jossa said, apparently figuring out that he wasn't going to answer her, "did we or did we not have a deal?"

Delfi wriggled on his shoulder, still trying to get free of the light cords. He swatted her thigh. "Stop that. Or I'll leave you like this. Joss, get over here and help, would you?"

"Jossa," she huffed. "And you expect me to come, just like that?"

She usually did. Generally speaking, when he teased Delfi or even just stayed in the same room with her for too long, he was actually trying to get Jossa out of her clothes. He didn't have time for that now. Very carefully, he dropped some of his interior shields, letting her feel what was going on under his skin. Letting her see that if she didn't give him a hand, he'd overload from the emotions Delfi was practically shoving down his throat—and then they'd all have much bigger problems than whatever her sister'd been trying to fix in the first place.

Jossa came over, stomping a little to prove she wasn't doing it because she really wanted to. Syrus rolled his eyes and held the strut so she could work on the cords. "There, that so hard?"

A fresh burst of anger took him in the ribs. He nearly choked on his own air.

"Words, woman," he growled once he caught his breath. "Told you a hundred times if I told you once. You and your sister. It's all too much subvocal. Shit like that will blow our cover right out into vacuum."

Jossa grumbled under her breath. He shot her a look. In those heeled boots, she wasn't much shorter than him, so it wasn't all that hard to catch her eye. Her mouth tightened. "I will not mount you here in public," she murmured quietly but firmly.

"I don't want you to." Delfi bit him again. He swatted her ass this time. "Stop that," he told her, then looked back at Jossa. "Wasn't even thinking of it." Although he was now. His dick was thoroughly on board for it. "Whatever you two were talking about before you got here, she nearly took a header off the table."

"She what?" Jossa jerked away, letting go of the cords she'd been unwrapping from Delfi's wrist. Delfi's arm dropped, free. Neither woman noticed.

Syrus lifted one foot, careful of balancing Delfi, and set his heel on Jossa's toes. She glared at him. She also shut up. He smiled at her. "So, what's the news? Cause I don't speak crazy."

He barely managed to get enough shields up in time to blunt her emotional attack. Snapping her in half sounded better and better every second he stood here.

Surprise burst over his back and down his neck and arm as Delfi used her free arm to brace herself on his shoulder while straightening out her spine. Syrus swayed to compensate and caught sight of the source of the latest emotional fluctuation, which speaking of, wasn't that a phrase that should earn him a few credits. He doubted the man standing in the walkway, dressed in synthleather and real silk, would pay him for it though. Light brown skin, lean body, clean-shaven face, and blond hair cut close to the head were all the impression Syrus got before Delfi's hand skidded off his shoulder. She landed back in her previous position with a *whoof*.

"Ladies, if he's bothering you at all, say the word. We don't allow noncon in here." The man's voice was smooth.

The fury in Syrus bubbled once and subsided. The monster beating at the lid of its prison in his head quieted suddenly. For half a second, he could think straight. Then the monster thrashed back to life, and Syrus had to grit his teeth on a growl as he hammered it back down where it belonged.

He needed to get rid of these two before they drove him insane. At least his contact was here. Finally.

"I don't do the noncon," he told the man. "Don't need to. Although if you'd taken too much longer, I'd have had to go find a whorehouse. Why the fuck do they keep them off the same level as the bars?"

The man's face twisted. Disgust crackled through the air of the booth. Syrus curled a lip in answer. Yes, he knew his choice of words gave him away. Considering the situation, the stupid fuck didn't have any room to be taking pot shots. Born a nehkeh, *Syrus* couldn't help it. This man *chose* to join the Kiprinog.

Apparently, the man knew enough to keep his mouth shut. Instead, he held out a hand to Jossa. "I'm Faler," he said. "Pleasure."

She leaned over and took his hand, sending out sparks of surprise when he half bowed and kissed her wrist. Syrus resisted the urge to yank her back. She'd just pitch another fit, and he'd lose his chance to warn her.

"Now," said Faler. "There's a private party being held in the back rooms. One less... violent." He looked over at the throng of people cheering a new set of fighters. "In the interest of being good hosts, my employer was wondering if you'd like to join?" He looked at Jossa, completely ignoring Syrus. "The view is very boring back there, but you would help to liven it up immensely. Might even meet someone who has more manners than a street Savage."

No, no, this man wasn't smart at all. Except he was, because Syrus couldn't *do* anything to him unless he wanted the whole deal to fall through.

He'd put too much work into setting up this meeting. Their lives were riding on this.

This man's life was now riding on whether they made the deal.

Delfi propped herself back up on Syrus's shoulder and dropped her chin on his head. He growled and looked up at her. She met his eyes and gave her head a tiny shake. On the emotional front, she was as communicative as a rock. Nothing leaked through her shields. Which was warning enough, in and of itself.

Right. Mind reader. Syrus shored up his internal shields, building the wall between himself and any sai who might be listening in, then looked back at the man. "Sounds like a lot more fun than anything happening here. What do you girls say?"

Delfi shook the arm still attached to the lights and harrumphed at them both. Jossa made a small *eep* noise and slipped around behind Syrus to help detangle that hand. Syrus made a point of not trying to watch her, since he'd only get an eyeful of Delfi's ass and his dick still wasn't too happy about being teased. Faler waited for them to finish, watching the fight below instead with a bored expression. Syrus couldn't tell what he might be thinking, even with the shitty state of his shields.

Then Delfi slapped him lightly on the shoulder and wiggled against his hold. Syrus gritted his teeth as her breasts swiped him across the head, told his dick to settle down, and stepped away from the table so he could set her on her feet without obstacle. Jossa watched him like a hunting bird the whole time. He couldn't resist pulling the younger of the two sisters close, letting her body slide against his chest and legs until she stood on her own. Yes. Very nice. Too bad he'd never actually been after her like Jossa thought.

Too bad she was so damaged she couldn't handle the thought of a man being interested in her.

Jossa wedged herself in between Syrus and her younger sister the second Delfi had all her weight on her feet. Heat blistered Syrus again, this time across his chest, but he let them both go. The time for teasing was over. Now it was time to find out whether they'd be stuck in the Empire till the Fleet devoured them all.

Faler came alive as the women approached, holding out his arm to Delfi in the way of highborn the Empire over. Oily anticipation mixed with something that sent stabbing pain straight through Syrus's lungs. Too late, he shouted at her in his mind. It was a trap, fuck it all.

Her arm already halfway to Faler's, Delfi swayed, staring at Syrus. Faler caught her, settling her hand in the crook of his arm.

Fuck. There went a solid chunk of their safety net. Syrus's old teammates had never been caught in that trap. He didn't even remember if it'd been tried on them after they'd brushed the gesture off the first time. The women on his team had been too nehkeh to react to it on an instinctive level. Just like Delfi was too much a noble to *not* take a man's arm when it was offered.

Syrus stepped up and snagged Jossa by the elbow before she could cause a fuss. She glared up at him but kept her emotions mostly to herself, which was the best he could ask for at this point.

"Come on," he muttered in her ear as Faler guided Delfi down the walkway. He didn't try to slip Jossa's hand over his arm like the Kiprinog man. These people knew what he was. And now they had an idea of what Delfi was. If he could keep them from realizing exactly what caliber of woman Jossa was, maybe he and the girls could get out of this with their proverbial arms and legs intact.

Jossa snorted and set off after her sister. Syrus shook his head and followed.

FIVE--SYRUS

We know the truth. The people of the Empire didn't just fall into Ancestor worship. Their continual ostracism of those who refuse to play brood mare and stud is as programmed into them as their lineage into their nanites. So why should we abide their rules at all?
  - Appulu of the Kiprinog, to his subordinates

"What was going on with you and Delfi?" Syrus leaned in close so he could speak in Jossa's ear as they entered a dimly lit hall. The noise was only a low thrum back here, but it should be enough to mask any pickup from surveillance equipment.

She looked up at him, scorn and anger nowhere in sight. Or in evidence to his sai. Instead, fear lurked in the shadows around her eyes, lapping at his skin in wavelets of acid pain. "There aren't any news feeds in the bar. Did you notice?"

He'd noticed. He also knew why. But why mention that when Delfi'd been distracted long before Jossa set foot in the place?

Jossa frowned at him. Right. She wanted an answer.

"People looking over their shoulders aren't as likely to get drunk and fight for the fun of it. Or bet on the fights. Then they'd fight because they're scared or angry instead of for fun or money, and that's how you get mobs in contained places," he murmured in her ear. "Doesn't explain what—"

Delfi stopped short. Syrus nearly ran right up the back of her. The look she gave him as he ground to a halt could've melted the paint right off the hull of their ship. He glared back and jerked his chin. *Look forward little girl*, he thought at her, *before you snap my last nerve.*

She huffed and turned around, leaning into Faler slightly as he pressed his free hand to a lockpad mounted to the wall. Syrus wondered what her reaction would be if he told her the truth about this guy's preferences in bed. Although, all things considered, he might be the safest person for her to rub up on since her late husband.

Syrus scratched at his short beard to hide his smile when Faler turned to look at him with raised eyebrows. Amusement and frustration rolled off the man in prickly waves. Syrus lifted a shoulder in reply. Guy was on his own.

A door formed in the wall in front of their guide. With a hiss and a quiet clunk, the sections irised out and away. Faler handed Delfi in first, watching her feet as she picked them up just a little too high and too carefully to clear the sill. Syrus followed, Jossa right behind him. Syrus looked around.

Small party was right. No party was more like it. Not that he'd expected anyone else. The space wasn't large enough to hold more than ten or fifteen people. Chairs, short couches, piles of cushions, low tables and high were placed strategically around the available floor space. No decorations for the holiday. Plenty of room. Only two people.

A man sat on a plush red couch along the far wall, fingers flying over a screen. To the left, another man stood next to a small table, arms folded as he watched the newcomers. The half-smile on his face looked semi-permanent. Syrus reached with his sai. Amusement mixed with no small amount of worry lapped at his skin in tingly waves. He wished he could claw the emotions out and throw them back at the man like Jossa could.

The man with the green eyes waved at them, gesturing towards the couch across from his. A table stood between the two pieces of furniture, covered in plates of food.

"Please," the man said. "Come in. Sit. Faler..." Reproach edged the man's voice. "Are you going to leave them standing in the door? Manners." He flashed a very white smile. "I am Rultru. This,"he gestured at the young man on the red couch, "is Dokil. Welcome."

Manners. Right. The bastard was waiting to see if the girls would react like typical highborn bitches, noses permanently stuck in the air. Hopefully Delfi'd heard his mental warning and passed it on to Jossa. They didn't need to give these fuckers any more ammunition.

Syrus felt the wash of curiosity ripple out from Jossa, then vanish as either she or Delfi clamped down on it. Handing the magbag and its blood samples off to Faler, Syrus followed Jossa over to the edge of the couch, which was a brilliant shade of blue. Once she was seated, he crouched by the table to load a small plate full of food. Hopefully his lack of manners would throw these people off their stride, and they wouldn't up the price too much.

By accident or design, Delfi did her part to muddy the waters. Staggering against Faler as he led her around to the couch, she mashed her breasts into his arm. The man recoiled before he could help himself, nearly dropping both bag and young woman. Delfi kept right on going, losing her grip on his sleeve.

Jossa yelped and lunged, colliding with Syrus's shoulder as she went. Syrus hunched over his plate and clamped down on the monster as it surged out of its pit. Let them think he was guarding his food. Better that than grabbing Delfi by the scruff of her neck and shaking her till she quit fucking around.

Jossa got Delfi under control and settled on the couch before Syrus was sure he could set the plate down without breaking the damn thing. Plopping herself next to her sister, the older woman grabbed a plate and started loading it up. Good. Nothing liquid or covered in sauces.

Delfi probably wasn't actually drunk, but she didn't need any more ways to make a literal mess of things.

Shaking his head, Syrus went back to fixing the food on his plate. The hair-trigger fury simmering under his skin settled slightly. Nowhere to aim the violence now. He needed these bastards too much to let himself cut loose.

His job done for now, Faler slipped through a door in the starboard wall, taking the magbag with him. Syrus made a mental note to keep an eye on the door. Fucker better not come out with a pulse gun or worse.

Setting the plate on the edge of the table between Jossa and Delfi, he started loading another one. Little balls of ground meat. Some sort of sauce based on fermented fruit and crushed beans. A couple slices of dark red pickled eggs. Arranging everything without making a mess gave him a chance to pull the last of the teeth from his temper and finish stuffing it back into its prison.

As he stood, he caught the eye of the man by the table. Rultru hadn't moved, but the high-singing readiness coming off him waned somewhat. The look in his eyes was less amused now. More assessing.

Syrus nudged at Delfi's leg with his knee. "Move over," he told her. They'd managed to sit next to each other while leaving a space in between, an unconscious habit they had yet to break. According to etiquette, he should sit between them.

Manners were for those who could afford them. He didn't come from that level of society.

"All done?" the young man on the red couch asked. "Or are you going to do a few backflips to cap it off?"

Delfi bared her teeth at him as she scooted over. Jossa laid a hand on her knee. Syrus snorted and popped a ball of ground meat in his mouth. Dokil waited another moment, then straightened and set the screen on the table. "The price is up," he said. "Three million more. Each."

Syrus stopped mid-chew. Jossa choked on her food. Surprise burst from her like a flash grenade, then sucked right back in as Delfi leaned over to pound on her sister's back. Syrus paused to see if any of the men showed signs of being affected. Nothing.

"Fuck that." He growled as Jossa caught her breath. "Since when?" That was a shit ton more than he'd expected for Delfi's slip up in the manners departments. This wasn't about him trying to bring highborn women through the Barb. This sort of money meant they were seriously trying to run him off this trip.

"Does it matter?" asked the man standing by the high table. "Our price is our price. You'll pay it or get out of our system."

He'd been dickering with the Kiprinog for months now, trying to set the terms of this deal. Number of people, size of the ship, whether they'd run their own ID scans of his and the girls' blood. They'd won the argument about the blood scan, but he'd come away with the ultimate win. Sure, they could take the money and sell him and the girls out. But he knew who Appulu, their leader, really was. Syrus'd sent back his final amendment to the terms last week, along with an attachment and the promise to out the head of their operation to every form of official justice he could find if they double-crossed him. They hadn't come up with any more bits of finicky bullshit after that.

So, what changed that made them brave again? Not even resentment over Delfi's unconscious display of class accounted for such a big hike in price. Unless...

He looked at Jossa. "Which system did they take this time?"

Mouth full, she stared at him with haunted eyes.

"Avesab," Delfi said carefully. Jossa swiveled her head like a bird to stare at her sister.

Syrus wanted to growl, but the Kiprinog men were watching. Predators looking for weakness in their prey. So instead, he sat back and ate another little ball of meat, dragging it through the puddle of sauce first. "Told you there's a reason they don't have news feeds in the bar."

So they wouldn't lose customers when a new war broke out or the Svis Konanuog took another system or who the fuck knew what else. And also to blindside business partners.

He might've had warning, if he'd had a screen on him when the news broke. But the jackass customs official had dragged ship inventory out so long that by the time Syrus left for the meet, he'd barely been able to stuff a protein roll in his mouth and glare at Delfi when she showed up in the airlock. He hadn't bothered wasting time renting one of the disposable screens for such a short trip out. Half the time, Delfi didn't bother. The crippled interfaces and slow data links pissed her off to no end.

He should have just shelled out for implants and called it good, but no. He'd been trying to save money and keep them off the data networks. It also would've meant finding someone he trusted to remove the Fleet hardware still attached to his and the girl's jawbones. Trust like that wasn't something any amount of money could buy.

Here went all their savings. Dumped down the black hole that was the Gatekeepers' system. He was going to have to do more than dip into the reserves for this. They needed to sell cargo he'd been planning to offload in the Seps Coalition and hope what was left would be enough to cushion them on the other side.

The Kiprinog men were still watching him. Syrus swallowed his food and set his plate on the table. Propping his arms on his knees, he laced his fingers together and looked at the young man on the red couch. "We had an agreement. How much do you think it's worth, what I have on you assholes?"

Both Kiprinog men drew in a breath and looked at each other. Syrus couldn't read the emotions off them, not with Delfi baking his side in low-grade outrage and the sudden struggle to keep his own fury under control.

Dokil picked up his screen and flicked his fingers over it once or twice, then showed it to Rultru. The man nodded.

"Two million," Dokil said, jaw set.

Delfi shifted towards Jossa and then away, just slightly. Syrus gritted his teeth as the tension in the room ratcheted up another notch or three. The Kiprinog men watched with hard shoulders and harder eyes, hands suspiciously close to the table. They probably had weapons stuck to the bottom. They'd figured out how much it would cost them to cover up the damage he could cause with his information and weighed it against what it was going to cost them to keep to the bargain and make this run. Now they were waiting for *him* to lose his cool. To give them an excuse to refuse the job—or better, shoot him right here.

Except if he lost his shit, he'd have to ask their bloody corpses for help. Bloody corpses were popular with the Kuchen, or Svis Konanuog, Fleet. They did sweet fuck all for someone trying to sneak through a Barbican. Even if killing them would be more fun than selling nearly half the cargo.

He ate another little ball of meat. "That's better. Operating costs, I can understand. Greed..." He sucked the sauce off his fingers. "Greed is just plain stupid." But he'd be adding to the data packet he'd put together and setting a timer for it to send out if they didn't deliver on their end of the deal. They'd already tried to fuck him over once. No guarantee they wouldn't try again.

It was a miracle Jossa hadn't pitched a fit yet. Did Delfi have her brain on lockdown or something?

Rultru relaxed, just slightly, and nodded. "The next window opens in thirty-six hours. You have until then to gather the extra money. If you don't..." He lifted a shoulder. "We can no longer help you."

Delfi curled a lip and snarled at him, but she kept her emotions low enough that Syrus doubted he would've felt them at all if he weren't nearly touching her. If he could have patted her on the head without sparking an actual temper tantrum, he would've. Maybe later, just to watch her blow up in safety. And then have Jossa to distract him.

The redhead's eyes flickered to him. He fed more power into the shields that walled off his thoughts and feelings from the rest of the world. She looked back at the men.

"Now," Dokil said. "If you would like to—"

"I would like an explanation please," Jossa said in a clear voice. "I'm afraid I don't understand the *much-increased* fee. Or the *incredibly* short time frame."

Syrus swiveled to look at her and, by virtue of proximity, Delfi. Jossa ignored him, all polite attention aimed at Dokil. Delfi caught Syrus's expression and rolled her eyes. He scowled at her. Had they planned this? Or was Jossa actually that dense? Sometimes it was hard to tell what bit of present-day logic would clash with the world she'd known three hundred years ago.

He wished Delfi could speak mind-to-mind to someone besides Jossa. Then she'd be able to let him know what the fuck she and her sister were up to.

The men of the organization gave Jossa identical looks of condescension. The tension in the room dropped another few degrees. Syrus could feel his ribs expand properly for the first time since they'd walked in.

"I thought most people were running for the Core," Jossa said, tucking one ankle behind the other as she set her plate aside and folded her hands over her knee. "We're still very far from Avesab. As far as I know, there is no direct path of travel from there to here. So..." She spread her hands, emanating calm interest. "Why the sudden increase?"

Dokil set the screen aside and gave her a look like she was a particularly stupid child. Jossa managed to keep her sai from flooding the room. Syrus decided to be glad Delfi was doing her job. He knew how Jossa felt about being looked at like that. For his part, he stuffed another ball of meat in his mouth, trying to step on his reaction to the sudden hostility. It wasn't so much the man's emotions. Fucker was flat. Dead almost. Which, considering the fact he'd felt like a normal person since they'd entered the room, was much more dangerous.

But not as dangerous as the monster that lived in Syrus's soul. He shoved the rage back down just as Delfi poked him in the arm. He glared at her. She glared right back.

"Hazard pay," Rultru said into the quiet. Confidence dripped from his words, saturating the air. "If you can't figure that out, woman, you might as well give this whole thing up as a lost cause. Tell your man here to aim for the Border. The Svis Konanuog haven't taken Korukkesab yet. That, or head back to whichever husbands you ran from and pray they have a better plan to protect your gold-plated ovaries."

Heat flared, bright and sharp. Jossa sat straighter, ready to send an insult right back. Delfi laid a hand on her sister's arm. Jossa stopped before her words escaped to open air.

And that was enough of that. Next thing, *he'd* be the one blowing up. Syrus wrestled his monster back into submission and stood, wiping the crumbs from his hand onto his pants legs. "Think I got it from here," he told their hosts. "I'll have everything ready on my end. Don't fucking lose the blood samples."

Jossa flared again but didn't say anything. Delfi must have really put a lock on her brain-to-tongue filter. Good. Jossa nudged Delfi in the side. Her sister huffed but stood, stepped around the table, and headed for the door. Syrus grabbed another ball of meat and dipped it in the sauce while he waited for Jossa to pick up her bag and pass him. Then he jerked his chin at the two fuming members of the Kiprinog and followed the women out.

Faler met them outside the door. He didn't hold his arm out for either woman. Instead, he stalked down the hallway, radiating bad temper like a faulty power core. Syrus gritted his teeth and resisted the urge to bury a knife in the man's back. Jossa and Delfi were probably dealing with him better, what with their bond and all.

Come to think of it, he'd rather strangle Jossa. It was amazing in and of itself that Roltru hadn't upped the fee again and called it a stupidity tax. That she hadn't pushed the issue was even more so.

Maybe Delfi had sponged the answers out of the man's brain for her.

"DNA?" Jossa asked quietly, dropping back to walk next to him. Her long legs matched his stride. The command in her voice would have done any noble House proud.

So much for Delfi getting answers for her. He wished knocking their heads together would make the complacency fall out.

Jossa elbowed him in the side, sending stabbing flares of frustration through his ribcage. He growled. She rolled her eyes. Ahead of them, Delfi twisted to look over her shoulder, mouth set in a firm line. Right. Quit bickering and act like adults.

Fuck that shit.

He clipped the knife hilt back to his belt and caught Jossa's elbow before she could use it again. "This ain't the place," he told her, jerking his chin at Faler. She walked in sullen silence until the Kiprinog man stopped to unlock a door.

"Roltru will contact you in eight hours to tell you the results of the blood tests and set up payment," he said. "Good day."

Syrus watched Jossa lean forward, clearly wanting to attach herself to Delfi before the younger woman stepped through the door. The redhead slipped out before Jossa made contact, then set her hands on her hips and turned to glare at Syrus. Or maybe Jossa. He wasn't sure.

Syrus waited for Jossa to exit before nodding to their guide, who gave him a flat look in reply, and stepping over the sill of the door.

Immediately, the sharp burn of fear set his nerves afire. Shielding. The Kiprinog had the damn place shielded against outside sai. And he hadn't noticed because he'd been so focused on not letting the crowd *inside* set him off. He held in the groan until the door shut behind him.

No buffer now. No shield he set up would hold against an entire city's worth of people all stacked on top of each other. It got worse every time he left and came back to it. It hadn't been this bad a few months ago. Or even a few weeks. On the Fleet, well. It hadn't mattered as much how often he killed someone in a fit of rage. In fact, he'd gotten enough challenges and war to keep himself mostly in check.

Mostly.

Until those last few weeks, after he found the women on that abandoned planet.

He waited for Rissa to make a smart remark and found himself grasping into the void. Of course she wasn't there. She never would be again.

"Hey!" Jossa snapped her fingers in his face. He grabbed for her wrist and squeezed, glaring.

"Pull yourself together," she told him. But without heat.

Syrus took a deep breath, then found a measure of sanity somewhere in the corner of his memories and pulled it over himself like a blanket. The fear permeating the base didn't go away, but his reaction eased. Focus. Focus on thinking. Focus, fuck it all.

"That," he said, hearing his voice rasp over the words. "That is exactly why they want hazard pay."

She frowned at him, then frowned harder when he wrapped an arm around her waist. The base-wide emotions faded from his awareness, replaced by a sort of suction. Of course. Delfi was dampening Jossa to the point where the Feel couldn't set him off. Smart woman.

A faint echo in his head, something like *damn right*. He jerked his head up to stare at Delfi. She lifted one corner of her mouth in a sarcastic smile.

Ok then. Deal with that later. "Come on. Let's get into clearer space."

There was nobody in earshot. Jossa raised an eyebrow, but when Syrus flicked his eyes back to the door, she shrugged and headed out.

His mind was wandering. He yanked it back to the job at hand. Get through the base and back to the ship. Lock himself in and figure out the extra payments. Fuck Jossa senseless at some point and maybe they'd be able to ignore the emanations of however many thousands of people in various states of panic. Emanations. There was a word worth a few credits.

They slipped out of the side hall and into one of the larger thoroughfares. People walked past. Some ran. Some trotted. Nobody lingered. Everyone spoke in hushed voices. The fear pressed at him, but with contact to Jossa—and Delfi by extension—the urgency was less.

He glanced over at Delfi feeling her way through the crowd. Looked like she'd found her mental feet. Must have been the strain of siphoning the whole damn base at once when the news broke that'd made her wobble. At least there wasn't any shaking or crying this time around. The first base they'd been on when news of the Fleet breaking through the Net hit, she'd been in bad shape. Fresh from having nearly died of injuries acquired when the Fleet soldiers raped her. He and Jossa'd had to scrape her off the floor and all but carry her to the new ship.

"Hazard pay?"

Right. Explanations. "It's a psychological thing. Use your brain, woman. The Fleet is halfway through conquering this hemisphere of the Empire, at least out at the borders. It's not far behind on the other side either. And after they're done with the borders, they'll turn inward. Once people learned the Net was there, mainly because of how bad a job it's doing at protecting the Empire, they reacted instead of thinking. Nobody's stopped reacting long enough to actually think about what's happening.

"So first people find out some long-dead Emperor actually *did* take measures to protect them from a threat so scary people call them Star Eaters. He even gave it a pretty name, Hadra's Net. And that might've been great, except the very first system the invaders hit along the Net, they blew right through. Now they're forcing their way between Barbicans that were never meant to link with each other at all. And they're doing it almost unopposed."

"Ilattesab," Delfi said over her shoulder, in the same careful voice she'd used to make sure she didn't spout He'la in the Kiprinog.

Syrus lifted a shoulder, though she couldn't see, and bent to dodge the wildly swaying metal pole covered with bangles and charms wielded by a frantic shopkeeper trying to ward off the street thugs rummaging through his storefront. "The military managed to implode that Barbican, but just the one so far," he said once he was safe from concussion. "The Fleet was only stalled for a month or so, and they hit the next three systems like a fucking supernova." Syrus had a feeling the Barbican implosion hadn't caught Quinn unawares. Especially seeing as he himself had handed the Fleet Second that particular tactic on a silver platter.

"The military isn't set up to defend the whole Net at once. They never expected to need it. But just the one so far. You see the news feeds after they pulled the other Barb through the Ilattesab wormhole?"

Jossa sighed, grief and sorrow oozing through Delfi's siphon and permeating the palm of his hand. "Yes. The neighboring Kizrardog had a fit. The Commons are *still* throwing the occasional riot over food shortages."

"Nobody's figured a way to stop the Svis Konanuog," Syrus said quietly. "People are starting to realize nobody can, not without shattering the Empire and its trade routes. These people have known the importance of their Barbican for years now. You can bet the other Gatekeepers-linked system does too."

"That still doesn't answer my earlier question. The Fleet—"

Syrus growled at her.

She tried again. "The Svis Konanuog are barely past the halfway point of that part of the Net. But that's just one system. There are plenty more they need to take before they have the Empire surrounded."

He shook his head and sidestepped a man dragging his protesting wife along while she tried to keep hold of the child sobbing in her arms.

Syrus used his free hand to tip the balance so the kid wouldn't fall and hit the deck, then looked back to Jossa. Delfi slowed so he was nearly walking on her heels. Syrus caught the edge of her boot once, as a warning. She snarled and trotted out of the way.

Jossa opened her mouth again. He held up a hand. "Think. When the news broke, what was your first reaction?"

Jossa twitched. Ahead, Delfi looked over her shoulder. Syrus wasn't sure if the glare was for him or her sister. He kept going anyway. "You thought of how it would affect *you* if this place went into full panic mode, didn't you?"

The whites of her eyes showed all the way around when she looked at him. He grinned at her, only a little forced. "Exactly. *They*"—he swept his hand out at the churning crowds—"thought of what will happen to them when the whole *Empire* panics. Listen. Any one of them talking about running?"

He waited while she listened to, and probably Felt, the crowd around them. He dodged a man with an armload of synthcot rolls muttering under his breath about blankets and cost of living and invading outsiders.

A street vendor nearby packed up the bowls, cartons, and pour spouts of his trade, talking in low tones with the young boy at his side. Syrus caught mention of tariffs the local rard was going to levy on imports from the nearest Ajiri planet. A woman came up behind them, jaw set and whites showing all the way around her eyes. She clutched a screen in one hand, the image of a baby wrapped in blankets clear at this angle. At the top of the screen an icon flashed. Paid in full for services rendered.

"They aren't," Jossa said before he could reach out and stab the woman. Syrus stomped on his anger and looked over at her. She met his eyes, mouth pressed together and gaze firm.

He nodded. "They got nowhere to go, and they know it. This and one other system. Only two Barbicans into the Gatekeepers and the Seps Coalition past that. If they could have gotten through, they would have years ago. No way they can make it before the Svis Konanuog roll over us."

"Anyone who knows of the Seps will head this way." Jossa stuttered to a stop and looked at him. Really looked at him for the first time all night. "They know they won't be safe in the Core."

"If they aren't blockaded out to begin with," Syrus said. He doubted anyone but the nobleborn would be allowed through the Barbs in the center of the Empire. The gates themselves had long been rigged to scan every ship that came through for any warm body, no matter how small. The Core was too overpopulated to let just anyone in. Despite the abysmal natural birth rate, the Empire couldn't avoid expanding. Not with the priesthood dictating population growth the way it did.

"This system will bottleneck from here to the Barbican," she said.

"Already has. What do you think that two-week wait for a parking spot was about?" He tightened his arm around her shoulders and pulled her back into motion. "We had a head start because we know what's coming. I skipped us past as many systems as I could on the way here. It helps that I know a couple of the non-legal ways to make it into the Gatekeepers and the Coalition. But this..." He waved a hand at the people running back and forth and up and down the corridor as they looked for safety. "This is just the beginning." The acid of their fear would get worse the longer this went on, corroding good sense and logic. *He* needed off this floating death trap before it reduced him to a raving lunatic. The *people* needed hope, or they'd literally tear themselves apart before the Fleet ever showed up.

Hope was exactly what they wouldn't get.

Oblivious of his train of thought, Jossa kept going. "If not right away, then—" Her face twisted in revulsion. She clutched at her stomach, bending over to crouch on her heels. "Oh no," she whispered.

Ahead, Delfi retched and bent over, gasping for breath.

"Oh *fuck* no," Syrus snarled, looking from one woman to the other.

"Jump, slash, sneak," Delfi croaked in Imperial Common. "Rats they come, rats they are. Skitter, skitter, cornered, dead. Do you feel the knife of gold?"

Oh fuck no.

Jossa whimpered and clutched at her stomach. A vendor nearby shouted a protest. The crowd moving past them parted and kept going, too intent on their own troubles.

"Bounty hunters," Jossa said, clawing at Syrus's pant leg to find her balance. "Coming. Kill orders."

Syrus grabbed her around the waist, gritting his teeth against the horror dragging at his arms. He snagged Delfi by the elbow and started moving. Bulling his way through the crowd, ignoring the yells and curses that followed him, he looked for a gap in the walls of the corridor. The bag on Jossa's arm slapped his leg.

"It's been seven months," he snapped at them both. "Seven *fucking* months, and you have to have one of your visions *now?*"

"If it saves your life, would you rather we didn't?" Jossa retched again. He had a flashback to dragging them naked through the hall of a stolen military ship… He squashed the memory. At least Jossa'd been there to translate. The one that happened later, just him and Delfi in a market—that had nearly cost all three of them their lives. Jossa'd been eating chalk tablets for weeks after.

"How far away?" There. A recycler trailing a wheeled cart of glass and rotting organic matter emerged from the gap between vendors. Syrus dodged the bot, nearly got his foot run over by the cart, and ducked into the alcove it had come out of.

"Too close," Jossa replied.

He shoved her towards the back of the little space, then pushed Delfi after her. "Stay out of my way."

"We can—"

"Throw up on them? No."

Delfi bared her teeth at him, but she grabbed Jossa by the arm and pulled her back against the wall. He spun to face the street outside, pulling his knife hilts and activating them. The liquid metal slithered and twisted before solidifying into blades.

Now he just had to hope the hunters were smart enough not to use guns on a base.

Six--Jossa

Let them whisper. We're the only ones who will ever know the truth of what we can do, because all who stand against us die.
- Armsmistress to isk Churus lis Kuchruis

Jossa put herself between Syrus and Delfi, pushing her sousi towards the back of the pocket hallway. The good thing about being on a space base was that there weren't any rooftops for people to leap off. Although she wished they could have made it closer to the ship and the dockside law enforcement before they'd been caught.

::Like *they'd* do anything,:: Delfi snapped along the mind bond. Jossa felt her sister's irritation as the younger woman stepped away and out, dodging Jossa's attempts at guarding her. Delfi threw the awareness back down the mental link. ::And don't you dare treat me like a child. I'm just as good as you in a fight.::

Out in the street, a tall man stopped and looked in their direction. Dark hair, dark clothes, olive skin. He didn't wear a uniform, but he moved like he should have. Syrus rotated the knife he held in one hand and shifted his weight to the balls of his feet. The aftertaste of the glee in the anticipation rolling off him nearly made Jossa dizzy.

Delfi unsnapped her own knives from her belt as she siphoned the emotion before Jossa could get too happy about the fight to come.

Stepping up behind Syrus, she let the weapons hang at her sides, ready, but not a direct threat.

Jossa sighed and pulled her own weapons. The blades she favored were lighter than the double-edged, partially serrated rectangle of metal Syrus liked and larger than the curved single-edged set Delfi favored. The skills she and Delfi had been taught at a young age had kept them alive in more than one sticky situation. She'd still rather they make it to a place where local authorities would have to do something about an altercation or risk the commerce of the base.

Syrus shot her a look over his shoulder as two more men appeared in the crowd outside, stationary in the flow of traffic. Delfi rolled her shoulders and settled her weight. ::If the authorities got involved, it's just as likely that we'd end up dealt the same hand as whoever these people are. Honestly, Joss.:: Affection trickled down the mind bond. ::You have too much faith in humanity.::

A fourth and fifth man joined the group of soon-to-be attackers. Jossa flexed her fingers and moved up on Syrus's other side. An argument with Delfi about reality versus hope wasn't what she needed right now.

"You two take the flanks," Syrus said as the men, apparently done making their plans, split and headed towards the alcove. One vanished from sight, probably going to sneak up the wall and come on them from the side. Another wandered in the other direction, towards a vendor clearly torn between packing up his display and attempting to make a few last sales.

::Sometimes,:: Delfi said. ::This man.::

::Sometimes?:: Jossa shot back.

But they'd do what he said. He knew it. They knew it. They were all too fond of breathing.

The four men coming at them from the front hit first, charging laterally across the main corridor with all the subtlety of a ship dropping through orbit. Syrus let the first pair make it three steps into the alcove before he exploded into action. Dodging the cut from a short tactical sword, he grabbed the other frontrunner's arm, twisted, and pulled.

Jossa was already moving, dodging the attacker's flying body. Planting her hands on the floor, feeling the hilts of her knives flatten to accommodate the move, she swung a foot out and around, catching the man at the ankle. He stumbled, the blade in his hand missing Syrus's shoulder by inches. Syrus kept going, taking the momentum left over from the throw and using it to keep turning. Face forward again, he grabbed the wrist of the one Jossa had knocked off balance and jammed his blade up under the man's armpit. Blood blossomed. Artery.

Jossa noticed this in passing. The man who'd tried to mask his movements near the vendor was coming for her. She popped to her feet, landing in a crouch as he swung his short sword through the air over her head. He overextended, probably surprised that she hadn't stood and taken the blow. Or maybe surprised to see a woman fighting at all.

She didn't give him a chance to recover. She lunged, moving forward and under his outstretched arm, dragging the edge of her knife over his ribcage. Her blade scraped over a shell of armor under the clothes. Ok then. Step forward with the hind leg, pivot on the balls of her feet, drive the tip of the blade into the uncovered side of his neck. Bad angle. Her teachers screamed at her through three hundred years of space and time.

But they also approved of the fact that she'd cut his arteries wide open.

There was a time for grace or even taking someone alive.

You couldn't do either while dead.

Panting, Jossa caught her balance and looked for the next targets.

There weren't any.

The other forward fighter and the man who'd backed him up lay between Syrus and Delfi. One of Delfi's knives stuck out of the first man's abdomen near the hip. A shiny wet spot, dark against the gray of the man's pants, proved that either she or Syrus had also gotten him in a femoral artery. The second attacker lay with his legs splayed oddly beneath him, a knife pinning his wrist to his companion's body. Delfi half-stood, half-crouched on the man's other arm, holding her second knife to his throat while she laid a palm over his head.

::Del?:: Jossa asked, forcing herself to look away and check for any more attackers. The vendor had fled, apparently deciding neither his wares nor his life were worth getting caught in a blood bath. A few people glanced into the pocket hall as they moved past, then walked even faster to get away. A little girl pointed, open mouthed. The man who had hold of her other hand picked her up and vanished into the crowd.

Jossa let her sai tag the people and settle into a background awareness, then turned her attention back to her sister.

::Stop him,:: Delfi said before Jossa could ask why she hadn't answered yet.

Rage bloomed, nearly knocking Jossa off her feet, then vanished as Delfi pulled her sister's shields back up for her. Teeth clenched on a subhuman growl, Jossa fought for her own emotions as she looked for the source of the anger.

Wet sounds of flesh hitting flesh. A squelch of blood. The crunch of a bone snapping.

Oh no.

::Del, you know I can't get close to him when he's like this. What are you doing?::

::Finding out who sent them. Get him before he decides we're in the way.:: Delfi didn't move. The man under her writhed, trying to pull his arm free of her boot. She dropped her weight, driving her knee into his gut and forcing the air from his lungs. ::Now, Joss!::

Jossa obeyed. Stepping over the bodies, she eased past the twitching legs of Delfi's victim and looked deeper into the hall. It was wide, as base hallways went. Probably to accommodate the recycle bins and the bots that serviced them. A door she hadn't noticed before was set into the wall opposite the bins. No keypad or locks. Probably an emergency exit or service tunnel that only opened for a bot's proximity pass. There was another door set in the rear wall of the hallway, the lockpad on it gray and dead.

And covered in blood spatter. The dark liquid shone dully in the dim overhead lights. Below it, crouched on the floor in front of the door, was Syrus.

No. Not crouched. Kneeling over a corpse, methodically pounding its face to a pulp.

Jossa took a deep breath and stepped forward, slow and easy like a cat. Clearing her mind of any thoughts of nehkeh or animals or violence, which cropped up as soon as she tried *not* to think of them, she groped for calming thoughts.

The peace of the mind bond answered her, tranquility in the face of the horror of a universe where Delfi hadn't saved her. She breathed a blessing in the direction of her sister, grabbed the feeling with both mental hands, and flung it towards the maddened nehkeh man like a catch rope. A lifeline to sanity.

He hesitated before the next blow. The one after that was slower. His rage, the force he emanated on a daily basis, dissipated against the implacable certainty that here was safety. Here was comfort. Here was a place where he didn't have to shake his fists, metaphorical or otherwise, and rant against a universe that hated him.

By the time Jossa was in touching distance, he'd stopped hitting the body. He sat back on his heels right over the corpse and slumped in place, breathing harshly. But he wasn't fighting.

Jossa buried her opinion of his behavior beneath another layer of shields, braced herself, and laid a hand on his shoulder.

He went stiff at her touch. His emotions, dampened but not erased, blew up her nerves with the force of a solar flare. Jossa clamped her lips together on the howl of outrage that threatened to tear out of her, clawing for the peace of the bond instead. ::Delfi!::

Images assaulted her. Someone wrapping her in chains. Drugs in her veins, cold and blinding. Men coming for her. A hole in her mind where Delfi should have been. Anger. Agony that had nothing to do with physical reality.

A face. Pale skin, wide almond eyes. Dark hair.

Gone.

The peace of the sousi link swamped her, swallowing the overflow of Syrus's mental state and replacing it with calm once more. Jossa found herself crouched next to Syrus, her forehead on his shoulder as he dug bloody fingers into her hip. "They're dead," she gasped into the tatters of his shirt. "Dead. We're done."

His grip tightened. He took a deep, shuddering breath, let it out, and finally relaxed. Jossa waited a moment to see if he'd lose control again, then looked up to meet his eyes.

They were still his eyes. Hard. Brown. The scar over one eyebrow only emphasizing the fact that he was a man who fought for his life and loved every minute of battle that came his way. Nehkeh. The word for his people boiled down to the same thing in any of the three languages of the Empire.

Savagery. Animal in human form. His people were many, but their place in the Empire was dictated by their bloodline. This little display was a prime example of *why* they were shunned.

Syrus curled a lip. He'd picked up on her train of thought. Letting go of her waist, he planted his hand on her chest and shoved. Jossa yelped as she went over backwards. "You," she snapped as he stood and stepped off the body. "A thank you would be nice!"

A fresh wave of anger hit her. She realized that Delfi had retracted the outstretched grace of the mind bond. He was on his own, and so was she. Jossa could have wept at the loss.

"What've you got?" Syrus asked Delfi as he went to stand over her. She turned to look at him, then leaned to the side and yanked the knife free of her captive's wrist. The man screamed. A surge of alarm blasted its way into the hall from the main street, then dissipated into the general anxiety. Jossa shuddered and watched as Delfi used one hand to force the man's head back and drew her knife across his throat with the other. Standing, the younger woman tugged her clothes back in order, shook a bit of blood off her hands, and looked over at the pile of meat that was the man Syrus beat to death. ::I think he already knows what this means,:: Delfi told Jossa. Her mental voice was hard. Clear. But no emotions leaked over the bond the way they should have.

"She says you know," Jossa said when Syrus looked at her.

He raised his eyebrows and looked back at Delfi, who was in the process of retrieving their abandoned weaponry from the various bodies it had been left in. "She's the one who had the fucking vision."

Right. Put everything on the Foreseer.

::If I had a choice about what I see, does he think I wouldn't have gotten more detail?:: Delfi grumbled, pulling the last knife free of a body and thumbing the switch. The living metal slithered and sank back into the hilt. She held it out to Jossa, who sighed and took it.

Her sister was right. The visions were sketchy at best and barely usable at worst. They had been ever since their days in the Churus lis Kuchruis. Her translations were clear enough, thank the Ancestors, but they didn't bring a lot of detail.

Yet she and her sister had still been valuable. Revered, even, for the warning they could give. Even more so after they'd escaped and joined up with Rui and the crew of the *Skatasi op Essi*, running from the hunters who would bring the sousi pair back to the Capitol.

"Hey." Syrus waved a hand in front of her face. "Quit with the memory thing."

Jossa rapped his hand with her knife hilt, but swallowed down her pain, trying to focus on the here and now. "Delfi doesn't get that much detail and you know it," she said. Then held up a hand before he could snap something else insulting. "You also know more than you want to let on."

If nothing else was clear, the images she'd caught from his emotions had told her that much.

Stubborn man usually knew more than he let on.

Syrus rolled his eyes, but whatever he felt wasn't strong enough to make it through both his shields and the ones Delfi still held over Jossa's mind. "Bounty hunters," he said. "Someone wanted me caught or dead." He toed the body of Delfi's prisoner. "Dead, most likely."

::How'd they find him?:: Delfi asked, suspicion and worry giving her words a staticky feel. Jossa frowned and passed the question along.

Syrus crouched to rifle through the corpse's pockets and came up with a hand-sized screen. It was the same sort of battered and worn rental screen Jossa had clipped to her belt. He turned it. A three-dimensional image of Syrus filled the display, its hair and beard shifting through various combinations of color and cut as they watched. Syrus snorted. "Figures. A bit surprised it took them this long."

Jossa glared at him. "So all the dead people, all the changing—" She stopped when he and Delfi both growled at her. "None of it mattered?"

"It's a lot harder to change your face," he snapped at her. "And the blood was more important." He wiggled his bloody fingers at her. "If I hadn't taken that part, we wouldn't have made it past the first system after our escape."

She huffed and crossed her arms. "And how long have you known there was a bounty out on you?"

He grinned, teeth white against his blood-spattered skin. "Twenty years, give or take."

::Duh,:: Delfi said, rolling her eyes physically as well mentally.

"So they're military?" Jossa asked, hoping Delfi would take her chagrin before Syrus picked up on too much of it. He'd never explained why he'd abandoned his unit. Nobody left the Karukap's service lightly, even in her time. From what she'd learned about this time, nobody left it *ever*.

He shook his head. "They'd be wearing insignia. Probably Uvlaku. Maybe not, considering." Right, because he'd been Uvlaku too. He knew how they worked.

::Anyone can change clothes,:: Delfi muttered.

Jossa passed that on for him. Syrus snorted and leaned down to pull at the shirt collar of the nearest body. The man's neck was bare. No glyph of rank there.

"And you've changed—" Jossa said.

"Damnit, woman!" Syrus clamped a hand over her mouth faster than any man had a right to move. She tried to yelp in surprise, struck him along the forearm with her knife hilt, and then went still.

She couldn't Feel any emotion from him. Not even through skin contact. He'd shut himself off completely from any outside reading.

He eased his hand off her face, then leaned over to whisper in her ear, breath warm on her skin. "They're not the last. And we're vulnerable. Shut up before you get us all caught again."

Her neck tingled. Her skin was on fire. Like the myth of the dog and the bell, being in proximity to him like this, bodies inches apart, set off some atavistic reaction in her. A part that remembered she was bred to be a concubine to Emperors. Specifically, to his line of Ancestry.

Months now. Months of panting, screaming ecstasy, conditioning herself to be aware of every inch of him in reach of her hands. Hips that fit between her legs. The touch of hands lined with scars, old and new.

"*Zoturyj nakekks neh!*" Delfi's snarl sounded tinny under the rush of Jossa's pulse in her ears. "*O'li jegah zo'li ra'eh zudieh sekkidl o'li lu ya'eo je'luhkoks neh!*" She wedged a slim arm between the two Feels and forced them apart through sheer stubbornness.

Jossa staggered back, nearly tripping over the body of the beaten man. Catching herself, she stood, staring at her infuriated sister. Delfi's face was as red as her hair, her fists clenched as her body shook with anger. Behind her, Syrus grinned as he adjusted his pants and mouthed, "Later then."

Jossa rolled her eyes and felt along the bond for her sister. ::Ok, fine. We're all the way across the hall from each other. You happy now?::

::No.:: Something echoed along behind the word, but Delfi blocked Jossa's reach for the subtext and kept going. ::But he has a point. The longer we stay here, the more likely someone will check to see what happened.::

Jossa sighed and clipped her knife back to her belt, then accepted the other hilt that Delfi held out to her. "Alright, ok. Let's get going." She looked at her companions and down at herself. "Lucky for us nobody here seems to mind a little blood."

Syrus looked at the shirt plastered to his muscled chest and shook his head. "Lucky for us the lighting is for shit and our clothes are dark," he corrected her. "Come on." And without waiting to see if they were following, he stepped out into the flow of traffic. As if leaving a pile of bodies in an alley were just a normal day.

Jossa took Delfi's outstretched hand, accepted the extra shielding her sister offered, and followed. It was sad that, even in this new era, she and Delfi still left a trail of dead in their wake. How far her Empire had fallen, that such a thing did not cause her to pray for the Ancestors' forgiveness?

Ancestors willing, with a fresh start in the Seps Coalition, these would be the last of those she had to kill.

Seven--Jossa

Some deal in stardust. Some in food. Others in untainted water. All have more hand in how a base runs than the local authorities, who are only there to curtail the worst excesses.
    - Head of Merchants Guild in Beyesab, to his son

Jossa wrapped a towel around her hair, twisted it up on top of her head, and padded through the ship, shivering as the air blowing through the ducts struck the skin left uncovered by her threadbare robe. She'd never understand why Syrus let the ship stay chilly even when hooked up to a base. Some days she missed planetside life with such an ache, she could feel the imaginary sunlight.

::I can disable the shield poles if you like,:: Delfi offered. ::Then you'll get nice and toasty.::

Jossa snorted and tucked her robe a little tighter around her body. ::Sure I would. We'd all fry.::

Delfi didn't answer. Jossa prodded along the mind bond for a response and got a string of numbers in return. Right. Her sister had gone to dig through the data feeds to see what she could find on their attackers. They'd agreed the Kiprinog were unlikely suspects. Unfortunately, that didn't leave much to go on.

Jossa stopped at her bunk, stepped over the disarray the customs man had made of the crates and oddments, and dug in the tiny dresser for clothes. She found a long shirt, buckled her belt around her hips, and laid a hand on the small crate of roughhewn goldwood that sat on a shelf in her closet. The box itself was nothing special. Its maker hadn't even bothered to sand down the splinters or seal the wood. Broken down and sold to a recycler, the box wouldn't have paid for a sweet cake from a market stand when she flew with Rui. She'd sold a crate like this three systems ago, empty, for a hundred thousand credits. In her past life, she would have counted herself rich if she'd had half that in her pockets. In this era, it was still a significant amount of money. Enough to keep the ship running for a few weeks at least, if she sold it to the right buyer.

But not enough to get herself and Delfi through this last Barbican.

Jossa sighed, then pushed the crate and its more innocuous contents back along the shelf and headed out of her bunk. Delfi continued to ignore her, attention on her work. Jossa stopped in the galley, heated a kettle of water, and popped two bags of dry herbs into silplat drinking pouches while she waited.

::Three,:: Delfi said absently.

::Three what?:: Jossa asked, wondering what her sister had found.

::Make three. He's up here.::

Jossa gritted her teeth and pulled out a third teardrop-shaped pouch. ::What, he doesn't have a bottle of gut-rot?::

Delfi laughed through the mind bond, sending waves of sarcasm mixed with genuine mirth to wash over her sister's mind. ::Gut-rot is for when you *don't* want to be able to think. Of course, you seem to have a different—:: She stopped. Jossa caught an image of a planet on the screen before Delfi pulled up her barriers, shielding her sister from the information.

Or maybe she was shielding herself from Syrus. Jossa rubbed her head and hoped the shields were meant for Syrus as well. She was sure Del didn't *mean* to cause pain when she did this, but that didn't always help when Jossa found herself groping for a presence she *knew* was there but wouldn't respond.

The kettle chimed. Jossa poured water into the three pouches, made sure the power to the heating unit was off, then gathered up the drinks and headed out of the galley.

The bridge was lit in blues and greens, with a bit of electrical white and warning orange here and there. Jossa eyed the orange lights, but they were all indicators that the base computers were trying to make connections for life support, power, and air processing. Jossa shuddered at the thought of what this place must charge those who were stupid enough to let their ships hook in.

::You'd need to bring a few thousand of those goldwood boxes,:: Delfi told her as she sat up and stretched.

Jossa handed one of the pouches over and set a second pouch on the console over Syrus's head. He picked it up, sipped, and made a face. "At least you remembered not to boil the leaves."

Jossa stepped on the urge to pour the contents of her pouch down the back of his neck. "What've you found?" she asked them.

Delfi sighed and turned back to the console, nearly leaning out of her chair as she worked the icons, physical buttons, and sliders on the screen. ::Not much. The man didn't—::

"Out loud," Syrus said. His voice was mild. So mild it set off alarms in Jossa's head. She let her sai surround him. Nothing. It wasn't just Delfi shielding her, then. He'd barricaded his mind, refusing to let them see or feel what was going on in his head.

Not good.

Delfi made a rude gesture, which he returned without looking up. Frustration crawled through the mind bond. Jossa patted her sister's shoulder. "Just tell me what you found," she said. These two would needle each other all day if she let them.

Her insides, traitorous as they were, turned warm at the thought of how she could put a stop to it. She didn't block fast enough, because

Syrus sat up and gave her a heated look. Delfi reached over to flick her on the wrist. Hard.

Jossa returned the favor by rapping her knuckles on her sister's head. ::Then do your job,:: she told Del. "Answers, not bickering please," she said aloud.

"Shweshe'o. Sheh'o weshor jehokshuks nih," Delfi said in a waspish voice. "Jeh kiprinog nih. Nishbudo'yj nihba?"

Jossa frowned. That wasn't good. They'd hardly been here a day. How had they managed to anger any of the local cartels?

"I caught the Kiprinog, cartels, and professional out of that," Syrus said as he set the pouch of tisane down and went back to working his screen. "Translate the rest."

Jossa stared at him. "Excuse me, milord?"

Anger flared like a small sun as Syrus turned his head to bare his teeth at her. Jossa lifted her pouch of hot liquid in warning. Who did he think he was, ordering her around? Still warlord of a Fleet of killers? Mass murderer of thousands?

Her *owner*?

::Technically, yes:: Delfi said, so emotionless that the words themselves were a knife. A pull, a tug, and Jossa's rage drained down the mind bond, leaving her head clear and her heart aching.

She sighed and rubbed at her nose with her free hand. "You don't have to demand," she told the man-shaped volcano in the pilot's chair. "You *could* pretend to be polite. I know you can manage that."

He didn't move, teeth still bared, hands tight over the console controls. Jossa waited, feeling his emotions wash over her, break against the barriers Delfi held for her, and vanish into whatever part of her being Delfi used as a repository for excess feeling.

Finally, after what felt like a small eon, he pressed an icon in the corner of his screen, flipped a toggle on the bank of lights above him, and sat back in his chair. "If you would translate, *please*, milady Jossalyn lis Churus isk Fuerrus."

Oh. So, it was like that then. She'd poked him about having been Warlord, so he reminded her that he did, in fact, own her indenture.

Behind her, Delfi smacked her forehead with an open palm and went back to digging through the data feeds for information. Jossa felt along the mind bond, but her sister had blocked her out completely, keeping the siphon going while offering nothing in return.

Jossa sighed. "She says that the men were hired anonymously, in this system. They never met or saw their employers. She thinks they were professionals. Maybe the cartels. But not military or private House security. "

"Not the Kiprinog either." Syrus tipped his head so he could watch Delfi's fingers fly across the console. "Did she find *anything?*"

Delfi made another rude gesture and kept working. "A'asheh zhuzhu ii'wehrich ritha nihba." she snapped when Jossa poked her in the shoulder.

Syrus snorted. "Him and want and dead? Yeah, got that one." He shrugged and went back to his own work. "The military isn't stupid enough to hire locals to take me out. They decide they really want me, they'll send a unit themselves."

"What about the rard in Vammesab?" Jossa asked. "Or the other rard in Chichesab?" They'd managed to avoid two civil wars between nobility on their travels through the Empire, but at the cost of replacing their identities. "Or the Freighter's Guild..." Those were the only ones she could think of as having the reach to hire anyone from halfway across the Empire.

"We're too small." Syrus flicked his fingers to expand a data feed and frowned. "Rards are too busy fighting each other to worry about independent ships that escaped. Freighters wouldn't care about us leaving. They're all going after the big merchant enterprises."

"Supposedly," Jossa said, feeling the itch between her shoulder blades at the remembered pain of repeatedly resetting her maruste.

He must have remembered too, because he rolled his shoulders.

Jossa sighed and stepped a little closer, dropping a hand down to scratch her fingernails lightly along his spine. He leaned into her touch briefly, but she couldn't catch any emotion before he pulled away. Whatever his thoughts on their situation, he'd locked them all up again. He was just a person-shaped presence to her sai, unreadable as a bot.

::I could have told you that,:: Delfi muttered.

::Not like you're a font of information either,:: Jossa replied.

Delfi threw up her hands, snarling. "Jeppa'yj! *Neh!* Dijoh lono'o nih. Galla shijuch phijeh I'gatsyruks nih. Jeh shappa okshuks neh!"

Well. That was worse than typical local toughs. Far, far worse.

"Hey." Syrus reached out and snapped his fingers in Jossa's face. "Names, a planet, and... transport? What else she say?"

"They used fake names, even with each other," Jossa said, trying to work out the implications as she translated. "They came in on a ship from the nearest planet. No—" She held up a hand before he could point out the obvious. "They didn't know the name of their ship. It dropped them and left."

He scowled and rubbed his thumb along a shiny spot on an armrest of the chair. "That's no fucking good."

"I know! What've you found?"

"A shit ton of nothing," Syrus muttered, crossing his arms and glaring at the console screens. "At least, nothing new."

Jossa eyed him, then felt along the bond for Delfi. She was still blocked off, ignoring Jossa as much as possible. ::Del.:: Jossa stretched the word into two syllables. ::Is he telling the truth?::

No answer.

Great.

She met his eyes. The skin around the corners crinkled in that way it did when he was looking for a reaction. Good or bad, he usually got it. If there was a man in the Empire better at irritating, teasing, and generally throwing water on a metaphorical oil fire, she hadn't found him yet.

That didn't mean she had to give him what he wanted. Doing *that* usually devolved into a maddened frenzy of skin and sweat and need. None of which would be helpful now.

Delfi's mental blow rang inside Jossa's head with all the force of a hammer striking a bell. Jossa staggered, caught herself on Syrus shoulder, then whirled to stare at her sousi. "What the fikek was that for?" she cried.

::No sex,:: Delfi snarled. ::Don't you dare!::

"I was thinking of how it *wouldn't* be useful, you bittek," Jossa nearly yelled. "If you hadn't block—"

Delfi walloped her again. Jossa lost her balance entirely. Someone's arm, muscled and hard, wrapped around her waist and guided her onto a solid surface.

Syrus.

She was in his lap, head still ringing and stars popping in front of her eyes.

Delfi barked a short word as she erupted from her seat. Slapping at Jossa's dangling feet, she shoved her way out of the bridge and down the hall.

"The fuck was all that about?" Syrus asked. His arm tightened around her waist as he rearranged her so she sat fully in his lap, facing away from him. She could feel his erection poking her in the backside. Heat built between her legs in answer.

"I have no idea," Jossa muttered, rocking her hips slightly. Traitor body.

"Hmm." He ran one hand from her knee to hip, rucking the hem of her long shirt, the fingers of his other hand played over her ribcage. "You going to make her tell you?"

She was. She would. Let Delfi cool down. Then find her, in mind or body, and figure out what set the silly girl off this time. Soon.

Syrus's fingers brushed the undersides of her breasts as the hand on her hip started working on her belt.

Soon. Just as soon as she was done with—

Cold water hit her across the head and shoulders. Jossa shrieked and lurched out of Syrus's hold. She landed hard against the console, groping for reality. The haze of shared lust vanished. Behind her, Syrus turned to a veritable inferno of rage.

"Jeh skaeksyj neh!" Delfi barked. Something hit the deck with a clang.

Jossa nearly slammed into the console again as Syrus lunged out of his chair. She scrabbled for her center of gravity, found it, and turned to see her sister standing in the middle of the bridge, low-pulse gun in one hand and a long knife in the other, a metal bowl rolling near her feet.

"Delfi," Jossa yelled. "What in—"

"Jeh. Skaeksyj," Delfi repeated as she thumbed the power on the gun all the way up.

Syrus stopped mid-grab. Jossa froze.

"The fuck did she just say?" Syrus growled.

Jossa had a feeling he'd understood, but answered anyway. "No sex."

He snarled.

Jossa rubbed at her face with both hands and sat down on the edge of the empty pilot's chair. "Del."

"It's funny," Syrus said, low and hoarse, "how you think you can tell me what to do."

Delfi made a noise like a feral cat, but she kept her eyes on Jossa. ::Not tonight,:: she said, sending the mind bond ringing. ::Not *at all* until we get through the Barbican.:: She raised the knife in warning when Jossa opened her mouth to answer. The air in the room was still, as empty as if none of them were sai at all. Jossa clutched at the pain under her ribs. Delfi had closed herself off. Completely. It hurt. Hurt more than Jossa could name. Tears brimmed in her eyes. She clamped her mouth shut, categorically *refusing* to give in to the childish need to cry.

::I can't, Joss.:: Delfi cracked open her shields across the bond, just a bit. Something else slipped through, but the younger woman patched the leak before Jossa could identify it. ::Too many people. Too many risks. We're almost there. Almost free of the Empire.:: Her eyes flicked from Syrus to Jossa and back. ::Almost free of *him*. Please.:: Delfi thumbed the power on the gun and flipped it around to give to Syrus butt first. ::I don't have it in me to keep you two from causing a base-wide orgy. Not tonight.::

She turned on her heel and vanished through the door, narrowing the mind bond to the barest trickle as she padded down the hall.

Jossa looked at Syrus. He stood, dripping wet, staring at the empty spot where Delfi had been. She couldn't see his face from this angle or read him through his shields. But the line of his shoulder, the way his muscles bunched, and the veins in his arms stood out. She didn't need to be a Feel to know what they meant.

He was inches from losing his temper. Bare seconds away from an explosion that would put his display in the alley to shame.

Jossa swallowed and stood. He clenched his free hand, knuckles white. Moving carefully, she did her best to ooze calm. She didn't know how good a job she was doing. She still had to try. Easing up next to him, she laid a hand over his on the gun.

Nothing. Nothing clear anyways.

Praying Delfi wouldn't abandon her entirely, praying to her Ancestors, offering promises to her Progeny if she lived through this, Jossa tried to slide her thumb between Syrus's hand and the butt of the gun. He didn't let her.

"Syrus," Jossa said softly. "Let me have it."

Nothing. He stood frozen. She could see his face now, head tilted to one side as he looked down the hall towards Delfi's bunk. The muscles in his jaw worked.

She tried again. "Syrus. Please. Give me the gun." She pressed harder with her thumb, careful of the power switch and the trigger.

He rocked back, caught himself, and looked down at her. Something in his eyes struck her. They weren't furious, the way she'd expected. She didn't have a name for the emotion that burned in his gaze. Whatever it was, it rendered him voiceless. Because of the effort to keep her from feeling it? Or because it affected him so? She couldn't tell. But he opened his hand, throat working as he swallowed hard. Jossa took the gun, checked that the power was indeed off, and tucked it into the back of her belt.

"I'm going to bed," she told him.

He rocked again, forward this time. His hand skimmed her hip. She gulped and stepped away.

"In my old bunk. Alone."

No answer. No sign of intelligent life at all. Would he let her go? For all their bickering and arguing, she was very well aware that he could overpower her in a heartbeat. If he decided he didn't want to obey Delfi's order, there wasn't much that would stop him—or, truth be told, herself—once they got going.

If he decided to attack Delfi instead?

Jossa's heart shuddered to a stop at the thought. No. Not when they were this close. Not after all she'd done to keep her sister safe.

But her one surefire way to do that had just dropped down a gravity well without heat shields.

"Syrus?" she asked again, carefully.

He squeezed both hands into fists, shut his eyes, and blew out a lungful of air. Then, without answering, he stalked out the door and down the hall. Jossa rushed to follow, heart in her throat and a frantic chant of ::Del, he's coming. Del! Del! Del!:: surging down the bond to hammer at Delfi's mental shield.

When he was ten feet from her door, Delfi yanked the shields aside, sent a blast of impotent fury through the bond, and then sucked it back just as quickly before slamming the shields back in place.

Jossa caught herself on the wall before she hit the deck. Clawing her way back to upright, she caught sight of Syrus. He stood, one hand on a lock pad, a door irising open behind him. Not Delfi's, Jossa realized. His.

He stepped through and pounded the lock from the other side.

Jossa let go of the wall, landing in a heap on the floor. As she stared at the closed door before her, she realized that things weren't about to change. They were standing on the edge of a new chapter in their lives, one where they were safe from the Empire and free of the need to hide.

But unless they could come up with the extra money to buy their way through this last Barbican, they'd be stuck with each other.

Not forever. Only until the Fleet finished swallowing the Empire whole.

Would she die in Delfi's arms? Would Delfi die in hers?

What would Syrus do, infected with the grief and insanity of a bereft Projective Feel who'd lost her sousi?

She hoped he killed her quickly, when the time came.

::Go to bed, Joss,:: Delfi said softly, slipping a phantom hand over the bond to offer a soft caress. ::We'll deal with it in the morning.::

Wiping at the tears running down her cheeks, Jossa obeyed.

EIGHT--SYRUS

*Mama, why is it called Natural Son Day when we're the
ones they want to have sai? What if the first natural baby
had been a girl?*
Who said it wasn't, dear?
> --conversation between Rissa and Alrurisi lis Tova
> af Mitachte, 3750.10.13

That night, he dreamt of the past. Another festival, years gone and
forgotten by any but the women honored during it. It was weird,
dreaming a memory. He didn't know if his subconscious was trying to
remind him of something or what. He sure as hell didn't like the
alternative.

Whatever the reason, the fact remained that he wasn't lying in bed,
tangled in sheets and Jossa. He was standing on the ramp of a ship,
covered in sweat, trying to breathe wet soup for air. Rissa panted
shallowly next to him, fanning herself with an oversized leaf she'd
found on the ground.

"How do you know that thing isn't poisonous?" he asked her as they
stepped down onto the dusty track that wound its way through the
docks. "Can't you find something else to use?"

"If it's poison," she replied, using the leaf to blow a small gust of
tepid air in his direction, "at least I won't die of heatstroke."

He shook his head and slapped at her hand when she tried to stick the leaf in his ear. "You'll be dead of something else, you don't knock that off."

She laughed and caught up with him, hooking her free arm through his. She didn't stop waving the leaf, though. He had to admit, the little bit of breeze it generated felt better than nothing.

Then they reached the end of their parking section and the empty area between the ships and the wall of the space port.

"Well shit," Syrus muttered.

"You didn't see this from the air?" Rissa glared up at him. "How did you not see this when we came in?"

The ball of white cellulose and silver tinsel was as big as Syrus. The thing would have looked much more impressive if it weren't for the muggy atmosphere. As it was, the paper wilted and curled in the damp, which made the object look far too much like an actual cell. The tinsel, cut in the shape of sperm, didn't so much shine under the layers of sticky paper as it barely glimmered.

Syrus wondered if the damn thing was flammable. It'd be fun to find out, despite the inevitable arrest that would follow.

"At least they didn't add the differentiation stage," Rissa said. "That's always nightmare inducing."

"Not as bad as the half-formed fetus ones." He steered her around the oversized zygote and towards the little booth manned by a couple of port guards. "And no, I didn't notice this shit from the air. You were griping at me about groceries."

"Well, for future reference, I'll go hungry if it means we get to avoid—Hello, sirs." She flipped from irritable to friendly between one word and the next, pasting a smile on her face and fluttering the leaf just a little faster. The two guards straightened. They even managed to make their sweat-soaked uniforms look halfway official.

Syrus rolled his eyes and pulled his arm free of hers to hunt through his pockets for the data crystal with their ship information. Some days he thought everyone had it wrong. Rissa's sai wasn't for seeing across vast distances. It was for getting people to do anything she wanted. Up to and including using actual manners around her instead of sending her packing.

He was proof positive.

The guards took the crystal, logged the information on their screens, and sent them on their way a lot faster than if he were on his own. They even managed tired smiles for Rissa, who twinkled back at them as she thanked them.

"One of these days, you'll do that in the wrong place and they'll peg you for highborn get," Syrus told her as they drifted along the edges of the markets, looking for a likely place to dive in. There weren't many.

The buffer zone on this side of the space port's wall was full of more giant cells, water misters, and umbrellas mounted on anti-grav units. Some were tethered in place over tables and chairs, others floating free. Almost every bit of shadow held a cluster of people. Near the openings to the streets of the city proper, a slow-moving river of bodies caught and swirled around their stationary counterparts. Even if he and Rissa could get to one of the outflowing tributaries, they'd still be stuck shoulder to shoulder with half the city.

"I hate Firstborn Son Day." Rissa's voice wasn't made for growling. She gave it a good try. "All these stupid, brainless idiots flapping around, patting each other on the head for an accident of timing."

Syrus pulled her away from a clump of young women who'd overheard. The heat had to be getting to them too, because aside from some sneering looks and narrowed eyes, they didn't show any signs of leaving their pool of shade to come after Rissa.

She let him steer her until she spotted a floating mister just ahead. Then Syrus let her park him at the edge of the thing's range. A pile of little boys played in the proto-puddle forming underneath the thing. She waded right through them, ignoring their protests as she tipped her face into the spray.

Syrus watched her, wondering whether she'd keep up the rant with so many little ears nearby. Hopefully not. She may have spent most of the past ten years locked in a cryo casket, but he knew better. Anything these kids heard would get parroted to their parents. Next thing they knew, the whole damn town would be up in arms looking for the heretics who dared blaspheme the holiday.

Fucking Natural Son Day. He'd like to hamstring whatever idiot decided to throw a party just because someone managed to get pregnant sans in vitro.

Rissa tapped him on the forehead, grinning. He scowled at her. "Knock it off."

Several of the kids stiffened in surprise. One looked like he was about to bolt. Rissa worked her way out of the pack and took Syrus's wrist in both hands. She knew what he meant. Not that it helped. Their distaste was nothing in the face of thousands of years of tradition. The weight of their culture, of her upbringing, was the neutron star sucking any good thing out of their shared pasts.

"Take that back." As if she could read his mind through his shields, Rissa tried to growl at him again. Then she smacked his shoulder with the wet leaf. "Got you, didn't I? And you got me?"

And look at the price they'd paid. Were paying. Life on the run. Him hunted by the military, a death sentence if they ever caught him without his team. A slower, longer death, if they realized how much of their top-secret equipment he'd stolen when he ran. Both of them hiding from her family and her husband.

He laid his free hand on the crown of her head and wobbled it back and forth. "Nothing you could do about it," he told her.

Their fate was sealed the minute she convinced him to leave that alley and follow her up the mountain to her family house.

"They wouldn't have taken you if it weren't for this idiotic holiday!" she snapped.

Yup. Too late to keep her from following that train of thought. Syrus sighed and went back to looking for a way into the markets that didn't involve climbing over half a hundred people.

Rissa made a rude gesture he *knew* he hadn't taught her. "If Al hadn't been born, Father wouldn't have had any excuse for selling you off."

Oh hell, she was actually going to do this *now*. In the open. On Natural Son Day. "Say it louder," he hissed in her ear. "I don't think the local nobility heard you."

She jerked free. "Well, why not do this now? Months, Sy. Months we've been dodging around this. We're as safe as we're going to get, and you *still* won't talk about anything that happened while I..." Tears welled in her eyes as she fisted both hands and pressed them to her mouth.

While she was stuck in cryo, sleeping as her father did everything in his power to sell *her* off to the first bastard who wanted a noble breeder for a wife.

Handed over to a man who beat her nearly to death just for the fun of it. Who *had* beat Onika to death, and the poor thing's only crime was that she'd had the bad luck to be joined at the hip with Rissa all the way to the marriage ceremony.

"Fuck, Riss, c'mere." Syrus tried to catch her by the shoulder and pull her close. She yanked away again, hunching in on herself, goosebumps covering her in defiance to the sheen of sweat that coated her body.

"Riss." He tried again, softening his voice into what she called his whisper-growl. "Let's get you into the shade. Then you can rip into me and I'll take it, and we can get on with the day, ok?"

She let him pull her into the shadow of the next giant zygote, both of them careful not to brush against the cellulose and tinsel. She pulled away when he tried to tuck her head into his shoulder. He snarled wordlessly.

"Too hot," she mumbled.

And too public, he realized. She hated being seen as vulnerable even more than he did.

So he let her be. "They still would've gotten rid of me. You know that." The requirement that the third child go into military service was only a convenient excuse. Syrus's presence had already cost her two marriage offers, both too much better men than the husband she'd ended up with.

The rumors had gotten stronger after her little brother was born. Fertile, some said. The women of the family were fertile. The rard had money. Power too. Enough to put a nehkeh to his daughter as a stud and then bribe the priests into faking the records later.

Her father'd nearly had a stroke when that one made its way to the family home. Those rumors combined with the Karukap trying to take away his Ancestors-blessed Natural Born son? The results were inevitable.

If he'd had any kind of brain back then, Syrus would have grabbed Rissa and run the minute the baby let out his first scream.

He leaned down to rest his forehead against hers. "Nothing you could have done," he told her again. The heat of her anger radiated off her body, baking him further. He rolled his head from side to side, feeling their skin stick and pull as their sweat tried to glue them together. "Maybe we'd have gotten free if the brat weren't born. Maybe. They'd have found us, though. Probably killed me."

Rissa froze, the acid lashing his extra sense. Quick as it appeared, she tamped it down. "I—"

Syrus reached into the dream and yanked himself back to consciousness before he had to live through any more of that conversation.

Before he had to listen to the promises they'd made each other and eventually broken.

Not her fault.

His for sure.

He lay there, tangled in sheets and sweating. Just as hot and sticky as that day, however many years and who knew how many planets ago.

Sweating because of the dream? Or because the room was too hot, too claustrophobic? He couldn't tell.

Pawing at the other side of the bed, he realized what was really wrong with the room. It wasn't hot, it was missing an extra body. At least on the Fleet, on the nights when memories fed the need for oblivion, there'd been the concubines. Fifteen walking distractions, each one as willing as she could be to help take his mind off the shit that was his life.

Some more willing than others.

All dead now.

He hadn't even known most of their names. But he'd memorized the feel of them. The noises they made when he touched them. The way they touched him back, especially when they took hold of him without his sai playing a part in it. He'd branded them all in his head, full color and sound, trying to lose himself before he looked around for the millionth time and wondered why Rissa wasn't mocking him or raging at him or whatever else he thought she'd be doing if she were still alive.

It got worse after he let his imaginary conscience have a name again, letting Rissa's memory out of storage to guide him through saving all their lives on the shadow base. After he decided to leave the Fleet and the shackles of addiction to blood and sex he'd let Quinn chain him with.

Then Jossa made her offer, and he'd finally been able to stop the replay. Away went his conscience, and here came sex. For months now, Jossa'd served where the market whores he'd been paying hadn't. Most nights they wore each other out so well he didn't have the energy to dream. Mornings, she was a ready distraction from the pain of waking.

About the time that thought rolled around, followed by a reimagining of long legs over his shoulders and breathy cries swallowed by a pillow, he decided that enough was enough.

He had no idea what the hell was wrong with Delfi. She'd tried to explain a couple times, but she couldn't make herself understood. If she'd tried harder to relearn Navlad, he might've tried harder to learn more than a few words of He'la. But she was still stuck in her rut. It didn't matter what language she used; he didn't take well to getting chewed out. The emotions boiling off her during her harangues were enough to make that part clear.

Interfering little witch. She was a damn telepath. She should've figured it out by now that having someone in bed, distracting him, kept the dreams from overloading his brain and running rampant through the ship.

He grabbed Jossa's abandoned pillow and chucked it blindly at the door. Then he kicked the rest of the sheets out of the way. They clung to his damp skin before pulling free. Swallowing down the panicky gasps as he finally fought free, he grabbed a shirt and went hunting for his last pair of pants that weren't full of holes or blood.

Rissa'd always taken care of him there too, saying engine grease and dirt were fine and all, but if he walked around in public covered in bloodstains or showing more skin through his knees than a dockside whore, they'd find themselves tossed in a prison cell before they could blink.

She was right. He'd still laughed at her. Sometimes she showed the remains of her upbringing in odd ways.

He wasn't laughing now. His balls hurt like fuck, his head was pounding, and it was far too early in the day to get drunk off his ass and find a whore to take care of him.

He stopped, one foot in a pant leg, the other propped on the edge of his mattress, and looked at the side of the bed that Jossa had occupied for the greater part of seven months.

Fuck. A whore wouldn't do it anyways. He was ruined for normal women.

Fuck.

Snarling under his breath about Feels and sai, he finished getting dressed, headed out into the hall, and pounded on the first door he passed. Delfi yelled in derogatory He'la, and something solid hit the door. He turned around and headed the other way, slamming his open palm on the door to Jossa's bunk. "Up," he shouted at the blank metal. "We got shit to do."

And fast too. Before the next pile of bounty hunters landed on his head. Bounty hunters that weren't as stupid as the first set. At least half the Guild roster was made up of Karukap deserters. People who knew how to hide knew how to hunt. The next batch could very well be the last, in all the wrong ways.

A groan, muffled by the door, was Jossa's only answer.

Syrus pounded on the door again. "Not fucking kidding, Joss. Get up."

A shuffling noise. A yelp. A thump. More scrabbling sounds. Something crashed. Down the hall, Delfi came stomping out of her bunk, hair a flaming mass around her head and nightshirt barely reaching her thighs. She carried a pillow in one hand and a wadded-up towel in the other. Grinding to a halt next to Syrus, she glared up at him.

"Good," he told her. "Get cleaned up. Get on the data feeds. See if you can remember anything else about those mercs."

She swung the pillow at him. It bounced off his shoulder. Growling, Syrus grabbed her by the wrist and yanked her in close. "Just do what you're fucking told," he said in her ear. His dick, having been disappointed once this morning, came to attention again as her breasts pillowed his arm. He shoved down on the lust before it could get loose and contaminate her.

More crashing noises from inside Jossa's bunk. Something struck the wall several times. Defi turned her head to look, and Syrus got a faceful of hair. It smelled good.

He didn't catch himself fast enough the second time. The young woman went ramrod stiff, tore out of his hold, and ran down the hall towards the head while holding the back of her nightshirt down with one hand.

The door irised open, revealing Jossa and what looked like the aftermath of a battle. Syrus stared at her, anger and lust fading. "The fuck happened to you?" he asked.

She clawed hair out of her face and pulled the shoulder of her tank top back up her arm. She had a scrape on her elbow, a blooming red mark on her forehead, and a tear down the abdomen of her shirt. "I slept in a junk shop," she yelled. "A verse fikekoj *junk shop!*"

Syrus looked past her at the room she'd claimed as her own and raised his eyebrows. "You could have moved it all out."

"And what? Get my head split open again by Delfi? Or better yet, have her standing over me like the Chataf Kuchru, tapping her foot and wanting to know why I was taking so long to get to bed?" Jossa turned halfway around and flung a hand out at the piles of crates, bales of cloth, assorted baskets, and bags full of random shit. "Yes, that would have gone well. I'd *still* be clearing this place out."

She had a point. Syrus looked at the piles of junk again, then at the tiny space she'd managed to clear on the bed. Oh yeah. Definitely should have ignored Delfi and made Jossa come sleep with him.

And where had that fucking piece of altruism come from anyways?

Jossa harrumphed, reminding him that she was still standing there, injured and leaking itchy irritation everywhere. "Did you have a *reason* for making me plow through a ton of stuff getting to the door?"

"Yes." Syrus yanked a thumb in the direction of the galley. "Get dressed. Eat. Then we need to load up the flit and sell some shit."

She stared at him. "We were attacked yesterday."

"Yes," Syrus eyed her, wondering when steam would start leaking out of her ears.

"We killed five people. You left a man with mush for a face." She flung up her hands, sending an icy draft of incredulity his way. "We don't even know why!"

"Because they tried to kill us."

She took a deep breath, then realized he was messing with her. "Oh," she spat, face flushing. "You!"

"Me." Syrus propped one hand against the edge of her door and leaned in, breathing the scent of her as it rose off her body. She smelled like herbs and caramel, warm and sharp. "Haven't you realized yet? People been trying to kill me since before I can remember."

"And for good reason."

Her neck was long. And thin. So easy to snap. All she had to do was finish up that thought with an explanation of how his status as Savage painted a target on his back. Just one word in that direction and he'd give up mind-blowing sex for some blood instead.

"You're an arrogant achek who gets off by winding people up and watching them explode in frustration," she said, apparently unaware of how close to death she was.

Syrus laughed and stood straight again. "Don't change facts. We've got to get the money for the Kiprinog, and we don't have time to sit around and wait. Now get dressed and pack up some of this"—he waved at the room full of trade goods—"so we can get going before someone else decides to try for a piece of me."

She growled, a real growl in her throat. "How do you even know we can raise the money?"

"Why the fuck you think I've got so much shit down in the hold? Not my first drop down this gravity well. Now, get moving."

She hit him with a lance of irritated anger and slapped her palm against the lock on her door. It irised shut.

Syrus laughed to himself and went to finish getting ready.

NINE--SYRUS

Whatever you do, don't get yourself stranded at the end of a Barbican chain. All the credits in the Empire won't help you then.
    - Head of Merchants Guild in Beyesab, to his son

Two hours later, Syrus tightened the tie-down on the last crate, tossed his go bag into the flit, and looked around for Jossa. She'd brought down several loads of trade goods, but not enough. Not near enough to cover her and Delfi's part of the increased price. She still wasn't used to the cost of living in a crumbling Empire. He'd have to drag her back up to her bunk and load them both down like pack animals. Assuming she turned up soon.

Where the fuck had she gotten off to anyways? They had work to do.

Almost, he reached out with his mind, thinking of asking Delfi to send her sister down. He stomped the urge flat before it grew past a half-formed idea. No. It was time he started cutting ties, for real. The plan was to leave them on the first Gatekeeper planet with their share of the freight money and cargo and then hightail it out past any known system. He needed to remember that he was on his own. No team. No backup. Self-sufficient and able to function without some hormonal she-person making his life miserable.

He paused between one step and the next on the stairs, waiting for Rissa or a ghost from the Fleet concubines to make an appearance in his memories. The blonde who'd liked bruises floated to the surface as he'd seen her last, black and blue from head to toe. Bleeding from every orifice and a few new ones as well. Elbows dislocated, knees shattered, fingers bent in all the wrong directions.

Begging for more through swollen lips.

Syrus snarled and took the rest of the stairs to the upper deck at a run. He nearly rammed himself headfirst into the box Jossa was carrying as she turned the corner from the corridor. He *did* manage to catch the thing when she let go in surprise. He didn't help her stay upright as she stumbled backward. Delfi did, popping out of the bridge just in time to keep her sister from landing on her ass.

If he'd had his hands free, Syrus would have clapped. Slowly. So they got the point.

Delfi cursed him as she helped her sousi regain her balance. Syrus looked at the box he'd taken from Jossa in the upset. Honey. Flower stamen used as spices, dye, or medicine depending on the buyer. Various odds and ends she'd picked up. And the box itself, kiln-dried wood from some Ajiri planet near the border that couldn't get its exports out system to save its collective life, thanks to the war between the rardog who wanted to claim ownership of its Barbican.

"You need more," Syrus told the women.

"What? That's five hundred thousand credits there." Jossa leaned over to point at the box. "At least. I checked prices here."

He took the last step up, forcing her back towards the bridge, and handed her the box. "It *should* be worth that much. Do you want to risk it though? End up with barely enough? Not get the money? Go put that on the flit. Then stay put, fuck it all."

Jossa sputtered at him as indignation and fury sizzled through the air around her. He curled a lip, stomped on the urge to push her down the stairs, and headed for her bunk. She could do what he told her, or not.

She obeyed. He loaded up two more boxes, each made of woods from other worlds, slung a net full of natural fabrics over one shoulder, and headed back down to the cargo hold.

Delfi stood in his way, arms crossed. He stopped. "What?"

"Zo'li iikeha'oh Jekkekseh nih," she told him. "Zo'li how iiwehrieh, o'li zo'li *iinehwehri* nih."

He understood the mention of Jossa, and then the promise to kill him if he hurt her. Delfi'd been making that promise for the past year. The rest of it was window dressing.

He bared his teeth at her. "You lose her, you'll be on the deck gibbering and screaming into the abyss. Good luck coming after me then." It'd get her out of his hair, at least. No sousi could lose their other half without losing their mind. The number that ever regained their sanity was so small as to not count as a statistic.

She hissed at him like a cat. But she couldn't hide the cascade of acid fear across the deck at their feet. The pain of it seared through Syrus's boots and up his legs.

She couldn't be afraid if she was dead. It was tempting. So very tempting to end her and her fear.

Syrus kicked the monster's claws off the edge of his psyche and back down the hole. Leaning down so he could meet her eyes, he said, "I made you two a deal. I get you to the Gatekeepers. Where you go after that is up to you. We are *this* close. I won't fuck it up if you don't."

She leaned back, fear still burning his feet through his boots, although her eyes flickered uncertainly. He stood straight. "Get the ship ready. Soon as we have the money, we're taking off."

Before she could come up with an answer, vocal or otherwise, he shouldered her back onto the bridge and headed down the stairs.

>>><<<

Jossa didn't speak as they left the ship. Instead, she stewed in her thoughts and fidgeted. Syrus did his best to ignore her. She was probably just trying to deal with the emotional load of who knew how many people. He sure was. The ship was small and fairly well insulated, all things considered. His sai had nowhere near the range or sensitivity hers did, but he still felt the crowds—and the closer they got to the main spindle of the base, the more insistent the press of humanity.

He couldn't block it off entirely, not that his shields would hold anyway. Tricky, finding the balance between staying aware enough of his surroundings to avoid another ambush and keeping his temper from rampaging him across the docks in an orgy of blood and death.

The last sounded like a lot of fun that ended with a pulse bolt turning his head into a cooked mess of brains.

To distract himself from imagining what he'd do to this place if he were still Warlord, he nudged Jossa with an elbow. A maelstrom of emotion damn near sucked his brain through his ears. He cursed and jerked away.

"Huh?" Jossa stared at him, eyes wide.

"Fuck," he growled. "For fuck's sake, woman—ask before you implode with it." A sense of questioning. That was all he could sort out from the mess she'd zapped him with.

She stared at him some more.

He pulled his shirtsleeve down over his hand, braced, and used his knuckles to lift her jaw and shut her mouth. The touch still pulled at him, but not as bad. "Ask," he told her again.

"Why didn't you fight them harder on the price?" she blurted. "It's insane. We'll be lucky if we don't have to come back and unload the whole ship!"

Syrus steered the flit around a pair of arguing engineer types while he waited to see if she was done. When he glanced back at her, she sat staring at him, cheeks flushed. But no emotions leaking. Delfi. Girl could do wonders.

"If this doesn't get us what we need, we can come back with another load tomorrow," he said. "Don't fuck this up, though." He'd been guiding their freight and investments towards this for months now. "We blow the trip today, going to have to make the sales the old-fashioned way."

The flit trundled out of the docking arm and into the main staging area of the docks. People milled around, loading and unloading rented mules, haggling with Base Ops over costs, and generally going about their business. Syrus bypassed the little kiosk with the rental screens; they wouldn't be able to take them into Atkive's place anyways.

"That doesn't answer my question." She leaned in. "Why?"

He sighed. He'd asked for it. "Yeah. It's a ridiculous amount of money. And yeah, snapping them in two would've been great." He glanced at her. "But then what?"

She opened her mouth.

"We'd be shit out of luck, that's what."

Jossa huffed and flopped back in her seat. "I'm so glad this place is too loud for anyone to hear you."

He bared his teeth at her, then guided the flit into the line for the upward couplings. "Fuck them. Point is, I figured they'd find a reason to pull this sort of shit. Knew for sure we were screwed when Delfi let Faler escort her like that. They pegged you for nobles' get and tacked on extra because they hate the highborn. Then—"

"What, so it's our fault?" Jossa twisted in her seat to glare at him. Heat flared, then vanished. Syrus resisted the urge to check the side of his head to see if any of his hair was burnt off.

"It's the way they are," he said. He could get involved in a blame game, or he could get her back on track. "The way things are. Everyone who can make money, will. Until they can't anymore. As I was saying..." He raised an eyebrow at her. "Letting them peg you as highborn would've been bad enough. But it was the news about the Svis Konanuog that really drove the price up."

Their turn came in line. Jossa clambered out of the flit, leaving a trail of irritation and ginger shampoo in her wake. Syrus inhaled, exhaled, and followed.

She was already halfway through hooking the flit to the grav tethers hanging from the ceiling. Syrus started in on his side. "Point is, I figured we'd end up paying more," he told her. "Just thought it'd be a last-ditch payoff to keep them from doing a blood draw right there."

That snapped her head up. "And that's the other thing! Why the blood? If they do a draw on us on the other side of the Barbican, what's to keep them from tossing us out an airlock when it doesn't match?"

Syrus ignored the question for the moment, focusing on the last link on his side of the vehicle. Nobody wanted to be in a flit when it lost its hold on a ceiling, any more than they wanted to pay damages for whatever it hit on the way down. The tethers sizzled and snapped into place. The flit rose three inches off deck.

"Nothing," he told her as they clambered back into the vehicle. "But they won't necessarily expect the blood to match either."

"Then why—" Jossa looked like she was about to say more, but Syrus cut her off by pulling on the control yoke. The flit lurched as the tethers pulled it up, then lifted to hover with its roll bar a foot from the ceiling. Jossa turned green and clapped a hand over her mouth. Syrus shook his head and set the flit into motion, trying to ignore the alarm and frustration tingling and zapping his arm.

Once she had herself back under control, Jossa tried to poke him. He swatted at her, then twisted the yoke to the side to avoid a run-in with the wall. "Knock it off. I gave them samples because they want to know who's *claiming* to come through the Barb.

He caught her raised eyebrow out of the corner of his eye as her skepticism skittered across his skin. He bared his teeth at another fucking idiot who figured he could slide his grav anchor past Syrus without affecting either coupling. The man backed off before he linked the two vehicles to each other.

"They're going to call the authorities on you, you keep making animal noises," Jossa warned him.

He did *not* snarl at her, although he wanted to. Instead, he answered the question she hadn't asked. "Look. We're going through back channels here. The Empire considers the Kiprinog a religious extremist group. No," he said before she could do more than get her back up about that. "Not everyone prays to their Ancestors. Don't look so shocked. These guys have been around longer than the priests. They're not legal. The agreement isn't legal. The Gatekeepers have their own reasons for using the Kiprinog ships to smuggle people away from the Empire. Now shut up. I'm trying not to get us killed."

Jossa lashed him once with frustration, then propped her elbow up on the side of the flit to watch the various lights, people, and transports slide past and below. Syrus kept his attention on where he was headed, doing his best to dodge floating decorations, random streamers shot up by packs of roaming boys, and the insulted glowfish floating in bubbles of water that dangled from tiny grav tethers.

Who the fuck decided a fish was a good way to celebrate anything?

The din faded as he turned this corner and that, spiraling up and around the corridors of the base and ducking down halls that would have been alleys in a planetside city. Moving deeper into the occupied space. Away from the small traders' markets geared towards the transient population attached to the docking bays. Closer to the permanent residences of those who kept the place running, could afford the prestige of living here, or couldn't escape now that they'd lost their way off.

Embossed and painted doorframes alternated with small piles of cloth that shifted and moved as the bodies beneath tried to find a more comfortable way to lie on the hard metal deck. An old woman squatted in a cross hall, holding a begging bowl of burled wood that would have paid for a month's rent in his birth city.

Traffic picked up as they neared their destination. More flits ran along the ceilings. The colors of the Merchants, Freighters, Whores, and Food Service Guilds were hung or painted on the walls and floors in front of the doors to the various offices. People in guild colors made up most of the crowd below, along with a healthy seasoning of independents like himself and Jossa, the bright synthsilks of whores looking for work, and apprentices rushing everywhere. The smells of hot oils, vegetables, and spices hit Syrus in the face. The corridor grew, heightening until it was twice as tall as down near the docks.

Jossa leaned over the edge and watched the crowds below. Syrus shifted so her weight wouldn't throw the flit too much off balance and kept his eyes peeled for the right set of tether links. A fresh clamor of voices yelling about booze and leave time pointed him in the right direction.

Him and at least twenty other people. Luckily, he didn't plan to set down in plain view of half the Shipyard's Entry Hall.

"Hey," Jossa said as they passed the gaping hole in the wall that led to the staging area for flits. "Aren't we setting down?"

He shook his head. "Next one."

She frowned at him. He ignored her.

The place he was looking for didn't look like a linkage at first. Around a corner from the main corridor, it was hidden behind a huge ova and sperm decoration made of pieced-together scraps. Little bits of metal hung off the tails of the stylized sperm, glittering dully in the glow from a nearby fish. Chromosomes.

He fucking hated First Natural Son Day. He hated the whole week leading up to it too. Another reason to get the fuck off this base before the actual holiday hit.

Sliding the flit sideways around the giant representation of the miracle of life as it should be, Syrus felt the grav tethers snag and hold on the linkage base. Jossa yipped in surprise, and then they were down, their fall halted as the tethers kicked in again.

"Really?" Jossa asked the air. "Some of this stuff is fragile."

"I'm sure Atkive will buy a broken pottery vase as easy as a whole one," Syrus told her as he hopped out of the flit and went to unhook the coupling. "Maybe more. Then he can say it was an antique and sell it off in bits."

Jossa rolled her eyes and got out to do her side. "I'm sure. You would know this how?"

"Done it before."

"You are just..." She stood there, radiating confusion and amazement. Syrus chuckled and popped the handle of the sled free of its housing, then yanked the slab of metal out of its slot in the flit. "Get that cover, would you?"

In a few minutes, they had the sled loaded and re-covered. Then they pushed the flit behind a recycle bin where two or three others waited, all with warning lights glowing. Syrus locked the vehicle down, activated its alarms, and they were off.

"Please tell me you only have one broker this time," Jossa said as they slipped into the stream of traffic and headed down the corridor, away from the docks and the large Merchant offices. "You found fifteen tiny little family shops in Ustesab, and it was absolutely ridiculous."

Syrus took a breath as someone passed them in a cloud of anxiety and agitation, then let it out once the worrier was out of range. A fraction of a second later, Jossa's shoulders eased. Hmm. Not enough help from Delfi?

"Just a couple," he told her. "We'll go to the inorganics guy first, then dump the rest of this on the one who wants to feed people exotic insect drool."

Jossa wrinkled her nose. "You are very confident this will work."

He should be. Not much to do while crossing solar system after solar system but keep the ship going, keep himself going, and dig through the data feeds looking for what was left of his old network of contacts, shills, and covers. It was all in pieces, of course, but he'd managed to stitch together enough of the whole, with new faces and names, to keep them flying and turn a profit. And set up this reserve of curiosities.

"It better," he told her as they maneuvered the sled around a larger one that looked to have lost power in the middle of the hall. "Didn't see you doing much research in the data feeds."

Her cheeks turned red. She looked away as embarrassment flared around her.

Eventually they found what he was looking for. A door, twice his height and covered in chipped paint in Merchants Guild colors. A man in a worn hip wrap of synthcot and beads sat on a stool next to the door, gray hair hanging in dreadlocks around his face and fingers stuck inside the glittering lights of a holo game. He shook the game off in a shower of sparks and stood as they approached. "What you want, strangers?"

"Atkive," Syrus told him. The man lost twenty years as he stood, going from seventy to about fifty. There was muscle under that translucent skin, lean and ragged though it was.

"Who's askin'?"

"Oropan," Syrus answered, giving the man his current alias. "Kirdar Oropan."

The man looked them over again, eyed Jossa, and then called up the holo game. A twist of his wrist, a flick of his fingers, and the lights turned from gold to blue. Behind him, the door opened, metal folding out and back like a many-petaled flower. A draft of air billowed out, full of the smells of pine, wool, and something musty. Syrus turned to Jossa. "You ready for this?"

She tapped him on the chest with one finger, sending a concentrated bolt of scorn to hiss and pop its way through his lungs. "What do you think?"

He swept a hand at the door. "After you."

She straightened, stuck her nose in the air, and marched forward. Syrus paused long enough to drop a credit slip in the doorman's hand, then followed her inside.

Ten--Jossa

*Why bother with physical arts when digital costs almost
nothing to store and transport? Because it's the tangible
arts that make you rich, that's why.*
    - smuggler of antiquities on Lobielnet

The room they entered was not what she'd expected, based on the rest
of the base. Wood panels, red-hued and glossy, were set at intervals
along the wall. Gold, copper, and silver inlay followed the loops and
whorls of the wood grain. Warm lights, not the standard base white,
floated here and there, illuminating the tiny entry and the short hall
between it and the room beyond, which was more brightly lit. Carpets
covered the deck plates, layered one upon the other. Some were single
colored while others had designs worked into the fabric. None were
new. All showed wear along the paths people usually walked.

A bot floated towards them, spindly arms reaching up. The blunted
tri-tip claws clasped Jossa's arm gently, then let go. Syrus moved away
before it could touch him.

Jossa Felt the ripple of humor and suspicion tickle the back of her
brain. Then a male voice said, "Apologies. It expects you to be wearing
over-clothing."

She looked up as a man stepped out of the hall ahead of them. With
light-tan skin and the pallor of someone who'd lived their whole life

out of natural light, dark eyes, and short-cropped blond hair, he had a sharp face and a myriad of tiny scars covering his exposed skin.

There wasn't much of that. He would have fit in with any of the low-level day workers swarming the corridor outside. He wore clean, neat clothes, the only concession to comfort being that his sleeves were rolled up. A com unit covered one wrist; a beaded bracelet hung from the other.

"Please. Come in. Doing business in the entry is far from professional." He waved a languid hand and turned to go back through the hall he'd come out of. "I trust you're going to make this worth my while?"

"Let's hope you make it worth ours," Syrus answered as he stepped forward, dragging the sled behind him. Jossa followed, keeping an eye on the crates threatening to topple off the sled.

They emerged into another opulent room. Instead of panels of inlaid wood, pictures lined the walls. Jossa squinted at the nearest one. It was raised, not seamless with the metal behind it. A lifted screen?

As she stepped further into the room, she saw that it *wasn't* a screen. It was a physical image. Broad strokes of color layered onto a fabric surface. He had an actual, real painting hanging on his wall, where anyone could come in and steal it.

Turning on her heel, she saw that it wasn't just the one picture. Every single image was a physical representation of a scene, an object, a person. Some seemed to be made of fabric and thread. Tapestry? Was that the word? Others were paintings. Others were grayscale. She couldn't imagine what medium might have been used in their creation.

Not since she'd lived in the Imperial palace had she seen such a display of art.

Her insides quaked. What had Syrus gotten them into? What business did they, posing as small-time smugglers, have trying to make a deal with a man who had access to such treasures? Rardog dealt with people like this. Officials high up the food chain. People with more money than sense. Syrus was a nehkeh, scraped out of the gutter. What business did he have even *knowing* Atkive?

"Hey." As if summoned by her thoughts, though more likely by her panic, Syrus spoke in her ear. "They're pretty and all, but we've got work to do." He took her elbow and pulled her away from the painting. Farther from it, she could see that it depicted mossy rocks on an Ajiri planet, sunlight crowning the flowers around their bases with gold.

She stumbled slightly as he guided her back to the sled, but she couldn't find it in herself to be frustrated with him. "They're beautiful," she breathed as she looked at Atkive. "Where did you? How..." She trailed off, not even having to act the ignorant rube. ::Delfi, did you *see* that?::

No answer.

"Here and there," the man replied. He hardly glanced at her, looking instead at Syrus. "Been a while, Oropan. You get tired of the last one?"

"They come and go," Syrus answered without looking at the man. He didn't look at Jossa either. Instead, he headed for the other end of the room, still dragging the sled. A large metal table stood, waiting. Jossa stopped short, trying to reconcile the utilitarian object with the rest of the room. Syrus solved the problem for her. Grabbing the top box off the pile on the sled, he dropped it on the table with a muffled clang. Then a larger crate. Soon he had half the load laid out.

The man followed behind Syrus, poking in some boxes and taking out this or that while ignoring others completely. "Market for decoratives is down," he said, setting the third statuette of wooden birds down on the table instead of back in the box. "People are more worried about feeding themselves than making their homes pretty."

Jossa frowned. The words and even the tone of the man's voice said disinterest. The emotions coming off him told another tale entirely. Anticipation beat at her shields, ran off, and slipped down the mind bond like rain. Excitement too, low grade and subtle—but rising. Never when he touched a piece of merchandise. Always when he spoke.

Why? What was it about the things she and Syrus brought that had this man practically quivering with glee?

"Honey," she said, sidling up next to Syrus. "Are you su—"

A heavy hand landed on her shoulder. Not Syrus's. Faint images tickled Jossa's mind as the man all but pulled her away from the nehkeh, giving her a none-too-gentle shove towards a nearby tapestry. "Why don't you leave the money to us," the buyer said. "No need to worry. We'll get it all sorted."

Jossa opened her mouth, ready to take the man's head off.

Syrus raised an eyebrow at her over Atkive's head.

Jossa snapped her mouth shut and settled for glaring at him instead of chucking the intricate bit of metalwork she'd picked up, all unknowing.

"Now." The buyer grabbed the jar from her, slammed it on the table, and planted a hand between her shoulder blades. "Best you get that translator looked at. Ain't got no place in business anyways. Might as well go look pretty."

::Delfi,:: Jossa called down the bond, glad she didn't have to force words through clenched teeth. ::There's going to be a bloodbath.::

Delfi pulled a solid handful of the rage burning through Jossa's veins over the bond to her side and set a few more shields in place. Then she went back to whatever she'd been doing. All without saying a word.

Jossa swallowed and went to look at the tapestry. Telling him that her translator worked fine, Fleet issued or not, wouldn't help. Breaking the man's nose wouldn't get them their money. Syrus would know if the step-father's child was stalling like the Customs official had. If there was one thing she could count on Syrus to do, it was see through excuses. Even though it seemed everyone on this Ancestors-cursed base was conspiring to keep them stuck here until the system computers managed to force a link to the ship.

Come to think of it, they probably were.

Jossa suppressed a shudder at the thought of what was happening and would happen to all the people trapped here. Then she sent a prayer to the Ancestors that Syrus would get a good price for their goods.

It seemed like he was. Jossa listened to the men haggle, glancing over every so often as Syrus or Atkive picked something up, looked it over, and commented on a price. Going back to the table was out of the question. The buyer kept moving around to block her. Every time she looked at Syrus, he'd shake his head at her. Just a little. Finally she gave up and turned her attention back to the tapestry.

It really was beautiful. A winter scene on an Ajiri planet, snow clinging to bare red branches worked in thicker yarn, bits of metallic thread in the icy water running beneath the trees. She couldn't tell if it was machine made or done by hand. Either way, it was in great condition. Not as old as the ones that had hung in the palace galleries. Some of *those* dated back to the Foundation of the Empire. Despite the care taken with them, years of sun exposure and movement between displays had faded their colors and worn the edges of the fabric. Paintings had fared better. Statuary best.

Jossa stopped halfway between the winter tapestry and a grayscale image of some mammal running across a plain. Wear. Why was the idea of wear bugging her?

She went back through her train of thought, then further back. The disturbance had started in the entryway. Something about the floor here itched her too.

She looked around. She could only see one door to this room, the one they'd come through. That didn't necessarily mean anything. Sometimes doors on bases hid in the seams between panels.

Panels. Wear on the carpets showing where people walked.

And a buyer who had more money than he should if he was taking on knickknacks and the odd piece of pottery from small-time merchants such as her and Syrus.

"How much is the bounty?" she demanded, turning on her heel to glare at the buyer. She hadn't remembered to ask Delfi whether she'd found that out last night. Stupid.

Syrus set down the box he was holding and dropped a hand to one of the knife hilts on his belt.

Atkive froze. "Excuse me?"

Alarm sizzled through the air. Not enough. He could just be afraid of the accusation.

Jossa set her jaw and glared at him. "Answer the question."

The man looked from her to Syrus and back. "You make assumptions, woman." There was the scorn. But no outrage. No remarks about her translator either. Interesting, that.

Jossa raised an eyebrow at him.

"You sure?" Syrus asked.

Was she? Delfi was the oracle. She herself was three hundred years away from her own time. The Empire was so fractured that the behavior she expected out of some was flipped on its head and habits she would have looked for in others gone entirely.

Oily smugness oozed across the floor and crept up her legs, bringing with it images of money.

"Yes," she spat, then launched herself at Atkive.

Two men burst out of the hall at the other end of the room, stun batons raised. She'd missed them. Too focused on the buyer to notice them in the morass of background emotions.

No matter. She had the boss. He didn't know how to fight. Grabbing the front of his shirt in one hand, she yanked and slammed her other palm into his nose, then brought a knee up into his gut. He doubled over, clutching at his face.

::Del,:: Jossa barked through the bond.

::What the?:: Delfi yelled, yanking on the surprise and fear before they overwhelmed Jossa.

::No time.:: Jossa stepped quickly behind the man and planted one booted foot in his rump. Brace and shove. He slammed into the wall face first. Not unconscious, but dazed.

Good enough for now.

Her sai barely warned her in time. The man who came for her was cold and clinical, but the frisson of anticipation betrayed him. She dropped. His stun baton whistled through the space where her head had been.

Her attacker was huge. Muscled like an ox and much, much faster. He swung at her on the backhand, aiming down at her head and shoulders. Jossa lunged for the space between his legs, sliding through and under the table before he could adjust course.

He made it around the corner about the time she found her feet on the other side. By then, she had her knife off her belt. She dodged the baton again, sliced across his midsection with the blade, and backed out into clear space. He followed, swinging.

Did the man know how to do anything other than throw his weight around?

Another swing.

Apparently not.

Jossa dodged, slid to the side, and struck at his hand when he grabbed for her. He shouted in pain. When he lunged for her again, she scored the knife along his palm.

"Finish it," Syrus snapped from somewhere near the door.

All right then. No leaving people alive to be questioned. The bruiser lashed out at her again. She ducked to the side. One stab in a kidney. Another stab as she came up behind him. Aorta. Her knife parted cloth, flesh, and stuck on the spine. She let go, dancing back as she reached for the second hilt on her belt.

The man turned. Jossa moved out of reach and crouched low, waiting to see if he'd go down.

Blood hit the floor in little *pat pat pats*. The man staggered towards her.

"Fucking hell," Syrus growled from behind her. "I said finish it."

Then a hand landed on her shoulder. Jossa felt her shields crumple like so much wet cellulose in the face of a volcano.

The last thing she remembered was a shriek of rage as she whirled, knife upraised.

ELEVEN--SYRUS

*Doesn't matter what's happening in the Empire. People
still need things to get from point A to point B.*
  -Freighters Guild saying

Syrus came to himself in the pause between one slice and another. He
stopped, gasping, as numb cold grabbed his mind in an iron grip and
pulled. Gone was the fury. Gone the fear. In their wake came emptiness,
vast and dark as space itself. He staggered, dropped whoever it was he
held, and clawed for reality.

The body he'd been cutting on was alive. It cried out but didn't
struggle when it hit the floor. Somehow he put together enough sanity
to look down and see carpet instead of infinite stars. He had no idea
how he managed it.

A woman. Dark of skin and hair. Tatters for a shirt. Blood seeping
from a bone-deep gash over one shoulder and another over her breast.

Part of him was pleased. He didn't know why. The monster wanted
blood. It always wanted blood. Why should it be happy that it failed to
kill on the first strike? Happier that it *stopped?*

Because I am happy, for you, whispered a voice in his head. A
woman's voice. The voice of the woman he'd injured?

No.

The void pulled on him again. Somewhere in his brain, the woman's voice pulled back. He didn't know how it worked. He didn't care.

He'd nearly cut Jossa in half. Without even realizing it. Fucking hell.

Someone *else* nearby moaned. He spun, knife lashing out before he could catch himself. He cut through empty air before realizing the person making noise was sprawled on the table.

Hired help, his memory told him. Atkive's man.

Ah. That made more sense.

A look around, then down, revealed the slumped form of Atkive on the other side of the table. He was reaching for something on the underside of the metal surface. A button.

Syrus dropped, slid sideways under the table, and slammed one booted foot into the man's ribcage. Atkive went over like a felled tree, wheezing and hacking in pain. By the time he recovered enough to struggle upright, Syrus had the man by the shirtfront and a knife to his throat. "Backup?" he snarled.

In answer, a deluge of acid filled the air. *Now* the monster roused from its stupor. Syrus shoved it back and down as fast as he could, barely stopping the knife blade before it penetrated the man's neck.

He bared his teeth. "Ain't coming now."

Atkive wet himself. Apparently he was dehydrated, because it stank to high heaven. Great.

"The fuck was all this?" Syrus snarled. "We had a deal." Not that he'd expected it to be completely honored, but an attempt on his life hadn't been on the to-do list either.

Maybe he should've listened when Jossa asked how many people wanted him dead.

Familiarity. Contempt. Stupid risk-taking.

Yup, he was checking all the boxes

Atkive laughed. It was a wet, sobbing sound devoid of humor. "Was good deal," he said. His words were mushy. His breathing forced. "You, they want dead. The woman?" He shrugged. "Someone always wants a woman."

This time Syrus caught the monster before it escaped its hole. He even managed to slam the lid on it before it could escape again.

The gaping void that was Jossa's presence probably had something to do with that.

"How much?" Syrus growled.

The man laughed again, head rolling on his shoulders. "Enough. Don't need to pay for transport, right?" The smile on his face was macabre, bloody. Staticky humor, bright and sharp, filtered through the air around him.

And Syrus understood. His reasoning for picking this man as their buyer had backfired. Bastard hated spending money if he didn't have to. Half the artwork Jossa'd been drooling over was forged. Well done, but still fake.

Keeping someone alive, arranging transport off the base, guards to make sure that whoever put up the bounty actually *got* the cargo and then paid were all expenses Atkive didn't want to handle. So far as Syrus knew, all the bounties on his head were for a live catch. Even the military wanted him breathing, if only so they could say they shot him themselves.

But it probably wasn't Quinn. Syrus had wondered if Quinn would want him back. The Fleet might be a hammer smashing through the Barbican networks like a child with a set of blocks. Quinn was far more subtle. Now that he had the keys to the Empire, so to speak, the Fleet Second would be able to have the techs put together a legit bounty.

But Quinn would want Syrus alive, so this attempt couldn't have been him. There were a few others Syrus had ticked off enough to want him dead. And some of them were patient enough to wait years for the chance to catch him.

The only good thing about the bounty was that nobody'd caught up with him until he and the girls were nearly out of the Empire.

Jossa groaned behind him. Syrus remembered that not only were they not in the clear yet, they still didn't have the money to pay the Kiprinog.

Fucking hell. No way they'd make it to their second meet today. But there was a way to make up for that.

Syrus bared his teeth and yanked Atkive in closer. "Cash," he barked. "Where is it?"

Atkive shook his head and cringed. Maybe because of the look on Syrus's face. Maybe because of the pain. Either way, his fear bloomed brighter.

Syrus snarled and raised the hand holding the knife.

"Wall," Atkive croaked, eyes going wider if that was possible. "In the wall."

"Show me." Syrus got his feet under him and stood before Atkive could do more than make a pathetic wiggle for escape. "Where?"

Shaking, the man pointed at the space between the winter scene and the running mammal. Syrus grinned wider and transferred his grip so he had Atkive by the shirt, then caught one of his hands and slapped it up against the wall.

A seam popped open, the panel slid aside, and the compartment behind was revealed. Neat rows of credit slips dangled from hooks set into the sides and ceiling of a space big enough to fit the loaded sled.

Atkive died quietly enough when Syrus dragged the knife across his neck. His fear faded more slowly, leaving ghosts and afterimages burned in Syrus's soul.

Jossa didn't make a sound. Probably not good, all things considered.

Syrus went back around the table and checked her pulse. The bleeding on her shoulder had slowed. She'd need stitches, but she'd live. He wanted to curse himself for losing control so badly, but there was no time.

Pulling a small med kit from his belt pouch, he cut off the sleeve and a good chunk of her shirt. Once he'd wrapped a synthskin bandage over the cut and sealed the edges, he stepped back and took a deep breath. Carefully, he picked her up and placed her on the sled. There was room, barely, though he had to half-curl her on her side to account for how tall she was.

Delfi'd done something. That was the only reason he could think of for Jossa to go from overload to person-shaped vegetable that fast. How it affected him, Syrus had no idea. But he'd take good luck where he could get it.

Going back to the hidden safe, he grabbed credits by the fistful, making sure they were all ringed together so he wouldn't lose any of the slippery bits of silplat and metal. Some he stuck in the secret pocket in his shirt. More went down his boots. A couple went into his belt pouches as bait for pickpockets. The rest he shoved down Jossa's boots, in her pouches, and clipped to the mag rings that edged her bra. No desire here. No lingering over skin and breasts. Get out get out get out. No time for anything else.

A final check to be sure that he wasn't bleeding all over the place, an adjustment of Jossa's shirt so it wouldn't look so much like she'd been cut open, and he was set.

Out through the hall, then the entry. The door guard was gone. No time to wonder why. Hopefully not off delivering news to whoever'd put the bounty out. Day workers still milled around the main corridor. He waited until a cluster of them left the Whores Guild next door, slipping out as they passed to keep them between him and the rest of the hall. No one noticed him.

He needed a bank screen. No point in having all this money if it got stolen between here and the ship.

There.

He left the cover of the workers and headed for the screen. Nice. Slow. Don't draw attention.

"Sir?"

Curiosity and worry gelled together, tapping at his consciousness with sticky hands.

Syrus stopped and looked back. A man, thin and nervous, with an Adam's apple the size of a baby's fist and bony outstretched hands. "Sir, is she ok?"

Jossa would be gratified to have someone worried for her. Syrus wanted to punch this guy in the face. "She's fine. Bringing her home."

Anger, low grade compared to what lived inside Syrus. It flared weakly under the weight of all the other emotions in the corridor. But the man's chin jutted out and his hands clenched.

"She's my wife," Syrus said, putting some steel in the words. He'd have the right to do what he liked if it were true, and this little fuck would know it. "She got in a tight spot. I'm taking her home and finding a physician."

Then, satisfied that he'd taken the wind out of the self-righteous little dickhead, Syrus turned away and headed for the bank screen. Come on, bastard. Go back to your day. I played the good husband. I didn't sell my woman so a john could cut her up.

Not for the first time, he wished he could project emotions worth a damn. Or that he could fake them. Swamping the man's worry with reassurance would have been a great way to lock in his cover.

There. The flat screen and slot for credit slips. Syrus checked on Jossa. Still alive. Still out of it. The stranger'd gone back to what he was doing, vanishing into the crowd just like any other sheep.

If he'd believed in a higher power, Syrus would have sent up a prayer of thanks.

Instead, he wiped his hand clean of blood with a sani-rag from the med kit, fished the credits out of his shirt pocket, wiped them as well, and palmed the screen active.

Five minutes later he'd emptied all his pockets, his boots, and retrieved the credits from Jossa as well, shielding her from the crowd with his body as he worked. The account was set up, timed to release the money to the Kiprinog ten minutes before the deadline. He was left with a single ring of high value credit slips and confirmation on his screen for the payment.

Another look around to be sure nobody was watching, a scan with his sai to catch anyone covert. Then he pulled the sled back into the crowd. The ring of credits hit the floor once he was a good distance away from the deposit kiosk. Someone would find them eventually. It might even be someone law abiding. He didn't really care.

They were nearly to the alley where he'd parked the flit when Jossa groaned and shifted. Alarm filled the air, stabbing Syrus with a thousand needles. He gritted his teeth and kept moving. Just a little ways now.

"Wha—" Jossa moaned. "Wha happ'n?"

"I lost my shit," Syrus said, turning to look at her. "And then so did you."

She didn't look at him. Her eyes were fixed on the ceiling.

Syrus sighed. Right. Sousi. She probably didn't even know he was nearby.

"Don't worry," he told her as he turned the corner into the alley. He wasn't sure why he bothered talking, but maybe it would bring her back to reality sooner. "Almost done. Get back to the ship and we're on our way."

"Oh. I don't know about that," said a voice he hadn't heard in over twenty years.

Syrus stopped. The sled, a victim of momentum, bumped into the small of his back. Jossa moaned again.

"Shit," he muttered. "I thought you died."

The woman seated on the front end of the flit leaned forward and rested her elbows on her knees. Her smile was a rictus. As far as his sai was concerned, she didn't exist.

Then he knew nothing more.

Twelve--Delfi

You know we won't live long enough to eat half of those.
Yeah, but they make me think of her.
  - Conversation between Rui and Denz, 3485.05.19

Delfi waited until the airlock closed behind the man and her sister before flopping into the copilot's chair, sticking her feet on the pilot's chair, and blowing a raspberry at the ceiling.

Some days. Some nights. Some eons. If she could push Jossa into a black hole, she might. Delfi squashed the idea as soon as it formed, blocking it from transferring across the mind bond. Jossa was talking to Syrus as they headed for the docks. If she caught that little tidbit, however much of a joke it might be—or worse, however serious it sometimes was—she'd turn right around and come up here, demanding an explanation.

Delfi didn't have that kind of argument in her at the moment.

The ceiling of the bridge was boring. Lights. Joins in the metal plates. The markings of emergency hatches and access panels. Fire suppression. All the things a ship needed to be considered spaceworthy.

Muttering, Delfi sat back up, dropped her feet to the deck, and glared at the information on the screen in front of her. Jossa was too fried by hormones to ask real questions about where they were going.

She'd spent the last eight months giving and receiving orgasms so truly legendary, any so-called fuerrus might very well die of jealousy. Ancestors, by the time the older concubines had danced Jossa into adulthood, the fuerrus Delfi'd been raised to serve needed a Feel in the room just to keep his usik up.

Delfi's insides twisted at the memories of metal at her back and shackles on her wrists, and shied away from the rest. Wrapping her arms around herself, she concentrated on breathing. In. Out. In. Out. Look at the pretty planet. It's green and blue and cloudy all over. She didn't know how Syrus had tapped into the feeds to make this data available, but he hadn't locked it down very well when he was done.

Unless he'd left it open on purpose. Sometimes Delfi suspected him of being far sneakier than a man had any right to be. Especially a man who couldn't control his temper to save his life.

Either way, here was the data on the Gatekeeper system. Two Ajiri planets, another two suitable for Kovavek use—although it didn't look like the locals had domed either the desert planet or the ice ball. Hmm. No notes on trade, traffic, or satellites. Not surprising, considering the secrecy of the place. Far more information than had ever been available in the era she'd grown up in.

Her old attempts to dig up hard data on the place had netted bare crumbs compared to what she had in front of her. Back then, Rui had tried to get them into the Coalition. They would've gone in with no cargo and no trade contacts, but they would've had their husbands and their family, and that was still worth more to her than any of the knickknacks and tchotchkes left on the ship.

Their application had been denied by a computer. No human had passed judgement on whether the ship would be allowed through. She knew. She'd checked the flags in the code when their answer came back.

If what Syrus said was true, the rules were even more stringent now.

And less, for some reason. Because the Kiprinog were able to promise them passage for a fee that could buy a starcruiser.

Delfi sighed and sat back in the chair, drumming her fingers on the armrest. In reality, she was no better off than Jossa. Not for lack of trying. Not even because the man hid information with the same instinct most people breathed. No, it was because the Gatekeepers and the Seps Coalition actively worked to keep people ignorant. And the Empire helped, not wanting to lose citizens to systems outside its control.

She laughed and stood, palming the screen off. It was right there in the name. What idiot, herself included, truly thought they could dig up what the Coalition didn't want found? Well, what idiot who didn't have the resources of the military or an Empire to back them up?

Delfi wandered off the bridge, pausing to wrap her hands around the upper sill of the door and stretch. Muscles complained, stuck too long in the same position. Her hair fell in her face. She blew at it in a futile effort to keep it out of her mouth.

Nope. Even her hair was against her today.

Grumbling to herself, Delfi clawed the mass back and away from her eyes, then headed to her bunk to find a scarf. In the back of her mind, Jossa's conversation with Syrus flowed like a slow river. Delfi paid less attention to it than she did to the pair's emotions.

She'd lost the trick of it right out of the cryo casket. Waking up to find herself naked and knee deep in men who'd happily rape her beyond death hadn't helped. Recovering from the attentions of said men wasn't easy, but she'd finally found her equilibrium. It was second nature again to be holding a steady pressure on Jossa, the constant pull just strong enough to bleed off the worst reactions to people around her, light enough to keep from turning her sister into a walking vegetable.

Delfi shuddered and dug in her dresser, pulling out a length of blue fabric. She held it to her mouth as she tried to scrub the memory of that last day of freedom out of her brain. Denz, his arms strong and huge, his body so very real against hers. Rui, angry and scared and very much ready to take it all on himself. He had. Literally.

Some days, she dreamed that he would walk into a random space port, grumbling about the trouble two women could cause and didn't they know he'd been waiting for them to show up? Then Denz would pick her up, she'd wrap her legs around his waist, and they'd laugh at the shouts of the crew as he took her away. Far, far away.

So much better than nightmares of shackles and blood. *Infinitely* better than the phantom touch of the nehkeh who was also Imperial, or the heat that burned in her veins as he and Jossa desecrated every memory she had of their past life.

::Del,:: Jossa asked, feeding comforts and worry down the mind bond. All hers. None of it ambient. ::Are you ok? Do I need to come back?::

Delfi slammed the drawer full of headscarves shut and shoved her thoughts down where Jossa couldn't reach them. ::No,:: she snapped. ::I'm fine. You stay put.::

::Del!.:: Delfi could almost see the frown on her sister's face. She could definitely feel Jossa's hurt. ::I'm just—::

::You're just out there with thousands of people trying to get into your mind, where someone is trying to kill the man and possibly us.:: Delfi pulled her shields into place, narrowing the thread of the bond to its smallest possible diameter. ::Keep your mind on staying alive.::

Silence.

Delfi wrapped the scarf around her head, tied it under one ear with such force she felt the circulation in her skull drop off, and stomped out of her bunk. The ship's computers were safe enough for now. But engines needed warming up before they could take off. If she did all the prep work and didn't activate the power crystals until the others were on their way back, they could get off base before the "day" of docking rolled over and the firewall came under attack again.

She had a spanner in one hand and a temperature gauge in the other before the guilt got to be too much to ignore. Biting her lip, she stared at the gauge. Levels were normal. Nothing needed coolant or seals checked or any of a million little chores that might make the next trip, their last trip, any more trouble than it should be.

Widening the gap in her shields slightly, she reached along the bond to slide a mental hand over Jossa's shoulder. ::I'm sorry,:: Delfi told her.

Jossa pressed her cheek to her shoulder. Delfi felt the contact through the bond. ::It's ok. You're right. I just—::

::Worry,:: Delfi said. ::I know.:: She paused to put the tools away and went to check the levels on the water tank. ::Show me the halls?:: She'd been too busy not giving in to the urge to cut the genitals off every man who looked at her twice to pay attention to the decorations. Just because she could leave and be ok didn't mean she always wanted to. Like right now. Someone needed to watch the place, and she was a liability during haggling.

But she was glad she'd left last night.

::If you'd just stayed on the ship...:: Jossa sighed.

Delfi slammed her hand against the hull. ::Enough! I wanted to know what was going on. I got to dance a bit. On a table even. Whatever his faults, he wasn't going to let me get hurt. If he did, he knew you'd—:: She cut the words off before she could finish reminding Jossa that she was prostituting herself. ::Please. What do things look like from the ceiling?::

Jossa opened her side of the bond, offering her eyes to her sister. Delfi took the apology as it was meant and slipped her awareness over to Jossa's mind.

::Huh,:: she said as the flit slid along the ceiling. ::What are the fish for?::

::Local custom?:: Jossa leaned out and looked over the edge of the flit so Delfi could see. ::So few colors,:: she said sadly.

Delfi drew the worst of the hurt off and away before Jossa started weeping on the heads of the people below. ::Different times. Different places. The Empire isn't what it was.::

::I know.:: Jossa had her own set of memories. Her own mourning. Delfi escaped Jossa's head before she could drown in the scent and feel of Rui. Not sexual. Not this. Jossa held the memory of him around her like an old blanket. Comfortable. Familiar.

Safe.

Delfi realized there were tears running down her cheeks. She wiped at them. They kept coming. Grabbing one end of her headscarf, she pressed it to her eyes. It wouldn't do to look like she'd been crying when the others got back. Syrus already gave her enough knowing looks when he found her tucked in the corners or behind the water tanks.

She hoped she hadn't left grief imprints in the engine room for him to read. She didn't need him knowing that much about her. Not unless he was going to open his mind and show her who the woman with dark eyes was.

She didn't know how long she crouched there, sniffling back snot and trying not to sob. It wasn't until familiar rage stabbed her in the hindbrain that she remembered her real job. The job she'd failed at. Yanking roughly, she pulled the fury over the bond, felt it stiffen all her limbs for a moment, and then let it lose itself in her core.

If Jossa noticed the slip, she didn't say anything. She went back to whatever she'd been doing. Delfi scrubbed at her face one last time, coughed at the clogged feeling in her throat, and went to find some cold water to wash her face as she listened.

She had just enough time to do one last sweep of the ship's computers before they got back. She wasn't a Crack, but she'd been married to one. Denz couldn't give her the ability to detect technology the way sensors found ships, understand code and spit it back out when she'd never seen it, or to never type the wrong letters. But he had taught her many things that could be done with normal human abilities. Things like thinking differently than modern coders and using that to her advantage.

She kept half her attention on Jossa and, by extension, Syrus as she worked, maintaining the siphon through the bond with only part of her brain.

She shouldn't have tried to multitask. She was just finishing the first auto-scan when blinding rage flooded the bond and slammed her back in her chair, knocking the air from her lungs and sending a shriek of fury up her throat to choke itself off behind clenched teeth. Before she could figure out where it came from, the feeling doubled. Pain scoured the inside of her skull, killing any chance of rational thought.

She bent double, clinging to the armrests of the chair as a flurry of thoughts battered her. Stupid man. *Fikekoj nehkeh*, thinking he had any right to touch her! Barbarian! She'd kill him! Tear him limb from—

Delfi fled her sister's mind. Diving deep, she took shelter in the abyss of her soul, where neither Jossa nor Syrus could force themselves on her. The anger chased her, too large for Jossa to control and too encompassing to be held by the bond. Delfi curled her mind up as small as she could to keep the rage from frying her and waited, breathing in shallow gasps as whatever it was that made her her sister's keeper ate the emotions.

Ate them. And went looking for more.

Broad hands, strong hands, found her in the vast emptiness. Not with strength or sharp blows. They reached through blackness and gently lifted her. Rearranged limbs and balanced her. A voice like gravel spoke softly.

Delfi realized she'd dragged Jossa into the void with her. Ancestors, she hadn't flattened her sousi so thoroughly since the day they'd gone into the cryo caskets. And then she'd been awake, aware of what she was doing.

How much damage had she done to her sister this time? To herself? She'd lost her language then. What consequence her actions now?

Delfi took a deep breath, trying to fight down the horror that thought engendered. She couldn't put that in Jossa's head. She couldn't. She had a job to do, a sousi to protect. Turning her sister into a screaming numbwit was not part of her job.

Once she was sure she had herself under control, Delfi felt out along the bond, smoothing a mental hand over Jossa's head. ::Joss,:: she said quietly.

::Hmmm?:: Jossa's voice was subdued, muted even. ::Delfi, why did you?::

::Next time you want to wake up in a lake of blood, I'll let you both go,:: Delfi promised, keeping the acid out of her voice as best she could.

::What?:: Jossa came a little more alive at that.

Could the woman be *any* more oblivious? ::The two of you were about to start a butchery in the Major Trade Quarter. And not the kind you sell the meat out of,:: Delfi snapped.

::Delfi, I—:: Jossa stopped, mind clinging to Delfi's phantom hands. ::I'm so sorry.::

::Don't be sorry,:: Delfi said, sighing aloud. ::You are you. And I am here to keep you *you*.::

A touch, soft and warm against her cheek. Minds this close, Delfi could feel the affection radiating off her sister as if she herself were an empath. She settled deeper in the pilot's chair, letting the warmth of that love envelop her.

::I'll try to do better,:: Jossa said.

Delfi rolled her eyes at the promise, nearly as old as their bond. ::You'll be you. And I'll keep you *you*,:: she replied. Just as old a promise.

::No.:: Jossa's mental voice was firm, and she tightened her mental grip on Delfi's hands. ::I—:: Alarm seared a path across Delfi's psyche. Anger followed, hard and sour. ::Delfi, there're more—::

And then she was gone.

THIRTEEN--DELFI

Those who had power before the Consolidation of the
Empire will ever find a way to keep that power.
-unknown

Delfi blew out of the ship in a rush of panic and desperation. She'd had just enough presence of mind to slap bloodlocks on every door and hatch she could think of before grabbing her weapons belt from her bunk, snatching a gun from the locker in Syrus's bunk, and sprinting for the main airlock.

Jossa wasn't dead. She couldn't be dead. There was no way. She wouldn't be quiet like this. Wouldn't be silent or even absent.

She would tear a hole in the center of Delfi's being and leave something so much more than absence behind. The abyss. The yawning darkness that swallowed everything Delfi threw at it. It would swallow her too, leaving only a shell behind. An automaton, without even the programming of a trash-bot.

Delfi clung to that belief with both hands and all the faith she'd ever had. Jossa couldn't be dead. She couldn't. And since she couldn't be dead, something else must have silenced her.

Once Delfi found out what, or who, had done this to her sister, she'd teach them what came of tampering with a sousi bond.

She bared her teeth and pounded down the short gangway that separated their ship from the docking arm.

Unfortunately, finding Jossa wasn't quite as simple as reaching with her mind while running blindly through the corridors. Delfi nearly smashed into a slow-moving flit loaded full of crates, spun into the broad back of a longshoreman carrying a coil of hose in both arms, and cringed away as he cursed her in trade pidgin.

She fetched up against the wall, metal cool on her back as she panted for breath and tried to get a grip on her thoughts. Pounding the side of her head with one hand, Delfi berated herself for her idiocy and took a few deep breaths. Jossa was alive. She could think it calmly now that she wasn't so blinded by panic. Jossa was alive, she'd tried to tell Delfi something, and—

The commercial shipyard's Guild Row. They'd been on their way back to the ship when something had happened.

Delfi lurched for the nearest public screen and called up the base news. A fire in the systems that controlled life support for the residencies. No. A man with electric shock hair and waving hands claiming to have seen winged aliens. Very much no. Someone needed to stop taking stardust.

Delfi slid her hand down the side of the screen, watching the feeds fly past. No, no, no.

Well, at least whatever it was hadn't caused a very public bloodbath.

Which, when she stopped to think about it, was almost more disturbing than if it had. Syrus wasn't one to simply *let* anyone take what he thought was his. And no matter his protests to the contrary, no matter his stated plans for their arrival in the Gatekeeper system, she knew better.

Until he said otherwise, she and her sister belonged to him, by something far deeper than mutual agreement or convenience of travel. It was in his blood and in theirs. They'd been bonded to his line in their infancy, raised to its service, and for all he'd denied his

Imperial heritage, he still owned them. He owned them, blood and bone. Not even a priest could naysay that.

Delfi shook herself hard to reset her thoughts and looked at the gangway. Go back? Use the better shielded resources of the ship's computer to reach the shadow feeds that informed cartels and people like the Kiprinog? Or find a quiet place, sink inside herself, and try to find Jossa through the bond?

Yes, that was a better plan than standing here in a public forum, advertising vulnerability.

Delfi took a deep breath, reminded herself that Jossa had to be alive, and headed back to the ship.

A hand landed on her shoulder just as she passed the line that marked the separation between docking arm and gangway. Delfi spun, slapping at the owner of the hand in a double blow meant to push the arm away and possibly shatter the person's elbow.

She succeeded in removing their touch. She didn't manage to break anything.

Which turned out to be a good thing, because the owner of the hand wore the light armor and insignia of the base law enforcement. Not the dock authorities responsible for making sure commerce ran smoothly. The full legal authority of the base as a whole.

A cluster of men stood behind the cop. They wore gray and brown, with thorns worked into the wire braids on their belts and waning quarter-moon insignia on the buckles. In the center of the grouping was a man with dark almond-shaped eyes and close-cropped dark hair. A commlink sat along one broad cheekbone. He wore gray and brown as well, although his clothes were finer. Embroidered in silver thread, the garments were held together not by buttons or buckles or even zippers but by tiny grav tethers that glowed with soft silver light, silhouetting the moon and thorns worked into their surfaces. A flex-screen wrapped a dark band around one wrist.

And floating there, right in the forefront of his mind, was the pale face that lived in Syrus's most guarded memories.

Delfi gulped.

The cop she'd slapped put a hand to his belt, unsnapping his stun baton. He didn't say anything, but he didn't need to. She'd laid violent hands on a man of the law who was, in turn, in service to the highborn standing behind him.

He was well within his rights to beat her bloody and drop her in a cell.

"That's enough," said the noble, lifting one hand slightly. "I think we can take it from here."

The cop looked at the noble and pressed his lips together, but he stood aside without more than a stiff nod. Delfi could have shrieked in frustration as he placed himself along the wall next to the entry to the gangway. Would it have killed him to simply walk away? Now, even if she were to take out the noble and his guards, she'd still have a witness to deal with. One that knew she'd been taken and by whom.

Of course, she could kill them all and run back to the ship.

Only that would leave Jossa behind. The idea of which was so laughable that Delfi actually giggled a little. Leave her sister. Right.

Jossa was alive. Jossa had to be alive. And that meant Delfi couldn't just abandon her.

The highborn man frowned slightly, stepping out from between his guards to examine her. The men moved to compensate, all but shoving themselves between their employer and Delfi. Decent guards then.

The noble glared at his men but didn't demand they move. "Who are you?" he asked. His voice didn't carry the strong accent of a Core noble. Neither did it have the fake fashionable overtones some of the current highborn cultivated. It was an average voice for a decidedly un-average man.

The image of the woman with pale skin and dark hair wasn't going away.

Delfi wanted to poke her fingers in his brain and find out why.

"Where is your man?"

Delfi started to snap at him but caught herself just in time. No Imperial. Right.

So she shut her mouth again, fully aware that it made her look like one of the poor fish hanging from the ceiling. At least she wasn't glowing.

One of the guards grabbed her by the upper arm. Another guard caught her by the shoulder. Delfi jerked in place as they started to turn her. No. She couldn't. She couldn't let a man do that to her again.

But turn her they did. She quivered, hands clutching the hem of her shirt as she fought to breathe evenly. Any second now. Any heartbeat, they'd yank her clothes off, pin her to the floor, and the noble would take her. Guarded by the cop not five feet away.

It was an irrational thought. Not even a modern highborn would be so stupid as to rape her in full view of anyone who walked by. The docking arm wasn't crowded, but it wasn't empty either.

She still quaked. Blood welled as her teeth sank through her lip.

Rough hands undid the hooks at the shoulder seams of her shirt, letting the back of the garment fall down and away. She knew what they saw. Her stolen maruste, bought at the price of another woman's life; although they could not know that. It told them her system of birth, her profession, her family line.

All the pertinent information of an Imperial's life. None of it verifiable if they ran a full scan of her blood. The nanites in her veins would lie for her, but her DNA wouldn't.

"It's a match, sir," one of the guards said.

"I can see that," the noble replied. "Close her up again."

Delfi held her breath until the guards were done redoing the hooks and didn't let it out until they turned her back around.

The noble watched her, arms crossed over his chest. She thought she saw pity in his gaze, although she wasn't sure she read that right. She stood, trying to gather her wits as she met those slightly sad eyes with her own, wondering why the pale young woman in his mind had been joined by the image of a gawky youth with bronze skin and a bald head.

Half a second before he spoke, she heard, *How long has he had this one?* His mouth said, "Get her in the ship." *He might be back soon,* he thought where he didn't know she could hear.

Still caught, Delfi screamed down the bond for Jossa as the guards all but dragged her up the gangway.

Jossa, of course, didn't answer.

>>><<<

The noble's guards didn't give her a choice about unlocking the ship. She struggled as they got closer to the airlock. She shattered one's kneecap. Planted her elbow in another's side. They caught her and pinned her arms as she whirled to run, so she was left with only her feet as weapons. Except every time she picked up a foot, she gave a little ground. The gangway wasn't all that long. So she twisted her head and snapped at the nearest guard's hand with her teeth. Someone grabbed her by the hair and yanked her head back.

She lost a few moments there to panic-infused memories.

"Quiet her," the noble snapped, just as she recovered from the feeling of being pinned by a large body. She found her limbs locked, one arm out and her palm stinging.

The airlock dinged and slid open. The sting in her palm, faint through the layers of worn-out false skin and blood, vanished. She clung to the feeling, a sensation she hadn't had *then*. She hadn't had use of her hands. She didn't now; but neither was she shackled. Not shackled. Not shackled. Not—

They hauled her inside the airlock. The heat and press of bodies, the smells of man flooding her brain with adrenaline so she couldn't scream anymore, just shake and gasp for air.

Then they slapped her hand on another keypad, and the inner airlock door slid open. She staggered forward in the arms of her captors, one to either side, then hung between the two impassive men, fighting the urge to vomit as she listened to the airlock slide shut behind her.

Trapped.

She did lose it then. Legs giving out beneath her, she dropped like a stone. The guards, unprepared for the dead weight of her body, lost their grip on her. Hard hands grabbed her by the shoulders and elbows as they rushed to recapture her. The impact knocked her forward on her knees before they pulled her upright again.

Somewhere in the echoing distance, she was aware of voices. What they said, she couldn't be sure. She couldn't even say for certain they were speaking aloud. Words jumbled through her head, one or two flaring into reality for a moment before the conversation moved past her.

Jossa was alive. Jossa had to be alive.

She would need her sousi. Her anchor.

Delfi wrapped herself around that certainty with arms, legs, and body. It was the one truth she could count on. She had a purpose. She had a reason to be. Protecting Jossa from the universe and the universe from Jossa. She couldn't do that if she was lying in a pool of her own vomit.

Gentle fingers touched her cheek. She flinched away.

I should have let her run while she had the chance, thought someone nearby. Out loud, the same person asked, softly, "He's hurt you so badly then?"

Who was this *he* the man spoke of?

The fingers moved under her chin and lifted. Delfi met dark brown eyes set in skin weathered by life on a planet under sunlight.

Should not have left this so long, the voice said. But his mouth didn't move to match it.

Delfi blinked and pulled her face away from the man's hand. Had she blacked out? No. She'd know if she'd been completely unconscious. She hoped.

"Mmmph," she said, trying to rub her face. Her hands came up short. She looked down. Gray and brown gloved fingers were wrapped around each forearm.

Almost, *almost*, she lost herself to panic again. A keening mewl rose in her throat. She pushed her toes against the deck, trying to back away.

"Let her go." The soft voice wasn't soft anymore. It held the edge of command.

"Sir," one of the guards said. She heard a more complete thought in his mind, to the effect of letting lunatics loose and being responsible for the damage done.

"Now."

Muttering in his head, although he kept his mouth shut, the guard let go. Half a second behind him, the other followed suit. Delfi staggered as she took all her weight on her feet again, then rubbed her hands over her forearms.

Not shackled. Not tied down. Free. Well, as free as possible given the circumstances.

The pale-faced woman danced around the edges of her sai again. Delfi turned to follow her and found herself looking at the highborn. He frowned at her, full lips pressed in a thin line.

She frowned back. Who was this man, to look at her like that? She wasn't a child anymore, to be patted on the head and pitied for her lot in life.

"What is your name?" the man asked before she worked herself up to a full rolling boil of anger. "How did you come to be here?"

What has he done to you?

She snapped bared teeth at him. He was the one invading. He was the one who had put her back in a place she'd spent a year trying to forget.

"O'li—" she started, then stopped as she heard the word. Her heart sank. Sometimes she forgot that Imperial no longer fell out of her mouth like a waterfall over a cliff.

Everyone around her tensed, leaning in, minds quiet as they waited for her next word.

Delfi crossed her arms and glowered at the noble.

"Speak, girl," one of the guards said, reaching out to lay a hand over her shoulder in warning. "This is Rard Almovak lis Tova af Mitachte. You will not be silent when he wants answers."

Delfi rocked back on her heels. House of Thorn Moon. Where had she heard that before? She knew she'd heard the name somewhere, but her brain was still too fogged with adrenaline and the last shreds of terror to be able to call up the information.

The noble, Almovak, narrowed his eyes and looked at his men. Delfi looked too and noticed that only two of the six stood with her and the rard. She could take them. She could probably take the others, wherever they were.

But would it be wise?

She looked at Almovak and frowned. His thoughts ran in a singular line. The gawky youth to the pale young woman and back to the youth. He was so focused on the two, she couldn't find a way around them to dig deeper in his mind.

But he was highborn. With enough power to merit a personal escort to their ship by one of the local authorities. That her blood ran bluer than his ever would was no defense. Not here. Definitely not *anywhere* in the Empire as it stood now. If she hurt him, well.

They were called foregone conclusions for a reason.

She took a deep breath, shoving the last of the panic attack into the abyss as she tried to think. Take out the guards. Avoid damaging the noble. Get out of the ship.

And then?

Then find Jossa. Everything else could come later.

The man opened his mouth to ask another question. Delfi settled her weight evenly over her feet. Before she could strike or he could speak, two of the guards appeared at the top of the stairs leading to the upper deck and the living quarters. They set their hands on the stair rail and slid down without touching the steps at all.

Delfi glared at them. Step-father's children, ruining her plan.

"Rarkut Almovak," said one of the men as they approached. "All the doors are bloodlocked."

Almovak raised an eyebrow and looked at Delfi. *Was she really escaping him?* he wondered.

She should probably let him keep thinking that she'd been running away when he caught her. But the idea grated. Besides, he'd figure it out soon enough. So instead of looking cowed and scared, she dredged up a feral grin from somewhere and waggled her hands near her face. The layer of false skin coating her skin felt loose along the grooves of her palm.

The noble shook his head. "Well then, it seems you'll have to oblige us once more..." He trailed off, obviously waiting for her to supply him with a name. A title. Something.

Nobles so hated not being able to carry out their supposed mannerly lives.

Delfi grinned wider.

"I do hope you will not struggle," the noble continued, covering his inward thoughts with outward calm. "I do not believe the stairs will be safe, else."

His men would truss her up like livestock if she tried. The two nearest her were at least planning on it.

Delfi propped her fists on her hips, flinched away as one of the men held a hand out to her, and glared at Almovak.

The youth cycled to the forefront of the noble's mind and stuck there. Delfi nearly reached out to turn the image this way and that, trying to figure out why the boy looked so familiar. Instead, she stood still as the noble stepped aside and gestured at the foot of the stairs where his men waited.

When she didn't take the invitation, one of the guards gave her a tiny shove. She snarled at him but got moving before they decided to follow through on tying her up.

"Dimtra and Lutik?" Almovak asked as they mounted the steps.

"Dimtra is checking the engine room," a guard replied. "Lutik has the upper deck."

"Very good." The noble fell silent, his feet quiet on the stairs as his thoughts were not.

The youth had harmed the highborn's family in some way. A way that ran so deep, the specifics of the event no longer mattered anymore. Just the consequences.

Delfi lost her grip on his thoughts as she came to the landing. A guard met her, hand on his stun baton. Delfi eyed him until one of the men behind her gave a second little shove. She had to move or be run over.

The fall from here to the cargo deck below would break her ankles. Stupid Syrus, not putting any large crates where she could jump on them.

Her chance to escape vanished as the guard in front of her took her by the elbow and pulled her out of the way. Delfi gritted her teeth and allowed him to maneuver her up the two short steps to the bridge door.

"Open it, if you please," the noble said.

Delfi looked at him.

Prey? he asked himself. *Or accomplice?*

He must not know much about Savages, to think Syrus would ever truly work with someone for the sake of it. To the nehkeh, everyone was prey. Surviving acquaintance with one was mainly a matter of keeping them from stabbing you in the back or shoving you out an airlock before you got away.

She couldn't answer the highborn though, except by action. So, she laid a hand on the keypad next to the door and watched as it irised open.

In a ficvid, this would be the moment where she learned that Syrus and Jossa had escaped their situation in the commercial shipyard's Guild Row in eeva suits, flown through the chaotic traffic outside the base, and reentered the ship through one of the external hatches while Delfi was busy with Almovak. They'd be waiting, weapons drawn, and the noble and his men would be no more. Then they could disengage from the base, escape. Be free.

An empty bridge stared back at Delfi, lights on the console dimmed, screens locked. No rescue. No Jossa.

Delfi swallowed a sob and allowed the guards to move her to the side as they made way for Almovak. There wasn't much space in the little room. One guard ended up in the forward part of the bridge, between the control consoles. Two others took up station on either side of the door, leaving the space near the chairs for Delfi and the noble.

None of the guards took their hands off their weapons.

The noble looked from the door Delfi had just unlocked to the darkened screens on the console. "I assume these will also answer to your hand?"

He was trying to goad her into showing off. Fool. How little he knew that she'd cut her teeth on far more subtle manipulation than this.

When she didn't move, his mouth quirked, and he propped a hip on one arm of the pilot's chair. By the time he got himself settled with his hands laced together over one knee, all humor was gone. His eyes were steady, although not quite hard, as he looked at her. "I will ask again, ma'am. Who are you?"

Delfi lifted her chin and looked back at him.

He sighed. "If you do not answer, I will have to bring you along to put you under the care of those who can get answers through means closed to me. I do not have time to wait for your temper to sweeten."

Oh, she'd talk all right. Ancestors help them understanding her.

Should she do it now? Was it worth throwing away that advantage? Not yet.

"I know you are not his first travelling companion," the man continued. That pale young woman in his mind reached out fine-boned hands and smiled sadly at her. "It would be safer for you to be away from him. If you will unlock the consoles, then we will be able to make sure he can no longer hurt you."

If only he knew. Delfi did her best to make her face look concerned and stared down at her hands clasped before her.

Good, he thought to himself. *I'm getting through. If I can just get her to talk, I can get her somewhere far away from that step-father's child and keep her safe. Maybe the Gatekeepers will allow her sanctuary.*

Delfi was saved from trying to hide a fit of laughter by the sound of feet on metal decking outside the bridge. Everyone in the room turned to look as one of the noble's men ducked through the doorway. In one hand, he carried a battered synthcot bag blazoned with the insignia of the Karukap.

Delfi's heart sank. Oh no. She knew that bag. She had no idea where Syrus had been keeping it this time, but it was the one thing that always came with them when they switched ships and identities. He kept the masker that changed their maruste in there. And the data crystals and hardware he'd ripped from their first stolen ship, a military vessel off the shadow base. If they lost all that—even if they escaped—life was going to get much, much harder.

Delfi did her best to wipe the concern from her face and replace it with curiosity. The longer she could keep the rard from grilling her as to the bag's contents, the better.

For his part, the rard took the proffered bag from his man. "It's clean?" he asked.

The guard nodded. "You need to look inside, sir."

Delfi winced as the aged zipper complained on being yanked open. Then winced again as the rard stuck his hand inside. Something clanked. Something else *crunched*. He froze, then opened the bag wider to peer inside. Questions sprouted in his mind, so jumbled and scattered that Delfi couldn't parse them all.

Then his wrist comm beeped. Frowning, the rard shut the bag and opened the alert, then tapped a few more times. His mouth twisted. Delfi caught an image of a dark alley and a flit loaded with empty crates, then a torrent of data and numbers. A jumbled confusion of *found him, what happened, where is he* ran through the noble's mind. Delfi choked on a gasp as the onslaught hit her unguarded sai and all but bowled her over.

Almovak looked up sharply. Delfi realized too late that she hadn't managed to hide her reaction. Ancestors' *balls*. She glared at him but didn't struggle when the guard standing between the consoles put a hand on her arm.

"Bring her," Almovak said, voice harder than it had been since he'd arrived. He zipped the bag up and handed it to one of the soldiers as he stood. One of the guards by the door led the way out. The noble followed him. The other guards sandwiched Delfi between them and herded her out.

She allowed it, feeling only the briefest of panicked moments as she was momentarily trapped between the men behind and the men still sorting themselves out on the stairs.

She still didn't know where Jossa was.

But if she stuck with the noble, she would soon.

Fourteen--Jossa

*If Cracks are so common as to almost not be sai, Nulls are
so rare as to be the same. How can someone be sai if their
sole ability is that of not existing?*
 - Question posed to the Karukap Mistress of Sai,
 on the use of Nulls

Jossa returned to the universe in fits and starts. From the foggy
awareness of hands on her, she progressed to the realization that there
were voices all speaking over and at each other. Emotions didn't come
for a while. Not until someone jostled her, someone else took her by
the arms, and she landed next to a familiar body that didn't so much
brace her as stay steady and immovable while she tried to claw her way
back to reason. Pain screamed down her arm and up her neck, cutting
through some of the fog, but leaving her with a different sort of
confusion.

What was wrong with her sai? The people around her—for there
must be people—were less than dim shadows to her sai. Why was she
stuck here, in this yawning blackness that pulled at the edges of her
soul and siphoned off everything that made her *her*?

More voices, tinny and far away. Something rumbled next to her. It
reminded her of a rockfall, grating and harsh and inevitable. She knew
the noise, but she couldn't remember why.

Movement. Smooth. Almost unnoticeable, if it weren't for inertia pressing her against a soft surface and occasionally side to side.

"I know you're awake." The first intelligible words she could make out.

Was she? Technically, she supposed. She could hear and think and was even beginning to comprehend. The pain in her shoulder and arm told her that much.

But why couldn't she *Feel?* She should be able to by now. She was often slightly deadened if she'd been sleeping and Delfi was regulating her before she woke. She was *usually* pleasantly numb after a night of—

Her mind shied away from the memories of what she and Syrus did before they both imploded in the ecstasy of lust. Instead, she reached down the mind bond for Delfi, sending questions ahead of her. The more aware she was, the more this felt like her sousi overcompensating for the press of the crowd. Except in a more dramatic manner than usual. Jossa couldn't really complain. But she wanted her sai back now please.

Delfi's presence was far, faint, and not at all responsive.

Fear sent adrenaline surging through Jossa's veins, kicking her brain into overdrive. She lurched up, hit some sort of barrier, and gasped in pain as it bounced her back into the hard body behind her. Then she found herself mewling, trying to protect her shoulder as it screamed again in agony.

Whoever was beneath her sucked in a breath. Frustration zapped her through the contact, bright and sharp.

Syrus.

"Looks like the vegetable's not a vegetable anymore," someone said. Male. Sarcastic voice. Not Syrus.

Jossa blinked, trying to clear her eyes. Blurry shapes resolved into forms, which further clarified to identifiable objects.

She tried to scrub at her eyes. Pain brought them up short. More pain. How in the universe had she gotten hurt?

"Keep that up," said a man with a hint of smoke in his words, "and you'll break your wrists."

"Why do you care if she breaks her fucking wrists?" a woman muttered. With effort, Jossa turned her head to look up. Blue eyes in a spacer-pale face glared at her. "Just means she'll have to suck him off instead of jerk him off," the woman continued.

"Don't need working hands to ride a dick," someone else said. Jossa craned her head around and saw a man with a shaved head and an impressive beard. He stood hipshot, both hands on the knife hilts clipped to his belt. A tase gun sat holstered along one leg.

"Forget her," the smoky voice said again. A man with a sharp face and scarred hands crouched near Jossa. A wide strap crossed his chest. The long muzzle of a snipe gun rose over one shoulder. He ignored her, looking instead at something else.

No. *Someone* else. Syrus—who, Jossa realized, still sat quietly behind her. Not limp. Waiting.

The man with the snipe gun reached out and slapped Syrus. Not gently. The blow had enough force to shift his body. Jossa grunted as she fought for balance against the shifting of her support, then gasped as her shoulder let her know its opinion of her antics.

"Quit faking," the man said. A hint of anger trickled through Jossa's extra senses. "We all know you're in there."

Syrus leaned forward then, pushing Jossa upright ahead of him. She put her hands down for balance, gasping as one arm refused to function properly, then yelped as she zapped her other hand on the anchor of a grav tether. He gave her a shove with one elbow. Balance gone entirely, body twisted around like a poorly coiled rope, she toppled over. She couldn't help crying out in pain as the tethers pulled on her arms. But at least she landed on her good shoulder.

Scorn and derision were often thought of as the same thing. Jossa would tell anyone who wasn't a Feel that they might seem similar, but they were very much different to her. Both washed over her, faint but clear enough. Syrus leavened the stranger's emotions with more than a bit of humor.

Ancestors behind, she wished he didn't find everything so funny.

Although she could have kissed him too, for helping prove that her sai was still working.

Someone snorted. A pair of worn boots stepped into Jossa's line of sight. The person crouched next to her. Hands took hold of her shoulder and opposite arm. Not gently, but not as aggressive as the man who'd struck Syrus. Pain swallowed her. She came back to reality screaming along the mind bond for Delfi. Screaming in actuality too.

She was also sitting upright. She realized it just as the people around her reacted, their bodies stiffening in panic, teeth bared and hands on weapons.

They were only afraid for a moment before rage took over.

Jossa almost didn't notice. She was still looking for Delfi, pushing through physical agony to reach for her sister. The bond was still there. But it was thin. So narrow that all she could tell was that it existed.

"Easy," Syrus said. His words were low. Calm. He shifted. Jossa felt him press an arm to hers. Residual fear, followed by rage, burned her skin and swamped her brain. Then both leeched away, drawn like the tide on an Ajiri world.

They didn't return in the next wave. Instead, the pseudo-grace of a false mind bond replaced them. It did not come easily. The feeling wavered, quivering without the full support of a true bond.

But it was enough to steady her. Jossa took it into herself, letting it wash away the feelings of the strangers. They'd dissolved into an argument while she was distracted, all waving hands and tense voices. The fact that they'd all gone fuzzy to her sai helped.

All except the woman who'd helped Jossa sit up. She stood now, watching them with one eye while keeping the other on Jossa and Syrus. The woman didn't exist at all.

A sense of questioning passed through the peace that Syrus offered. Did she have this? Was she able to keep herself in line?

In answer, Jossa leaned away from him, focusing on the calm. The grace of a soul bond, even though it wasn't real. She could make it real. She could hold this feeling, at least for a little while. The longer she held it, the easier it was for Syrus to take it and rebound it back to her. Provided neither of them lost touch with the feeling—admittedly not likely, given their captors—they'd be ok.

Come on, Delfi, figure it out! Help!

After a few deep breaths, Jossa realized the argument among their captors had quieted. They stood, resentful and mutinous but no longer afraid or raging. Looking up, she saw that every single one of them was staring at *her*.

Oh dear.

Jossa twisted around to look at Syrus, sending him questions and curiosity and praying to the Ancestors he'd be able to understand her. The look he flicked her way might have been reassurance. It also could have been contempt.

"Bitch," the blonde woman spat. "Fucking noble sai bitch." She stepped forward, hand raised.

The other woman caught the blonde by the wrist and swung her around on her own momentum. "We don't have time for this. Get out and check the next hall." She jerked her chin at the sharp-faced man. "You too."

The pair glowered but stalked off. Once they'd vanished through a door at the far end of the tiny room, the woman turned back to Syrus and Jossa. "Well," she said. "Not quite what I expected."

Syrus snorted and leaned back. Jossa shifted as far as she could in order to keep him in view as she eyed the woman. The woman watched her in return, dark brows raised over suspicious eyes, an arched nose, and thin lips. She had shaved either side of her head, leaving a long fall of hair down the middle of her skull, tied back in a way Jossa couldn't identify at the moment. The others on the woman's team watched her. Every move she made set off a tiny cascade of adjustments in the people behind her.

Jossa couldn't feel anything coming off this woman. The others were muted again, their initial surge of fear and rage having died down to almost nothing.

If it weren't for the way they spoke, she might've almost believed they'd calmed down. But she'd learned a bit about nehkeh over the past year. If Syrus was any indication, no nehkeh ever truly calmed down.

It hit her then, as she stretched with her sai and found that he was the only one at all clear to her. She had her gift. The bond still lived. And she wasn't crowned, which was the other common method of suppressing sai. Unlikely that this group had managed to find a... Jossa looked around... abandoned office with anti-sai shielding in the walls. That meant something else was blocking her ability to get a read on their captors. Unless they were all shielding themselves with equal degrees of skill.

She tilted her head and squinted at the leader, who still watched her through narrowed eyes. "Null?" Jossa asked.

The woman blinked. One of the men behind her cursed.

Syrus barked out a laugh.

When the man with the beard stepped forward, fist raised, Syrus kicked him in the kneecap. "Stay the fuck back," he snarled at the man.

"Told you we should have shackled his feet," the man with the smoky voice said. He finally moved out where Jossa could see him. Wide cheekbones, square jaw, narrow chin and mouth, his face was an odd amalgam of parts that made a memorable whole.

"Yeah, yeah." The woman in charge crouched so she was eye-to-eye with Jossa. "Or stun him from ten feet away and never give him the chance to kick you."

"Is that what you did?" Jossa asked. "Stunned us in the middle of the corridor?"

The woman snorted and looked at Syrus. "Picked a winner here. Hope the other one's smarter than this."

Jossa felt Syrus suddenly come into focus behind her. She didn't get images or words. Nothing so concrete. But there was a definite sense of attention.

Very carefully, she didn't turn to look at him. She had no idea what these people knew about her. And she'd already given away too much. Besides, she didn't like the implications of the woman's words. Not just the bit about his having chosen her, Jossa. But the knowledge that she wasn't his only travel companion.

::Delfi,:: she called down the bond, not sure if her sister could hear. ::We have trouble. Are you safe?::

Nothing.

Jossa sucked in a breath as quietly as she could and grabbed hold of the bond in both hands. The false grace Syrus had given her was fading quickly.

"... think we should just get off this dump." That was the man with the beard. Their captors had gone back to talking amongst themselves while Jossa was distracted. "We got him. The bitches are icing on the cake at this point. Fuck, we even got one of them too."

The group looked down at the prisoners, then went back to their conversation, voices much quieter this time. Their emotions, however, rose—even with the numbing influence of the Null woman.

Jossa scooted back as far as her tethers would allow, using her good arm to compensate for the bad, and leaned towards Syrus. "Who are they?" she asked as quietly as she could manage.

He turned his head to look at her but didn't answer.

Jossa glared at him.

"He hasn't told you about us?" The man with the smoke in his voice came to crouch in front of her. Out of kicking range, she noticed. "Fancy that."

While Jossa was still puzzling out the meaning of the phrase, he unclipped a hilt from his belt and activated it. Liquid metal flowed, then solidified into a narrow blade, single-edged and curved at the tip.

"Pity," the man said. "He's got a lot of stories to tell." His lip curled. A pulse of anger hit Jossa in the feet.

"Shit or get off the pot, Fieltar," the woman in charge told him. "We don't have time for games."

He growled. "We don't have time for anything if we want to get this done. Agadi, you making any progress over there?"

The man with the beard snarled something unintelligible and flung a hand up in a rude gesture. Jossa realized he was working on a screen. Still close enough to the group for them to cover him, but not really part of the conversation.

"Ok," Jossa said. "Since it doesn't look like he's ready with whatever he's doing, would someone mind telling me what in the *universe* is going on here?" She twisted her head around to look at Syrus, gritting her teeth as her shoulder complained. "You, for example," she said. "You could start talking."

"Oh, I like you." The woman came over to stand near Fieltar. "Go on then." She nudged Syrus's boot with her own. "Tell her what's going on."

Syrus kicked out slightly. Whether he was in earnest or not, Jossa couldn't tell. He'd locked himself down again.

Fieltar leaned forward, hands clenched into fists on his knees. "Twenty years we been hunting this one. Bounty is big, but too much work for most. Not us. Not since we had to go after him anyway. But he got hisself declared dead, and we had to move on or starve.

"And here he turns up, alive and kicking. Dancing through Barbs like he didn't do nothing at all. Like he don't have fucking debts to pay." He leaned in to jab a finger in Syrus's forehead. "Well, now we have you. We'll finally get what you owe us."

Jossa could finally feel the man clearly through the Null field. Pure, unadulterated fury boiled the air around him, shoving images of fights, minor squabbles, beatings by someone in authority, and nights of starvation into Jossa's face. She bowed her head against the torrent, gasping as she tried to find the calm, the peace that would carry her through the firestorm.

"Tarva, you're gonna want to up the field," Syrus said quietly. "Unless you want us all dead."

She heard someone sneer. Fools. Idiots. Didn't they know what they were dealing with? Why, if she'd had charge of this group, not one of these idiots would've had the *chance* to lose their temper in such an unprofessional manner. Why she'd—

The anger vanished. Swallowed up and flattened by a burst of nothingness that knocked her back against Syrus. She mewled and curled up as best she could with the shackles pulling on her arms, then reversed course to ease her injured shoulder. "Wha—?" She gasped.

The woman, Tarva, made a thoughtful noise.

Jossa lifted her head from Syrus's abdomen to look at her.

At the whole group of them, actually. Even Agadi, hands wrapped around his cracked screen, watched her. They reminded her of a pack of wolfdrakes that'd just sighted prey.

"Let me guess," Syrus said, his voice harsh in the heavy silence. "You saw a new bounty on me. Figured it'd be a great chance to get some of your own back." He leaned forward. Jossa had to struggle to sit up or find herself with a face full of his belt buckle. "Curious part is you picked her up. What you need dead weight for?"

Tarva shrugged and leaned back. "They mean something to you. Apparently they mean something to whoever you stole them from too. Going to get our money's worth out of you."

Jossa couldn't help laughing. "Mean something? To *him?*"

Syrus snarled. She flapped her good hand at him. "Oh, now that is just rich. Us! Him!"

He hit her with a lance of frustration and something that felt like *shut up* through her leg where it touched his. She almost obeyed. But by now she was laughing too hard to even talk properly.

"You mentioned the other one," Syrus said after a moment.

"Yes."

"And your plan right now?"

"What," snapped Agadi, "so you can ruin it?"

Exasperation rolled off Syrus and up Jossa's leg, somewhat muting her humor. Only somewhat. She coughed a couple times, lost a couple more giggles as she sat back up, and shook her head. "You can't leave without my sousi," she said as she caught her breath.

Every head in the room turned to look at her. Jossa squared her shoulders and met Syrus's eyes before transferring her gaze to the woman leading the bounty hunters. "I'm too strong a Feel. You take me away from her, away from this base..." Jossa shrugged. "Your sai better be strong enough to offset the results. By the time you make it halfway to the Barbican, I'll have lost control. We will *all* die in blood and fury."

"You're very sure of that," Fieltar said, narrow mouth thinning as he glared down at her.

"I have seen the results," Jossa said. "If you want to collect the bounty on his head, so be it. As for any bounty on mine, whoever gave it should have made it clear we come together or not at all."

And oh, how it hurt to expose herself like that. But they had to know. She couldn't let them think either of them was disposable. Couldn't let them think they'd get away with separating her from her sousi.

She didn't look at Syrus again. She didn't want to know what he thought of her taking initiative like this and opening such a gaping hole for these people to shoot through.

Their captors were silent for a long moment. Finally, Tarva stepped back to Agadi, waving a hand at Fieltar in some sort of signal. "How much did you get?" she asked the tech as he unclipped another screen from his belt.

"Not enough," the man replied. "Let me see what saved before it went crunch."

The woman nodded and came back over to stand next to Fieltar. "Here's the deal," she said, crossing her arms as she looked down at Jossa and Syrus. "Some rard has the docks blocked off for the time being. Once he clears out, we're putting you on the ship. Then, and only then, we'll see if it's feasible to track down your sousi. If not..." She shrugged. "Well, we have ways of controlling sai. Ways that don't give me headaches."

Jossa's mouth went dry. Terror grabbed her spine with icy hands. They didn't need her awake for shipping. Stupid, stupid, stupid! What good her revenge on waking if she ended up halfway across the empire?

::Delfi!:: she screamed down the mind bond, throwing her end as wide as it would go. ::Now is a good time to answer!::

The blonde woman and the man with the sharp face ran into the room, skidding to a halt just before they slammed into the table. "Fucking highborn," the man spat.

"They're here," the woman said. "And they've got enough firepower to blow an armada out of the sky."

"Fuck." Tarva grabbed for the knife on her belt and ran for the door. "Nadi, Banuo, guard those two and make sure they don't kick a fuss. Agadi, leave it."

Something struck the door to the room three times. A voice full of authority called, "Open in the name of isk Tova af Mitachte! Open immediately."

"Isk Tova af Mitachte don't run this base," Nadi snarled. "Isk Kallura lis Kerute do. What the fuck do they think they're doing?"

"A daughter of isk Tova married the heir of isk Kallura," Syrus told the ceiling. "You're supposed to be a scout, Nadi. You forget how to do your job?"

Tarva grabbed Nadi's hand as it cleared the woman's belt pouch. Three tiny blades shimmered dull green between the woman's gloved fingers. "Don't," Tarva said. "He's baiting you. Think!"

The people outside pounded on the door again. "Open in the name of isk Tova af Mitachte! Last warning."

"I'm not a big fan of being paralyzed while my eyes ooze out my head." Banuo pulled his tase gun and thumbed the power switch. The indicator light turned bright orange. "We let them in, yeah?"

Jossa scooted back as best she could, trying to find the wall. Her shoulder, half-forgotten in the rush of fresh terror, made its presence known again. She looked down at it as the crew around her armed up. Her shirt was in tatters. Two wide stripes of synthskin were stuck longways across her collarbone and chest. Bright red spots of blood had seeped through the field bandage, but so far none had made it past the seal. "What?" she started to ask.

"Not important right now," Syrus told her. He leaned in slightly, bracing her as she found the wall. Frustration mixed with resignation passed to her through the contact. Was that... sadness in the background? Why sadness?

Then he straightened, and the emotions were gone, locked up in his shields or dampened by the Null field.

"Alright," Tarva yelled. "We're coming!"

::Del!:: Jossa tried again to reach her sister. These people had guns. Tase guns, yes—but still, even those could be lethal.

"Need to borrow a cup of sucrose?" Fieltar muttered as he came to stand in front of the prisoners. The others spread themselves out. Agadi eased up to the door and slapped the lock panel from the side, out of the way of whoever might come charging through.

The rard's men didn't *quite* rush in like air through a depressurized hull, but they did move with purpose. Weapons trained on the bounty hunters, they spilled through the door, spreading out to make way for others. Suddenly, Jossa had a new appreciation for the claustrophobic. Such a small space was *not* meant to hold this many people.

::Delfi, disfesa, any time you wish to answer,:: she called along the mind bond. ::I am about to be buried in men.::

Someone at the back of the pack of House guards said, "Sir, this is not—"

"I don't *care* if it's a good idea," another voice snapped back. "I'm doing it."

Jossa could well imagine the look a good bodyguard would give his charge at that moment.

Tarva stepped forward. The man covering her shoved the muzzle of his gun into her chest. She ignored him. "Whoever's in charge of this might as well get in here." She bared her teeth at the man in front of her. "Since you came out of your golden tower and all."

The guards all bristled. Syrus made a hoarse noise that might have been a laugh.

But the ranks of men parted, making way for someone else. He wore gray and brown, but more elaborate in the trimmings. Bands of silver embroidery at the cuff and shoulder seams. Glowing miniature grav tethers holding the upper shoulders together. There was a sigil worked into the surface of the tethers, silhouetted against their light, but Jossa couldn't tell what it might be.

He had dark eyes, canted at the corners. Sharp features and a strong jaw, mellowed by age but not lost to fat and loose skin. With a straight back and hands fisted at his hips, he was the complete image of a noble who did not know what it was to be thwarted. He passed Tarva as if she weren't even there. His guards all made abortive efforts to stop him. He didn't notice them either.

His eyes were fixed on Syrus. Tarva's own sai muted the man's emotions down to dull embers, but even if Jossa weren't a sai, she would have been able to feel the impotent rage that burned the man's eyes to cinders in his face. He fairly shook with it. The closer he got, the more stilted his movement, the deeper the flush in his cheeks.

She half expected spittle to form on his lips.

Jossa couldn't help it. She cringed back, trying to make herself small. Hoping he wouldn't notice her when he finally vented his temper on Syrus.

Fieltar, tall and broader than the noble, stayed where he was as the man rounded the table. Tarva stepped forward before the rard could plow into the other bounty hunter. "Sir," the woman said in an even voice. "These are our lawful tags."

"You will release them to my men," the rard said to Fieltar. He didn't even look at Tarva. "They are now in the custody of isk Tova af Mitatchte. Untether them."

Perfect. So not only was this man adding another layer of confusion and complexity to the awfulness of this day, Jossa was about to be the prisoner of yet another arrogant achek with more manpower at his beck and call than sanity in his brain. She didn't know who she'd shoot first, had she a gun in her hands. Syrus for getting her into this, the rard for his attitude, or Tarva for threatening her and Delfi's chance at safety.

She waited for Delfi to remind her that a gun had more than one shot and she could get them all if she moved fast enough.

Silence.

"And I'm telling you that if you want to take them, you'll do so over our dead bodies." The conversation had moved on while Jossa was lost in thought. Tarva had both hands on her belt now, fingers white with the strength of her grip on it.

The noble puffed himself up like an insulted cat, then bulled forward, into and past the woman. He stopped inches away from Fieltar, shaking a finger in the taller man's face. "You breathe the air of this base by a rard's will! You think you can hold them? You think you will make it out of this room without my blessing, much less off the base?"

The bounty hunters moved as a single unit. Fieltar whipped something long and flexible off his belt, stretching it between both hands in a glowing green cord of light. Tarva lunged for the rard, caught him by the back of the shirt, and turned. Feet braced, hips rotating, she threw him across the table in the middle of the room.

A guard grabbed for her. Fieltar tossed his cord of light around the man's wrist. A slip, a twist, a yank, and somehow the tall nehkeh had the guard turned around, his arm hitched up behind his back. A loop of glowing green ran around his neck. Before the guard could get away, Fieltar captured his other wrist and hitched it to the guard's neck as well.

Gasping and choking, the guard staggered back. Jossa couldn't see what was happening with the others, not from this angle. But nearly half the highborn's retinue was down, and the rest were a fair way to wiping the floor with their shiny livery.

"What's all this?" a new voice shouted, hard and demanding. Jossa looked away from the struggle among the guards and hunters in time to see another rard step through the door. He too wore gray and brown trimmed in silver. He too was accompanied by guards who looked none too pleased that their charge had wandered into a dangerous situation.

The fresh men turned the tide against the bounty hunters. Nadi fell with a cry of frustration, struggling until the guard held a stun baton to her neck. Agadi took out two in rapid succession before the third caught him a solid baton blow to the skull.

"Enough!" Tarva barked.

Her people froze, then went down under the weight of the highborns' men. Fieltar hit his knees next to her, gasping as the guard held him by the hair and the threat of the baton along his face.

The nobleman on the table, still nameless, thrashed in Tarva's grasp. She shifted to keep her hold on him as she met the newest intruder's eyes, then very deliberately stepped back and away.

Syrus pressed himself to Jossa's side and then eased away, leaving smug humor behind.

Yes, yes, she wanted to tell him. That was one of your tricks.

Question was, did he want her to see *more* than simply the similarities between himself and the bounty hunters' leader? Or did he just enjoy being an insufferable achek?

"Peace, brother," the new noble said as the man on the table lurched to his feet.

Spitting epithets, the enraged rard lunged for Tarva. She dodged back and around Fieltar, halting near Jossa and Syrus. Numbness pressed at Jossa's temples, pushing against her eardrums. The world echoed strangely, feeling flat and somehow colorless.

Jossa might have hugged Tarva if the woman weren't so set on collecting that bounty. The last thing anyone needed with this much testosterone in the air was to have the local Feel losing her mind and infecting them all.

"I'll have you flogged," the first rard said, finally finding his words as his brother steadied him on his feet. "Flogged in the halls! I'll take the skin from your back, you bittek, and cut it into strips so fine no dedaf-priest will ever put it together again. Then I'll space you, you hear? Slow depressurization. You'll be screaming for mercy by the time I'm done with you, you *asjokochek!*" He devolved back into curses, far more creative than any highborn Jossa had ever known.

Tarva stood still, waiting. Jossa didn't dare look up to check the expression on the woman's face. Neither did she risk meeting the eyes of either rard. Instead, she lowered her head to her knees, hunched her shoulders as best she could, and waited to see what would happen. Far better to appear small and helpless than let anyone know she might be able to fight back.

So long as Syrus kept his mouth shut about her, she might have a chance.

::Del,:: she called along the mind bond again. ::We've got more trouble.::

Very old, very familiar trouble too, if her guess was correct.

She prayed fervently that it wasn't.

FIFTEEN--SYRUS

Hunters pay bonds on their bounties. It's just the way it is. Any hunter who can't put up the percentage doesn't belong in the game. Any hunter who won't is a cheat and a thief and isn't to be trusted.
- Head of the Bounty Hunters Guild in Merjesab

Syrus didn't need faces or mannerisms—and wasn't that a word worth a few credits—to recognize the fuckers with the sticks up their asses. There were thousands of rardog in the Empire. They came in all shapes, colors and sizes. No. It wasn't their appearance, nearly thirty years older than the last time he'd seen either of the brothers, that tipped him off.

He'd known he was fucked the minute the first guard in isk Tova af Mitachte livery walked through the door. Fucked up the ass, fucked sideways, it didn't matter which. He might've been able to handle Tarva and her crew. Or at least escape later. Maybe even convince them that taking Jossa was a monumental mistake, although she'd been doing a good job of screwing that seed of a plan to hell and gone. But now?

Fucked.

"Control yourself," Almovak, younger of the two brothers, told Jirdis. "You're sinking to his level."

Jirdis's eyes flared, but he let his guards ease him back to the door, one checking the rard for any injuries Tarva might've given him.

Syrus could've told them the man was fine. She'd hardly touched the bastard. Now, if *he'd* managed to wrap his hands around the fucker's neck, none of them would need to listen to the man's bitching. He'd be dead.

And you'd have a whole other mess on your hands, a voice in his head told him softly. *Worse than it is right now.*

Syrus froze, trying to figure out when Rissa'd gotten free of her prison. What the *hell?*

Carefully, doing his best not to let the rage show on his face, he grabbed the scraps of his unwanted conscience and stuffed her back down with the monster, where she belonged.

A boot scuffed across metal decking; then Almovak was there, crouched so he could meet Syrus's eyes. Tarva growled something, but it was at Fiel, so Syrus ignored her. He wished he dared tell her to turn the Null field off, but that was too dangerous—for so many reasons he could hardly count them. The likelihood of everyone ending up a puddle of gore leaking through the seams in the deck was only the least of their problems right now.

The thought made him laugh. To think, a time when losing his temper *wasn't* the worst thing that could happen.

Almovak frowned. "I fail to see what's funny, *nehkeh.*"

Syrus laughed harder. The room around him went quiet. Even Jossa, her anxiety tingling his leg through the fabric, went flat and still.

"You dare laugh at a rard?" One of Jirdis's guards stepped forward, stun baton raised.

Syrus dodged, caught the blow on one shoulder, and leaned back against the wall, still laughing. The man brought the baton back for another hit. Syrus decided to sit still for this one. He was enjoying the irony too much.

It never landed.

"Don't damage the goods," Tarva growled softly. Louder, she said, "Milord, I paid a bond on these bounties."

Syrus wondered if anyone else heard what she didn't say. That she'd take him and Jossa out of here if she had to kill everyone in the base.

She'd always been determined like that. Probably why she was still alive.

He shoved the memories of agonized screams away, dragging his focus back to the room around him. Almovak was standing again, eyeing Tarva like she was a piece of rotten fruit in his salad. The guard she'd kept from striking Syrus glared at her, rotating the hand still holding the stun baton. Jirdis's guards had apparently gotten their rard out into the main hall. The highborn's cursing was muffled but still audible. And around them, back on their feet and with eyes wary, ranged the rest of Tarva's crew.

Once upon a time he would have known which way they'd jump in a fight.

"What was the price?" Almovak asked.

Syrus jerked his head up. Jossa's surprise peppered his leg with pinpricks of pain. Tarva blinked. "Twelve million," she said. She didn't add the honorific. Almovak didn't seem to notice. His eyebrows climbed for his hairline. One of the guards breathed out a curse.

"For *him?*" a man asked.

Tarva crossed her arms and glared at the noble in front of her. Almovak drew himself up, insult in every line of his body. Then he looked down at Syrus. At Jossa. Syrus glared up at him, daring him to say something about the worth of a nehkeh.

Instead Almovak shook his head and motioned for one of the guards to step closer. To Tarva, he said "Come to the manor, if you will..."

"Captain," she supplied.

He nodded. "Captain. No harm to you or yours. We'll even have a physician take a look at some of the bruises, if you'd like. We can talk prices there." He crouched again, facing Jossa this time. She flinched away when he reached to touch her face. Sighing, he pulled his hand back. "I don't know what you've done to her, Syrus. I would have thought you knew better than to mistreat either woman so."

Jossa lurched forward. Syrus threw himself to the side, knocking her off balance before she could blurt the words he *knew* were about to come out of her mouth.

Then a stun baton struck him in the back of the head and for the longest time, he knew only pain.

SIXTEEN--SYRUS

Only the dedda-priests may treat someone's maruste after death. Only they know the secrets of making the frozen nanites answer to a family's touch while also making the skin pliable and soft so it can be stretched onto an eljabibi and placed in the shrine.
   -"Strictures of the Navlad Funerary Rites," High Priest Rolluston

By the time the transport reached the bottom of the base, Syrus was mostly aware of his surroundings. The stomach-rolling motion of the vehicle slipping from the spindle to the Noble's Fist that capped this end of the base brought him all the way around. Gravity flipped, then realigned as the grav tethers adjusted to the up-down direction predominate in the Fist, and then they were off again.

Past the guards, through the small viewports in the transport, Syrus could see the near endless expanse of the Fist's ceiling. Shimmering metallic blue in the false daylight emitted by thousands upon thousands of tiny lights, it was dotted with vents, exposed piping, valves, and the other assorted bits of base infrastructure that couldn't be completely covered by panels and pretty paint.

Then the transport tilted again, one side at a time. Syrus caught a glimpse of huge fields of grass broken up by stands of trees. Tiny dots of color clustered in herds, or flocks, or whatever the fuck they were, ran from the shadow of the transport as it switched from a hall-crawler to independent flight.

Syrus leaned back and stared at the roof of the transport as the view vanished into painted metal. Fake. All of it.

"Makes you wonder," Tarva said, nudging him none too gently in the knee with one booted foot.

Syrus ignored her. She wouldn't badger him into old habits and old banter. It was a trap anyways.

"I said—" She drew her foot back for a real kick. Syrus jerked his knee out of the way at the last second. Her boot skidded along his leg to his hip before she recovered. She didn't finish the question.

The guards around them shifted nervously. The hum of stun batons in close quarters rose a notch.

Syrus closed his eyes and tried to sleep.

>>><<<

Twenty minutes later, the vehicle landed on a paved square of gray in the middle of a field of grass. Other transports landed around them, guards leaping out to make sure their highborn passengers didn't trip and fall flat on their faces. Syrus didn't bother trying to leave his seat until he'd seen Jossa and Delfi taken over the small rise that shielded the landing field from the mansion beyond. Jossa lolled in Banuo's arms, unconscious. Delfi fought and scratched and spat the whole way.

How had Jossa ended up unconscious? He didn't like that he'd missed whatever led to that. Or Delfi's arrival. Although the two events were probably related. Stupid sousi. The whole breed was exhibit A for lack of control.

"You had them since you ran off?" Tarva asked as she unclipped the flight harness around him.

Syrus snorted. "You get a massive concussion when the factory exploded, or you just get stupid with age?"

That earned him another blow to the head. He missed the fine details of exiting the transport and making it up the slope as his ears rang and stars popped in front of his eyes.

On topping the rise, he goaded her into hitting him harder.

"Get moving," one of the guards said, giving Syrus a shove towards the wide steps leading to the double doors of inlaid wood and ocean shells. "Now."

Syrus obeyed. It wasn't mounting the stairs that made him balk. It was the assault of his memories. The heat of the false sun, the scuff of boots on stone, and the smell of so much vegetation in the air threatened to catapult him back in time. To a time when he *had* a conscience to keep him from fucking up. To a time when he'd had, if not a right, then the privilege of coming up a set of stairs like this.

Everyone on the lawn was waiting for his reaction. He could guess what Jirdis wanted. And Tarva's crew. But Almovak? Now there was a puzzle. The man just stood there, hands behind his back, framed by the tall pillars of the mansion's front entry. His face was impassive as he looked down at Syrus. Even if Tarva turned off her Null field, Syrus doubted he'd know what the man was feeling until too late.

Should have gone military, some part of him thought. Not his conscience. His conscience knew better than to prod Syrus with the whys and wherefores of how Almovak had risen to a higher duty than the one his position as baby of the family had slated him for.

Then Almovak and Jirdis were in front of him and Tarva behind. The guards ranged around them, hands still on weapons. Syrus stopped at the top step and eyed Almovak. The man eyed him back, then nodded at one of his men. "Put him in the solar," he said.

"I'm not giving you the key," Tarva said.

Jirdis, predictably, came alive like a cat tossed in water. "You speak to a rard," he snarled. "Know your place, woman."

Tarva didn't look away from Almovak. "None of your guards could take him anyways, 'f he gets loose."

The rard, who still looked far too old for Syrus's last memory of him, raised an eyebrow. "And you could?"

Tarva bared her teeth in a feral smile. She shouldn't look so much like a predator bird, but she did. The guards around them shifted, their attention finding a new focus. Syrus smoothed his face before any of them could see the laugh threatening to escape. She'd always been good at the nonverbal communication shit.

Almovak shook his head and looked back to Syrus. "The solar," he said again. "Have her shackle him." To Tarva he said, "I would speak to you alone, after."

"Go on," Syrus told her. "Price me out by the weight bone-in. You'll get more than if you wait for them to cut me up into roasts."

Jirdis's face twisted. Almovak's mouth tightened. Tarva laughed and clapped a hand on his shoulder, shoving him past the rardog. "You haven't changed, you know that?"

Syrus followed the guard and thought about all the ways she was wrong. And all the ways she was right.

>>><<<

The room where they parked him was glassed in on three sides. Four stories high, its walls took in light, refracted it through the patterns cut into the panes, and bounced the results across dozens of mirrors hung from the struts and beams that crossed and recrossed in the air overhead. The glass dimmed partway up, keeping the people inside from being blinded the minute they walked in.

The air was heavy, wet, and warm. Orchids of all colors clung to the columns of blue and gold that lined the one solid wall. In the far corner, a trickle of water landed in a small pond. A tiny creature—half ferret, half something else—looked up from washing its face in the pond, chirruped in alarm, and ran off into the flowers.

"Spikeferret," Syrus said. "That's great. Sure this isn't a zoo?"

The question wasn't directed at anyone in particular. Tarva answered anyway. "If it is, then you're home."

He gave her a half grin. "And so are you."

She swatted him upside the head. Not as hard this time. "Fuck, woman," Syrus snarled as he caught his balance. "I like my brain intact."

She snorted and shoved him towards the heavy wooden table in the center of the room. "Nothing left for me to damage," she said as she nodded at one of the guards. "Chair."

The guard didn't move. "Milord said something solid."

Tarva waved a hand around. "You see anything solid in here? No. Your rard is a moron who's never taken a prisoner in his life if he thinks *this* room will hold *this* man. "

The guard looked uncertain. Syrus nearly rolled his eyes. Trust Tarva to ignore the possibility of hacking down half an acre of orchids and sticking him to the wall.

Then he saw her eyeing the flowers and rubbing her hand. Right. He'd forgotten. She was baseborn, allergic to the fucking things. He did open his mouth then, to remind her that allergic reactions passed but his being her prisoner would pass even faster. She must have seen something in his eyes she didn't like, because she grabbed a chair from the table with one hand and slammed it into the backs of his knees.

Syrus sat and tried not to call it a fall. The guards pulled their tase guns, holding them at the ready as Tarva unlinked his shackles and then attached the anchors to the floor, one on either side of the chair. Then she popped the smaller, curved cuffs from their hiding place in the shackles and attached his wrists to the arms of the chair. Syrus didn't fight her on it. It wasn't worth another brain-jarring punch.

Done, she stalked past the guards and over to the door. It irised open just before she got there. Banuo stepped through. She stopped to murmur something to him, then continued on her way. Ban grinned and stalked over to stand between the guards.

So much for trying to escape. Syrus stretched his neck to either side, trying to work out the kinks, and settled in to wait.

>>><<<

Time passed. The false sunlight of the Fist shifted and moved. Lights played along the walls and the floor as the mirrors above rotated and swung gently. Almovak's men kept half their attention on Banuo. Ban, for his part, kept his mouth shut. Syrus'd wondered if the fucker would ever learn to stop needling prisoners. Tarva must've beaten some sense into him; that or Nadi'd refused him access long enough to drill discretion into his stubborn skull.

The ferret creature came back eventually, chittered at him, and went on with whatever it'd been doing by the little pond. Then it gamboled off into the flowers again, and the room was silent. Syrus tried to remember where he'd learned the word "gamboled" and decided that was a memory best left alone for now.

The door opened abruptly some two hours later. The guards looked away from Syrus for the first time since Tarva had left, alarm and wariness blooming in the air around them. Ban didn't look over at all. Syrus grumbled to himself and leaned forward to see who it was.

A woman walked in, full skirts brushing the door frame before the metal panels could slide all the way back into the wall. Behind her was a girl. Young, slim, carrying a tray. Syrus didn't register any more than that.

He was too busy trying to restart his heart.

The nearest guard stepped into her path, one hand raised. She spoke. Syrus knew that much. But his attention was stuck on her face, not her words. Pointed chin. The almost translucent skin of someone who'd spent most of their life in space. Dark hair pulled back and around to frame her face, tiny grav-tethered gems floating in a cascade around her shoulders. And her eyes. Huge. Dark. Tilted up at the corners and framed by long lashes. Windows to a soul.

Windows to the wrong soul. The angle of her jaw was slightly off. Her lips weren't full enough. The cheekbones were too wide. And her eyes weren't quite almond enough, although they were still the most familiar thing about her. She stood wrong, held her shoulders wrong. Superficially everything was there. But the core, the substance of the woman she resembled? He didn't see her.

The guards swiveled to face him. Banuo's eyebrows rose. The woman blanched and stepped back. The serving girl nearly dropped her tray. Fear—zinging, tingling, and burning—drove itself into his brain.

A sound, low and grinding, filled the room around him. One of the guards stepped forward, baton raised, mouth firmed in... anger? Determination?

Syrus realized that *he* was the source of the noise. A growling whine that reverberated in his chest and up his throat. His shoulders strained. He'd leaned forward, pulling against the shackles that held him to the chair. The monster thrashed in its prison, beating at the lid to its hole as it screamed to be let loose. His conscience did nothing to stop it.

Something pale and thin hit the table nearby, slithering into Syrus's line of sight. He froze, staring at it, lying folded and puddled and nearly hanging off the edge of the polished wood surface. The growl in his throat deepened as he leaned away.

"You do yourself no favors, acting like that," someone said. Syrus whipped his head around. Almovak. The rard stood at the other end of the table. The serving girl set the tray down in front of him. The woman, the quasi-ghost, bobbed a quick curtsy and fled, shepherding the servant before her. Syrus followed them with his eyes, then looked back at the bit of leather hanging off the table. Proof positive that no matter the similarities, the woman wasn't who he'd first thought she was.

Two guards flanked the rard. One set something on the table. Battered, scuffed, and torn, the insignia of the Karukap barely visible on its side, the bag was as sorry a piece of work as anything could be after twenty years hard use.

Syrus's heart didn't quite stop, but it did stutter slightly. He'd wondered and dreamed this moment in a thousand variations, although he'd usually expected Rissa's mother to be the one confronting him, not Almovak.

Almovak ignored the bag for the moment. The cup of liquid he'd poured for himself steamed, releasing earthy spices and bright citrus into the air. It smelled like home, which was ridiculous, because the last real home Syrus'd had was dead and gone.

"I would pour for you," Almovak said. "But seeing as you are inhibited at the moment, it seems a pointless gesture."

"But taunting me about it isn't, right?" Syrus asked. Watching the rard kept him from focusing on the leather Almovak had thrown at him. He couldn't get a read on the other man, not with the residual acid contaminating the air. The guards didn't help, radiating determination and scorn in equal measure.

Was the rard smart enough to figure out how to blunt his emotions so Syrus couldn't read them? Or was he just that calm about this whole thing?

Almovak sipped, frowned, and poured a healthy dose of cream into his cup. Sipped again and sighed. "Not as good as the blend from home. But then, processing does detract somewhat from the flavor."

"Get on with it," Syrus told him. "I'm not interested in your fucking games."

Almovak met his eyes over the cup as the guards shifted uneasily. Syrus raised an eyebrow.

A thin smile pulled at the man's mouth. He took another sip of the tea, set the cup aside, and leaned over to brace both hands on the surface of the table. "Why don't you tell me about that." He nodded at the leather.

Syrus looked at it. The patterns of dark glyphs and light scars. The fine grain. The neat edges. The weeks of work it had taken to get exactly right. The dissonance of it being so far from a perfect example of its kind.

"And then," Almovak's voice turned hard, fury and bleak hope sending shards of icy pain through the air, "tell me why it was hidden in a *hole* on your ship."

The shackles on Syrus's wrists had little leeway in them. But enough for him to turn his hand and snag the thing with his fingers. The sheet of fine leather slid, buttery soft, off the table and into his lap. Syrus felt the breath catch in his throat. Felt his pulse speed up. The monster slammed itself against the lid on its prison, over and over and over, keeping time with the rising beat of his heart.

"Tell me!" Almovak's voice cut the air in a hoarse roar, full of every emotion Syrus fought to hold in. "Why did you hide my sister's *skin* like a piece of trash?"

SEVENTEEN--DELFI

But Father, why? He's a stain on the house, he's
contaminated Rissa beyond all hope—
Don't question me, boy! You are no longer in a position to
care about the direction of this family!
- Conversation between Jirdis and Karudis lis
  Tova af Mitachte

A man stood over Delfi when she finally woke. Face free of age wrinkles and weathering, his mind churned with data. Heart rate, respiratory rate. Oxygen saturation. Nothing about where she was or how she'd gotten there.

A light blinded her eyes. She cried out, trying to cover her face with her hands. She came up short.

Pupil dilation, good.

"Do you know the date?" the man asked.

Delfi opened her mouth to reply, remembered that she couldn't answer properly, and shut it again. When he kept looking at her, she nodded.

He raised his eyebrows and waited.

She glowered.

"I believe she may be a mute," said a half-familiar voice just out of sight.

Delfi craned her neck around. The rard stood there, flanked by his guards. She frowned at him, trying to remember how she'd gotten into this situation. Right. She was a captive. She'd been stuck in his flit surrounded by guards while he'd taken the rest of his men into some random room in an abandoned back hall of the base. Then he'd come out with even more men and several strangers, plus Syrus and Jossa.

At which point Delfi herself had lost her everloving mind, because Jossa was right there but the bond was still completely empty—and how could that be? If she could just get to her sister, touch her, look into her eyes, she could prove to both of them that everything was ok. The bond was fine. They were fine.

And of course, it hadn't worked. The last echoes of pain at the back of her head told her that much.

"'S'at so," the medic answered the rard, voice absent as he marked things off on the screen. "Well, looks like her mind is intact at least." He looked up. "Unless you wish imaging, milord?"

The rard shook his head. "Take a blood sample, though. Tarard Jirdis is putting in a call for a marus-priest to come and parse it."

Delfi's stomach sank. A marus-priest? Oh, that was not good at all. Escape just went from impending to emergent.

The medic drew himself up. "Milord, the facilities here are more than up to the task of parsing what few glyphs the women have in their maruste. I do not think it—"

"Do not touch the blood samples." The rard's voice was hard as titanium. *No chances*, his mind said. *No mistakes. Everything put on temple record.* "You will make the draws, and they will be put in stasis under *my* bloodlock. I will bring the priest down when he arrives."

The medic bowed his head. "As you say, milord." The things running through his head, however, were much less polite.

Delfi clutched at the cool metal under her hands. She'd *heard* them. Both of them. Which meant that whatever had been blocking her sai earlier was gone.

::Jossa,:: she called along the mind bond, careful as could be.

No answer. Delfi nearly choked on the air in her throat. Why was it still not working?

"When is the other expected to wake?" the rard asked the medic, oblivious to the mental anguish of the young woman on the table.

"Shortly, milord," the medic replied. "The damage was severe, but localized. I don't advise any... rush to be put on her recovery though. Without a known baseline, we may not know if all the repairs have taken as fully as they should."

The rard sighed and waved the medic's caution aside. "Yes, yes. You do your job. I'll see to the rest."

The medic bowed and went back to checking things off on his screen.

Delfi decided now was as good a time as any to try sitting up. About halfway to upright, she realized why she couldn't put her hands to better use. They were attached to rails on either side of her.

"Woah, hey now!" The medic set the screen aside and put his hands on her shoulders. Too late. She glared at him. He tried pushing her back anyways, gently. She bared her teeth and tightened her stomach and refused to let him move her.

She was *not* panicking. She wasn't. She was breathing normally, thank you.

"Please ma'am, I'm not done checking you over," the medic said. "Please, lie back."

Bodies pressing and men growling and rage and lust invading her mind.

Why were her hands stuck? She couldn't move her hands! No! No, she needed to fight. Jossa. She had to protect Jossa. She'd *failed* Joss and now she was paying the price and she needed her hands—why weren't her hands free? What she deserved, failing. Should she fight at all?

"Easy, easy." An unfamiliar voice. Husky, low. Like velvet against her ears. Fingers, work roughed and large, around her wrists.

She screamed, trying to jerk away. ::Jossa!::

Nothing.

And then her hands were free. No longer pulling against an immovable will. She struck out. Found flesh. Scrabbled, and found skin and cloth. Someone grunted. Someone else cursed.

"Shhh..." Someone else this time. A presence near her knees. A low chant of a child's lullaby in her mind. Delfi uncurled her hands. Free. Loose. Not shackled and tethered. Not on a floor in a room full of enraged men and gory remains.

"Hey, hey." The woman's voice again. A knife wrapped in cloth, sharp edges not entirely covered. "Easy now."

"Milord?" The medic again. Delfi flinched, even though his mind contained only a running series of pitying remarks mixed with clinical analysis.

"Back away," the rard replied.

Delfi cracked an eye open.

A woman stood next to her. Blond hair, icy blue eyes full of sympathy and pity. She held her hands palm out so Delfi could see there were no weapons.

Delfi looked down. She was wearing her own clothes, thank the Ancestors. And sitting on what looked to be the mattress of a medunit. She checked. Yes, there was the hood behind her. And the tower unit with readouts and data feeds chirping away merrily.

A med ward. Not a tiny room full of blood and death.

"Hey," the woman said quietly. "You in there?"

Delfi narrowed her eyes at the woman. Really? Someone had a panic attack and the best she could come up with was "You in there?"

"Looks like." The man's voice again. Delfi nearly twisted herself off the bed looking for him. The woman made a little noise and steadied her. The man stood near the medic, thumbs hooked in his belt loops and an unreadable expression on his face.

Delfi pushed with her mind. Nothing. Her thoughts slid along an invisible wall and skidded off to the side, catching the medic instead. His brain was full of calculations. Nothing helpful there. Not from the hunters either, although she might be able to break through given time. Their shields weren't as solid as Syrus's.

"I told you not to startle her," the rard said from the other side of the medic. "The nehkeh's already damaged her enough. Bringing her out of it will be hard enough without adding to her trauma."

The medic drew himself up, insult in every line of his body. "Milord, are you comparing me to a *nehkeh?*"

Both men missed the tension that wrote itself across the faces of the unknown man and woman. It was gone as fast as it appeared.

"I am *saying*," the rard said, "that we need to provide a safe environment in which she can recover. If you are unable to do that without panicking her further—"

"That won't matter for long." A new woman stepped around the curtain that hid Delfi's little section of the med ward from what she assumed was the medunit next to her. "I've registered our catch with the guild, milord."

Delfi tried to see what was on the new woman's mind. What did she have planned, that she was so confident she could walk out of here without the rard stopping her? There was no wall to slide off of. No barrier whatsoever. The woman's mind didn't exist at all!

Which was preposterous, because her body was right there. Tall, with pale skin, although not spacer pale. Fine lines around hard brown eyes put her in her middle years. A slightly hooked nose and a thin mouth completed the face of a woman who was used to fighting for her rightful share of anything, and wasn't afraid to do it either. The horse's mane haircut and worn clothes just drove home the point.

The rard drew himself up straight. "Our deal was contingent on the information the nehkeh man could give."

"Our deal for *him*," the woman replied. Something passed through her eyes too fast for Delfi to identify. "You have no use for the women."

"There is a priest coming to parse their bloodwork and confirm their identities against the samples that were provided with the bounty sheets. In the meantime, if I might interest you and your team in some refreshments? While we finalize the details?"

The blonde woman snorted. The other woman waved a hand at her. The blonde subsided.

"My people stay here," said the woman in charge.

The man with his thumbs in his belt loops grinned. The blond settled her weight further onto her heels.

The rard shook his head. "As you wish." He tapped at the commlink implant along one cheekbone and smiled at the woman. "My brother will come down to supervise in my stead. In the meantime, I'll leave some of my men in the main room. To assist if they cause any trouble."

Delfi reached again, hoping to hear smug background chatter in his mind to the effect of cutting her plan off at the knees and preventing her from stealing the prisoners. Even he was blank to her. Just... dead space. As if he didn't exist.

Alarm clutched her heart. Was this...? It couldn't be. How could he have vanished when he'd been so easy to read before?

Delfi tried to push towards the new woman instead, to Read her intentions. She didn't find a mental wall. Or internal commentary.

Nothing. Absolutely nothing.

"Very well," the new woman said, face smooth.

Oh. Oh! Delfi watched the rard speak to the medic and the woman whisper something to the tall man who'd stayed so quiet. He nodded. The rard stepped up to hold the curtain aside, and then they were gone.

The man and the blond woman, whose names she still didn't know, watched the curtain for a moment or two before turning their attention back to Delfi. She ignored the man and told herself she wasn't a coward. She *wasn't*. She was just... prudent. No point in possibly triggering a reaction by antagonizing him.

Not that she thought the woman was any better, aside from the fact that she didn't own the proper equipment to rape her prisoner. Delfi swallowed the lump in her throat and gave the blonde a more careful look. There was something in her eyes. It didn't show when she looked at a person directly, but when she forgot to hide it, when she looked off to the side, there it was.

Did the man know that his teammate was not entirely sane?

Delfi stretched out a mental hand, fearing what she'd find now that the other woman was gone, but not seeing a way around it. If he purposely compensated for the woman's instability, that was one thing. If he didn't know, he needed to—

Nothing. Again, her thoughts slid along the mental barrier and off into nothingness.

Delfi withdrew before he could notice her prodding. That answered one question. Since she'd been able to Hear the rard at the ship and at least sense the two in front of her, that meant the woman in charge of the hunters was likely a Null. A Projective one at that.

Perfect. Just what this mess needed was someone who didn't exist to others' sai.

"Well," the blonde said, standing straight again. "Looks like it's just us again." She leaned in, baring too-white teeth in a smile, all sympathy and concern gone. "So. You ready to stop playing dumb, little girl?"

Delfi hissed at her.

Elsewhere in the room, something *thudded*.

Jossa lurched from quiet presence in the mind bond to full-blown panic. *A coffin! She was in a coffin!*

Delfi doubled over, gasping as she tried to get a handle on the panic. ::You always jump right into worst-case scenario, you know that,:: she snapped as she widened the bond to let the excess fear get suctioned through. She shoved irritation at her sister, genuine and manufactured, to serve as replacement.

Jossa went still. The thumping stopped. The man stuck his head past the curtain into the main room. "What's going on?" he asked.

"Other patient's awake," said the medic.

Jossa had stopped panicking, but her mind raced as she came down off the adrenaline high. Delfi caught a thread of the circular logic.

Coffins were for the bodies of dead people. People who'd already had the skin taken from their backs and their heads removed for the priests' ceremonies. If her body were in a coffin for cremation, she'd never know it anyways. Therefore, she had to be alive, right? But what if—

Delfi huffed a wordless sigh through the mind bond and rested a phantom hand on Jossa's forehead. ::Sometimes your imagination worries me,:: she said.

::There was a Null!::

::Yes,:: Delfi said. ::There is a Null. She's gone now. Or else we wouldn't be talking, would we?:: Sometimes, her sister. She loved Jossa dearly, but sometimes. Taking care of her was more like shepherding a small child around the universe. Too bad Jossa thought it was the other way around.

Delfi heard the muffled beep of a medunit acknowledging a command, then the voice of the medic. He echoed oddly in her ears. Not quite clear to her physical hearing, very much so to her mental, transmitted as it was by Jossa and the still-open mind bond.

"There you are." Interest and concern touched her gently, bringing with them an impression of numbers, calculations, and forecasts of recovery.

::I see how it is. You calm down for a man you don't know, but not for me.:: Delfi huffed to Jossa but kept her amusement on her own side of the bond.

Jossa replied with a mental eyeroll as the medic started his checks.

Delfi looked down at her hands where they clutched the mattress. She should check on her sister in person. But the male bounty hunter still stood between herself and freedom, and she couldn't make herself let go. She didn't think the blonde woman would bother talking her down a second time.

::Where are we?:: Jossa asked as the medic made the necessary pokes and prods.

::We're not prisoners yet,:: Delfi muttered. ::Don't push it.::

::What's that supposed to mean?::

::It means that we may or may not be back to being brood mares, depending on how negotiations go.:: Delfi eyed the two bounty hunters, then the medunit she sat on. Did it have any weaknesses? No seams that she could see. No easy access to wiring. Pity. If she could get to a live current and then... what? Make one of the guards stand still long enough to pull it out and jam it into her skin?

A low glimmer of light caught her eye. Delfi leaned over carefully and looked. Two silver metal sheets, each with a cord affixed to the back by a knob of silplat. Tucked into its own notch in the medunit was a power crystal the size of a baby's fist. The cords ran into it from either side.

Emergency defib pads, in case the patient couldn't make it into the medunit before their heart gave out. Hmm.

::Del!:: Jossa's voice held a note of frustration.

"Ok, that's enough." The blonde woman set a hand on Delfi's shoulder. Delfi blinked and looked at her. Then realized that she'd hopped off the medunit mattress and started for the curtain. The man stayed back, eyes thoughtful.

Thank the Ancestors for small favors.

::Del, what did they do to you!?:: Less frustration. More righteous anger now. The medic's voice lifted, placating and worried at the same time, as he tried to get Jossa to stay in place.

Delfi batted at the woman trying to get between her and the curtains and got her hands wrenched behind her back as a reward. "I said," the woman growled, "that's enough. Don't make me hurt you, little girl."

Delfi froze. That speech pattern. The cadence. She sounded like—

::Delfi! Answer me.:: And then, out loud: "Please leave me alone, sir. I need to get to her."

"So. You *are* sousi. How interesting." The man's voice was icy. Clear. Delfi felt Jossa's mind churn as she tried to come to grips with the fact that she hadn't noticed a new person entering the room. The medic said something deferential and fell silent.

::Joss?:: Delfi lurched against the woman holding her and didn't get anywhere. ::Joss, who is it?::

::I-I don't know. But he is a rard. And he *hates* Syrus.::

Delfi breathed out a laugh. ::Who doesn't?::

::I think he's related to the local rard?:: Jossa didn't sound sure at all, but the emotions boiling inside her mind were reaching a critical point. Delfi bled them off again.

"You going to behave?" The woman holding Delfi gave her another yank on the wrists. Delfi didn't answer, trying to listen for the new rard. From his initial announcement, he'd dropped his words down to more conversational levels.

"You aren't trapped with nehkeh trash anymore. You're safe here. If he hadn't killed the men sent for him a few days ago, you would've been safe sooner." Delfi could feel the earnestness in those words, thanks to her sousi. He meant it. He wanted to keep them safe. Contained maybe, but safe.

Poor man. He had no idea what would happen if he managed to keep them.

"Hey," the blonde hissed. "Listen, you little bitch. I have better things to do than play top for you."

"Nadi," her companion said, voice full of warning.

The woman's grip eased, but she didn't let go.

Delfi ignored her, all her attention on the rard with Jossa. *He* wasn't shielded or otherwise blocked from sai. His mind was open, painfully so. He believed everything he said. He His mind fairly burst with imaginings of things Syrus must have done to her and Jossa. The things he planned to do in retribution were equally vivid. And far too elaborate to be explained by worry for two strange women.

Jossa kept playing her part. "Truly?" she asked the man. "I am relieved, milord."

::Gag me, please,:: Delfi muttered.

::If only,:: Jossa shot back. But she let Delfi listen in via the bond. "Pardon, milord," Jossa said meekly. "Please, pardon. My sister. If I could see my sister?"

A murmur of assent. Delfi straightened and tried to compose her face. Not for Jossa, who fairly trilled with anticipation and worry. But for the rard, who felt much more open to suggestion than the first one. Maybe she could sway him. Look pitiful enough to make him bring her and Jossa out of here and away from the too-watchful guards.

Delfi reached for the curtain. Why wait? She could check on Jossa herself and then—

A yank on her arm stopped her. Nadi, eyes chips of blue ice, smiled at her. "I don't think so. You stay here."

Delfi twisted her wrist, trying to break the woman's hold. But the woman moved with her, grip tightening.

The curtain slid aside, a whisper of fabric on fabric and the hum of anti-grav generators. Jossa stood there, one hand on the arm of a man in silver and brown, surprise on her face. Behind them stood two guards in the now-familiar House livery.

For the first time since Delfi had woken up, something slipped through the blonde woman's shields. Something dark, twisted, and jagged around the edges. It wasn't a thought, and it wasn't an emotion. It was beyond either, primal.

The woman, Nadi, would happily eviscerate this man given the slightest chance.

So far as Delfi was concerned, that made two of them.

"Just what do you think you're doing, woman?" the man barked. "Let go at once."

Something else shivered through the woman's shields, to be interpreted by Jossa this time. Frustration and... urgency?

Then she was back to being a blank wall, and Delfi didn't even have skin contact to aid in possible mind reading. Nadi raised her hands. "As you command, milord."

The rard missed the sarcasm in the woman's voice. Instead, he stepped closer and took both of Delfi's hands in his. "Miss, I do hope you are feeling better. My brother says you were being held aboard that ship, locked in by the nehkeh. I am Tarard Jirdis lis Tova af Mitachte. You'll be safe with us now." His thumbs rubbed gently along her skin. Then he dropped his hold on her and turned to Jossa.

She stayed stock-still as he cupped her head. "And you, my dear. Forced into his service. Rest assured, you won't be his doxie anymore."

::Shoot me now,:: Jossa hissed through the bond.

::Me first!::

Jossa hunched her shoulders, twisting her fingers together in front of her. "Indeed, milord. I am most grateful to be free."

::Free as a caged bird,:: Delfi muttered, doing her best to keep her face straight.

Next to her, Nadi snorted. "Lady, you aren't free. You're coming with us. Bounty, remember?"

Jirdis turned on his heel, Jossa forgotten. "You have a very high opinion of yourself, woman."

Nadi's face twisted. The other bounty hunter, who'd been watching the byplay, set a hand on her shoulder. "Excuse us please, milord," he said to the rard. "It's been a long day. And we *have* been chasing these two across most of the sector."

::Ok,:: Jossa said, biting her lip and looking down as the rard turned back to her. ::I'm ready to get out of here. Before they start trying to count the eggs in our ovaries.::

"These two?" the rard asked, the picture of incredulity. "Not to say that some women can't be led astray, but surely the only crime these two are guilty of is enduring too long in the company of an animal." He peered at Delfi next. She bit the inside of her cheek to keep from snarling at him. "No doubt my brother is in discussion with your"—he made a face—"captain over whether you must really bring them to whatever misguided fool set the bounty."

::Tase guns,:: Delfi told Jossa as she eased sideways, closer to the medunit and away from the cluster of people arguing somewhat politely about who owned whom. ::But I'm on the wrong side of my people. A stun baton, *maybe*. They'll notice me trying to take it. If I can get to the defibs—:: She stopped moving as the rard and the bounty hunters all turned to look at her.

"... bounty is a bounty," the male hunter said. "Not for us to wonder why, milord."

"Besides," Nadi cut in. "We've paid the bond. Registered the catch with the Guild too. Captain let your brother know."

Jirdis drew himself up, ready to deliver what would surely be an edict for the ages. Delfi slipped her hands behind her back and felt along the housing of the medunit, trying to find the defib pads. Jossa eased backwards herself, closer to the guards, all innocence.

Behind *them*, the door hissed open. Delfi couldn't see past all the people in her way as whoever it was came in. A pause, and then it hissed shut again.

"Father?" A woman's voice. Relatively young. Hesitant. Delfi reached and found a mind churning with too many thoughts and images to sort through properly. A flash of familiar brown eyes, another of the woman leading the bounty hunters, and then a wall of orchids. Not much to go on.

Jirdis turned to step through his guard detail. Jossa swung wide to make way for him. "Lanet?" the highborn asked. "How did it go?"

"Ready," the male bounty hunter murmured, almost too low to hear.

Nadi pressed something along her cheekbone. A hidden comm? "Whatever sick fuck uses a snake and a skull and thorn bushes better've given us the right maruste for these two," she replied just as quietly.

The rard stilled but didn't turn around, instead pushing the curtain further aside and stepping out a little. "Here now. I told you that you didn't have to go along with your uncle's plan."

"I know, Father. But the sooner all this is resolved, the better."

::Joss?:: Delfi pushed carefully at her sister through the bond. Jossa was rigid, both physically and mentally. ::Joss, what is it?::

Jossa wavered in place, mind clutching at the bond. ::Snakes and skulls. Skulls and thorns. What use a sousi pair?:: Her mental voice was hoarse. Her brain had drifted off between the stars.

"Joss!" Delfi lurched for her sister's arm and pulled, trying to shake her back to life.

Every mind around her, even the bounty hunters', turned towards her.

Jossa stared at the rard's back, resplendent in his fine clothing, blind to Delfi's attempts.

"What's this now?" Jirdis turned around, saw them, and came back inside the little curtained area around the medunit.

"Hey." Nadi reached out a hand and snapped her fingers under Jossa's nose. "You in there?"

"What's the matter, Father? Should I call the medic back?" The young woman pushed the curtain aside and stepped up next to her father.

It was Delfi's turn to freeze.

Enormous eyes, dark and canted up just slightly on the outer corners. Face pale although tinted warm, like the last light of sunset filtered through a haze of fog. Pointed chin, wide cheekbones, slight build. She wore a noblewoman's clothes. Not the same color as the ones in Syrus's memory. Not covered in blood, as Delfi sometimes saw her. Not tangled with the mangled limbs of another girl.

But that face.

Delfi had thought that face was dead. Or an imagining, never real to start with. Some figment of an imagination that craved a woman's touch, overlaid on every woman he mounted. A forbidden face? She'd wondered once.

Maybe a concubine of the Fleet, dead before she and Jossa arrived? The blood and the other body seemed to support that theory.

Once, when she lay awake at night waiting for Syrus to start dreaming so she could slip inside his defenses and look for answers to the secrets he kept, Delfi'd thought that maybe it was the face of a woman he'd left behind on some distant planet. That she stayed there still, waiting for him to return.

She'd never been able to keep a foothold in Syrus's mind long enough to find out.

::Del!:: Jossa's voice rang inside her skull. ::Del! Snap out of it!:: Alarm and fear mixed with a questioning demand shoved through the bond, tracing Delfi's neurons with fire before dropping into the abyss.

Delfi came back to reality to find Jossa right in front of her, panic welling to overflowing as she shook her sousi. Around them, the others spoke or shouted as their personalities dictated. Over Jossa's shoulder, Delfi could see the young woman from Syrus's mind. Jirdis, her father, stood in front of her, one arm out to keep her back. Or, more likely, to shield her. From the death grip she had on her father's shoulder and the hand clutched to her chest, she didn't look like she planned to go anywhere.

::Delfi, what is it?:: Jossa's fingernails nearly gouged the skin from Delfi's shoulders through the thin cloth of her shirt.

::I've seen her,:: Delfi whispered.

"Seen her where?"

"Fucking hell." Nadi spat the words with all the feeling of an angry bajbar.

Jirdis recoiled, pushing his daughter further back. Revulsion ricocheted from him to Jossa to Delfi as he stared at Nadi. "You! You're—"

"Nice one," said the male bounty hunter, reaching for his belt.

"Shit."

"Not helping!"

"Run," Jirdis told his daughter, pushing her back again, then pushing the guard. "Get her out of here."

::Time to go,:: Jossa snapped. She lunged for the male bounty hunter, wrenched the stun baton from his belt and brought it down over Nadi's head. She staggered back.

Delfi stared at the woman from Syrus's memories as the guards hustled her out the door, trying to figure out what was wrong with her face. What dissonance ran through her mind, that she could be and yet not be the girl Syrus thought of so often?

"Del!" Jossa whipped the baton out again, cracking the male bounty hunter across the wrist as he reached for his tase gun, then did the same to Nadi. She punched a surge of terror and frustration down the mind bond. Delfi cried out as it hit her brain.

But it worked. She refocused on the here and now. Jirdis was gone, probably with his daughter to the guard station. Jossa held the two nehkeh at bay, keeping them from drawing their stronger weapons, but that would only last as long as they thought she was worth more in one piece than in several. Delfi couldn't find an opening to jump in without getting zapped or caught.

Her eyes snagged on the medunit. Right. Defibs. She lunged for the unit, dodging around Nadi's swinging arm. Grabbing the cord that connected the pads, she fumbled with the power unit. Where was On, where was On? She needed this thing on!

Where? Where? There!

"What the fuck you doing bitch? Ow!"

::Hurry,:: Jossa grunted, sending Delfi an image of the scene behind her. She was losing ground. And nowhere near able to steal a long-range weapon from either attacker.

The light on the power cell settled from a rapid blink to a steady glow. Delfi grabbed the cords near the pads. Good. Now if she could jump one of—

An arm wrapped around her neck from behind and hauled. Praying she'd gotten it right, Delfi flailed and shrieked, careful to keep her hands apart. Growling under his breath, the man shifted his grip to pin her arms instead.

In the half second of transition, she slapped her hands back and up. Contact.

He let go. He couldn't help it. People had an instinctual urge to claw things off their faces.

The power cell gave a warning beep. The charge hit the pad. The man toppled. She leapt clear of his jerking legs and bent to grab his tase gun from its holster.

::Little help over here!:: Jossa yelped as she took a hit from Nadi and nearly tripped over the man. Oblivious to or not caring about the fact that Delfi was armed, Nadi drove the stun baton towards Jossa's back.

The charged bullet hit Nadi in the neck, shorting out her thoughts in a burst of pain. She dropped. Jossa found her balance again.

::Run!:: Delfi told her as she shot the gaping medic in the throat. ::Now!::

Eighteen--Syrus

You haven't seen superhuman until you've seen a sai throw
herself under a crashing ship to save her sousi.
-unknown

Hard hands grabbed Syrus by the hair and jaw, yanking his eyes away from the leather. Heat seared across his nerves. Despair so deep it opened up sinkholes in his mind. Syrus gasped and fought for reality. His monster burst from its prison, howling its rage at the invasion of emotions. Syrus sent his sanity scrambling after it. He couldn't lose control. Not here. Not *now*.

He owed her that much, for the little brother she'd loved so much.

"Milord!"

"Milord, no!"

Syrus clenched his teeth to keep from biting at the unfamiliar hands. Why? Why not show these fucking assholes how close to being an animal he *really* was?

The monster agreed. Bite and tear and rend. Make them fear. Use it as fuel. Escape. Escape and teach everyone what it meant to take a Savage prisoner.

Show them the error of their ways.

Something struck him across the face. Electricity buzzed along his nerves. He tipped sideways in the chair, wobbled, then landed back along the correct line of gravity. Snarling, he lunged for the stun baton before Banuo could hit him a second time.

The blow landed. Syrus rocked again.

But the monster settled.

"Rard Mitachte," said a calm voice somewhere out of eyesight. "I believe I warned you about speaking to the prisoner without myself present?"

Syrus slewed his head around. Tarva stood in the doorway, hands behind her back in a formal military rest, a wry smile on her face. He grinned back, knowing it to be a feral expression. Not something that belonged on a human face.

No matter. He didn't quite qualify for humanity.

Almovak stepped back, panting as he twitched his shirtsleeves straight. "Indeed," he said. "But as I believe I told *you*, I am Rard in this house, Captain."

She bowed from the waist, just slightly. "Then, as I'm sure you and your men are capable of controlling a fully enraged nehkeh, I shall stand aside. Ban." She turned to her teammate. "Go let Agadi know we're on our way."

And get out of here before you make things worse. Unspoken, but the three former Uvlaku knew what she meant. Ban was supposed to keep the rard from doing exactly what he'd done. Stupid fucker just couldn't resist the chance to muck things up. Idiot. How Tarva'd kept him alive all this time, Syrus had no clue. Probably sheer desperation and Nadi hypnotizing him or some shit like that. He laughed.

Ban growled and cuffed him over the head, then danced back as the guards stepped forward.

"Now," Tarva snapped.

Syrus chuckled again as Ban stalked out of the room.

"I fail to see what warrants such humor," Almovak said once the bounty hunter was gone.

Syrus shook his head and sat back. His heart rate dropped a little further. The adrenaline hadn't quite bled out of his system yet, but he could see sanity again. "Nothing you need to worry about," he told the rard.

Almovak leaned down so he could meet Syrus's eyes. His face was hard. He looked like his father had, just before the old man invented yet another way to punish the unwanted child in his House. "You," said Almovak, "are my prisoner. You have a long history of throwing a spanner in my family's plans. Yes, I am worried. When I am worried, I take measures." He stood straight again. "Convince me not to take those measures, if you please."

Syrus laughed again. "You know, it's hard to take you seriously considering last time I saw you, you'd barely learned to stop wiping your nose on your sleeve."

For that, he got another blow to the head. This time the baton's charge was set somewhere higher than a light zap. Stars and sparkles popped in front of his eyes.

"And last time I saw you, you'd been drugged and packed up in a casket lest you contaminate the rest of the House on your way out." Almovak leaned forward. "Look how far you've come."

Tarva barked out a laugh. Syrus snorted. "I've had my ups and downs." He looked at Tarva. "Speaking of. The bounty. Who's so mad at me they'd rather spend money on me than buy a new frigate? And how in hell did you get the money to pay the bond?"

Something in her eyes shifted. Something he couldn't identify. An emotion he'd never seen in her before, unless twenty years had dulled his memories of her.

Pounding fists, enraged screaming, and bloody teeth filled his mind. No, he doubted he'd forgotten much about Tarva, except how hard she was to kill.

"I am curious as well," Almovak said, lacing his hands together and leaning forward. "He is worth far more to us, of course, but if you have some insights as to who else wishes his head..." He trailed off. Smart. The snot-nosed boy had grown.

Wouldn't save him if Tarva decided to drag her bounties out of here over a pile of bodies.

The woman shrugged and spread her hands. "No clue."

Syrus snorted. Almovak raised both eyebrows. "I assume you would have done some research before taking a job this significant. The money is good, but is the buyer good for the money?"

Tarva bared her teeth and leaned forward. "Trade secrets, milord," she said, her voice coated in sucrose. "Do I know the first thing about keeping a solar system in line? No. And I wouldn't ask either, unless I were planning to take over governance of said solar system."

Syrus mimed pulling a credit slip from an invisible pocket and tossing it at her. She flashed him her teeth in acknowledgement of the old joke, but she didn't look away from Almovak.

"It seems we're at an impasse then," the rard said. "I cannot turn him over to you. He is needed in my sector."

Syrus blinked. The fuck?

"But, if you had someone we could contact, I might be able to reach out. See if the bounty could be transferred to my name. In which case, I would pay, you would have your bond back, and we'd all be happy."

Tarva's eyes shifted again. Her face went smooth, then thoughtful so fast Syrus almost missed it. Suddenly he understood. Fuck. She'd never taken the bounty on him. Never paid its bond. She planned to kill him, slow. Nothing more. Nothing less.

The girls, on the other hand. She'd probably taken their bounties to pay for the cost of catching him.

Syrus glanced at Almovak. Tell him? No. The second he realized the real stakes in this game, he'd throw the polite mask out the window and fuck the consequences. Tarva and her crew would tear the place to pieces to keep Syrus, the girls would be forfeit, and the whole past year would go down a gravity well without heat shields.

The other two kept making polite business noises at each other as they tried to talk their way around Tarva's nonexistent bounty tags and whatever waited for Syrus in isk Tova af Mitachte territory. Syrus wondered which would be the best option. Leave the girls, go with Tarva and die? Or talk himself into Almovak's good graces and probably still die?

He reached for Rissa and found nothing. He'd shoved her too far down, faced with her family like this. That or she was hiding. Even his monster was no help. It wanted to rip these shackles off the chair and kill everyone. Same same, nothing new there.

"... a bush planted in a skull, with a snake in the branches," Tarva barked, throwing her hands in the air.

Syrus stared at her. "Say that again."

She sneered. "You go wandering in your head? Bad habit."

He curled a lip at her. "What do you fucking care if I did? You're not the one getting bargained over."

Almovak pinched the bridge of his nose. "Captain Tarva, you two are free to squabble like children *if* we come to a satisfactory arrangement. In the meantime, if you would kindly oblige so he will *shut up?*"

Syrus laughed.

Tarva rolled her eyes. "I *said*, I can't help him. Unless he knows of a House with a tree growing out of a skull as its crest. And a snake in the branches."

Well shit. Fucking shit. Fucking shit on fire. How could he not have put it together earlier? Why hadn't he expected it in the first place? He hadn't killed Quinn. Hadn't killed the bastard's wives either. Bad call on his part. Hell, Jossa'd been smarter than him on that score. If he'd listened to her, the asshole couldn't have done this. How long? he wondered. How long had it taken Quinn to snap out of the Frenzy and come up with this plan?

"I take it you know this crest?" Almovak asked, voice dry.

Syrus laughed, straining the tethers on his shackles as he leaned over and gasped for air. "It's perfect," he choked out between wheezes. "It's too fucking perfect."

Tarva's fist landed on the back of his head like a mule kick. Syrus toppled, chair and all, rolling awkwardly as the shackles hit the end of the grav tether holding him to the floor. People shouted. The guards rushed in. Blood trickled down the inside of his nose. It might be broken again.

He didn't care. It was too rich. Here he was, scum of the universe. Trash, filth, animal. Less than human. And everyone wanted him. His old House, his old team. The Fleet about to devour the Empire whole.

And him, tied to a fucking chair, able to do sweet fuck all about any of it.

Except run, a voice whispered in his ear. *Run the same direction you were going already.*

My luck, he thought at the voice, *they'll decide they want to use me too.*

"Hey!" Someone grabbed him and hauled him upright, chair and all. Tarva's face hove into view, full of fury. Real fury. "You miserable piece of shit," she whispered. Then, louder: "We aren't laughing."

Syrus opened his mouth to answer.

Every comm in the room squawked at once. The guards stepped back to answer. Tarva winced in the way of someone who'd had a comm implant try to blow their ear out. Almovak lifted his wrist to check the readout on the flex-screen.

"Hey," Syrus said under his breath. Tarva looked at him. "I know exactly who put the bounty out," he told her. "You take me to him. Talk to him, kill me after. I don't care. But he'll have better work for you than sniping bounties under a fake name while the universe sets itself on fire."

Tarva stared at him.

"I spent the past three years killing every Imperial fuck who crossed my path," Syrus hissed. "You want a bit of your own back?"

Of course, if Quinn wanted him for the reasons he suspected, Syrus would be able to make sure she never got her chance at revenge. Or not, depending on how much she tortured him along the way. Although he did deserve it.

"Apparently the women you've been keeping have decided they don't wish for our hospitality," Almovak said, coming over to stand next to Tarva. "What did you do to them, to make them so skittish of aid offered?"

Syrus ignored him and focused on Tarva, who still watched him with narrowed eyes. "You don't bring all three of us in, man who put that bounty out will send his own people." He leaned forward. "He's got plenty." He tilted his head to one side. "Can your crew take on an armada? Do you *want* to, over some money and your pride? They have a tendency to fuck corpses."

Almovak breathed a curse. The guards around them muttered. Tarva's lips thinned. Smoke practically poured out her ears.

"Sooner rather than later," Syrus reminded her. "Two thirds of your bounty is getting away."

"No." Almovak reached for Tarva's arm. "He is in *my* custody. You are not taking him anywhere without my—"

Tarva slammed her elbow back. It struck Almovak full in the mouth. He staggered back, grabbing the table for balance. The guards rushed in. Tarva punched Almovak again, sending him flying. The rard skidded across the polished floor of the solar and slammed into the wall.

One of the guards lunged for Tarva. She kicked him in the chest. He stumbled into Syrus, tried to catch his balance on the back of the chair, then dragged the whole thing down when Tarva shot him in the chest with a tase bullet.

The ferret creature ran out of the flowers, squealing in alarm.

Syrus snarled. The others ignored him, focusing on opponents who could fight. Every time someone got close enough, he stuck out a foot hoping to kneecap them. Or at least trip them.

Another guard landed on the floor, carotid artery spewing blood. Syrus flinched as it hit him smack in the face. Fucking hell. Bastard better not have any diseases.

The next guard landed out of sight. Then Tarva again, bending down to examine Syrus with cold eyes. "You shitting me?" she asked.

Syrus spat and glared up at her. "Which part?"

She growled and tilted her head to one side. "Fiel, report."

Syrus wiggled his arms in the shackles as she waited for a reply. Had the chair broken when he fell? It looked too expensive to be that cheap.

"Fiel," Tarva barked.

Syrus laughed and spat again. "Lemme guess. No answer?"

That earned him a kick in the gut. He curled around her boot, gasping.

"They must have installed better comm blockers since we were here last," Tarva muttered. "You know anything about that?"

Syrus coughed and tried to straighten out. His diaphragm complained, loudly. Breathing lightly, he looked up at her. "I haven't been in this part of space for twenty fucking years, Tar. The hell you think I'd know what they have in this shithole?"

She pulled her foot back. He kept going. "Doubt they'd cripple their own comms though." A cough, then another. Tarva set her foot down and growled. He grinned. "Bet I know what happened."

Out in the hall, people shouted. A woman screamed. He could hear noise coming from the glassed-in side of the room as well. Guards covering that avenue of escape? Assuming that direction *had* a way out.

Tarva crouched and grabbed a fistful of Syrus's hair. He yelled in pain as she used it to pull him upright, chair and all. "Shut the fuck up," she growled at him. "What's this big secret?"

More shouts and screams. Closer now. Syrus bared his teeth at his old teammate. "Really should have done a blood draw on the women."

Tarva frowned and yanked his head around. "The fuck is that supposed to mean?"

The door to the hall slid open with quiet ease, completely at odds with the chaos it let in. Three guards burst through the opening as soon as it was wide enough. None of them faced inwards.

The one on the right dropped first, dying silently as blood fountained from his neck. The one in the middle doubled over, groaning and clutching his abdomen. The third tried to flee. Someone landed on his back like a tree cat, wrapping strong legs around his shoulders and bare arms around his head. A twist, a crunch, and the body toppled. Delfi rode him to the ground, jumping free at the last second.

And froze. Jossa crouched next to her, a knife in either hand. She had a light bandage around her shoulder but seemed fine otherwise.

Syrus would have happily shot them both. "The fuck you doing here?" he yelled.

Delfi ignored him. The look Jossa gave him was pure murder. "Escaping," she snarled. "Not that you're much good at it."

Tarva threw back her head and laughed.

Both women stared at her.

"It's too rich," the bounty hunter said. "Not only do you collect women like toys, you take the ones who know how to fight." She pulled a knife hilt from her boot and activated it. A wide blade slithered into being, straight but for the curved tip. "You have a type, you know that, Sy?"

Jossa's eyebrows shot up.

Syrus spread his hands so she could see the shackles and shrugged.

Delfi charged, coming in low.

Tarva met her halfway, driving her blade down at the younger woman's exposed back. Jossa lunged in, blocking the strike with her own knife. Delfi slid under them both. Once past Tarva, she popped to her feet and kicked. Her heel caught Tarva behind the knees. The nehkeh woman went down in a controlled fall, rolling past Jossa.

Delfi spun and ran for Syrus, bloody knife in one hand and a synthleather pouch in the other. She skidded to a halt next to him and overturned the pouch in his lap. A handful of credit slips, two dim power crystals, and a four-inch-long hex bolt bounced off Syrus's legs and landed on the floor. The shackle key nearly followed them, but

Delfi snatched it out of the air and stuck it in the shackle so fast Syrus hoped she didn't bust the tines.

Over by the door, Jossa lost control of Tarva. The nehkeh woman threw the former concubine off with a twist and a heave, slamming Jossa into the wall hard enough to force a cry of pain out of her.

"Faster," Syrus snarled to Delfi.

The shackle clicked and popped open. Tarva charged.

Jossa hit her from the side in a tackle that had nothing of grace but enough power to knock the other woman off her stride. Syrus ducked his head and hunched his shoulders, and they both bowled into him.

The chair went over backwards, rolled, and broke with a crack. Syrus grunted in pain as the arm still stuck to the chair wrenched in its socket. Delfi growled something in He'la and came scrambling back, keys still clutched in her hand.

Tarva froze halfway to her feet, staring. Jossa, crouched an arm's length away, groaned. Syrus took the chance to knock his head against the floor and curse Delfi for an absentminded fool.

A distracted absentminded fool, Rissa reminded him as Delfi landed on her knees next to him. *One who is helping you.*

"Yeah, yeah," he muttered as the shackle popped open. Delfi yelped a warning. Syrus looked up.

Here came Tarva.

Syrus rolled to the side, kicking shattered bits of chair away as he grabbed for a knife on his belt.

Nothing. Right. Shit.

Tarva turned the botched attack into a low-swinging strike. Syrus dodged the blade, grabbed her wrist as it passed him, and yanked. Tarva came down; his other hand came up. He backhanded her across the temple and then drove his fist into the side of her head three times in rapid succession. Just to be sure.

Then he let go and rolled to his feet. Tarva landed in a heap, knife loose in her hand. Syrus kicked it out of the way. She moaned and wobbled to her knees, hands looking for some bit of anatomy to grab and pummel. Syrus backed up out of reach.

"We gotta go," he told Jossa and Delfi.

"Really?" Jossa snapped, easing around Tarva. "Thank you for stating the obvious."

Delfi rolled her eyes and headed for the door. Syrus let Jossa pass him, then crouched to look Tarva in the eye. "I was serious about the job offer, by the way," he told her.

She stared at him as she wove back and forth on her knees, one pupil blown wide open, the other pinned down to a dot of darkness in the brown of her iris. Her hand clenched and unclenched, looking for the weapon she no longer held.

Syrus shook his head and stood up. "You'd have done the same," he said, then turned to go.

Jossa's wide eyes and Delfi's shocked face were all the warning he got. Before he could put full weight on his forward foot, before he could turn, agony screamed across the back of his knee. His leg gave. Dropped right out from under him. He turned as he fell, gasping in pain.

Tarva broke her fall with her hands, a blade of living metal jutting out from under the flex-screen wrapped around one wrist. She bared her teeth at him in a feral smile, then *urped* and tried to catch her balance again.

Jossa and Delfi blew past him, moving as a single unit. Silent and graceful as cats, they stabbed down. Tarva screeched and collapsed, a blade sticking out of each shoulder joint. Jossa grabbed a fistful of the woman's long mohawk and pulled her upright, tendons and whipcord muscle standing out under her bloody skin.

"No," Syrus barked as Delfi yanked her knife out of Tarva's shoulder and aimed it at her throat.

The redhead froze, glaring at him.

Tarva laughed, broken and low. "Jus' do it," she slurred.

Syrus shifted so he could get his good leg under him. "No," he told them again. Not again. He could excuse himself the first time. Not now.

"Won't. Ever. Shtop," Tarva told him.

"We don't have time for this," Jossa muttered, then drove Tarva face-first into the floor. The nehkeh woman went limp.

Delfi came over and held out a hand. Syrus took it, getting a burning surge of fury, fear, and frustration up his arm as a reward. But she managed to get him up onto his good leg, so that was something. Jossa came and ducked under his other arm. Blank. No wonder Delfi's emotions were hitting so hard. She was putting everything into keeping Jossa level.

Together the three of them hopped and hobbled out of the room.

"Why the fuck did you come for me?" Syrus asked as they passed the bodies of two guards outside the door. A third man lay at the end of the hall, green and gold livery stained with blood.

"Because without you," Jossa grunted as she helped him maneuver over the splayed legs of the dead guard, "we wouldn't be able to pay the Kiprinog to get through the gate." She looked up at him. "You didn't lose the money, did you?"

"Some of it," he grunted, leaning against a wall as Delfi ducked her head around to check. "Where we headed anyway?"

"Escape pods," Jossa said, incredulity sparking bright around her. Incredulity. How much was that word worth? he wondered.

Oblivious to the rambling of his mind, Jossa kept talking. "What do you mean, *some* of it? There were *stacks* of credits in that safe."

"Surprised you remember." Syrus tried putting some weight on his leg and nearly took them both down in a heap. Nope. That wasn't happening. Hamstring? Lateral ligaments? Whatever it was, it wasn't working. Fucking bitch.

Jossa snorted. Her wry humor poked him in the ribs. "I remember everything up to the rage. Then it gets... fuzzy."

Syrus shook his head and hobbled on. "How many did you kill in here anyways?" How many were left alive to come after them? Where were Tarva's people? Agadi'd be back on their ship, prepping departure. Was Ban too far away to make it back in time?

He fucking hoped so.

"The med ward is on the first level in the public side of the house," Jossa told him. "Not here in the family rooms. The Uv—"

"No." Twenty years couldn't kill that habit.

She huffed. "Tarva only had two people watching us. The House guards were so surprised to see women with weapons, they hardly fought."

Ah. So they'd taken out pretty much every guard except those who were off duty or outside.

They turned a corner. The hall widened, crossing with another to form a largish atrium. At the opposite side of the room, the lights of a grav lift blinked through glass etched with the symbol of the base's ruling House overlaid by the glyphs for "guest."

The girls stopped. Syrus did his best to resist putting weight on his bad leg.

"*Odavek*," Jossa muttered. "Company."

"How many?" Syrus asked.

"Better to ask what they're armed with and do they want you alive," she replied as she pulled him forward. Delfi trotted ahead, ranging from side to side like a sheepdog.

"Shit," Syrus muttered, putting a little more power into his forward hops. It was tricky, moving like this without putting too much weight on either his leg or Jossa. "Jirdis wants to skin me, and not to make an Obijaf lis Ralchuroj for the family shrine."

Someone shouted a command down one of the halls. Someone else answered from the other direction. At least there wasn't anyone *behind* them.

"Let's not stand here waiting," Syrus growled. "Move."

They moved. Delfi eased into the atrium, back to the near wall. It didn't save her.

Jossa croaked a warning. Half a second later, Syrus felt it too.

Ahead and to the right, a man in gray and brown livery emerged from the corridor. Behind him came another. Expecting a guard, Syrus didn't recognize him until too late. Jirdis brought his weapon up and fired, a snarl of hate twisting his features and searing the air in the atrium to superheated plasma.

Delfi went down, twitching. The tase bullet that'd taken her in the chest clattered to the floor, its charge spent. Syrus was the only one that heard the tiny noise.

Everyone else was too busy paying attention to the screaming banshee that'd just landed in the middle of them.

The coronal flare emanating off her was so strong, it even overwhelmed his monster. Somehow, Syrus found his brain again, managing to claw his way upright from where she'd dropped him. Men shouted orders. Jirdis tried to countermand them. Jossa cut through the guards like they didn't even exist. A couple shots from their tase guns hit the wall near his head. Syrus ignored them, hopping and dragging himself towards Delfi. She lay oblivious to the chaos around her, still twitching in little spasmodic jerks.

"You!" Jirdis roared.

Syrus looked up from grabbing a handful of Delfi's shirt. The rard had escaped his guards a moment, though they were trying to pull him back out of danger. Their determination was bright and hard, underscoring the fury boiling off the highborn. "I will have a reckoning of you!" Jirdis shouted as he aimed his gun square at Syrus. The indicator shone bright red. Highest charge. Death intended.

"You will have a reckoning of *me*," Jossa screeched as she pulled her blade out of a guard's throat and lunged for Jirdis. Another guard stepped forward at the last moment, taking her strike to the shoulder as the rest mobbed their rard.

Syrus left her to it. Taking a larger handful of Delfi's shirt, he half lunged, half hopped along the wall towards the grav shaft. The cross corridor put a gap in his path, but he made it with an extra-hard push and no little determination.

A tase bullet took him in the shoulder just as he made it to the back wall of the atrium. He lost hold of Delfi, his arm numb, the muscles of his neck and shoulder seizing in painful knots. Too low a charge. The guards weren't aiming to kill. More fool them.

The etched glass panel slid aside when he punched the button.

More screams. More bodies hitting the floor behind him. Fewer sounds of fighting. Not long now.

He turned around, braced himself with his ass and his hands and even his bad leg, and took careful aim. A shove with his good foot, hard but steady, pushed the unconscious woman's body into the grav lift. His bad leg screamed in agony. His shoulder added to the complaints. He ignored both, watching the ends of Delfi's red hair and the tips of her boots vanish from sight, ripped away by gravity.

Jossa's wordless scream was the only warning he got. One second he was catching his breath; the next, she had him by the shirt and almost halfway off the floor.

Adrenaline. It did amazing things.

"What did you *do!*?" she demanded. Heat and acid raced up his nerves in equal measure. His brain turned to a cauldron of fury and fear.

Syrus snarled. "The hell you think I did, you psychotic bitch? Saved her!"

"And herein lies the problem. He would destroy the world and claim he saved it. Nehkeh. They're only good for one thing." Jirdis's face, blood-spattered and flushed, appeared over Jossa's shoulder.

She stiffened, choking slightly, and looked down.

Syrus looked too.

Three inches of metal showed through the skin of her upper abdomen and the rags of her med ward–issued shirt.

"Well," Jirdis said. "There's only one way to deal with filth. And with those that spread it." The metal vanished. Jossa lost hold of Syrus. He hit the floor, legs tangling with her feet.

He didn't even notice the pain. He was staring at four inches of metal this time. Higher and to the right. Rich blood flowed as Jirdis twisted the knife. Jossa screamed.

Kidney.

Another stab. Other side. Liver? Syrus tried to stop the calculations in his head, but the monster wouldn't let go. Wouldn't let him look away.

"So here I am," Jirdis said, still in that calm, reasonable voice. Syrus couldn't *feel* him though. His sai had gone numb. "Doing what should have been done to start with. What I should have done to start with instead of leaving it to third-party hirelings. Ridding our House of filth." Jirdis stabbed again. Met Syrus's eyes as he pulled the knife out and wrapped an arm around Jossa's torso, then positioned the knife over her chest. "And those who spread it."

The blade slid in.

The screaming in his head wasn't the monster. It wasn't him, either. It kept going, a wordless keen that no human throat could possibly sustain. It went on as Jirdis pulled the knife from Jossa's heart. It rose as he let go. Crested when she landed in a heap of blood and too-long limbs sprawled over Syrus's feet.

And fell silent as Jirdis bent down, knife at the ready, reaching for Syrus's head.

It wasn't Syrus who spoke then. He swam in caustic rivers of rage and frustration over his pinned and damaged leg.

"You always were a posturing, bombastic achek, Jir." Syrus heard the words come out of his mouth. The cadence was all wrong, but oh, so familiar. He watched his hand move, still tingling, but strong enough to take hold of Jirdis's shirtfront and yank him in close. His other hand lashed out, palm first.

Now he felt the rard. Surprise and fear subsumed the rage, leaving a broken wreck in their wake. The noble's knife fell from nerveless fingers. Syrus grabbed it and stabbed up. It was awkward from this angle. But it was enough. The fine embroidered cloth of Jirdis's House finery, already splashed red with blood, split. A foul stench, not imaginary in the least, filled the air. The quivering bowels of the rard spilled out along the polished floor like so many noodles from a bowl.

Syrus stared. At some point, he'd regained control of his body. Even the monster was back in its hole. He was left with a possibly dead noble. And a woman who was absolutely dying.

Shit.

He pulled his good leg out from under Jossa, dragging himself over and around so his back was to the grav shaft. Careful as he could, he hooked his hands under her arms and pulled her close. Blood flowed, pooling, running, and staining everything. He ignored it. He wrapped an arm around her torso, reached up and slapped the button for the door again, then rolled backwards, giving himself to gravity.

Interlude

At seventeen twenty-three on 3786.10.10, the gravity shaft running through the center of the Kallura lis Kerute Guest House registered a body entering it. Then, approximately one and a half standard minutes later, two more. The second entry was flagged with a warning in the system, as the two people falling through the many lower decks of the Nobles' Fist were not logged in the system as registered guests of the House that controlled the base. Neither, for that matter, was the first person, who was nearing the end of the tube's gravity field.

Code ran. Processors worked. The computers checked for any systemic or localized emergencies that might have required evacuation of the Guest House. They also looked for alerts in other sectors of the base, threats that could possibly affect the Fist.

Several power crystals flashed alarms for the human manning the Main House guard station. Before he managed to set down his bowl of noodles and turn off the celebratory porn on his personal screen, the computers had already passed judgement on the three unknowns.

They were in the escape tubes. Meant specifically for use in times of distress and accessible by any in need. When hailed, the family guesting in the House did not immediately answer. On the screens, the med ward glyph alternated with the alert icon for a fire. The sensors that monitored entry to the tubes indicated the presence of blood. Blood of more than one type and genetic signature.

Clearly, something emergent had happened.

The computer turned on the tube's anti-gravity generators.

The change happened slowly. The better to cushion the fall of possibly unconscious bodies. A thousand yards from the bottom of the shaft, the pull of gravity on the people within the tube lessened. It affected the single body first, allowing the other two to catch up slightly. But then they reached the lower gravity field and slowed as well.

It progressed in stages. First lessening gravity, then negating it almost entirely. They still fell, but not so fast as to injure them on landing.

Land they did. The computers sent the signal to the escape ship docked at the bottom of the tube. The ship woke, running its own protocols as the base computer prepared to unlock the docking clamps.

As the guard slid his chair over to the bank of alerts to see which one had gone off, the hatch in the dorsal hull of the ship opened. It was large, meant to accommodate people of all sizes and whatever configuration of limbs they might be falling in.

Anti-gravity generators built into the deck directly below the hatch emerged from their recessed hiding places and turned on, catching the first body in a gentle but implacable grip. The generators, mobile and portable as needed, slid to the side, carrying their passenger aft through the ship. Sensors didn't read blood, but the pulse was thready and breathing compromised.

The guard in the station frowned at his panel and toggled open a channel to the Guest House. Nobody answered his first query. Nor the second.

As the next set of anti-grav generators in the ship readied themselves for their next load, the guard tried one last time. A voice answered. Female. High with panic. She stuttered a reply to his rote question, confirming name and location.

The generators caught the bodies falling together. The hatch closed again, and the base ordered the docking clamps released. They did so, pushing slightly to send the escape ship clear of the various arrays and sensors and other bits that extruded from the bottom-most surface of the Nobles' Fist like so many questing tentacles.

The ship, meant as it was for escape above all else, only waited long enough for its own sensors to announce that it was in the clear. Then its engines, powered on along with the rest of the systems at the first sign of trouble, ignited fully. The ship shot off.

Just as the guard in the base realized he was speaking to a member of isk Kallura lis Kerute, the anti-grav generators slid the first body into a waiting medunit.

The second set of generators were not so efficient in their task. The two bodies could not be separated, but copious amounts of blood were detected. Protocol insisted on a medunit but, lacking the ability to put both bodies in a single unit, the generators defaulted to the next set of instructions.

They set their burden down. Gently. A survey-bot popped out of its housing in the floor and trundled over. One body was non-responsive to its prodding. The next had an elevated heart rate, was wheezing slightly, and made a noise when the proboscis was extended.

Another probe, carefully, this time by means of a sensor rod tipped in soft silplat. Another noise from the body. Movement. More noise.

After forty-seven seconds, the body—male, according to the sensors—moved. It detached from the other body, a female, and shifted so they lay separate.

More blood seeped into the seams between deck plates and under the bearings of the anti-grav generators.

By this point, the ship was speeding away from the base, epirb binging away on all channels. The guard in the base told his mistress to get to the safe room of the Guest House and wait for household guard detail to arrive. She agreed, then told him in no uncertain terms that if they didn't bring a fully qualified medic, two mobile medunits for the injured and three of their heaviest sets of shackles for the newest set of captives, her husband would personally shove the guard out the nearest airlock.

The guard put in the orders, flagged everything with the highest level of urgency, and looked up to find the eldest son of the House standing in the door to the guard room. "What has happened to my wife?" the rard asked.

The guard gulped.

On the ship, the first medunit sealed itself and started its assessment of injuries to the first body inside. The male finished easing his injured leg out from under the second female and tapped the bot on the dorsal surface of its outer casing. "You," he said.

The bot could listen but not vocalize. It wiggled its probes in response. The ship's computer made a notation in its automatic log of events.

"Pick her up, get her in a pod." The male pointed at the female body.

The ship obeyed, reactivating the anti-grav generators and their field. The male's foot caught on the edge, floating six inches off the deck. It dropped as the generators rolled away, carrying the body with them. The little bot registered the trail of blood left behind as something to be cleaned and sanitized. More bots popped out of the deck. Some full of liquids. Others equipped with cloth bottoms or wire bristle appendages. They attacked the puddle of blood.

The male moved towards the pilot's area of the ship, pulling himself by the arms and pushing with one foot. The other foot dragged, limp. Stress and pain indicators bloomed in his scent signature. The ship did not have a true cockpit, or a bridge. Two seats and a bank of directive input mechanisms. The ship monitored him. The anti-grav generators came back, having inserted the female body into her medunit with a minimum of fuss. They rolled through the blood on their way forward, leaving behind a trail of spatter as droplets lifted and then fell again once the anti-grav field moved on. The cleaning bots turned circles and tried to keep up.

The male struck at the generators as they surrounded him. Then he caught hold of the edge of the pilot's chair as they activated their field.

For a moment he floated, until they moved aft again, sure of their burden.

He came to rest on the deck violently, first his chest, then hips and legs. The ship made a recording of the noise he made and inserted it into the log. Its processors translated the vocalization as "Fucking hell." The computer worked for a nanosecond, then inserted an exclamation point into the log as well, for the sake of thoroughness.

By the time the generators rolled back a second time, the little bots virtually spinning to keep up with the now-tacky trail of blood, the man had the housing off the base of the control panel. Indicators said his heart rate was still rising. The survey-bot tasted the sweat trickling down the male's arm and found decreased levels of adrenaline. His respiratory symptoms were worsening as well.

The man took hold of the edges of the hole he'd made in the housing as the anti-grav generators floated him for a third time. His grip was weaker now. The ship blasted a shrill alarm as he pulled himself forward and let go of the housing with one hand, then pushed that hand into the wiring and cables and crystal boards that made up the brain of the ship.

Just as the generators started off again, he pulled his hand back out. The survey-bot registered a cluster of wires and a small net of crystals caught in his fingers.

The ship shouted a virtual alarm across all the frequencies it had been using to declare the epirb signal.

Nobody heard. The epirb was disconnected. As the man allowed the generators to carry him over the half-cleaned pool of blood and slide him onto the cushioned bed of the medunit, he pulled the crystal net apart, leaving it in pieces on the floor. The cleaning bots sucked the bits up. They were not programed to notice anything but mess and not-mess. The little survey-bot poked frantically at his hand as he traveled, until the anti-grav generators lifted him up out of reach and slid him onto the cushioned bed of one of the upper-level medunits.

The ship traveled on.

Nineteen--Delfi

Ere we leave on this lonely flight,
Through the boundless skies of night,
Careful now, you wastrel wretch;
That hand which you so quickly stretch
Can be your ruin, may be your boon,
When alone you walk a lifeless moon.
      - first lines of isk Detriog lis Osagil, a play

A smooth surface of pale silplat greeted Delfi as she opened her eyes. The light was soft, a dim presence at the edges of her vision. Delfi blinked, bringing her eyes into focus.

Familiar script covered the curved surface above her. The traditional reassurances and warnings that waited for every invalid, from now back to the dawn of time.

It's all right. This is a medunit. You are safe. You had -[Insert Injury or Illness Here]-. You have been in this unit for five hours, thirty-six minutes and eight seconds. The lid will unseal in 5... 4... 3...

She did so *hate* waking up in medunits.

Delfi sighed, stretched her toes, and lifted her chin. The seal on the unit broke, letting air both out and in. The outer air smelled faintly of cleaners and scorched wiring.

::Jossa,:: she called along the mind bond. ::Joss, where are you?::

No answer.

She was out of the unit and halfway across the floor before she realized she'd moved. She felt Jossa's presence, faint and far away, just as momentum overtook reason. She stumbled, rolling the rest of the way across the metal beneath her to fetch up against another medunit.

Delfi groaned and rubbed her shoulder where it had struck the unit. ::Joss? Where are you?::

Still no answer.

She tried to think. What was the last thing that happened? Joss'd had Syrus, the miserable bastard. And they were all trying to get out of the building. A building... where?

She looked around. She was in a room, clean and white and shaped like a lozenge. Aside from the red lights of the medunits, there were very few points of color. A House sigil, emblazoned in green on a lavender pillow sitting on a padded bench. A curtain hung across the back of the room, watered silk, abstract swirls of green and lavender shifting across its electro-stiffened surface. The solid door next to it had "lavatory" written in green. The chairs at the other end of the room were covered in lavender fabric.

Chairs.

The open metal panel between them had a mess of wires dribbling out of the hole. A bank of lights blinked above and on the walls to either side of the chairs.

Delfi twisted around as something hissed nearby. A section of the floor rose, a hexagonal object of the same pale metal as the deck. It had to be a deck. Because this had to be a ship.

Escape. Escape pods. Or ships, rather. That was what they'd been doing before.

Before what?

The bot trundled over, tiny metal protuberances emerging from its body and waving in her direction. It tapped her on the back of the hand she'd let rest on her leg as she took stock of her situation. Delfi frowned and turned her hand palm up. The little bot sent the probe skittering gently up her wrist. It paused over her pulse, then moved back down over her palm before retracting the probe.

Then it sat and blinked at her, little green lights marching in formation over its carapace.

Delfi snorted and turned back to the medunit. It wouldn't open when she pushed on the lid. Nor when she banged on it, although she knew that wouldn't help matters. She hoped Syrus was in this one. She hoped the banging woke him up and made him angry.

The pale face of a young woman, dark eyes huge and full of fear. The churn of her thoughts as she tried to get a grip on the events around her as they happened far too fast.

Delfi pressed her forehead to the surface of the medunit and reached along the mind bond for her sousi.

Silence still. But Jossa's presence was strong enough for now, so she let the peace of the bond wrap around her, cushioning the horror that still ate at her soul.

How could the woman exist? Who was she? And why did that family hate Syrus? So many questions. And no answers to be had.

Delfi looked over at the control console of the ship. Syrus must have pulled something out of it. Her first thought was data storage. A miraculous bank of answers that he didn't want her to find. She snorted and shook her head. Even for him, that was unlikely.

Grunting a little at the stiffness in her joints and the tension of muscles that didn't want to cooperate, Delfi levered herself upright and headed for the nose of the ship. On inspection, which involved getting back on her knees and more complaints from her abused muscles—and really, what *had* they hit her with—she was able to peer at the cluster of wires and the place they should have been.

Smears of blood covered the deck nearest the console, as well as the mass of wires spilling out of it. Delfi lifted the mass carefully and looked.

Navigation. Communications. Ancestors, the only thing that she was sure these *didn't* go to was life support. And that only because if life support were down, the ship would be dark. Drifting dead in space and headed who knew where at what rate of speed.

Without a hand light, which didn't seem forthcoming, she wouldn't be able to figure out how mutilated the systems were. Shaking her head, she set the wires down and levered herself up into one of the chairs instead. The controls answered to her hand easily enough, which argued further for this being an escape pod and not a personal or House vessel. The answer to the question of what'd been pulled sat there on the screen, bright as a star and twice as obvious. Delfi could have pounded her head against the console at her own stupidity.

Epirb. Of course. When going on the run, don't leave a navigational beacon in place, especially not one with the singular purpose of screaming for help on all available frequencies. He'd reached in and yanked it, along with everything around it, rather than remove it properly.

But why hadn't he just engaged the ship's evasive protocols? Every escape pod she'd ever trained on before she and Jossa ran from isk Churus lis Kuchruis had been equipped with a programmed response to escape from attack. That'd been when the Empire was mostly stable. At peace. Now? In a solar system bordering the most secretive Barb in the network, while the Empire was at war with itself and under active invasion?

They'd be idiots of the highest order not to be prepared to hide.

She looked down at the wires. The little bot trundled around quietly. It had a friend, an even smaller hexagonal body with rolling synthcot peeking out from the underside of its casing. The little bot pushed at the mess of wires. She'd dropped them in a slightly different position. Now that it had access, the bot was trying to clean the tiny bits of dried blood from the deck.

Delfi frowned. Of all the things to put in an escape ship, why would someone install cleaning bots? She understood the survey-bot. And the banks of medunits. But cleaning bots? Either someone was a germophobe or noble habits really *had* changed while she and Jossa slept.

The little bot whirred once, louder, then backed away from the mass of wires. Delfi watched it move across the deck and fit itself into its slot along the hull.

Shaking her head, she turned back to the console.

Life support status, excellent. Navigation, not fully functional but acceptable for now. The ship was headed for some place called Altruen, whatever that was. The coordinates read fifteen degrees off the direct line of travel between the Barbican and the trading base. A backup base? A bolt-hole for the noble family? Another, larger ship held in localized flight pattern near the Barb? The system didn't know, and she couldn't force a connection to the data streams with the communications gutted as they were.

She had to get back inside the console and tidy up the mess of wires, making sure everything that should be plugged in before she found what she was looking for. Fixing the epirb error message was easy enough. Going through the system to find the other protocols took a bit longer. Activating the evasion routine was as simple as hitting the big green button.

Several alerts rolled across the screen, letting her know that the connections to the nav-sats were blocked. Four backup epirbs lit up, ejected, and traced trajectories over the screens. She force-paused the program before it could send out all twenty. She had no idea where they were supposed to meet the Kiprinog. Until Syrus woke up, she wouldn't even know if that was still on the table, much less if he knew the coordinates. Better to not give up too many tricks.

Next order of business then. See if she could get out of these rags and into something that didn't keep sending her into flashbacks of the shadow base.

Delfi started to slip out of the chair, then stopped perched halfway off the seat. Jossa. When would Jossa wake?

It didn't take the computer long to answer her query. When it did, she slid the rest of the way off the chair and landed with a *thud* on the deck. Forty-five hours? Almost two *days!* What *happened* while she was unconscious? How could Jossa have taken so much damage that even a medunit couldn't have her up in a few hours?

Delfi nearly gave in to the temptation to pull up the override controls and force the units open. Good sense stopped her before she managed to get back into the chair and type in the command. It could kill Jossa. Permanent harm to Syrus was less a burden to the conscience. But Jossa?

She'd failed again. What had she done while they nearly killed Jossa? What good had she been, either in the fight or managing her sister's emotions? She'd been unconscious and falling through a grav shaft. Useless.

She crawled aft on shaking hands, hot tears dripping down her cheeks as she sucked in air and rattled out sobs. She didn't know which unit sheltered Jossa. She didn't care. She wanted to be nearer Jossa's mind. Close by in case her sister, out of all expectation, woke.

She'd failed. Again. And again.

She pulled her knees up to her chest, leaned against the medunit, and cried.

>>><<<

She woke to a hand on her shoulder. Huge palm, long fingers, warm. Not Jossa.

Delfi lurched to her feet, scrabbling for a knife. A weapon. Anything. She came up dry. Then the gravity of the ship reasserted control over her body and she tipped over, a graceless heap of limbs.

Syrus caught her by the shoulders and eased her into a sitting position. She pushed at his mind, looking for any mockery.

Nothing. He was shielded. She should have expected that.

"Don't bother," he said as she batted at his chest in a futile effort to get him away. "Your medunit should've kept you at least another eight hours, this the shape you're in." He looked over her shoulder at the closed lid of the unit she'd fallen asleep on. "You force your way out?"

Delfi shook her head, hard. She would have, had it been possible.

He snorted and let go of her, then sat back on his heels. "See you found the ship's evasive mode. Good." He settled his hands over one knee, but Delfi noticed he didn't lock his fingers. The better to grab a knife in case she went crazy. "So. You sitting on the floor because you *like* torturing yourself?"

She glared at him.

He scowled. "You got shocked, you little bitch. That fucker hit you with enough volts to put *me* down. Which is what he meant to do, if his aim weren't for shit. The medunit might say you're ok, but lying on the deck in a fucking ball isn't going to help. You, me, *or* Jossa."

Delfi snarled and scrambled forward, fingers reaching for his throat. He caught her by the shoulders, his face a mask she couldn't read. She beat at him with her hands. Tried to bring her feet into play as well. He flipped her up and over, wrapped an arm around her torso, and pinned her feet with his legs. "Shhhh," he murmured in her ear. "Shhhh. Easy."

Easy? Easy!? She'd show him easy! She'd pop his eyes out of his skull and play Two Bounces with them! She'd kick his balls all the way up to his chin! He wanted her to calm down. To calm *down?* He had no clue what she was going through right now! Ancestors cursed, goat-brained *adafek!*

Something pushed at her. Gently. Slowly. Wrapping her in a blanket of warmth and softness. She paused her thrashing, panting out air and feeling it drag at her lungs on the inhale. Syrus kept her legs pinned. His fingers worked slow circles across her wrists and the backs of her hands as he made soft *shhhing* noises in her ear.

What did he think she was? Some sort of animal to be tamed?

She was about to start struggling again when a new layer of warmth enveloped her. Her breath caught, then eased. She realized tears were running down her cheeks.

And that she was not quieting down of her own volition.

"Easy," Syrus murmured when she stiffened again. Another layer of calm. Of comfort. "Just breathe."

She wanted to keep resisting. She did. But she hadn't felt this safe in a long time. Not with Jossa, who treated her like twice-broken porcelain. Not during their travels across the Empire, with her sister and this man climbing each other at the drop of a hat. She should be mad about that. She tried to be mad about it. But her body remembered what it was like to be held by Denz. To be wrapped in love and know her husband wanted her for *her*, and not because he was dependent on her or saw her as a path to a throne. Just her.

She settled deeper into the embrace and let the peace flow around her.

And slept.

TWENTY--SYRUS

As smart as we've made computers, you'd think they'd be able to run a program without a babysitter.
*   - Denz to Delfi*

Inch by inch, Syrus let go of his hold on the false grace. He hadn't been sure it would work. Both because she was supposed to be the Stable half of her bond with Jossa and because she'd actively fought the calming. But it was either try or let the monster out to play.

He'd put too much fucking work into getting them across the Empire for things to end in blood and death not two days from the end of the trip.

He waited for Rissa to mock him. To laugh and tell him to go right on fooling himself as to why he was doing this. Ask him why he worried about killing a girl who was such a monumental pain in his ass. His conscience stayed quiet. Apparently she'd decided to leave him to his own devices. His and the monster's.

But he'd managed to overwhelm the beast with the false bond and send it down to quiescence. He probably couldn't do it again anytime soon. Knowing it was possible to quiet the thing that raged in his skin somehow made it harder than just shoving it into a corner of his mind. It was harder to trap something that could see the net underneath its feet.

His monster was more cunning than he remembered to give it credit for.

Syrus pulled the last dregs of emotion into his skin and waited. Delfi breathed softly, only a slight hitch left over from crying. She was warm, pliable and, with the remnants of the false bond echoing in both their veins, she felt so, so right in his arms.

He squashed the reflexive recoil at that thought, focusing instead on sitting. Listening for any sign that his shields had cracked. That she'd picked up on his thoughts. Any sign of waking.

Nothing.

It took some maneuvering, but he managed to get his feet under him so he could stand. A charge-stiffened curtain hung across the aft end of the cabin. He shouldered it aside and found a set of bunks built into the bulkhead. Four. No noble pride here. For all the comparative luxury of this ship, it was still an escape pod. It didn't have *room* for palatial sleeping chambers and beds large enough to sleep six. The noble using it to escape would have to share with any family or advisors or even guards who made it aboard.

Syrus set Delfi on the lowest starboard bunk, making sure her limbs didn't tangle and that her torso wasn't twisted around in a corkscrew. She slept like a fucking spinecat and was twice as prickly when she woke up. Eventually she'd wind up half sprawled, half curled up, maybe even hanging off the mattress. For now, this would do. Pulling the blankets off the upper bunk, Syrus laid them over her, made sure the pillow was in place under her head, and went back to work.

The light on Jossa's medunit glowed a dull, angry red. She wasn't getting out of there anytime soon. Syrus nearly rapped his knuckles on the angled surface of the unit's hood. He stopped halfway through the gesture. That sort of thing was what Uvlaku did for each other while they were healing up. To remind their teammates that someone was out there.

She was not his team. He was not guarding her back *or* guarding against her escape.

The tiny bridge in the nose of the ship was mostly intact. Either Delfi'd made more repairs than he'd first thought or he hadn't done much damage when he yanked the primary epirb. He sat down, ready to check the systems' status and start laying in a course for the rendezvous. Then he noticed the code scrolling down the screens. Shit. Shit. Shit. Shit. Someone was in the nav system. Deep inside and rerouting the ship.

Had to be Agadi. If it were isk Kallura or isk Tova, they wouldn't need to change course. This thing was still headed for the approved safe zone.

He crouched between the pilot's chair and the console. A little jimmying and the panel came off. Some careful sorting of the wiring, tracing contact points to crystals and control boards, and he found the data transponder. A careful yank and he had it loose in its port. The console above his head beeped and warned him that it had lost connection to the nav-sats. Would he please try to reconnect?

Fat fucking chance.

Back in the chair, he took a look at how far Agadi'd made it into the systems. They were either fucked or they were fucked up the ass. One way or another, he had to hope the man's style hadn't changed much in the twenty years since they'd last worked together.

He doubted it. Cracks might be able to see patterns in code and break things open faster than most people could even read, but their weakness was that they relied too much on the sai. Let it carve channels and paths in their thinking and lead the user into the same sorts of attacks and defenses.

Work against the same Crack long enough and the operator on the other end of the code would run into the same pitfalls.

The usual chatter from base auto-systems scrolled down the screen. Confirmation of departure, conditions of departure, so on and so forth. A few attempts at hailing, also by the automatic systems. Standard for an escape pod or ship sent off with theoretically precious cargo in an emergency situation.

An alphanumeric soup listed the designation of every nav beacon they passed along with their headings in relation to the ship. Also routine.

A little over five hours in, the ship flipped from "panic, help-me" mode to the evasive maneuvers. So Delfi hadn't been awake long before his medunit spat him out. Good to know.

A lull. Maybe an hour? About right for Agadi to find their ship again. He tipped his hand with a scrambled signal. A brute force attack on the computer and the nav systems. Out of range before the crack was completed.

Had it disconnected before planting a flare in the systems, screaming their location on Agadi's personal channel?

He should wake Delfi up and have her help him check. She'd taken to modern technology like a babe to its mother's breast. Sometimes he suspected she absorbed other people's talents by proximity, but he didn't have enough saiog around to test the theory. Whichever way it worked, she'd picked up enough from that Crack husband of hers and somehow kept hold of it through three hundred years of cryo to make computers cave to her will in a way Syrus himself had never quite managed.

But she needed to sleep herself out. He was good enough to look for Agadi's signature in the code and lay in a new course for the rendezvous with Kiprinog. Several, since there were still decoy-drones attached to the ship waiting to lead any followers off into the weeds. Smart girl, not only activating the evasion protocols but keeping some of the decoys in reserve.

Agadi knew the tactic. Nobility got these souped-up escape pods from the military to start with. Once the drones were out, the Crack would have to sort through all the signals and digital junk they broadcast before he found the right one. In the meantime, Syrus would be pulling away. Closer and closer to freedom.

He hoped.

If he and Delfi could get Agadi's fissures in the system patched up and the ship on course.

Speaking of. He brought up the nav system and punched in the coordinates for the meet. The computer beeped at him, letting him know it couldn't connect to the nav-sats and was he sure he wanted to risk flying into a sun? Or a planet? Or who knew what else? He checked the ship's last known coordinates, pulled up the maps cached in the system memory on another screen, and told the computer to go fuck itself, because he'd had to learn how to pilot blind before they take him off the trainee leash and stuck him in the Uvlaku harness. But first, turn the ship.

The computer didn't have a clue what he was saying, but it took typed commands well enough. It beeped the whole way about "where are the nav-sats, why are you flying blind you stupid meat sack," but it followed orders. Eventually he'd have to put the transponder back in its socket because he couldn't bring this thing in to the right spot entirely without the sats. Or without being able to yell at the Kiprinog people not to shoot.

It would be close. He hadn't been out so long that they couldn't make it to the rendezvous in time, but neither could they afford any more delays.

He refused to think his Ancestors or those of the girls'd had any part to play in the ship's direction after it'd left the Fist. Most noble escape vessels aimed to get the passengers either out of the system entirely or to a possible rescue ship waiting for evacuees. Usually, that was closer to the Barbs. It had been a gamble, hoping that this one wasn't set to land on a planet or go deeper in system. Although, considering the quirks of this particular system, he wouldn't be surprised if this thing ended up having access codes to go straight through the Barb and into the Gatekeepers' territory. Something to check on after he finished patching up Agadi's work.

A pity to lose the ship they'd been travelling on. A bigger pity to lose the cargo that was supposed to be their cushion on getting to the

Gatekeepers. Hopefully, once they were on the Kiprinog ship, he could find a secure data connection and tap into some of the credit accounts he'd kept stocked under the various names he and the girls had used on their way across the Empire.

It'd be tricky. He'd had to make sure most of those identities were declared dead before he could move on to acquiring the next set. He'd funneled as much money into new accounts as he could before dumping the bodies, but cleaning out the accounts completely would have raised too many flags. It'd be dangerous. He still didn't know how Tarva or isk Tova af Mitachte had found him. The accounts might be tapped. Might be locked.

Better the Kiprinog systems take the brunt of any fallout than leave this ship vulnerable.

The bag, though. He'd been counting on the bag. The maruste reader and masker. The cloned data drives with the military encryptions and codes that let him force Barbs to his will without using his blood and tripping possible alarms. He could have bartered those to the Seps Coalition and bought passage through several systems on the information those data crystals carried. Even out of date or changed, they'd still be useful to someone. The military didn't have the resources for the total system overhaul they'd need to lock down the data crystals' access. Not if they wanted to hold the Empire together.

The so-called Emperor currently on the throne sure couldn't.

The nobility wouldn't.

Worse was the loss of the masker. He could've wiped the girls' backs clean of maruste. His too. A fresh start in more ways than one. Nobody would know where they came from without a blood scan. Gatekeepers despised Imperials on general principal. He wasn't looking forward to that aspect of things being harder.

Syrus shook his head. He'd survived before without most of the advantages carried in that bag. He'd manage again.

It'd just be a little harder. And easier, once he was away from the influence of the local nobility. Provided he could get through the Barbican before Agadi got control of the ship again. Tarva and her people would follow him into a star if it gave them a reasonable chance of catching up. Too bad he couldn't trick them into aiming for one.

For a moment, he wasn't sitting in a highborn's escape ship. He wasn't surrounded by signs of wealth and assurances of safety. He was across a dirty landing pad, the whistle of dry wind nearly blocking the noise coming over the comms. The cuts and scratches all over his hands burned, grit stung his cheeks, and the sun overhead turned the entire space port into a giant griddle.

The wind couldn't block out the frantic screams echoing inside his skull. The heat had nothing to do with the sudden tightness of his skin encasing his body like an eeva suit three sizes too small. And the grit working its way around the edges of his goggles was in no way related to the acid burn of tears in his eyes.

The screaming in his ears changed pitch and tone as the ramp on his stolen ship closed. Instead of the echoes reaching across light years, the noise was near. Still enraged. Still desperate. He heard the explosion through the comms before he saw the results out the forward viewport of the ship. Far below and far out of range, he'd watched the buildings blossom with orange, yellow, and dull green flame. Caught sight of far-flung bits of metal and people.

He'd done the only thing he could.

It just hadn't been enough to keep them from following him.

Hard silplat creaked under his hands. His teeth squeaked and grated. A muscle in his neck seized and stuck that way.

Syrus pried his fingers loose from the arm rests and twisted, working his mouth open and shut in a futile effort to loosen the tension. Not until he stood and stretched, palms flat on the bulkhead above him, was he able to bring himself all the way back to the present time and place.

He hadn't just left them to die. He'd tried to kill them.

No. They'd never stop hunting him for that.

Syrus sat back down and pulled up the code he'd quarantined, looking for tell-tales. When Delfi woke up he could put her to work too. He should get her up now, really, but she'd be in no shape to think, much less keep ahead of his old teammate when they finally plugged the transponder back in.

They were safe enough for a few hours. Not much longer, because this ship was built to get its passengers very far away from danger, very fast. But he had a little time. Time to clean some of Agadi's code out of the computers. Time for Delfi to wake up and check his work.

Time to get out of these blood-soaked clothes and find some food.

Syrus stood and went to the port side bulkhead. The counter there didn't have a sink. No chance to waste running water. But the cupboards had sealed teardrop pouches and bricks of preserved food stores. The upper cupboards had changes of clothes in gray-purple and green, spare blankets, and random other shit that might or might not come in handy. Ten minutes later he'd shed his clothes, gotten as much of the dried blood off his skin as he could manage without an actual shower, and taken another blanket back to Delfi. She didn't show any signs of waking up soon, but he pulled her head back up onto the mattress and made sure she wouldn't roll off entirely the next time she turned over. Back in the forward cabin, he rummaged through the food, broke a block of meat paste in half, then activated the heat charge on a pouch of kafe and took both back to the console.

Time to get to work.

>>><<<

Two hours later, the alert chirped at him, reminding him of imminent fiery death in a star if he didn't give the ship a new heading. He set up three layers of the strongest blocks he could come up with around the code he'd been working on, sectioning everything but the barest nav computer essentials into a partition the computer couldn't remember existed.

Then he plugged the transponder back in just long enough to confirm the course he'd laid in. Looked like he hadn't failed his teachers after all. Still headed the right direction. Still going fast enough to make it to the meet on time. He yanked the crystal and went back to checking code. Either he'd caught all the fissures Agadi'd put in or the man hadn't gotten to nearly as many weak spots as Syrus'd thought.

They had maybe another three, four hours before the ship had to make a course correction or risk slamming into a moon, but he'd bought them some time at least. Grumbling to himself about heavy sleepers and useless hands, Syrus turned the chair around, ready to head back to the bunks. He needed Delfi out here and helping.

Maybe she caught the thought through her dreams. Maybe she had strangely good timing. He wasn't halfway out of his seat before a thud, followed by a muffled curse, announced the fact that she'd woken up.

"Get over here, will you," he called through the curtain. "Need you to check my work."

Delfi shoved the stiff curtain out of the way and stomped out into the middle of the cabin. Irritation skittered across Syrus's face and chest as she glared and gestured rudely at him. Worry followed on its heels, although that wasn't aimed at him. That was all for Jossa. It still nipped and pulled at his skin.

The monster roused slightly, interested. He shoved it back down. He didn't know why that side of him always showed up when Delfi prodded him.

Delfi stalked over to Jossa's medunit and stood, glaring at it. He hadn't taken a good look at her earlier. Too focused on getting her calmed down. Now he saw deep shadows under her eyes, a sallow cast to her skin. The slight tremor in her fingers.

Not as bad as when he first found her, inches from death in a cryo casket. Not the best he'd ever seen her, either.

She swayed, staring down at the angles of the medunit hood before her, hands outstretched as if she could make the thing work faster by force of will alone. Wouldn't that be a trick? There were stories of people who could do that. Tales of extreme cases of sai. Myths, or legend or whatever the fuck people wanted to call it. He slotted them right next to aliens under the heading of "old jenaf horror stories."

But if anyone could will someone into healing—if anyone should have the right to—it was the healthy half of a wounded sousi bond pair.

Syrus growled and snapped his fingers. "Hey. You. Get some clothes on." He pointed at the cupboard with the spares. "Then get over here and earn your air."

Delfi turned her head. Just her head. Like an insect. Or a night bird. The look she gave him would have scared a roomful of veteran Uvlaku.

He was still sorting through his reaction to that thought, the automatic relation of their current situation to his old comrades, when she struck him. Her nails scored bright lines of pain over his cheek. The heat she breathed out baked his eyes and seared the ends of his nerves.

He planted a shoulder in her solar plexus and bowled her over backwards, pinning her wrists to the floor above her head and stretching his full length over her legs to keep her from kneeing him in the balls.

She hissed at him. He wasn't fooled. Her fury mutated straight to panic the instant she realized he'd pinned her. He couldn't let her up, though. Not until he knew she would keep herself under control.

"That was uncalled for," he growled in her ear, fighting for clarity through the acid eating at his skin. "Don't make me break your fingers. Need them to make sure there aren't any fissures in the computer before I plug the transponder back in."

She went completely still, although the terror kept rising. "A'appa'ih?" she breathed in his ear, setting it prickling with her surprise.

"They won't let us go," he said, easing his weight off her slightly. He needed her to listen, not have a panic attack. If she didn't clue in quick, he wouldn't need to worry about her trying to kill him. She'd go off to that place where she hid when the memories took control of her brain, and then she'd be fucking useless.

A fine balance this, scaring her just enough to make her listen but not enough to damage her further. Part of him hated having to do it.

The rest of him just wanted it over with.

"Tarva, isk Tova af Mitachte. They're going to come after us," he told her, shifting further away but not letting her hands go. "Need your brain though." He tried for a wry smile and wasn't sure he'd succeeded. Fuck, but this was easier with Joss. "I'm checking things a line at a time. Need you to go over it after me. Gonna need them to keep Agadi out after we plug the transponder in and turn on the nav. Only got so much time before we miss the meet."

She lay there, anger fading to an itchy dry heat that lent strength to the dull wash of her fear against his senses. But her eyes were sane. At the moment, that was all he could ask for.

"Now, I'm going to stand up. You come after me, I might decide you're better off staying in the medunit till we get through the Barb. Got me?"

Her glare told him she understood just fine.

Syrus shook his head and stood, pulling her along by the arms. She didn't fight him, letting him support her till she had her feet under her. Then he let go and headed back to the pilot's seat. "Clothes." He pointed at the cupboard again. "And food." He pointed at the food storage. "Then take this second screen and start from the top. Only have a couple hours till we have to make a course adjustment."

He listened as she rummaged through the cupboards and made frustrated noises to herself. He wasn't convinced. She wasn't shielding her emotions from him. Sure, some of it was real. But the ebb and flow of her fear dominated as she tried to get herself under control. Residual reaction to being pinned. He shouldn't have done it.

He shouldn't have done a lot of things that needed to be done in the name of survival.

Finally she came up to the nose-cum-cockpit, bare feet slapping on the deck plates. Plopping herself down in the seat with a harrumph, she pulled her feet up to sit cross-legged and started sucking on what looked like a pouch of purple juice. She had the other half slab of meat paste too, gnawing bits off the edges between sips of juice.

He raised an eyebrow at her. She grinned at him with purple-stained teeth and gums.

Syrus shook his head and turned back to the screen in front of him. "I quarantined most of the code Agadi got to," he told her. "Look it over. Fast. I'm going to make sure he didn't get to anything I couldn't cordon off before I pulled the transponder. Then start setting up defenses. But don't lag. Only have three hours to get this done."

He didn't have to tell her to stay the fuck out of his head so she wouldn't pick up random bits of code. He'd locked his internal shields in place and added enough layers that a military sai wouldn't be able to get through.

"Jeh," Delfi said, then took another slurp of juice.

Syrus frowned at her. He knew that one. "No?"

The grin again. And an evil glint in her eyes as determination pooled in the air around her. "Jeh," she repeated.

Syrus sat back and rubbed at the bridge of his nose. "This should be good. Why not?"

Determination pushed at him like a weight. Syrus growled and shoved back. Delfi wouldn't be able to Feel it like Jossa, but he had enough projection that she'd know what he was doing.

She braced and redoubled the emotion. He had to give her points. She knew exactly how to get to him.

"Don't have time to play fucking games," he told her. "Either do the work or—"

She reached for the keypad on the console.

He slapped her hand away. "Don't close that out. You do, we have to start all over. No fucking way."

She hissed at him and waved her hands in the direction of the medunits.

"Words," he told her. "Use your fucking words, girl." And about time she did. There was a time and a place for the pantomime bullshit. This wasn't it. Although she should probably pay him for even knowing that word.

Her face turned as red as her hair. She clenched her fists. The juice pack squirted purple liquid that narrowly missed spattering all over the exposed wires between the two chairs.

And her emotions went from controlled attack to a wild blossom of everything imaginable, all lashing around like some tentacled sea creature.

Syrus's monster made another attempt at freedom and ran smack into the lid he'd welded over its hole. That didn't stop it from trying to fight its way free.

All he needed was for Rissa to come out of hiding and give him a little unwanted advice and the circus would be complete.

Rissa.

Jossa.

Ah.

Syrus pried his hands off the armrests of the chair. Lacing his fingers together so he wouldn't wrap them around the girl's neck, he braced his elbows on his knees. "Listen to me," he said in the calmest voice he could manage. He had to be a rock. An oasis in her frustration. This wouldn't work otherwise. His external shields were in tatters. But they might have a chance if he proved he could control himself.

She stared at him. The tentacles kept whipping around her, wrapping around his body, trying to pull him into the vortex.

Somehow Syrus made his mouth move to form words instead of a roar of agony. "You have the language. It's in your head."

Despair and desperation bitch-slapped him across the face. He braced himself in the chair before the blow could knock him to the floor. Fucking hell, but she knew how to wound a Feel.

"You do," he insisted. "You understand me. When I am actively shielding, you know what I'm saying. You read inanimate words wherever you see them."

More lashes. At his shoulders and across his torso. Fear and self-loathing joined the mix. He sucked in a breath and tried to remember that it was a very bad idea to kill the person he was trying to help. Even if she was flaying his brain to pieces.

"When you bother to try, you make yourself understood."

She glared at him.

"You want to keep using Jossa as a crutch, go ahead. Charades will only get you so far." He turned back to the code. She could do the fucking work or not. If he plugged the transponder back in and they died because some remote program hooked into the system and depressurized the cabin, he'd use the last of his oxygen to laugh at her.

The bitch.

Twenty-One--Syrus

You know how lucky we are to have found her? We can't throw her to that rabid beast; he'll eat her alive. Keep her. Save her so she'll be of real use later.
   - Kemvate Echoda to Kemvate Afutov, in charge of new recruits

He watched her from the corner of his eye as she finished the juice pouch and the slab of meat paste. He couldn't tell what the fuck she was feeling. She'd sucked it all inside and put up about fifty layers of internal shields to keep it there.

When she stood and turned a hesitant circle next to him, he looked up. "What?"

She showed him the empty pouch and food wrapper. He let a smile work its way across his face. "What?"

She stomped her foot.

He grinned wider. She thought she'd win.

He wagged a finger at her when she tightened her grip on the trash. "How childish are you going to be about this?"

She stopped. Her knuckles went white. He knew if he looked at her face he'd probably start laughing. It was tempting. But she'd managed to keep her emotions in check this time, so that was progress.

"W-wwe," she started. Then stopped. He felt the prickles of frustration before she locked it back down.

"Go slow," he told her.

"Wa-Waaaaassste." She forced the word out between gritted teeth. It was accented and garbled all to pieces, but fuck if she didn't manage it.

He lifted a shoulder. "Haven't seen one. Just drop it. Bots come for it fast enough."

Nothing. He glanced at her face. She gave him a look of purest disbelief.

He spread his hands. "I dare you."

"Kiddach," she snapped. Then took a deep breath that expanded her entire upper body. Blowing it out in a long exhale, she dropped the pouch and wrapper. Brushing her hands across the front of her shirt, she sat back down. "Ch-Chiiilluhd," she said this time.

He leaned back and clapped. Slowly.

A bot popped out of its place hidden in the decking and zoomed over. The crumbs vanished under the edge of its housing.

Delfi threw her hands in the air and muttered something Jossa usually translated as "smug bastard."

Syrus didn't bother hiding his grin.

Delfi opened her mouth again, then stopped and glowered at the floor. Syrus went back to work. She'd figure out how to say what she wanted in her own time.

He'd just checked their projected course against the timer on a different screen when the tenor of the emotions around her shifted. Harder, closer—they didn't quite form a wall, but not differentiated enough to be readable either. Frowning, he looked over at her. She had her feet up on the seat, heels hooked over the edge, toes curled in, and arms wrapped around her knees. Her eyes stared at something he couldn't see. Till he tapped her on the elbow. Then she focused on him.

"Wh-Wh—" She grimaced and bit her lip, frustration shivering through the air around her.

Syrus sat back and set his elbows on the armrests of the chair.

"Wh-Whooo-ooo?" Delfi forced the word out slowly, the last noise an exhalation of determination and fear in equal measure.

Fear. Why fear?

But her question meant that he didn't have time to think on that. He didn't have much time at all, really. Certainly none to spend on explanations. But if he didn't give her something, she'd put on another half-hour show of indignant antics and they'd be that much closer to blowing any chances of survival straight down a gravity well.

He'd just have to face the reality of what they'd just lived through.

Of whom they'd just escaped.

He could lie. He could refuse to answer. She couldn't *make* him do anything. Any more than she'd been able to pry the truth of Rissa out of his head before he'd shut his atrophied conscience up in a box and thrown away the key.

Last time he'd put her in her place about this bullshit, she'd tried to climb him like a fucking tree. Then Jossa'd come looking for the commotion and completely misinterpreted. That hadn't turned out so bad in the end. Sure, he'd had to close any memories of Rissa out of his waking thoughts so Delfi wouldn't pick up on her while he was blowing his brains out with Jossa. Had to go back to living like he had on the Fleet. But it'd saved him a bunch of money with the Whore's Guild. With the added bonus of ruining him for normal women once he dropped these two off with the Gatekeepers.

He reminded his dick that the current object of its obsession was stuck in a medunit for the unknown future and that—

A silplat pouch slapped him in the face. Delfi's fist came next, so close behind the pouch that Syrus didn't have a chance to block it.

She was tiny, but she put all her hundred twenty pounds of weight behind that punch. His nose crunched. Pain exploded in his head. The silplat pouch landed on the floor with a sad little *splat* of cold kafe.

Syrus lashed out, catching her in the stomach with his palm and tossing her backwards. She fetched up against the co-pilot's seat, staggered, and stood there with her feet braced. Volcanic fury, acid fear, and something hard and shining radiated off the young woman, all but knocking him over. Syrus clenched his fists and concentrated on *not* pummeling this fey creature into bloody paste. He needed her. Jossa needed her.

His monster was of the opinion that he'd be better off killing them both right now.

Come now, a soft voice whispered in his inner ear. *You both know better than this.*

He knew better. His monster just kept clawing its way out of its hole.

"Uppalith," Delfi breathed, sagging into the seat. *"Uppalijaoth, nashe..."*

And suddenly Syrus understood what she'd actually meant when she'd asked "Who?"

Fuck.

Delfi stared at him, then over at Jossa's medunit, then back at him. He could see a thousand questions in her eyes. Feel a million facets of emotion in the air around him. But only one thing really mattered.

Truth.

He sighed and eased back into the pilot's seat. A quick check told him that yes, he'd lost control of all his shields, internal and external. The externals were useless anyways. He left them down. Slowly, carefully, he built the internal ones back up, patching weak spots, bracing the most important joins, and making sure there were no cracks to be found.

His monster quieted, slinking back to its home without complaint. His conscience did not protest.

Finally, when he was sure his mind was as close to impenetrable as it could be, he looked back up at Delfi. She'd rearranged herself, feet crossed at the ankle and tucked back under her seat, hands fisted together in her lap. Her eyes were hard. Bright spots of color flew on her cheeks.

"Wh-Wh-Who?" she asked again, voice clear and nearly unaccented despite the stammer.

Syrus glanced at the countdown on the screen, then sighed and rubbed at his forehead. He had to do this fast. But he also had to do it right. "Short version, cause I would *really* like to avoid flying into the sun or running over a sat. Jossa told you about Rissa?"

Delfi's head flew back, her nostrils flared. Syrus couldn't read the emotion coming off her. He didn't try.

This was going to be hard enough.

He took a deep breath. And laughed it out. This was fucking ridiculous, getting tied up in knots over what to say. Why the hell was he spending so much time on just the right words, said just the right way? It wouldn't change her opinion of him.

Just get this shit over with already.

"That was her family. Well, her brothers. And her niece."

Delfi just looked at him, tension in every line of her body. She wasn't going to take that as the whole explanation. Not if the emotions still fracturing the air around her were anything to go by.

But he couldn't make his mouth open on the next part. Couldn't suck in enough air to send through his vocal cords. Couldn't—

Couldn't do a lot of things, it seemed.

Almovak's words came back to him. "Why did you hide my sister's *skin* like a piece of trash?"

"Ah—" Delfi growled and tried again. "Ah-ahl. All."

Bare feet appeared in his line of sight. Then Delfi's face, as she crouched on her heels and looked up at him. "All," she said again.

Syrus barked a laugh. "All of it? You sure? It's a long fucking story."

And you won't tell her half of it, his conscience whispered.

He ignored the voice. Delfi wouldn't look away. She didn't seem to have picked up on the commentary, though.

"She found me in a puddle of blood in a back alley of the Capitol," he said. "She and Onika. Got no fucking clue why they took a shine to me, but they did."

Then he told her the rest. He told her about nearly killing Rissa in that alley. The revelation that her sousi could detect other sai. The family's reaction to his presence on their doorstep.

Karudis, Rissa's father, had nearly thrown him down the mountainside with his own two hands. Alrurisi, her mother, had spoken for Syrus. Saying that they didn't have to keep him in the House itself. Another sai, an unexpected sai, could be useful. Take him in. Raise him to loyalty. Use him to better the family's position in the sector. Nobody would look for a male, and a nehkeh at that, to be the Feel feeding information to the family.

They'd activated his maruste and added the mark of ownership. He was to guard the sousi pair. He was to keep them safe. That was the excuse they'd give people for a boy too tall and too strong.

He told her how the House moved to the Northern Hemisphere, to the winter estate. How he was kicked out to pasture with the livestock.

He didn't tell her about screaming at the sky, scaring the sheep with his fury. He didn't explain how he'd cursed Rissa for dragging him from everything he knew and not letting him go back.

But he did tell her that all the offers for Rissa's hand had dried up. Not even her status as sai with a sousi was enough to tempt possible spouses. Not with the sector hovering on the edge of war, the Svis Konanuog coming closer and closer, and rumors of a nehkeh boy dogging her heels.

Delfi watched him through the whole thing, though she eventually eased down so she knelt instead of crouched.

At some point, she sucked in all her emotions, surface and deeper feeling both, and locked them up tight. Did she realize the danger? Or was she actually reacting to the history itself?

"M-More," she said when he paused. "All."

"Gonna have to learn a few more words," he told her. "That's not going to cut it, other side of the Barb."

She bared her teeth at him.

He shook his head. "Rest of it is simpler," he told her. "Alrurisi got pregnant. No priests needed. Almovak was born. Karudis decided that before he could marry Rissa off, he needed to get the military off his back."

Delfi looked at him, face blank.

"The Karukap? Third child rule?"

She shook her head.

"Right," he said. "Well, it's mandatory now, not just custom like it used to be. Fleet's too close for the military to let people beg off with 'He's my heir' or 'She's the first sai in four generations.' Lucky for Karudis"—Syrus felt his mouth twist on the word—"the sick fuck had an actual bargaining chip."

The military retriever hadn't even paused when Karudis made the offer. Syrus had seen the unfamiliar ship touch down behind the estate, and half an hour later a servant summoned him to the house.

Syrus glossed over the details, gritting his teeth as Delfi's impatience scraped at his skin with dry, coarse bristles. He just told her that he'd been taken. His old ownership glyph invalidated and the new one put in place below it. Lifelong commitment this time. No way to be cut loose when Rissa and Okini went off to whatever rard claimed them in marriage.

"Eventually Karudis found someone to marry Rissa and Okini, her sousi. Out past the Net in a dead-end chain of Barbs. First I heard of it was when Rissa managed to get a message to me." Syrus looked down at his hands and realized he'd clenched them so hard the knuckles were white. He opened them and laced his fingers together instead. "Fuck was beating them. Torture, you name it."

Delfi made a noise but kept a grip on her emotions, so he ignored it and kept going. "By the time I got there, Rissa's sousi was dead. Rissa wasn't much better off."

Horror swamped him. Something keened in his ears. Gravity pulled at him, threatening to yank him out of his seat and crush him to the deck.

Somehow, he managed to lift his head against the force of it. The monster in him thrashed, but not in rage. Syrus wanted to thrash too, just to prove he could.

Delfi stared at him, hands pressed to her mouth, eyes huge, face chalky. She was so rigid she was actually shivering with the tension.

Fucking hell. He had to fix this before she lost it. He expected this sort of bullshit out of Jossa. Delfi? She was supposed to be able to fucking deal with this sort of stuff.

You just told her half a sousi pair died, you idiot. With her *sousi almost dead in a medunit not ten feet away.*

Being lit on fire while a black hole compressed you down to atoms was *not* a fun feeling. Especially since it wasn't physically happening.

"Del," he growled, bracing his hands on his knees so he wouldn't end up flat on the floor. "Get your shit together."

More heat. More gravity. Were his elbows buckling?

Don't touch. Don't touch or you'll both be lost. Don't shake her, don't haul her back to the medunit and stuff her in. *Don't* try to space her.

The scariest part wasn't that his conscience had abandoned her post as the voice of reason. It wasn't that the monster didn't want her gone. It was that *he*, on his own, cared if she pulled out of it.

"Del," he barked. "I got her out! I got her out and she lived, you hear?"

The localized gravity field eased. Slipped sideways. Then vanished. Syrus sucked in a breath and shook his head, trying to clear it. "Fuck," he spat. Then again, "Fuck!"

He didn't see her coming till it was almost too late. Shying away from her reaching fingers, he slapped at her wrists, sending them off to the side.

"You touch me, girl, it'll be the last thing you ever do."

He expected her to try anyways, to prove that she didn't take orders. Normally, she would.

She sat back down, still staring at him. "Sheh?" she demanded.

"I don't know what the fuck that one means," he snapped.

She growled and dropped her head backwards so she could glare at the ceiling.

"I got her out," he told her. It might be the answer she wanted. It might not. He needed to finish this and see if the ship stocked liquor. "Got us both out of there. Took years, but I got her back to herself." He spread his hands. "All that fuckery about sousi not being able to live without each other, it's shit.

"Few years later, her husband's people found us. Took her. Nearly killed me. By the time I healed up and followed, Fleet'd made it to his world."

Delfi squeaked, then slapped a hand over her mouth.

Syrus snorted. "The rest of it, well..." He looked back at the medunit that held Jossa. "You know that too."

"All," Delfi said, drawing the word out with the effort of saying it.

He glared at her. "I don't fucking know it."

Delfi swatted him on the shoulder. She'd managed to pull her feelings back in. He felt the sting of contact. Nothing more. "Giiirrl?" she asked.

Syrus frowned at her. What girl? Oh. Right. He'd almost forgotten, in all the remembering.

"Girrl," Delfi repeated. "Jir—" She stopped, obviously trying to work the words out of her mouth in some sort of order. "Ath-fath—"

"Father?"

She nodded.

Well. That explained a lot. Syrus pinched the bridge of his nose. It exploded in pain, reminding him that he needed see about setting it soon. "I knew Jirdis married. He's forty-eight fucking years old. Of course he's married. His daughter married to the local rard's heir. Almovak must've had her come in on the off chance he could use her looks against me—" He stopped when Delfi made a questioning noise. "Yeah, she was upstairs. Probably before she went running to her father."

An affirmative this time. Well, that fit.

The console beeped at him, reminding him that it didn't have a data transponder and would he *please* just let it do its job properly? Delfi stared at it like it was a bajbar come out of the ground to chew her leg off. Syrus snorted. Apparently she'd forgotten their situation, what with all the talking.

"Here," he told her as he pulled up the navigation display on a screen he hadn't used so far. "Watch that. Keep an eye on the code. Make sure nobody gets in and redirects us away from those coordinates." He stabbed a finger at the destination marker on the map. "Better yet..." He opened up the little menu of decoy beacons and their chosen targets. Two or three looked like they'd follow the same flight path long enough to confuse a pursuer. "I'm going to plug in the transponder crystal. I say 'go,' send these two"—he pointed at the decoy listings—"off. You got five seconds, got me? Then I yank the crystal."

She glared at him.

"Not kidding, Del. Agadi's a Crack. Can't let him have access to the system. Hell, this is dangerous enough. Wasting time on all this history."

She scowled and threw hot, stabbing needles his way. He must be getting immune to her; the emotions barely registered.

"Just watch the screens, ok? And pray I got the technical parts working right."

She made a couple of pissy noises and leaned forward, hands hovering over the keypads on the console.

He'd take it.

They had to do a little maneuvering so he could get down in front of the opening into the console's guts. Somehow he ended up on his knees with one of her feet planted behind him and her other knee up on the opposite chair. Tension all but quivered through her, vibrating into his skin and making his teeth ache. He worked his jaw a couple times to ease it before saying, "Ready?"

"Khe."

He knew that one. Good to go. Reaching into the internal workings of the console was easier now that he had some practice. In short order, the crystal was seated back in its housing, glowing a faint blue green. "Navigation good?" he called up to her.

A pause.

One second. Two. Shit, he hoped she hadn't fudged a keystroke. That was almost the last thing they needed.

"Khe."

Thank fuck. "K. Go the decoys."

He could hear her fingers tapping above him this time. She said something that sounded affirmative, but he didn't know the word. The zap of pleasure and joy that hit his exposed hip seemed fairly intentional, though. "Pulling the plug."

The same affirmative. He wiggled the transponder crystal until the light went out and started backing out of the hole. Alarm ripped up his side. What the hell?

He pulled out and sat up all at once. Delfi *oofed* as his head stuck her in the stomach. For a second she wobbled, and then she lost the war with her center of gravity and half fell, half folded over him.

And that was about the last straw.

Syrus stood and turned, managing to toss the young woman back into the pilot's seat on the way up. She landed in a heap, squawking outrage. He ignored her, more worried about not tangling his feet in all the wires still straggling out of the console. A glance at the screens showed that everything was fine. No new attacks that he could see. Course laid in and doing fine. Indicators on the decoys showing green.

What the hell was she all panicked over anyway?

"Look," he snapped. "You go over the code again. Make *absolutely* sure Agadi didn't get in this time. Put up as many firewalls and traps as you can think of. Closer we get, more we need that transponder connected full time. They're all going to land on us like a cruiser out of orbit if we don't get through the Barb. Get to the Gatekeepers, we'll have some breathing room. Maybe not much though, so we can't afford to get lazy."

"O'zo?" Delfi frowned up at him.

"Yes, we," he told her. "Almovak's connected to isk Kallura lis Kerute. The Gatekeepers might open the Barb for him outside of schedule. Tarva will have contacts on the other side. I give it three days. Maybe less. Then I move on. You two need to decide if you'll sit there and wait for fire to rain down out of the sky, or if you're coming along."

Oh hell, what did he just say? And why? It wasn't logical. They were bait. He could leave them and run. Tarva, at the least, wanted them for bounty. If Jirdis lived, he might leave them alone. His hate was all aimed in Syrus's direction. Almovak would get slowed down trying to decide if he should bring them home and put them to use.

Really, it was better to drop them and run faster through the Seps Coalition Barbs.

So why the fuck had he offered to take them along? Again?

Delfi peered up at him, alarm, surprise, and curiosity rippling around her, bursting tiny bubbles of ice against his skin. He saw the flush rising along her neck to her face. The quiver of an eyelash as she blinked, probably trying to decide if he'd lost his mind.

He had. He really had.

Before she could reach out or speak or do anything else to cement the reality of his lunacy, Syrus turned away and headed for the food storage cupboards. A little rummaging in the back corners netted him a tiny pouch of amber-colored liquid labeled "Fire." He cracked the seal, squeezed the contents into his mouth, and savored the burn down his throat as he dug around for another pouch.

He found three and emptied them all. Delfi stood where he'd left her, watching.

Tossing the last pouch on the deck nearest the cleaning bot's hiding spot, Syrus stood. "Check the code and have it done soon. Wake me for the next course correction."

Before she could refuse or complain *again*, he slipped around the stiffened curtain separating the main cabin from the sleeping area.

Fuck, but he hoped the booze was strong enough to let him sleep without dreams.

He doubted it.

TWENTY-TWO--SYRUS

The existence of so-called "Siphon" saiog is only a myth. Those who seem to display this trait are merely extremely sensitive Receiver-type sai, with minds flexible enough to absorb whatever knowledge they glean in addition to their Feel, Hear, or Sight abilities.
    - Professor Ibilu, Imperial University, Advanced Sai Studies

Syrus watched Delfi slip behind the curtain and waited to make sure she wouldn't come back out with a blanket to set up camp next to Jossa's medunit.

After a minute or so, he checked, stretching his sai out carefully. She was even *more* tired than he'd thought. The buzz and churn of her feelings had quieted to almost nothing. She was asleep. Good. He wasn't. Fuck, but he needed a drink. Shouldn't have downed the entire stock of liquor in one go.

While he was at it, he needed sleep too. Keeping the monster from marching him up to the proto-bridge and knocking the girl into the next system took too much concentration for sleep. He'd spent most of the off-shift staring at the ceiling and trying to ignore the roil of her emotions. Being stuck in this flying box with the Seer was about as comfortable as rubbing sand in his eyes.

She couldn't help it. For so many reasons, she couldn't help it. That didn't make putting up with her any easier. Telling her to shield would have been the same as telling her to stop feeling altogether. She spent so much time with her shields up as it was, she needed a little space to let loose and give her emotions some leeway. Otherwise she'd self-combust or implode at the worst possible moment and probably get them all killed.

As it was, she hadn't let herself go nearly as much as he wished. Because she was the Stable one and had better inherent control on herself than he'd thought? Or because she'd actually started healing, really healing, from the trauma of the shadow base?

He doubted *that*. Very much. Which meant that the volcano he'd been watching build for the past few months was still likely to blow at the worst possible moment. Knowing their collective luck, she'd finally lance her wound in some public place and land them all in a bloodbath of epic proportions.

Proportions. Now there was a word someone should pay him for.

Liquor. He really wished there was some liquor left.

But there wasn't. So he rolled his shoulders and went back to work.

Delfi'd gotten most of it. All the major systems were ok. She'd left one set of minor files in quarantine. He finished picking through them, pulling out a couple of the more subtle fissures Agadi'd left. Done, he slid the programs over to the co-pilot's side of the console and pulled up the table of decoy drones. They'd have to be careful with these. If he didn't use enough, Agadi'd hardly have to try to figure out which signal was real. Too many, and they wouldn't have any in reserve in case things went bad later.

He chose four by their default headings and told the ship to load them but not send them off just yet. No sense in giving Agadi, or whatever nobles were following, any more warning than he had to.

He checked the chrono. Five hours and change till he needed to start actively steering this thing. Just enough time to catch up on some sleep. He made sure the chrono was set to wake him in time, then turned his chair and propped his feet on the other seat. He gave the girl maybe two hours, two and a half tops, before her anxiety knocked her out of REM and back out here to make his life a living hell.

For a wonder, he got all five remaining hours.

The alarm bleating out of four separate speakers woke him. Cursing, he dropped his feet off the co-pilot's seat and leaned over to look at the screens on the console. Behind him, surprise bounced through the cabin, mutating to the high thrill of anxiety and fear mixed together. Delfi came running up. "Keha'oks nihba?"

"We got ten minutes till we need to plug the transponder back in. Take a piss, grab all the food you can, and siddown," he told her as he flicked screens here and there.

She hissed and lashed him with heat and something else that seemed to suck at whatever moisture the anger left behind. It took him a moment to realize she was embarrassed.

Delfi. Embarrassed. If there were time, he'd stick a note in the ship's log just to mark the day.

But they didn't have time. "Get it done," he snapped. "Or else you can get all this set up and *I'll* use the head first."

A few soft thuds of stomping feet and the door behind him slid open, then shut. He shook his head, brought up the drones' launch sequence, and went to go find his own food.

Nine minutes later, he knelt between the two chairs again, a pile of food packages and liquid pouches to either side and Delfi half standing over him.

"Ready?"

"Yee-auh."

Close enough. "K." He leaned into the console. "Three, two..."

The transponder crystal lit up. Her hand slapped the screen over his head. Something in the system chirped once, twice, four times in quick succession.

They coordinated his exit better this time. Delfi dropped into the co-pilot's chair, hands already flying across the screen as he clambered into to pilot's seat. His screens were already lighting up with alerts.

Fuck Agadi. And Tarva too. He should've made absolutely sure the entire team was dead when he blew that factory.

"Don't fucking care about your language," he told Delfi. "Something you can't handle, let me know."

She made a small noise, bent to grab a pouch of liquid at random, and dropped it in her lap. One smooth motion, one hand still working the screens.

Ok then. He turned to his own work.

Time to see if they could outwit an active Crack.

>>><<<

They managed it. Barely. Agadi—and Syrus had to assume it was still Agadi instead of some pet Crack the nobles had on hand—got control of the nav systems three times in the next eight hours. First, he tried to run them into the system's solar collectors, or near enough. Guarded as the things were by mag nets and shields, the ship would end up stuck in an invisible web, unable to move until someone came along to inspect and empty it. That one might have been a noble's work, but Syrus doubted it.

Delfi spat and hissed and fairly bristled with terrified fury as she tried to work her way around the man's style of code. Syrus was right there with her, the itching crawl under his skin all the worse for the fact that it wasn't the woman next to him setting it off.

Agadi'd always been a tough bastard, rooted in front of a screen though he might be. It'd be a fight, but it was a fight the monster wanted. That Syrus agreed with the creature made it all the harder to tamp down.

By the time they got control of steering back and sent off another couple of drones, including one to follow the course they *would* have taken if Agadi'd had his way, there were three background programs running, set to pop up annoying flags and false fissures. Bug bites all of them, but they looked real at first. He and Delfi wasted more time slapping them down before Syrus remembered the trick of them and cobbled together a string of code to swat the things out of the system and alert him if anything was really wrong.

They lost three more drones the next time Agadi made it in. Delfi was the one who noticed the minor course corrections popping up in answer to altered data coming in from the nav buoys. Slowly, ever so slowly, the ship was turning in a wide circle.

Syrus took care of that one. He knew the coordinates they needed to end up at, and Delfi didn't. Whatever she said to the screen as he fought the nav system over entering the correct destination, he didn't think it was "Ancestors bless." But she managed to put up a filter between the ship and incoming buoy transmissions while he got the correct heading entered and locked, giving them another hour of breathing space to deal with all the tiny incursions that kept cropping up.

By the time they'd worked their way through half the liquid stimulants and the knots in his shoulders threatened to become permanent points of pain, Syrus decided that killing Agadi would be too good for the man. Not quickly. Skinning him alive would be a start. Deboning his fingers and feet would be a great second step. Jamming broken data crystals and fried contact wires in every orifice, then jacking the whole thing into a variable power array would be a beautiful ending. See how well he manipulated code fed straight into his brain.

Syrus didn't realize he was listing the planned torture methods off out loud until humor popped against his side and spread the slow warmth of approval across his skin. He glanced over to find Delfi grinning at him. It was a vicious, animal expression he didn't think he'd ever seen her wear before.

He gave her his own smile full of teeth and got back to work, one eye on the chrono in the corner of his main screen.

Almost there. Just another couple—

Alarms blared. The code on the screens crawled sideways.

Delfi snarled. The ship was headed straight for the Barb, all communications cut, including the emergency channel. Fucking Agadi. Probably figured on letting the Border Guard catch the escape ship at the border and then grabbing their prisoners out of lockup.

Tarva must be getting desperate, if she was willing to risk exposing her crew like that.

Bitch.

>>><<<

An hour and a half later, a couple rushed trips to the head, three more drones, and a whole new set of muscles he hadn't known existed all tied in knots, Syrus was too tired to even cuss. He'd had to cut communications on almost all channels. Too many ways to let Agadi in otherwise.

Delfi swayed in her seat, hands braced on the edge of the console as her eyes tracked code across the screen. Shit. Should've made her sleep longer, taken care of the first few attacks himself and had her come out to spell him. If she was reading one word in twenty correctly, he'd be surprised.

He checked the chrono again. Not enough time for either of them to get some rest. Their subroutines were doing a fair job of finding micro fissures in the system and walling them off, but some of the little fuckers were growing and adapting beyond the abilities of anything he and Del could write. If they didn't run over the top of the Kiprinog ship soon, that trip into the side of the Barbican array would go from Looming Threat to Immediate Danger very quickly.

Come on, you blind fucks, he yelled at empty space. Find the fly buzzing around your head.

And how in the hell would you know, if you've got all the channels blocked? another part of his brain asked.

Fuck. Fuck!

"Need to open comms again," he told Del. "We're too close."

She gaped at him and made a full-body "What the hell are you thinking?" gesture that involved halfway standing up, flailing her arms, and what sounded like an attempt to say "What the fuck" but just came out "Ffff-!" instead.

"I know," he snapped, dropping his shields slightly so she could see the frustrated argument going on in his head. "But it's that or we trip over them, don't know it, and they blow us to bits."

She sagged back into her chair and thumped her head against the headrest, eyes closed.

He waited.

Something beeped as another micro fissure tried to grow past the bounds of the trap programs.

With a sigh worthy of the worst two-credit actress, Delfi rubbed at her eyes and sat up. Scooping up a pouch of liquid stimulant, she squeezed half the thing into her mouth and held it out in his direction.

Snorting, he took it from her, finished it off, and tossed it back towards the cleaning bot's hiding place. "Ready?"

She rolled her hand in a "move it along" sort of way, then rested her fingers in place over the screen.

He checked their destination coordinates, told the ship to pick up speed, and started reopening communications channels again.

All hell broke loose.

He caught a glimpse of Delfi's mouth moving, maybe in silent prayer, and then the only thing he saw for a long time was code, the shift of coordinates on the nav screen, and the steadily changing chrono as it taunted them through space and time.

>>><<<

Half an hour and a thousand automated incursions later, the coordinates on the screen marking the ship's position finally started to come in line with the rendezvous coords. If someone could play tug-the-rope with a computer and several thousand tons of metal, he and Delfi were at least managing to hold their own. Just a little further. A little more.

The ship shuddered once, twice, and then the comm screens lit up with alerts and panic buttons and all the other things a computer used to tell the stupid humans whose brains were too fogged with code that someone was trying to talk to them.

Syrus had just enough presence of mind to reach out and grab Delfi's hands before she could cancel all the alerts and lock the incoming frequency out of the system.

"No." He choked as his throat stuck shut, protesting use after so long. "Check with your mind. I'll look at the sensor data." Those particular screens had been blank for so long, he hadn't so much as glanced at them since they'd plugged the transponder back in. Either Tarva was staying out of range, or she had the best masking tech he'd seen since the shadow base.

Delfi sat back, eyes glazing over as she stretched out her mind.

He pulled the data feed over and blinked a few times to make his eyes focus. Little gray icons marked with the glyphs of the Gatekeepers hovered in a rough semi-circle in front of a cluster of the tiny white blips that marked their own position. Scattered here and there were other markers, some with the Imperial sigil, some only showing ID sequences of private vessels.

That was a shit ton of ships. He'd expected a decent-sized fleet, given the importance of the Barbican to both sides of the gate. But the Gatekeepers had a whole armada sitting between the Barb and anyone who might try to get through.

Fuck.

"Skaeksyj," Delfi growled.

"What?" he snapped. "Who are they?"

Had Agadi finally pulled a trick without being caught? Was Tarva sitting in that cluster of ships, faking this exchange? Maybe Agadi'd just been toying with them to buy time to building a voice frequency masker. Or the nobles got smart and laid a trap here rather than trying to track them all over the system.

"Sh... sheeee..." Delfi dissolved into the cough and bark of He'la. "Sheel!"

Shielded. Probably not the nobles then. If they hadn't used a sai back on the base, they didn't have one to use out here.

Probably.

Tarva didn't read as shielded at all. She just flat didn't exist to sai senses.

Yanking his attention away from the girl, he toggled open the comms just as the alarm flashed another warning. "This is EP-5746 receiving."

The alarm died aborning. The flashing lights on the console went dark.

Delfi sucked in a breath and tucked her hands under her legs. Good girl.

"EP-5746, this is the *Panris op Akuev*, sending." One of the white blips marked with its name and the sigil of the Freighters Guild lit up on the nav screen. "State your business."

"Kirdar Oropan," Syrus said. "EP-5746. Three on board, including me. One in a medunit. Supposed to be meeting up with Jaskuto. He there?"

No answer. Syrus checked the comm indicator. The light was green. Neither he nor Delfi had managed to disable the system that he knew of during their checks. Was something wrong outside the ship?

Next to him, a tremor ran through the air, too low to get a good read on.

"Kirdar Oropan, please confirm your identity." The person on the other end of the line still sounded businesslike. Syrus felt the skin on the back of his neck tighten. A routine request shouldn't have taken so long.

Delfi shifted in place. He looked over. She raised a hand, waggled it at him, then pointed at the pad in the center of the console.

He curled a lip. Did she think he was a fucking idiot? He knew what they wanted him to do. They needed a blood scan.

He was trying to come up with a good reason to avoid it until he knew for sure who this was.

"Run diagnostics on the external arrays," he told Delfi. It probably wouldn't give him anything. "See if there's any indication *they* are who they say they are."

"Kirdar Oropan, if you do not provide an ID, extreme measures will be taken. This is restricted space."

If that *wasn't* Tarva spoofing a voice over a fake comm frequency and the bastard on the other end of the connection used his fucking name one more time over an open comm line, he was going to strangle someone.

"Five seconds," the voice on the other end of the line said. "I must tell you that we do not concern ourselves with salvage."

He'd take his chances with Tarva, all things considered.

Syrus slapped his hand down on the pad, hard. He was *definitely* killing someone when they made it aboard that ship. On principle alone. And also because the stupid fuck on the other end of the comm had used most of those five seconds to blow hot air into vacuum.

"Identity confirmed," said the person on the other side. "Please confirm your passengers' identifications."

Too late, he checked his palm. The false skin that'd covered it looked almost rippled in places. The edges were starting to peel. Shit. Had the sensor found *any* of the stolen DNA or nanites to read?

Delfi put her hand on the pad before he could make her show him her palm.

"Can't do the last one," Syrus told the man on the other end of the comm. Too late to worry about the fake identities. "She's locked up tight in a medunit."

"Hold please."

"I just want to talk to Jaskuto," Syrus snapped. The edge of the console creaked under his hand. Stupid flimsy piece of shit.

No answer from the *Panris*.

Syrus sat back and pinched the bridge of his nose, running through the litany of foul language he'd picked up over the years and trying to find one to fit the cocksucker on the other end of the line.

There were a lot of choices. Cocksucker still fit best.

He laughed at the thought and straightened. Catching Delfi's raised eyebrows, he shrugged. "You'll get it eventually," he told her.

"This is Jaskuto."

Delfi jumped. Surprise popped and skittered around her. Syrus growled at the speaker and opened the comm. But the bastard on the other end wasn't done. "I am sorry to say, sir, but the offer of transport has been rescinded."

Syrus stared at the console, then at Delfi. She scowled, deliberately let go of the reins she was keeping on her frustration so it could rake him across the face, then tucked it away again just as fast.

Girl had a point.

Syrus checked the chrono in the upper corner of the main screen, did some mental math, and opened the comm again. "The money was set to transfer automatically twelve hours ago."

Their pause was too long. "We have not received a transmission of funds," the man said. "I regret to inform you, sir, but the offer has been rescinded."

Those sons of bitches and their self-righteous lies! Fucking *bastards!*

Delfi slapped him in the arm. Lightly. The feel of knives dipped in acid nearly immobilized him, vanishing into the touch of frozen metal before he really registered the pain. He nearly turned around and ripped her hand off. "Fuck, woman," he growled at her. "Keep your fucking—"

She slapped him again. Harder and across the face this time. Then she pointed at Jossa's medunit. Determination rang out like a bell, sending tremors of heat and little splashes of acid fear through the cabin.

Syrus clamped down on his initial reaction, which was to twist her hand off, and stared at the medunit instead.

They were in an escape vessel. With a medunit in use.

The Gatekeepers' contacts on this side of the Barbican never lost an opportunity to build good will, as they called it.

Syrus spun the seat and opened the comms for a third time. "I don't give a flying fuck about the offer or the money. I've got a critically injured woman here, and I'm in a lawfully registered escape shuttle. You're going to pick us up."

The man's voice was skeptical. "There is no distress signal coming from your vessel. Furthermore—"

"Understood," said a new voice, somewhere out of the normal range for voice pickup. Then, louder, it said, "Welcome, Kirdar Oropan. If you will turn over nav control to us, we will have your ship in a docking bay shortly."

Syrus, mouth half open to rip the first man a new asshole, stopped. Ok then. Someone had either gotten the money and knew lying was a good way to get in trouble with Gatekeepers, or there was an even bigger problem about to land on their heads.

He had a feeling he knew what it might be.

No help for it now. He'd made this bed for all three of them. Time to see if they fit.

The comm went silent. He toggled it closed from his end, then got to work on setting up navigation for remote interface. He and Delfi had scrambled it to hell and gone while they were trying to keep Agadi out of the system. He worked as fast as he could. He shook his head when Delfi moved to help. "Still shielded?" He would have asked if she heard any blank spots, but that only worked to find Tarva in a crowd, not in deep space.

She tilted her head, eyes drifting out of focus. "Y-Yyye."

"Shit. Ok, give me a hand then."

By the time they were done, the indicator light on the screen was blinking so fast it was nearly strobing. The officious little bastard on the other end of the comms kept up a litany of complaints. Finally, Syrus was able to shift the indicator over. It blinked green, then steadied. The prick on comms shut up.

All around them, the ship hummed with quiet efficiency as whoever had finally captured them brought the little vessel in like a fish on a line.

> Syrus

TWENTY-THREE--SYRUS

When we set up the tenets of the state religion, back when it was just another way to keep the saiog from rebelling, we discounted the vehemence of reaction from those who subscribed to the remnants of old faiths.
  -"A History of Faith in the Navlad Empire," High Priest Rolluston

Syrus didn't waste time wondering whether he'd made the right choice. There was too much to do. He stood. "Come on," he told Delfi. "Get to work."

She huffed, lashed him with frustration and impatience, and crossed her arms. Syrus stopped and looked back at her from prying the curtain back between the main cabin and the sleeping quarters. "What?" he asked. "You want to meet them with a hug and a smile and wait for the dagger between the ribs? We need to prove we're not hiding anything."

She cringed but stayed where she was.

Syrus sighed and yanked the curtain the rest of the way back.

"Mo-Monnnnn." The *slap* of a bare foot on the deck. Then she finished, "H-H-Hooow monneey?"

Syrus turned around. "Money? What? Oh."

That's right. She hadn't been there. She'd been off getting caught by Almovak. The bastard.

"Tarva didn't catch us till after we went to the trader," he told her. "We got the money."

She managed a noise that sounded like a cross between a baby-bird screech and "Arg." Complete with full-body exclamation marks.

Syrus snorted. "Fucking trader we went to wanted to sell us out. We killed him, found his safe, and stole half his cash. I set up a dummy account to send the money on a timer. That way, if things went to shit—"

Delfi gestured broadly at the cabin around them and gave him a "No fucking wonder" sort of look. Her emotions were too highly charged to get a clear read on them.

Syrus crouched to examine the control panel on Jossa's medunit. "Fine, yes. We landed in a pile of shit. Didn't want to lose the money, though. Don't know about you, but I'm not interested in staying in this system any longer than I have to.

"Good news is the buyer had enough on hand to cover all our fares. We'll do whatever dance we need to do once the Kiprinog have us, wait till they leave us alone on the ship, and I'll see if I can get access to the data feeds before we clear the Barbican. I can try to get all the money out of the accounts. Don't know the conversion rate over there, but it'll be better than showing up with nothing but the clothes on our backs."

He looked up at Delfi, who'd come over to watch what he was doing. Her crossed arms boosted her already impressive breasts, the ship-issued clothes hugged every line of her body, and her hips were nearly at face height with Syrus.

He wasn't as tempted as he'd expected. She all but vibrated as she stared at the surface of the medunit. Hard to think of sex with the human equivalent of a stun baton. Disturbing, actually. On an infinity of levels.

He poked her in the knee just to make her human again.

She reacted predictably. Dropping her fist and her weight onto his shoulder in a blow that might have knocked him over if he hadn't expected an attack of some kind.

The tsunami of acid fear *did* surprise him. He came back to himself with his hands stuffed inside the galley cupboard, looking for a knife to cut the sai from his head.

The fuck? The fucking *hell* was *that?*

He dropped the silplat ladle in his right hand, the fork in his left, and twisted on the balls of his feet to look at Delfi. She cowered against the medunit, hands clinging to the lid, head down between her elbows. A fountain of curling red hair and her quivering back were all he could see of her.

The biting fear still flooded the cabin. His monster wanted to eat it and turn it into rage. But the urge was a small force against the weight of "what the fuck" Syrus was using to keep it down.

"Del," he said softly. "What is it?"

Usually she spat at him like a kitten when he used Jossa's nickname for her. Now she hunched in on herself further and mewled.

No, not in on herself. Against the medunit. The medunit holding her sister. Who may or may not survive the next hour or so, depending on who had control of their nav system.

Syrus breathed out a "Fucking sousi" and stood to walk over to her. Carefully. The same way he'd approach a feral animal. Delfi didn't flinch or lash out as he crouched next to her. She quivered, and her emotions spiked slightly when he laid a hand on her shoulder, but otherwise she gave no sign that she was aware of his presence.

"Del," he said again, trying to soften his voice as the monster fought its way free of the hole. "Need you to stand up. Don't have much time."

Not much time at all to make a decision about letting loose and killing the first person who cracked the hull. Considering circumstances, he figured he was safe enough to fight alongside Delfi. Provided he could get her moving.

"Del." He ran his palm down her back, feeling the edges of her shoulder blade too sharp under his hand, counting her ribs where they connected to her vertebrae. The acid etched his fingerprints through the skin and down into muscle. His nerves were on fire. On fire and... being pulled out of his arms? Yes. It fucking hurt, the way her guilt literally dragged at him. Which checked out, when he thought about it.

"Come on, Del."

Another quiver.

He ran his hand down her back again, biting down on the hiss of pain as he lost feeling to the elbow.

He didn't have time for this bullshit.

Delfi yelped in surprise when he leaned forward, wrapped his arms around her at the hip and shoulder, and stood. She caught him in the jaw with her elbow and the leg with her heels. Carrying her to the co-pilot's seat was an exercise in endurance. By the time he managed to set her down, he wanted to scream in agony. The monster boiled in his veins, cooking him from the inside out to match the outside-in treatment of Delfi's emotions.

They'd crack the hull and find a charred-out husk in place of a man.

Delfi landed in the seat a little harder than he'd planned but didn't fall over. Syrus wrapped one hand in her hair and laid the other on her shoulder. "Wake up, girl," he told her. "Not dead yet. Not you. Not me. Not even Jossa, though she gave it a good try. See that red light?" He used her hair to turn her head so she could see the red light on the medunit.

Delfi sucked in a breath.

Around them, the ship gave a great, grinding crunch. Time'd just run out.

Syrus pulled Delfi's head around again and peeled one of her scarves off her skull. She stared at him as he used his teeth to undo the knot she'd tied in it.

"They're going to open that seal in a second. You listening?" Thank fuck, she actually looked like she was. He worked fast, gathering up the mass of her hair and twisting it into a coiled knot at the back of her head. "Hold that."

Blinking, eyes darting between the medunit and the hatch in the roof of the cabin, she reached back and held her hair. Syrus shook out the scarf, folded it, and wrapped it around her head. It looked ridiculous, but so long as it did the job, he didn't care. Neither would she, once she understood. "Here you keep your hair up and covered. Gatekeepers always have at least one rep with the Kiprinog, so they'll be judging us right off. Between their religions—yes, plural—and being sure they know where you come from, it's best to keep your hair up.

"Just remember, maruste aren't about pride for them, they're—" He stopped and searched for a word. "Shame. They take in Imperials, but they don't want them. Anyone with an activated maruste is second, third class even. Was going to erase them entirely, but shit happens."

Her mouth twisted, and wry humor prickled his fingers.

"Yeah, yeah." He stopped as something hit the top of the ship with a loud *thud.* "I get it. Point is, keep your head down and your mouth *shut.* Meant to have more time to explain this. Didn't think they'd be coming in for a chat." He shrugged. "Life's a bitch. Anyone wants to see your back, let them. Don't react when they think about how pitiful you are, or stupid or anything else; got me? They got their rules, we're their guests, and it's better for everyone if we don't make trouble." He tightened the knot on her scarf and tucked the ends under.

Delfi pointed at his hair and raised her eyebrows.

Someone struck the hatch set in the ceiling. Deliberately, not just the random noises of machinery.

"They just want my hair pulled back. Women get the head covers." Before she could growl something about *that,* he leaned over and punched the exit sequence into the control panel. The system beeped and gave him a "hatch blocked" alter. He growled and hunted for the external comms button. Finding it, he snapped, "Hatch won't open if you're on top of it."

Delfi appeared at his side as if by magic, worry emanating from her in jittery waves. He looked down at her. "Easy, ok? Tarva would have just opened it up and shot us. Probably. Almovak wouldn't be standing around being polite either. I gutted his brother."

For a wonder, she calmed down a bit.

A series of scuffling noises above them told him that whoever was up there, they'd gotten the hint. He waited another thirty seconds and hit the exit sequence again. This time the icon turned green as it chirped acknowledgment. Delfi froze, staring at the hatch again. Syrus shook his head and herded the young woman over near her sister's medunit, ignoring the zings of anxiety she gave him as he pushed her gently into place. Just in time. The hatch opened with a hiss and a *clunk*. Someone stuck their hand down where he could see it, waving upwards in obvious invitation.

That was new. He'd expected an assault team. Why the hell did they want himself and Delfi *out*? The hand gave another wave and then vanished, and a ladder telescoped down from the housing around the hatch.

Well, still nothing he could do about a trap from in here. Maybe they were fucked if they left the ship, but they'd be fucked up the ass if they didn't.

"Go on." Syrus nudged Delfi in the shoulder. By rights, he should have gone first. But if he did, she'd probably plaster herself to Jossa's medunit and refuse to leave the ship.

The look and feelings she gave him told him his guess was right on the mark. He bared his teeth and pushed her a little harder. "Or should I carry you?"

"Are you coming, Kirdar Oropan?" someone called in heavily accented trade tongue.

"Yeah."

When he went to take her by the elbow, Delfi slapped at his hand and headed for the ladder. She paused as her head cleared the hatch but kept going before Syrus had to swat her on the ass.

Muffled voices, all male, echoed through the opening as he mounted the ladder behind her. Syrus climbed till he could see over the edge of the hatch and looked around.

They were in a large landing bay. Not a Navlad ship, if the lines and angles were any indication. Dull gold letters gleamed under the lights. White paint on the walls and deck showed the "stalls" for ships to park in. A few already sat there, quiet and empty. No bustle. No shouting back and forth.

And yet, he couldn't quite make his feet move. Just over a year ago, he'd come out of another ship to another dubious welcoming party and ended the day nearly dead of his own hubris.

If there was a time to be praying—if he were the sort to pray at all— he'd long since passed it.

"Is he coming?" someone asked.

"Should be. He wouldn't have sent his woman ahead if he didn't think it was safe." That was the fucker who'd tried to turn him away.

Curiosity, wary alarm, and anticipation swirled up through the air. Syrus sighed, threw up all the interior and exterior shields he could manage, and finished climbing the ladder. If he didn't get down there, Delfi would start knocking heads together just to prove that she was *no one's* woman, least of all his.

He paused at the top of the steps set against the side of the ship and put a hand on his hip where a knife hilt usually sat. He'd lost his weapons somewhere between gutting Jirdis and landing in the ship. He should have dug something better than a butter knife out of the cupboards on the ship.

"Leto?"

Eight men stood at the base of the stairs. Two in the uniform worn by medics the Empire over. Five with guns drawn in an easy hold position in front of them, barrels aimed at the deck. Another with no weapons but a flinty expression on his face as his hand hovered near Delfi's elbow. And the last, standing at the base of the stairs, eyebrows pulled together in a puzzled frown.

"Leto? Leto Arkon?"

Syrus blinked at the man. Maybe in his late forties, medium height, pale skin weathered by time spent planetside, close-cropped blond hair and ears that reminded Syrus of some of the double-handled jugs he'd carted around the lis Tova family compound in his childhood. The man had smile lines on his face and a white strip of cloth half hidden behind the collar of his black shirt. He looked familiar somehow. But Syrus hadn't used that name in almost twenty-five years. Not since the last time he'd come through the Gatekeepers.

"Markos?"

The man's face lit up. Joy bloomed in the air around him. "Ha! I thought it might be you!" He bounded halfway up the steps and clamped Syrus in a bear hug. "It's good to see you!"

Syrus remembered the hug. He thought he might have a couple cracked ribs. Laughing, he hugged the man back, doing his best to return the injuries.

"Oof." Markos let go and leaned back. "Just as strong as ever." He narrowed hazel eyes and frowned. "You haven't aged a day."

An exaggeration. They both knew it. But since the seventeen-year-old kid Syrus once knew had crow's feet around his eyes and gray at the temples, it was close enough. "And you got old," he told Markos. "The fuck they have you doing out here sifting through the dregs?"

Markos rolled his eyes. "That hasn't changed either. Come, come! We'll get you settled, and you can tell me where you found the interstellar Fountain of Youth."

Syrus followed the man down two steps before his code-drunk brain caught up with the rest of him. "Wait. Just like that?"

Markos turned to look up at him, puzzlement through the joy that surrounded him. "I'm sorry?"

Syrus glared at him. "Just like that? I get the fucking runaround coming in. Get told the passage I booked and *paid* for is suddenly unavailable and boom, here we are? Off our ship even. What's the game?"

Markos placed a hand on his heart, all injured innocence. "Leto! For shame! Why would I be anything but honest?" He tugged at his collar. "I am a man of the cloth now. I don't need to lie to you. Or anyone for that matter."

"If I may," said another voice. Syrus looked down at the man who'd tried to turn them away. Clean shaven, neatly dressed, and hair clipped short, he stood at the base of the stair with his arms crossed and a scowl on his face. It looked permanent.

Next to him, Delfi eyed the man like a snake about to strike.

Fuck, woman, he thought at her. *Don't start trouble.*

She glanced up at him, wrinkled her nose, and went back to watching the man.

The man didn't notice the exchange, short as it was. "I am Jaskuto. I'm the Kiprinog's primary contact with the Gatekeepers." He gestured at Markos. "I believe I may be able to clarify matters."

Syrus looked at Markos, who shrugged. "I am a man of the cloth."

Jaskuto's scowl deepened, and a sour tang colored the air around him.

Syrus laughed and clapped Markos on the shoulder. "Man of the cloth indeed. Never thought you had it in you. Let me down, before 'my woman' punches your liaison in the throat."

Jaskuto spun to look at Delfi, who bared her teeth at him. Markos chuckled and finished going down the steps. Syrus followed. As soon as he stepped off the last riser, the two medics brushed past him and headed up the stairs, a tangle of harness and silplat boards held between them.

"They'll get your—excuse me, *the* other woman off the ship just fine," Markos said before either Syrus or Delfi could go after them. "She is in a standard Imperial medunit, correct?"

Syrus looked over and saw the portable capsule waiting just below the ship. "Not sure. It might detach. Escape shuttle and that shit." He ignored the disapproval radiating off of Jaskuto. "But she's been in there long enough that she ought to be safe to move, if it's fast."

Markos nodded. "The infirmary isn't far, for obvious reasons. She'll be in good hands." The way he slanted his eyes over to Delfi said that he hadn't missed the young woman's anxiety. "Now, explanation time."

Jaskuto started to speak. Syrus snorted and cut him off. "You got overruled, didn't you?"

The man shut his mouth with a click.

"Probably with the same logic I was about to use, yeah?" Syrus looked at Markos as Delfi went to cling to the railing of the stairs and watch the medics descend into the ship.

Markos's eyes crinkled. "If you mean the logic that they have no way to hide the fact that they took your auto-pay if they want to continue doing business with us, then yes." The humor drained from his face when he turned to look at Jaskuto, replaced with iron determination that rang like a bell in Syrus's head. "Promises given are promises kept. Your organization made a promise to this man and his companions. Reneging on that promise on the basis of fear is cowardly and will be reported to your superiors."

"I took my orders *from* my superiors on this," Jaskuto growled, heat rippling the air around him.

Markos frowned. "Then it will be reported to *their* superiors. We need you far less than you need us, young man."

Syrus couldn't resist. "If you need to know who the head of the Kiprinog is," he said to Markos, "I can tell you." He looked at Jaskuto. "I've known who he is for years."

As predicted, the Kiprinog man's attention and hostility shifted from Markos to Syrus. Syrus bared his teeth again to remind the little shit just what he was dealing with.

Jaskuto blanched.

"Now." Markos clapped his hands, apparently forgetting that he was giving Jaskuto a lecture on the basics of integrity. "Let's get you settled. Jaskuto, can you let the bridge know that we've reached our *expected* cargo load and are ready to depart? Ask them for an ETC to the Barb as well. Thank you."

Syrus watched the man stalk off towards one of the blocky communications towers that lined the walkway down the center of the landing bay. "He's too stupid to understand the politics of the truth, isn't he?"

Humor bubbled and popped against his skin, mixed with the hissing slide of scorn. "You do him an injustice. He's not stupid. He's willfully ignorant of consequences. As all his kind are."

Syrus turned to raise an eyebrow at the other man.

Markos's mouth twitched up at the corner. "I remember another man like him. Not with the same consequences in his future, but—"

"I thought there was only one consequence for sin, no matter what the variety."

Markos flapped a hand. "Yes, yes. At the root, it's the same. The manifestations on the mortal side of life tend to be different, though. In his case, he's so concerned with fighting his particular battle, it blinds him to the larger war."

Syrus shifted so he could keep an eye on Delfi, who'd practically climbed halfway up the outside of the railing edging the steps. "And what war is that, priest?"

"When those who devour the stars come, he will find that they will not martyr him for his cause as he has anticipated his struggle against the Empire ending. His choices will be survival or annihilation. His ideals will hold no place in that equation." No humor now. No sarcasm. Nothing in voice or emotion but straight sincerity. "He will learn the truth of what I just told him. We don't need you. Your politics, your approbation, or even your permission. But you need us. More and more every day."

And there was no arguing with that.

TWENTY-FOUR--SYRUS

You think they're not sending spies to our side of the
Barbican? They are! Sire, I don't care what the treaties
say! We need to know what they're up to.
- Isloste Boret to the Fuerrus Boloto, 0576.12.08

Markos stalled them in the hangar long enough for the medics to
unload Jossa's medunit. He used the time to wrangle Delfi's name out
of her. It took almost a full minute for the young woman to force the
word out of her mouth. Less than that for Jaskuto to call attention to
himself again. Syrus nearly laughed when Delfi elbowed the obnoxious
little fuck. These Kiprinog people could be even more prejudiced and
stupid about women than the nobility. He wasn't sure if Delfi'd done a
deep enough read on any of them to figure out the reasons.

She'd probably run screaming when she clued in.

The trip to the infirmary didn't take long, Thank fuck, because his
brain was still thinking in code and his fingers kept wanting to twitch
over a keypad. He focused on his surroundings instead, wondering if
every ship that'd taken his old team through the Gatekeepers'
Barbicans was as odd as this one.

For all this was supposed to be a Kiprinog ship and under Imperial
authority, the Gatekeepers held more influence than he'd thought.
Hell, this was a Gatekeeper ship, complete with ramped inclines and

curved walls that no Navlad ship ever had. It almost felt like a Fleet ship, except for the lack of snakes and thorns covering the walls.

The infirmary was as sterile as any other, even the *Edde Belo's*. White and light gray metal walls were set with glowing panels of light. Cupboards were mounted everywhere but the ceiling, each with its own lock indicator blinking slowly at the corners of the doors. The ceiling was painted too. A long line segment with a short crossbar at one end and a snake in navy blue wrapped around both. Syrus had never seen anything like it, even in the parts of Gatekeeper space he'd been through before.

Granted, he'd never had to infiltrate an infirmary. Maybe he'd recognize the symbol otherwise.

He did recognize the things bolted to the floor of the room. Row upon row of medunits. Some in the Imperial style, angular and solid. Some in a style he didn't recognize, an odd blend of curves and square angles as the snake and cross. Others were sleek, like fast aero ships. They reminded him of the units the Fleet used. Now wasn't that a disturbing thought?

Others were odd. Like someone had started installing the base of a unit but forgotten to add the part that actually held a person. He closed his mouth on the questions. Curiosity could get him killed if he let these people know he was paying that much attention to their medical care. They might decide it was a state secret or some fucked-up nonsense.

He'd heard of stranger.

Delfi pushed past him as they came through the door and set a straight course for one of the Imperial medunits. The only one, Syrus saw, that was in use. Yellowish-green light traced its seams' angles. He'd missed the switch. Or maybe the medics here had a way to speed up the healing process.

Either way, they weren't prying Delfi loose from that unit without some sort of lever and maybe explosives.

Fucking sousi.

"What was that?" Markos's voice was mild, but the interest in his eyes was sharp. This close, Syrus could feel the cool effervescent mix of amusement and curiosity along the side of his body closest to the man.

He decided that stepping away would just give the fucker another reason to gloat.

"Why?" he asked, because the Gatekeeper brother kept looking at him like he expected an answer.

"Why... what?" Markos's emotions didn't shift a hair.

"Why are we out? I've been through to the Seps Coalition more than once. You people never let anyone off their ship." He swiveled to look the man in the face. "So why?"

The bubble of curiosity vanished, leaving behind something Syrus couldn't identify. Markos's eyes lightened, and he tipped his head slightly but gave no other visible reaction.

Syrus waited.

Eventually the other man looked away, towards Jossa's medunit. It wasn't all that far down the room. Delfi was practically glued to it, forcing the medics to work around her. Checking readings, Syrus guessed. Making adjustments?

"We'll be travelling about twelve hours," Markos said after a moment, his voice quiet. "Then we'll be through the Gate and on our way to Duftorst Station. Have you thought of what you'll do after the waiting period is over?"

Syrus started to bark, "What waiting period?" but one of the men working on Jossa's medunit stepped around Delfi and headed their way. His emotions were as controlled as Markos's.

"Sir." The medic came to a stop in front of them, checking the movement of his fist to shoulder halfway through the salute. It moved his shirt just enough for the high collar to reveal a Karukap rank mark on the side of his neck. Well, that answered that. A runaway soldier. "We have a status on the woman in the medunit," the man went on, apparently oblivious to Syrus's assessment of him. His emotions didn't flicker from the steady thrum of earnest concern and worry. So. Kiprinog, but not a woman-hater like some of them. Had he come to the Gatekeepers like that? Or were they wearing him down?

Syrus held up a finger before the man could open his mouth again and looked over at Delfi. She leaned hard against the medunit, watching them, her gaze wary. When he met her eyes, something flared to life in them. He couldn't identify it by sight or Feel her from halfway across the room. She stiffened, gripping the raised edges on Jossa's medunit with whitened fingers when he crooked his finger at her. Syrus glared and opened a tiny, very tiny, crack in his shields— hard to do with exhaustion pulling at his control—pushing *get over here so you can hear what he has to say about Jossa* at her as hard as he could.

She flinched again but straightened and came over. Slowly. The medic turned to see who Syrus was looking at. Embarrassment soured the air, burning its way up Syrus's sinuses. "Apologies, sir. I didn't realize she would—"

"Don't worry about it," Syrus said before the embarrassment could turn to speculation. "We've been traveling together a while. They got to be friends. You know how women are."

Delfi came up just as he said that last bit. She lashed him with a whip of dull anger before pulling her shields back in place and turning her attention to the medic, all attentive concern.

Syrus gritted his teeth and focused on the medic as well, who looked back and forth between the two of them, a faint frown on his face.

"The report," Markos said quietly, "if you will, Tomas."

"Right. Of course. I'm sorry, sir." The medic drew himself straight and nearly saluted again, stopping himself just in time. "The medunit is one of the most efficient I've ever seen, sir," he said, meeting first Syrus's eyes and then Markos's. "Sensors indicate the extent of the damage was severe. Despite that, in the days the subject has been inside—"

Delfi made a little mewling noise as a fission of anxiety seeped from her pores. Her face turned red as she stopped herself from speaking with visible effort.

The medic must have read that as embarrassment. He looked at Delfi, face softer than it had been. "Don't worry," he told her. "Your friend is all but ready to wake up. According to the readings, the unit is giving her the last few minor repairs. After that, it's a final diagnostic and she'll be up and about." He eyed Syrus, expression suddenly sharp. "Although I wouldn't advise any strenuous activity for some time, sir. Unit-repaired tissue has the same fragility as freshly healed wounds. It won't hold up during... athletic activity."

Syrus told himself that breaking the man's jaw wouldn't do any good. The fucking nerve, thinking that Syrus would undo all the work of putting Jossa's insides back... inside for the sake of sex.

Wouldn't you though? the voice in him asked, sly and oily. *This is the longest you've gone without nailing her to some solid surface since she first started sleeping in your bunk. I'm surprised you're not going into withdrawals already, seeing how much fun you two have exploding each other's brains. What's it going to be like if they decide to take the risk and stop travelling with you? Poor Syrus, what woman will ever measure up to her?*

Syrus took his conscience and stuffed her down to a corner of his mind that never saw the light of day. She was right, the bitch.

A faint mental *pthththbth* was the reply to that little thought.

"Leto." Markos nudged him with an elbow. Syrus looked down at the other man a beat too late. Damn fake names.

Markos ignored the slip. "Are you amenable to the course of treatment?"

All three of them were watching him. Probably knew he hadn't heard a word past "athletic."

Syrus growled and glared at the medic. "Repeat."

His tone of voice, one usually used on young soldiers and those about to be disciplined, worked. The medic lifted his chin. "Since we've already got you out of your ship, the tests needed to enter Gatekeeper space can be carried out on all three of you now as opposed to on arrival. The medunits on the ship and the one with your... companion here can give us a baseline for your state of health. Our review of the data should be done by the time we're through the Barbican. The innocks can be done on you two"—he nodded at Delfi—"now and we can monitor you for any adverse reaction while in transit. Just in case."

Just in case either one of them went into anaphylactic shock or had a seizure or who the fuck knew what else. Syrus glanced at Markos, who shook his head slightly, warning in his eyes. Ok then. No telling the peon that Syrus'd been back and forth through the Barb who knew how many times already, without innocks or exams either. Got it.

Delfi opened her mouth, either to object or give some other opinion. Syrus laid a hand on her shoulder. She clammed up, glaring up at him past a few stray curls of hair.

"Do it," Syrus told the medic. "How long will it take?"

The medic shrugged. "Not long. An hour or so each."

"Right. We do it here, or?"

"Actually," Markos said as he looked at Syrus. "If you'll come with me, we can straighten out some of the details of your travel on the other side. Once Miss Delfi is done with her exam, they can take care of you."

Syrus looked at the man, who smiled benignly, not a single emotion fizzing past his skin.

Bastard just wanted to give the medic a chance to question Delfi without a monitor around.

Good fucking luck with that.

A snag occurred to him. Tightening his grip on Delfi, he waited until she met his eyes. "You good with this?"

You going to keep your cool and not yank his tonsils out if he needs to give you a thorough check? Cracking open his shields was just as hard the second time. She rewarded him with the pop-fizz of fear, though she squelched it quickly.

Just don't let on you're sai. And keep your mouth shut. He squeezed her shoulder again, then patted it. *Don't worry. He's not interested in testing your plumbing.*

She really did need to control her temper better, he mused as heat baked his hand and he turned to follow Markos out of the infirmary. He kept the thought locked up safe where she couldn't Hear it. Her face was enough of a giveaway as it was.

>>><<<

Markos didn't speak again for a while, leading Syrus through a maze of curved, angled, and rising corridors. He followed, still fighting the twitch in his fingers that said he should be throwing out code. He hooked his thumbs in his pockets to keep them still.

Finally they came out into a large room. The far wall was convex, puffing out from the floor like some sort of bubble. Its surface shone with far-off stars and the gleam of reflected interior lights. The edges of the bubble showed a seam where they met the walls of the room, the telltale gray of the seal only faintly visible. Well, he'd wondered who built the ship. This answered that pretty definitively. How the hell'd it ended up being used as a Kiprinog ship though? Fleet, Empire, the outer Edge planets, none of them were this crazy.

"Magnificent, isn't it?" Markos went to stand in front of the enormous window and laced his hands together behind his back. "Reminds you how small we are in the universe."

"Reminds me that some lunatics put actual windows in their ships instead of projecting the display like sane people who *don't* want to risk the seal breaking. Or disintegrating. Or whatever it is the seal on these things does when overstressed."

Markos laughed. "You cross an empire full of people who hate you on principal. You pick fights for fun and sometimes profit. And yet show you the stars, real and true instead of sanitized and digital, and you turn into a little old lady."

Syrus snorted. "Sure. Says the man who turns to pudding at the sight of arachnids."

Markos shrugged and looked out at the expanse of stars beyond the window.

Syrus settled in next to him. The man had a point. It was an awesome view; not that anyone would give him a credit slip for knowing the original meaning of that word. He'd seen the universe stretched out around him many times, in many ways. But there was something about all those points of light going on and on, further than the eye could see or most minds comprehend. And yes, there was something different about looking at it through an actual window instead of a projection set in a wall.

Beautiful view or not, Syrus wasn't surprised when Markos drew in a deep breath and opened his mouth to speak.

"Are you having sex with them?"

Syrus swiveled to stare at the man. "The fuck does it matter to you?"

Markos met his gaze, blue-gray eyes steady and stern.

No answer. Just that look. Fucking annoying priest.

Fucking annoying *stubborn* priest. Who had a major say in what happened to him and the girls while on this ship. And probably after. A lot of power to stir up a lot of shit.

Syrus sighed and looked back out at the stars. "Thought you wanted to talk about what we were doing next."

"This has to do with your plans."

Well, there was a concession he hadn't expected. Syrus tilted his head and raised his eyebrows, but apparently Markos wasn't willing to give any more ground than he had. Odd, that. None of his past trips through the Barb included an interrogation like this. There'd been women on his team then. Why now? What did it matter to the man what he and Jossa got up to—and what he and Delfi *didn't*?

"Why don't you come out and say what you mean?" Syrus said after another minute of silence. "Or is that collar around your neck fake?" Markos's religion valued honesty. Before he gave up information that may or may not bite him in the ass later, Syrus wanted to see how well the man followed it.

Markos snorted and looked back out the window. "Wasn't born a priest. Wasn't one when you first knew me. Think we have personality transplants when we take our vows?"

"I think you're a priest of a Brotherhood on a Gatekeepers ship crewed by fucking religious rebels. I think you weren't sent here because you bow nice and stick your ass in the air while you do it."

Markos laughed. "Come now. You know better than that!"

"Do I?" Syrus turned to look fully at the man. "Aside from the religions you claim, how different is your Brotherhood from the Kiprinog? Both trafficking people. Neither welcome in Imperial space." Both made entirely of men. That last one hung in the air between them like a poisonous cloud. Syrus knew the mandates of Markos's religion. Knew why the Gatekeepers and Seps Coalition beyond refused entry to the Kiprinog members unless they disavowed its cause. On the political level, those made sense. Why invite people who lived to stir shit up into the carefully kept bubble of safety without some assurances for their long-term behavior?

"There are rumors," Syrus said quietly, "of rites the church novices are required to undergo. To prove that they're—"

"And are there rumors of the punishments for that behavior?" Markos's voice was tight, his eyes hard. Tiny heat shimmers wavered through the air around him to lick at Syrus's skin.

Syrus leaned back on his heels and smirked. "There are." He shrugged a shoulder. "Well, there were. Nice to know you're honest enough to admit the issue exists."

Markos's eyes widened just a fraction, and his hands tightened. Sharp surprise replaced the heat of anger. Then it vanished. Markos sighed and shook his head. "This is not a matter to joke about. Or provoke. I know—knew you as well as anyone. I'm here on this particular ship because we do not allow Imperial ships through the Barbican at all, but our treaty does not allow the vessels we use for transport to be crewed by Gatekeeper folk." He pulled his longish hair aside and bent his head so Syrus could see the small silplat square stuck just behind his ear. "My presence quite literally keeps the ship running."

He looked up again.

"You are lucky that I was the brother assigned to this particular run. Next trip goes to the followers of Mohammed. They are far, far less forgiving of..." He waved a hand in a vague sort of way.

Syrus frowned. "And I'm back to my original question, Markos. Why the fuck does it matter what I am to those women?"

"It matters what you may have *done* to them."

Oh. Well shit.

That made more sense.

"They are going to be checking the list of injuries that the medunits repaired while the women were in them," Markos continued, as if Syrus were a small child. "Will they find vaginal or anal trauma?"

Syrus waited for his conscience to smack him upside the skull with a torrent of memories, but nothing came. That was almost more disturbing than the echoes of screaming and the spray patterns of blood on walls engraved with snakes and thorns.

"I said, will they—"

"I heard you the first time," Syrus snapped. "No. Maybe. It's been..." He ran the numbers in his head. "Been three or four days since I nailed Joss to any solid surface." He held up a hand when Markos glowered. "She agreed to it. Her fucking idea even." Now wasn't *that* an unfortunate choice of words?

Markos shut his mouth, but his glare didn't go anywhere.

"And no," Syrus continued. "I haven't touched Delfi." Not for lack of trying on her part. Better to keep that bit quiet. None of the shit that'd happened to her, or her fucked-up way of coping, was any of Markos's business. Not only that, but saying more would fly dangerously close to a shit ton of information he'd rather stay locked in his head. Not even the girls knew everything about their time on the *Edde Belo*, and that was the way it should stay.

"Her behavior towards you seems combative," Markos said. "And her reactions to myself and Jaskuto are concerning."

Syrus snorted, remembering how Delfi'd imposed the moratorium on sex back on the Customs base. It seemed like fucking ages since she'd stormed off the bridge and back to her bunk.

"Ahem." Markos snapped his fingers quietly.

Syrus yanked his eyes away from the stars on the other side of the window and looked at the man. "Delfi's made of piss and vinegar. She doesn't like me much. Jossa and I pulled her out of a... bad situation. She's not looking to end up in similar. Now. Since you've gone and interrogated me before I've slept, eaten, gotten washed up or anything, mind telling me what all the fuss is about the girls? Better, what's it got to do with our plans going forward?"

Markos crossed his arms. "If they wish, they will be offered sanctuary at the monastery of the brothers. Till they are healed in body and soul and ready to find their feet in the Coalition."

But no sanctuary for him, Syrus noticed. He shoved his irritation down and tried to think rationally. His monster was quiet. So was Rissa. That was good, because he didn't need either chipping in on this. Tell Markos about the bounty on his and the girls' heads? Man already knew the local nobility was after them. No one else could have tried to strong arm the Kiprinog into refusing transport.

Tarva and her crew were more dangerous, though. Fieltar was from the Seps Coalition. Although the man had been a boy when his family left the protected systems, he knew ways to get through the Barbicans that none of the others on the crew could manage. Hopefully, whatever'd happened to him back in the Guest House had put Fiel out of commission for a good long time, if not permanently.

Here he was then, back to the same problem. Follow through on the original plan? Let the girls off with Markos right through the Barb, in a place where they'd be relatively safe? Or face the fact that whatever political power the Brotherhoods had in the Gatekeepers, he'd never known anyone in the sects to be militant? They'd give sanctuary, yes. But could they hold that against the sort of assault Tarva would make on the place?

He doubted it.

"You do that," he said finally, "and you might find your precious monastery under assault."

Markos stiffened. Syrus went on before the priest could get a word out. "Bounty on our heads. All three of us. Most just want me dead. Those two, though. They're valuable to certain people. Lot more than I am. People will come for them. And they won't play nice if they think you're going to turtle up and refuse to let the girls go.

"Told Del already. They're better off coming further into the Seps with me."

Markos didn't lose a bit of his indignation. Was that suspicion curling across the floor around him? Whatever it was, Syrus felt like someone was systematically pulling the nerves from his body.

"Let me put this another way," Markos said, voice cold. "Unless we are absolutely *sure* that you are not hurting them, those two will not be joining you in whatever future travels you have planned."

Well, that was about the dumbest thing he could have said, Rissa muttered quietly.

Syrus ignored her. The rush of blood in his ears. The snarl of the monster's rage flooding his veins. They pulled his focus. Washed the world in black spots and red afterimages.

Acid fear stung his arms, face, and torso. The monster gobbled it up and went looking for more, a low growl building in its throat.

Syrus gathered the scraps it left behind and clung to reality, using them as an anchor while he looked for the source. For Markos.

The priest stood stock-still, face blank, eyes dilated, pulse fluttering under the sun-weathered skin of his exposed neck. His kept his hands splayed open at his sides. Smart. Smarter, not to have run.

Somehow that helped. Helped shove the growling, snarling *thing* back into the hole it was supposed to live in. The fear bit deeper into his mind, no longer dulled by rage. Syrus stole it before the monster could get hold of it, using it to give his mental muscles the strength to shove the lid over the hole and lock it down tight.

Markos had the girls' best interests at heart. Markos was a priest to a god that had nothing to do with fucked-up Ancestors and their just as fucked-up Progeny. He believed in his calling. He wouldn't see the girls as assets to be used the way Quinn would. Or anyone in the Empire.

Still. He'd made some assumptions that needed to be corrected. Syrus unlocked his jaw. "Who are you to dictate what we do? Whole point of leaving the Empire was to be free. Isn't that the deal? A system, a planet. Fuck, even a base or hollowed-out asteroid where anyone can find a home and be free?"

There, let him chew on his own false advertising. Maybe it'd slow the man down enough for Syrus to get his heart rate back under control.

When are you ever under control?

Syrus growled at her and looked back out at the stars beyond the window, hunting for the brighter specks of light that signified—and wasn't that a word—man-made satellites masquerading as stars. One of those was the frame of the Barbican. It should be brighter than the rest, given their nearness. But he couldn't see it. Maybe it was on the other side of the sh—

"If you were normal immigrants," Markos said, not a trace of emotion in his voice, "then yes, that promise would be for you. You, and they, would be given orientation and aimed at the destination we believe might best suit your temperament. But our rules are more strict now than the last time you passed through the Gate." The twitch of his lips said he suspected that Syrus had been through since, but not in any way that could be tracked. "Even the usual newcomers are checked for abuse and pulled aside if we believe there is cause for worry.

"None of those people are you."

"What's that supposed to mean?" Syrus turned to look at the man. Markos's emotions were locked down again, but the gleam in his eye was clear. This wasn't going to be good.

"Aside from the fact that you and yours have, on multiple past occasions, entered the Gatekeepers and Seps Coalition on false pretenses, under fake identities? With the sole purpose of stealing our secrets and in some cases, tech?"

Syrus glared at the man. "They're not mine."

Not anymore, his conscience reminded him.

Markos kept going, oblivious to the shouting match going on in Syrus's head, just as serene as if he weren't dropping seeker bombs all over Syrus's plans. "We may not use the nanites in our blood," he said. "We do not subscribe to the beliefs that your people hold. That does not mean we don't have the tools to sequence DNA. Or parse the data from your nanites."

Well shit. That was something he could have used back when he was making stealth runs inside the Gatekeepers for the military. His old superiors couldn't have known, or his team would have been given some other cover. Or a better masking tech.

Like what, complete blood transfusion?

He ignored the criticism and refocused on Markos, who was still a closed box as far as his emotions went.

"Why would you care about nanites?" Syrus asked.

The twist of Markos's mouth said that he understood what Syrus really meant. "We live apart from the Empire. That does not mean we ignore it. Our people have been crossing the border since before the first consolidation of your boundaries, when your people—"

"Not my people."

"Yours by default, my friend. Seeing as you were not born to *us*."

Syrus clenched his jaw but didn't protest. Man had a point.

"Every layer of your society," Markos continued, "has been seeded with our spies. It's far easier for us, of course, than it is for you."

Yes, yes, Syrus wanted to say. I get it. You are engaging in basic diplomacy and covering your asses in case things go to shit. Get on with it.

But saying all that wouldn't speed this up any. In fact, it might just close off the flow of information entirely. Lacking any other weapons right now, information might be the only thing that saved his hide once he was inside the borders of the Coalition.

You want to hold on to that thought, Rissa said quietly. *He's not the only one who knows things.*

Truth.

The problem would be getting in a position to make the things he knew most valuable at the right moment. And not getting shot afterwards.

"So," he asked instead, "If you people have all this knowledge, all these spies. Why haven't you used what they're telling you about the Svis Konanuog invasion and closed your Barbs?"

Markos shrugged and looked out at the stars, something flickering across his face too fast for Syrus to read. Regret? Fear? With the man walled up as he was, there was no way to tell. "It's not my area," the priest said. "Although I will remind you of the tenats of my faith."

"Yours isn't the only faith in the Gatekeepers," Syrus replied, "or the Coalition. Don't think I can't remember that they're actually two separate entities." He hid a smile at Markos's reaction to the word. Wasn't just Tarva who'd owe him money for words. "And unless you've had a massive fucking shake-up in your politics, no single one of the three major religions you people like to fight about has enough clout to dictate policy in the face of cold reality."

Markos laughed. "True. But. Still not my area. My order merely facilitates travel and offers rest to those who need it before moving on."

"You mean policing who's allowed through the Barbs and who's left out in vacuum."

Markos looked back at Syrus. "Exactly. Which brings me to the point." Now he turned fully to look up at the nehkeh man, eyes serious and face carefully blank. "Did you know that your companions have previously applied to enter the Gatekeeper system?

Syrus stared at him.

"They applied from a different ship under different names, together with five others."

Fucking shit on a stick. Why hadn't either of them ever said anything?

Markos's lips tightened. "The most interesting part is that they made those applications over three hundred years ago."

Even the monster lay quiet, waiting to see what the next bomb would be. There had to be another one. This couldn't be Markos's end game.

"I will not ask where you found them," the other man said. "It is not the concern of my order where the refugees come from. Only that they are cared for." He stopped when Syrus snorted, then continued, just as calm as before, "Once you are inside the Coalition, there will be questions. They will want to know how a man of the last true Emperor's lineage came to have two Imperial concubines in his possession."

"They're not—"

Markos kept talking, eyes narrowed and mouth a thin line in his face. "That is not how your people see it. Therefore, it is not how mine will see it.

"Make your plans, Syrus lis Tova af Mitachte." Syrus's real name dropped like a stone in the quiet of the room. "Go where you will in the Coalition. If the women are approved by the medics, if they choose to accompany you, fine. But know that when the people who ask these questions decide that it is time for answers, you will be called back. Or tracked down and brought in. You've done much damage to us in the past. You will have to pay it back."

Syrus stared at the man, jaw working and fingers twitching, but not to type code. The bastard. The motherfucking, hypocritical bastard. No wonder he'd overridden the Kiprinog rep to allow them on board. No *wonder*. Fucking shit-eating prick! How long had he known? How long?

Looks like you just jumped out of decaying orbit and dropped yourself into a sun, Rissa muttered.

She was so helpful, stating the obvious.

But where was the monster, ready to tear the priest limb from limb?

Maybe you're not so much pissed as disappointed that your brilliant escape plan just got blown to bits?

"You may return to the infirmary to discuss whatever innocks you need with the medics," Markos said, almost carefully. "I expect there won't be many, considering past exposures."

Syrus glared at him.

Markos ignored it. "You are not a prisoner, but there are sections of the ship where you are not allowed."

"No shit." The words sounded like gravel, even to Syrus's ears.

"No shit," Markos agreed, inclining his head, then gestured again at the door leading out of the room. A younger man in the ship's uniform stood there, hands folded behind his back. "Go. Let the medics do their work, get some actual food in your stomach. For the love of everyone's nose, take a shower. And if you will take an old friend's advice, think of what you might be able to tell the council that will make them look more favorably on you."

Syrus ground his teeth and turned on his heel. He knew exactly what he had of value. And it wasn't the accounts he still hadn't accessed. If he even wanted to risk opening a connection to the data feeds from whatever terminal they let him near.

There was no help for it. He'd hoped to fade away. To be just one of many people running from the wars. The Fleet. Quinn. They were the only bargaining chips he had to avoid a cell. Or a breeding program. Or whatever the Seps had planned for the misbegotten child of a long-dead line.

Fuck.

Twenty-Five--Delfi

If we build a society and imbed it with a religion that emphasizes that society's inability to survive without its priesthood, it doesn't matter how far afield they stray. They will always return to the fold.
  - unknown author, Imperial Records 0532.09.21

They separated her from Syrus very easily. She didn't care so much about that as the equal ease with which they steered her away from Jossa's medunit.

All it took was for the medic to step between Delfi and the medunit, another to offer food, and for her traitorous stomach to growl very loudly. Her abbreviated meal aboard the escape ship had been a long time ago.

The two men had her bundled down the length of the room and into a small office before she had a chance to do more than lay her fingers on the outer shell of the medunit. The head medic parked himself on one chair while the other slipped back out the door, and she realized she'd been tricked.

She wasn't sure what kept her from punching the man and running back into the main room. The look in Syrus's eyes as he left with the priest? Or his words to her before they were taken from the safety of their ship? Whichever it was, she managed to remember that she was supposed to be the stable one. The one who didn't run mad the minute she was separated from Jossa.

Right. At the moment, she felt as sane and stable as a rabid bajbar.

Maybe that was part of the problem. Whatever she was feeling, she had to give these people the impression that she *wasn't* part of a sousi bond. She'd already raised too many suspicions. Paid too much attention to the medunit keeping Jossa alive at the expense of everyone around her.

They were inches. *Inches* from freedom. The best way she could keep Jossa safe in the long run was by pretending they were nothing more to each other than travelling companions.

Which meant playing a good little woman and not causing a scene.

The medic sat, still waiting for her to come to a decision. She wondered how many sousi pairings he'd seen in the past. The way he'd spoken to Syrus and Markos meant he was probably military. Even in her own time, the military'd kept a monopoly on sai, even more so than the nobility.

She held out a mental hand, trying to feel his mind. He had shields, though not as good as Syrus's. She touched his surface thoughts, dipped a millimeter into his subconscious, and found her sai skating off into the ether.

Delfi landed in the second chair with a thud, trying to wrap her brain around what she'd found in the medic's head. No wonder the men back on the base had been so dismissive. No wonder Jaskuto was so antagonistic towards Syrus and Markos.

Kiprinog.

Anathema to everything the Empire stood for.

It wasn't just their preferences. She'd seen those before. Even in isk Churusimpir lis Kuchrog lis isk Fuerrus, there had been carefully hidden relationships. Friendships passed off to the Chataf Kuchru and Emperor as pseudo-sousi, sacrilegious though they were. She'd found more after their escape. Women *and* men. Most were much more circumspect than even the women of the harem. The men most of all.

A woman had few legal or societal recourses to avoid the men in her life making free with her reproductive system, no matter her inclinations. Who cared what a woman wanted when she could be forced anyways? You didn't need a woman lucid, or even conscious, to make use of the oh-so-valuable womb inside her.

From what she'd seen back then, and again in this man's mind, the dangers were even greater for men who turned their backs on the line between Ancestors and Progeny. They didn't have uteri or ovaries to save them. Death came swift and without trial for any who strayed from the righteous path.

The Kiprinog weren't just smugglers. They were a heretical army doing their best to undermine the Empire itself.

Jossa's brain might explode when she woke up and found out.

Ancestor's behind, let them be off this ship before that happened.

"I thought we could start with introductions," the medic said aloud.

Delfi blinked at him. "Aaah." Great. Make him think you're a babbling idiot.

"My name is Karakof." The medic held out a hand for her to take.

Delfi eyed it. This again. Why couldn't they let her stay anonymous? Nondescript? Safer for everyone involved that way.

Less embarrassing too.

Karakof seemed to understand her hesitancy. He set his hand back on his desk. "That's ok. We don't see many fresh faces. I get a little—"

"Here we are." The second medic shouldered his way through the door almost before it finished opening. He carried a silplat tray loaded down with plates, a bowl, and two cups. One held liquid, the other eating utensils. The smell that followed him into the room was enough to make Delfi's stomach start growling all over again.

Karakof sat back to make room so the other man could set the tray down on the desk. The medic made sure everything was in place, gave Delfi a half bow, and vanished from the room as quickly as he'd appeared. She blinked at the door as it slid shut.

"Nojach is a bit... fast for the rest of us. But he does his job well. Please. Eat. Do you mind if I join you?" He tapped a finger on the chrono displayed in one corner of the desk's screen. "I haven't gotten a chance yet today."

There were two empty plates on the tray. Obviously Nojach had assumed his colleague would join Delfi's meal. It'd be almost the pinnacle of rudeness to refuse. She handed him an empty plate and offered the cup with eating utensils before selecting her own and digging in.

Twenty minutes, three soft flat circles of bread wrapped around meat strips—actual *meat*—fermented dairy, and chopped vegetables, and Delfi could finally feel her stomach unstick from her backbone.

Of course, that was when her exhaustion made itself fully known. And when Karakof started in with the questions.

She took back every nice thing she'd been thinking about him. The sheer impudence of the man, asking about whom she'd had sex with, the nature of old scars, what she knew of *Jossa's* relations and *her* scars. She wanted to scream at him. Ask what he thought he was doing, prying at her like this. Why did he have to pull up old hurts, ask her to lay them bare, and then salt the wounds?

For once, she blessed her inability to speak in anything but He'la. Luckily, Karakof hadn't been there for her stuttering attempt to give Markos her name. Let him think her a mute. She wasn't going to play his games, no matter how well meaning he might be. Not without him unshielding his mind so she could read his full intent.

He wouldn't.

So she wouldn't either.

Finally, he ran out of ways to rephrase the questions and sat there pinching the bridge of his nose. "Ma'am, I understand that what I'm asking is extremely intrusive and not at all the norm. Please understand that I am only trying to help. If he was the source of your injuries—"

Delfi shook her head before she could stop herself.

"Alright then. Even so. Your medunit reports a physical history of assault of your..." He faltered to a stop. "If he has raped either of you, he must be held accountable."

Rape? Where did a man of his inclinations get the right to talk about *rape*? What did he know of it anyways, not being a woman or sai? Delfi bared her teeth at him and grabbed the last of the soft bread rounds, dipping it in the fermented dairy and taking a very large, very uncouth bite. Then she chewed. Loudly and with her mouth open.

It took more energy than she'd expected, and she waved in her seat as her vision grayed around the edges.

Karakof appeared beside her in the next instant, one hand on her shoulder to steady her. "I'm sorry. I assumed that since the medunit let you out, you were in better shape." Two fingers pressed to the underside of her wrist. "We can put you back in. Check for any damage it may have missed."

No. No! She'd spent too much time locked in caskets and medunits as it was. This was just fatigue from fighting Agadi for control of the escape ship. Shaking her head, she pulled her hand away from the medic, set down her food, laid her head on the edge of the desk, and gave a soft but obvious snore.

Karakof's shielding slipped slightly. Just enough for her to hear him think *well I'm an idiot* before he pulled up the walls again. "Right, got it. Many, many apologies. I don't blame you in the least. We can put you up in one of the bunks if you'd like. We don't have passenger quarters, but we aren't at full crew occupancy. Would that be amenable?"

She hauled herself upright and nodded.

"Do you need assistance?" He half stood, half crouched next to her, one hand on her elbow and the other out for her to take. This time she did give him her hand, bracing her weight against his as she found her feet. She managed a smile for him, took a step towards the door, and swayed again.

Arg!

"Here." Karakof took firmer hold of her elbow and punched the button for the door. "Let's get you a glide-chair."

She wanted to argue, but the idea of not having to walk however far between here and a bed was too tempting. She waited while the head medic summoned Nojach again, let them help her into a glide-chair, and dozed the entire way to the bunk. They collaborated to bundle her into bed and wrap her in covers.

Then sleep clobbered her over the head, and she knew no more.

>>><<<

She was out long enough for dreams to set in, run their course, and leave only faint impressions of angular white surfaces, soft fur, and a rumble like thunder in her bones. Wakefulness came in stages, giving her the time to adjust to her surroundings and assess the noise of the room around her. And to feel along the bond for Jossa's presence.

Still nothing.

That occasioned a bit of crying. If she dampened more than one of the pillows and got snot all over the corner of one blanket, well, there was no one here to judge her for it, and she wasn't ruining bedding for anyone who would need it in the near future. All the blankets carried the odor of stale air about them when she appropriated them from their assigned mattresses. The pillows were crisp and undented by use.

Once she'd wiped her eyes, tested the bond again, and satisfied herself that Jossa was truly out of reach for the foreseeable future, she swung her feet down over the edge of her mattress and looked around.

She was in the bunk closest to the door. On one side was a small open section of floor, barely large enough for two people to pass shoulder to shoulder. From where she sat, she could see a door meant to open off the far side of the space. The symbols for lavatory and showers were blazoned on its surface. Leaning around the end of her bunk, she saw that a door opposite the showers would let her into storage. She snorted. They could keep their spare blankets and pillows and whatnot. She was more than happy to see the possibility of an actual shower in her future.

Looking the other way, she found bunks stacked two high lining both walls all the way to the rear of the room.

On the back wall, in the place usually reserved for Ancestral shrines on ships big enough to have crew bunks in the first place, was a sigil of a stylized conical tree.

Well, if she hadn't known already what the Kiprinog stood for, that would have given her a very clear idea. They'd put their namesake tree, the best-known symbol of their predilections, right there in the name. And then painted it all over their ship for good measure. Honestly, did they not worry the least bit about the Imperial Border Guard catching them? They'd find themselves flayed, castrated, and sent to work in the temples as mutes before they could even think to run.

Arrogant idiots.

Arrogant idiots who had helped her and treated her with care.

Nothing she could do about any of that now. She turned her attention to what she could change. The greasy feel of her hair and the faint stink of day-old sweat in her clothes. Her *uncomfortable clothes.*

She had some feeling for reptiles trying to shed their skin. The seams of her shirt, too small in the bust, too short in the waist and too tight in the shoulders, rubbed her into itchy claustrophobia wherever they touched. Her skirt, already little more than a wide belt, was rucked up around her hips. She wanted a shower, but she *really* didn't want to put this outfit back on. Had anyone thought to bring her spare clothes?

No way to know but to look.

Delfi unwound herself from her blanket and stood, then pulled and wiggled until she had the hem of the skirt down where it belonged. She ended up nearly tripping into the small entryway before she managed all the gyrations. A small stool nearly finished her as she caught her knee against it and tried to back up rather than fall over. A pile of folded cloth and a hand-sized screen thudded gently to the floor.

She checked the screen first. No damage. It did give her a small apologetic message stating that this was all that Nojach could find in stores that had any hope of fitting her.

Delfi set the screen aside and picked up the bundle. A loose shirt of green silk, its sleeves big enough to furnish fabric for a whole other garment. And a pair of off-white medward pants that she already knew would be too long in the leg and too tight in the hip.

Then she noticed that there was a second stool, also holding a burden. A plate domed in swirling mist, a temperature seal blinking orange at the top.

However much she'd eaten while in Karakof's office, the time spent sleeping must have negated its presence in her stomach. She dropped the clothes, flicked open the seal, and inhaled the spicy steam as it billowed upwards to disperse against the underside of the bunk directly above. Ten minutes later, she'd cleaned the small platter of meat, sauce, and most of those soft rounds of bread. Full and feeling much better for the rest she'd gotten, she stretched a hand towards the shirt.

Then she stopped. Her fingers were covered in red smudges leftover from the meat sauce.

For that matter, her face felt sticky too. Fine example of a lady she was, eating like a pig at the trough.

Sighing, she got up to look for a cloth to wipe her hands on. And came up dry. The blankets would stain as badly as the shirt or pants. Food murder with evidence left in plain sight was a poor way to repay the hospitality given so far.

But there was the door marked showers, and if that wasn't a hint, she didn't know what was. Plucking the heat seal carefully from the blankets on the bunk, she left it and the plate by the door to the corridor, where neither could mar the clean clothes. Then she elbowed the lockpad for the door to the head and marched on through. Full *and* clean. If only Jossa would wake, the day would be complete.

>>><<<

The decadence of this ship extended to the bathing facilities. Well, comparative decadence. Jossa had told her of the bathing pool in Syrus's quarters on the Fleet flagship, and this was nothing like that. But the extended timer on the hot water meant she'd be able to take her first proper shower in weeks. Not since the last bathhouse she'd found planetside had she really felt like her hair was clean.

Delfi winced and shivered as she slipped through the curtain hiding the shower stall. Syrus had taken her, not Jossa to bathhouses. They were excellent places to find whichever hapless captains Syrus would steal identities from. Although Delfi had refused to tag any of the women for herself or Jossa. Not after that first time.

She scrubbed her back, trying not to wonder where Syrus had picked up the woman who had given her this current maruste. It was a good thing the life the woman'd led had been so ordinary. Now Delfi was stuck with her story, and it looked like she was stuck with Syrus too.

Stay with him? Keep travelling with him? Why in the universe would he even *make* that offer? He tolerated them, they tried not to provoke his killing rages, Jossa turned herself into a rabbit on his usik, and that was about the extent of things. This was supposed to be a temporary arrangement. Get across the Empire. Get into the Gatekeepers system. Go their separate ways, preferably with a nice stack of credit chips to cushion the fall.

The credits weren't going to happen. That was the least of their problems right now.

How was she supposed to decide this? How could she even think of it seriously? It wasn't that she didn't trust him. It was that somehow, she did. He did what he said he would do. He kept his word. She could even account for his hair-trigger temper and plan accordingly for his intermittent fits of rage. In spite of what he and Jossa did to her, she still trusted him. And that scared her far more than any threat he posed.

She'd soaped and rinsed her hair and was just starting in on scrubbing she didn't know how many days of sweat and fear from her body when the door at the far end of the showers slid open and someone padded quietly into the room. Delfi froze, suds dripping from her hand and onto the foot she'd propped against the opposite wall of the tiny shower stall.

No. Not in here. Not trapped in a tiny box. Already naked. A target. No escape.

She looked up. Nothing but blank ceiling, beaded with condensation from rising steam. She looked around. The walls of the stall were more than a foot taller than her and lacked any sort of hand or foot hold. Where would she run to anyway, if she managed to climb up and into the gap between the top of the stall and the ceiling?

The curtain across the front of the stall yielded similar results. Run out? Into full view of whatever man had come to harm her?

Bait, a corner of her brain whispered, traitorous and sly. You were put in here as bait. They aren't all blasphemers. It's a statistical impossibility. You're the first woman they've had aboard in ages. What did you think they were doing, being kind? No. They set you up.

Delfi cringed against the wall behind her. Shower spray splashed over her head, running down her nose and chest. Water was such a pathetic camouflage.

The fuck?

Realization pushed all the air out of her lungs, nearly knocking her feet from under her. Syrus. Not one of the men. Not one of the blasphemers. Just Syrus.

She pushed, but he walled off his mind as soon as he finished the thought.

Would he stay quiet? Or would he call her out? He'd never bothered her when she used the facilities on the ship, but then there hadn't been much opportunity for a situation like this. Jossa'd made sure of that.

Here and now? Well.

"You realize the rabbit act is only pissing me off." Whatever he picked up in her emotions, his voice gave nothing away. The echoes and angles in the room made it hard to tell where he was, but Delfi thought he might still be up near the doors. "Been a long day," he continued, either oblivious or ignoring whatever signals her emotions gave him. "You want to make it out of here in one piece, you suck it in. Or get out and come back when I'm done."

The fear vanished. Delfi found herself clutching the piece of soap so hard that its silplat netting dug valleys in her skin. That *nehkeh*. That total—! Dictating to *her*, when she'd been here first, whether she could finish getting clean or not. All he had to do was pretend to have a bit of decency.

He'd called her rabbit.

She'd show him *rabbit*. There was a reason it was the sigil of a concubine.

Delfi flung open the curtain that separated her stall from the rest of the room and found herself almost nose to naked chest with Syrus.

He jerked back, apparently not expecting her to call his bluff so quickly. Before the sane corner of her mind could ask what she thought she was doing, Delfi stuck her nose in the air and stood straight. Then stayed like that, trying to quiet the screaming in her soul as her instincts caught up with events.

She was trained for this. Raised to it. She had to pull his attention away from Jossa. Keep him from going back to her when she woke. Because sure as Progeny followed Ancestors, he'd manage to talk her into staying with him.

Under his thumb.

And other parts.

Ultimately, he was right. It was safer to keep running than to stay on the border where hunters and nobles alike could track them. His old team had chased them all the way here. Eventually they'd find a way through the Barbican. And then the chase would start all over again.

Siphoning Jossa while she was with Rui had never been this hard. Not even before, when Jossa had sold herself to keep them fed and clothed while they ran. But this? A year now. A full year and change. A year of him mounting Jossa. A year of siphoning off their combined emotional overflow. A *year* of torture, agony. Of crying in the dark and gasping with need that wasn't hers. A year of missing her husband, her rock in more ways than Jossa could ever be. A year of feeling lost.

And he wanted her to walk willingly into the trap that he called safety.

She couldn't. She just *couldn't* go back to living as their emotional sponge. Oh, she could trust him all right. He kept his word, and he'd continue his bargain with Jossa, and who knew when it would end. She'd only survived because there'd been an end in sight. That didn't mean she had to bow her head and take what they threw at her. Not anymore.

The thoughts passed in and out of her mind in less time than it took to draw a full breath. Syrus recovered even faster, shifting his weight so he could look her up and down. She could see it in the way his mouth twisted and his eyes narrowed. Even though he kept his thoughts shielded, she knew enough about men to know what was going through his head.

Do it, she wanted to shriek in whichever language would come out of her mouth. Just get it over with.

"Well, aren't you a sight," he said finally, setting his hands on the rolled and tucked edges of the towel tucked around his hips. Delfi looked, following the vee of muscle from his hip bones to where it vanished behind white cloth, then gulped and looked back at his face. That was a very large lump under there.

His eyes met hers, full of smug satisfaction. The rest of his face was doing... something else. Something she didn't recognize. Little white lines showed at the corners of his mouth. His nostrils flared. A muscle worked in his neck.

She was getting to him.

She was getting to him, the terrified part of her shrieked. What in the Ancestors' names was she thinking?

Delfi cocked her hips, folded her arms under her breasts, feeling damp skin catch and stick, and managed to force a smile as she yanked her shields into place. She couldn't afford to let him feel her emotions, and she couldn't speak Imperial fast enough to make an attempt worthwhile. But if he couldn't read the invitation in her body language, he was at least ten kinds of idiot.

He was many things. Idiot wasn't one of them.

She stayed put as he prowled forward, his own bare feet making hardly any noise. She shifted her crossed arms when he stopped in front of her, pushing her breasts up slightly as she tried to swallow the scream fighting free of her lungs.

Sanity. She was doing this for her sanity. And safety. Sanity and safety, and Jossa would just have to live with sharing and get past the idea that her little sister needed protection from the big, bad nehkeh.

She was already covered in gooseflesh. A little more wouldn't show. At least she hoped so, as Syrus leaned in close enough to share his breath with hers, reaching with one hand to push a wet piece of hair from her forehead.

"You know what you're getting into?" he asked, voice rough like an avalanche of rocks falling down a mountain. "You do this, there's no going back."

Delfi knew *exactly* what she was getting into. She'd been living it secondhand for far too long.

She sucked in a breath, smelling sweat and humid heat and the odd spice of his aftershave, three days old. He finished tucking the hair behind her ear, ran a knuckle down the side of her neck to the hollow between her collarbones, and stopped.

Delfi's heart pounded in her chest. She could do this. She could hold on, keep her shields up, and—

He laid his palm flat on her chest and shoved. Delfi stumbled backwards. Only the narrowness of the stall saved her from landing on her ass as she flailed for purchase along the walls.

"No," he said, stepping back and away.

No? No!? How *could* he?

Delfi pushed herself upright and aimed herself at the retreating man like a particularly clumsy missile.

He spun and caught her before she mashed her face into his arm. Then he wrapped one hand around her shoulder, the other around her waist and pushed again, somehow setting her back on her feet.

Delfi stared at him, shivering—either with rage or fear, she wasn't sure. How *could* he? she cried in her head. He wouldn't hear her, but that didn't matter. He'd had her sister. Over and over and over. He'd grown up with a sousi pairing. He had to have taken at least one of them at some point. Probably both, knowing his appetites. So why? Why had he refused her all those months ago, when she first tried to seduce him? Why did he refuse to end her suffering *now*?

"Get back in the shower," he said, not meeting her eyes. The lump under his towel was even bigger than before. It twitched. Delfi realized she wasn't shielding herself as well as she'd thought.

"Rinse off, get back to your bunk," he continued as if his body weren't reacting to her at all. As if she hadn't exposed herself in so many more ways than one.

She should do what he said. Take the rags of her dignity, finish cleaning her body as she couldn't her soul, and pretend this never happened. He obviously planned to. He was already walking away, assuming she'd obey him.

She almost did.

Like a good little concubine.

Like Jossa did so often now, little though she realized it, coming and coming when called and leaving when sent away. Jossa, who did it all in the name of protecting Delfi.

Who should be the one doing the protecting.

Delfi gritted her teeth and stepped forward, hand outstretched for his towel.

She found herself back in the shower, water splashing over her head, as a huge warm weight blanketed her from neck to knee.

She gasped and got a mouthful of water. Choking and coughing, she tried to get her bearings. What the—

"You don't want this," Syrus growled in her ear. "You think you do. Or you think you have to, but you don't. And you shouldn't. You keep using your body, sex, to shield yourself? Someone will take you up on it." His breath was hot against her neck. There was nothing seductive about him now. "Get it through your thick skull, woman. You're only hurting yourself."

Delfi gulped and gasped. She couldn't breathe. Couldn't breathe! His chest against hers. Couldn't take a full breath. She was stuck. Trapped! Again!

She pushed frantically with mind and hands, looking for escape, for a crack in his armor. A way to get him off, get him off, get him off!

Her vision dimmed around the edges, the sound of the water vanishing into the din that filled her ears. She thrashed and found herself grinding against the length of his usik, that eager and all-too-willing bit of his anatomy that made his every denial a lie.

He wanted her after all. And he could take her.

Unless she fought.

She hammered at his shields, hearing him grunt but not actually hearing it. Somehow she found a soft spot. His snarl cut through the keen growing in her throat. She ignored it, pushing harder and harder against that point of weakness. Heat built under her skin, fury and reluctant lust all at once.

She screamed. Attacked again.

And was through.

The young woman with the pale face and tumble of black hair stared up at her with eyes full of desperation. She was so badly beaten she shouldn't even be alive. Blood stained the white sheets around her hips and thighs. Her legs were tangled with someone else's, the darker skin torn and the muscles beneath pulped, white bone sticking out in jagged spikes. The young woman's fingers bent in directions fingers should never bend as she reached up. An echo of *You came* whispered in the air around her head, half a second before her cracked and bleeding lips formed the words aloud.

Delfi saw her own arms reach for the young woman. But they weren't her arms. They were Syrus's.

Always wi—

And then she was back in the shower. On the floor. Just like Rissa.

But unlike Rissa, she had no Syrus to pick her up.

He was gone.

TWENTY-SIX--SYRUS

*Nehkeh fall in one of two categories when they give in to
their true nature. Rutting bulls or raging bulls. Pray for
one who rages. They kill faster than the ones in rut.*
  - Karukap Mistress of Sai on working with Uvlaku
  units

Syrus stopped inches from the door leading into the main hall, fist
raised to punch a hole through the lockpad. Only the realization that
he was naked stopped him. Fucking bitch. Fucking. Messed-up. *Bitch.*
Who the fuck did she think she was, pushing things like that?

Admit it, you're mainly upset that she broke into your head.

He took his imaginary conscience by the throat and stuffed her so
far down the hole, she wasn't even a glimmer at the edge of his
thoughts. Bitch, what did she think she was doing, undermining him
like that? When he needed sanity most?

Women. Why the hell did he mess with them at all?

Still growling, he pressed his knuckles against the door. He could
barely feel it. He laid his other hand, palm open, against it as well. Then
he leaned forward and touched his forehead to the cool metal.

Cold reality.

Just what he needed. Fuck, he'd nearly ripped Delfi to bits. Worse,
he'd almost let the lust take over.

She'd felt it too, though she probably didn't realize what it was.

He thumped his head against the metal and sighed. Girl had no idea what kind of trouble she'd just dodged. No idea the road she had yet to walk, recovering from what the Fleet's soldiers had done to her. Nothing he said seemed to get through to her either.

He stayed like that until his forehead and the spot on the door were about the same temperature. The vibration in his bones vanished when he took his palm off the smooth metal surface. The ship's generators must be powerful, to make the whole thing hum like this. Or maybe just badly insulated. Shaking his head and massaging his knuckles, he looked around the room.

Shit. He hadn't remembered to bring his clothes back in with him. Not the towel either.

Then he noticed something hanging off the edge of the bunk opposite the one he'd slept in. Cloth. He went over and picked it up. Clothes. Shirt, pants, socks. Not what he'd been wearing when they'd landed in the docking bay.

Well fine, he didn't need the old clothes anymore. Someone else could get them out of the showers. Knowing Delfi, she'd come after him with a stool. Or try to strangle him with her towel. Or who the hell knew what else.

Worse, she'd look at him and turn back into that gibbering little creature what forgot it had a spine.

He'd had enough of finding women huddled in corners, terrified out of their wits. Rissa. Jossa. Now Delfi. Somehow he always had to drag them out and push them into life again.

Except when they were too dead. Then he had to carry their ghosts instead.

He wasn't interested in adding any more voices to his conscience.

The door to the bunk slid open behind him. His balls, already pained and angry at being denied, tried to crawl up into his abdomen when the cooler air of the hallway hit. Syrus grit his teeth and turned around.

Markos stood in the entry. Emotionally, he might as well not've been there at all. But from the look in his eyes and the thin line of his mouth, Syrus could tell the shit would only get deeper.

"What?" he growled.

"Get dressed," Markos answered in a level voice. "Your welcome aboard this ship has been rescinded."

"The fuck?"

Markos kept looking at him, mouth pressed even tighter. As if he'd paid dearly for speaking at all and didn't want to waste any more words.

Syrus took a breath and tried to speak like a human instead of bellowing like a wounded animal. He managed. Barely. "What? The? Fuck? I paid to get through the Barbican. You—"

"You will still go through. You must do so back in your ship. Once on the other side, your future in the Coalition will be decided by a disciplinary council. Guards are waiting to ensure that you make it to your vessel."

Syrus grabbed the man by his oh-so-priestly collar and dragged him across the threshold. The acid burn of fear seared his hand and settled in through his pores, mixing with the caustic boil trickling out along his nerves. Teeth bared, Syrus slammed Markos against the wall. Then again for good measure.

He didn't need his conscience to tell him how stupid this was. He knew it.

Didn't mean he cared.

"Why?" he growled.

"You are not to be trusted around the women." Markos's words were slow and slurred, probably because most of his attention was going into keeping his shields up. Syrus almost told him not to bother while they were touching. Right now, he needed to focus on the auditory input, not tactile. The longer he could starve his monster of fuel, the better.

"Not to be *trusted?*"

"Did you think we would allow you to roam the ship unsupervised?"

Syrus stared, trying to come up with something, anything, besides the bubble and hiss of the monster sizzling through his body.

Syrus shifted his grip from the priest's collar to his throat and squeezed. Acid etched patterns in the skin of his hands, flowing along every ridge and furrow to burn deep through the dermal layer. The monster would transmute it soon. But for a moment, he had some sanity.

"Why?" Even speaking was an effort.

Markos choked and coughed. "Be-Because." He brought his hands up, digging at the tendon in Syrus's wrist, groping for his elbow.

Syrus ignored the priest's attempts to escape and leaned in. "Where are your vows now, holy man? Where are your guesting laws? Your *honor?*"

"With her," Markos rasped, crooked fingers clawing at Syrus's hand around his throat. "Del—"

Syrus dropped him.

Markos tried to keep his feet but skidded on the water puddle that'd formed at Syrus's feet. He landed on his ass with a grunt. At least he stayed there. Smart man.

"Now you listen to me, you self-righteous ass." Syrus crouched to look the man in the eye. It took almost everything he had not to throttle him again. He had enough sanity left to know what killing Markos would mean and just enough self-control to keep the monster from doing it for him. Instead, he leaned in, uncomfortably close. Markos tried to inch away.

Syrus followed. "That bitch has been a thorn in my side from day one. She's been trying to crawl into bed with me almost as long. *She* just came prancing up to *me* naked. And I'm the one sitting before a review board?" The last words came out in a roar, ringing off the bare metal walls and slapping him in the eardrums. Markos went a shade paler.

But he didn't try to get away. "You could have walked away." The breath of his words etched shards of criticism into Syrus's very bones. He twisted so Syrus could see the comm unit and keyed in a sequence. The tiny screen played out the events in the showers from up high. The cam couldn't see inside the stall itself, but its mike picked up Delfi's cries anyway, including her sobs after Syrus stormed out.

"You should have walked away," Markos said. "Instead, you assaulted her."

Syrus got halfway through picking the man up and throwing him at the nearest bunk before he wrenched control of his body away from the monster. Off balance, he staggered and fell. He didn't drop Markos, though, so they landed in a tangled heap of gasping pain, probable cracked ribs, and frustrated rage. Syrus pulled free, kicking at the priest in an effort to get the man away or propel himself away before the monster could do worse.

They lay there, propped up on their elbows and panting.

Syrus stared at the ceiling with its square metal panels interrupted by the odd corner hexagon of a fire-suppression nozzle, air ducts and, yes, surveillance cameras.

Shit.

So much for escape. So much for freedom in the Coalition. He'd fucked himself up the ass. Just for trying to do right by a traumatized young woman.

"If you people were so worried about her safety," he said once he had his voice back, "then why'd you put me in a bunk that shared a shower with her? Or tell me she was in the other bunk?"

He'd checked the door in the wall opposite the showers. It led to a small storage closet with spare sheets, pillows, and a rack of cleaning bots waiting deployment. And he hadn't worried about who was using one of the stalls until he'd recognized Delfi's particular flavor of fear. Fucking hell. Why *hadn't* he just turned around right then?

Why hadn't one of them come out to take care of the water he'd tracked in?

"That is something I plan to look into," Markos said, pausing to catch his breath after each word. "You—" He coughed. Syrus glanced over. The priest kept his eyes on the ceiling. "You," Markos continued, "should have never been put in this position. Either of you."

Syrus shifted his eyes back to the panels above. The monster in his veins was still there but lay quiet. Waiting, he supposed, to see if it had another chance at control.

He shoved at it, trying to push it back to the corner of his brain where it lived, if not down the hole.

"Somebody set me up."

Guilt flashed through the air and vanished, taking a bit of the color from the world along the way. Syrus frowned and sat up to get a better look at Markos. Was it his imagination or was the priest flushing slightly?

"Somebody," Syrus said, still watching carefully, "who wanted an excuse to punish me."

Yes, that was definitely a red face. Syrus just couldn't tell if it was embarrassment or anger for being caught.

"Was that the plan then?" Syrus growled. "Lock me down so the Gatekeepers and the Coalition won't have to track me down later? Easier to use a weapon awaiting *trial*, isn't it?"

Markos shook his head and sat up too. Slowly, wincing in pain and favoring one side. He made it upright—listing sideways, but he made it. "I have my instructions," he said, the words broken by wheezing coughs. When he tried to straighten his spine and open his lungs for breath, he winced and flinched. "My Brotherhood cannot protect me from the vagaries of politics at large. Not if we want to save as many as we can before the Fleet arrives."

Syrus snarled and came all the way to his feet. "Fuck your order. Fuck your politics. You people want me to fight for you? Whole Coalition can go to Hell."

Ah. There's the nehkeh we all know and revile, Rissa whispered, slinking free of the hole. *What are you going to do now? Go back to the Empire and wait for the Fleet to find you? Or isk Tova? Or Tarva and her crew?*

No. He wouldn't wait. He didn't have to. He'd go back to his ship all right. Soon as the docking bay opened in Gatekeeper space, he'd be gone. Jossa and Delfi could stay here and rot for all he cared. These do-gooders wanted to shelter the girls? Fine. They could see how much trouble those two really were. See who needed protecting once Delfi opened her mouth around the wrong person and someone tried to kill her for a witchborn.

Fuck all of them.

Syrus scooped the new set of clothes off the bunk and yanked them on. Markos stayed where he was, a void of feeling, his face blank as he watched. Shoving his foot in the second boot and wrapping the pliable silplat top around his calf, Syrus gave the man he'd once thought of as a friend a last poisonous look, reined in the monster as tight as he could, and punched the lockpad for the exit door. It opened to reveal two men armored and armed with stun batons.

Then, finally, Markos rose to his feet, leaning against the bunks for support as he held his ribs with one arm. "God's grace on you," he whispered.

Syrus only had a second to feel the sorrow leeching through the air. Then the door slid shut, leaving him standing in the hall between two Kiprinog guards. Still damp. Still pissed.

And very much determined that he was never, ever going to let anyone lock him down ever again. Empire, Fleet, women, Seps Coalition.

They wanted him, they'd better be ready to die in droves to catch him.

INTERLUDE II

Panris op Akuev Logs

3786.10.12.1951-

ETA to Barbican fold: four minutes.

ETA to Duftorst Station: three hours, five minutes

Panris op Akuev Internal Communications Log.

Crew Quarters 152: It's done. Subject is on his way back to ship of origin.

Bridge Log, Captain's Note: Subject observed walking towards hangar bay in company of guards. Success of mission acknowledged.

Crew Quarters 152: Let the record state also that I most vehemently protest this course of action. Both how it was accomplished and its intended purpose.

Bridge: Your objection is noted. It has been entered in the logs again. Please see attached note of counter-argument.

Bridge Status Log, Captain's Note: The kristaf-priest from the Order of Kristoph is a single representative of Gatekeepers and Seps Coalition. *Panris op Akuev* is a registered Imperial vessel, not under jurisdiction of Seps Coalition until such time as it passes through the Barbican. While in Imperial space, it must abide by Imperial laws, including the rightful reclamation of stolen property.

Camera 356: Priest observed to pound closed fist against wall. Appears to be injured.

Crew Quarters 152: As a courtesy and in respect for your station, medics are being dispatched to your position and a medunit prepared for you. You may await their arrival or meet them along the way.

Crew Quarters 152: Status of the other subjects?

Camera 15: Captain is noted to pause, look at guests occupying space near the door, and step to one side.

Bridge: Subject One is still in medunit. Medics will update you more completely as to expected time of awakening. Subject Two remains in lavatory. Not visible on camera due to being in shower stall. Note that you will owe the Kiprinog for not involving us in the operation.

Crew Quarters 152: Acknowledged. Take it up with the father on arrival.

-3786.10.12.1955

3786.10.12.1956-

Data access logs for Infirmary, unauthorized user log in. Data accessed, status of female subject occupying medunit 23-A. Report viewed.

Age: unknown

Sex: female

Time to release from unit: five minutes

Chief Medic's Office: What do you think you're doing?

Crew Quarters 152: Checking on my charges before you put me under and deliver me to my people in a body bag.

Chief Medic's Office: Markos, you idiot. We're going to heal you, not kill you. No matter what the captain says, we are still healers.

Crew Quarters 152: Then tell me the status of the woman before your less-than-honorable brethren sedate me.

Camera 824: Two men in medic's uniform approaching door to crew quarters 152.

Chief Medic's Office: You know this is going in the permanent ship's logs? And you'll only be out twenty minutes or so, if I'm any judge of cracked ribs.

Crew Quarters 152: Answer the question.

Chief Medic's Office: Repairs were more extensive than expected, given the unusual circumstances. She will be awake by the time we are through the Barbican. Able to move around before docking. Long-term viability will have to be determined at a later date. Our units aren't equipped for some of the injuries seen. Good thing she landed in a noble's medunit. We'll ask her about her relationship with the nehkeh. See if we can find out what he did to the other girl while they travelled.

Camera 356: Door opens. Subject leaning against wall. Medics move to support. One opens kit, injects subject.

Subject removed from Quarters and transferred to Infirmary.

-3786.10.12.1959

3786.10.12.2001-

Communications Logs access by unknown user. Authorization level admin.

Delete logs from 3786.10.12.1956 to 3786.10.12.2001?

|| Yes ||

TWENTY-SEVEN--DELFI

Your sister can stick her nose somewhere else. This thing we have? It's just ours. Ours from the start and ours till the end.
- Denz to Delfi, the night he asked her to marry him

The nice thing about crying in the shower was that it hid the tears running down one's face. Not that there was anyone to see. But it was the principle of the thing. At least, that was what Delfi told herself as she huddled in the corner and sobbed until she choked, coughed, and gasped in lungfuls of wet air, only to start all over again.

She didn't realize how long she'd been in there until something in the ceiling beeped and the stream of water guttered out. A draft of chill air followed. She shivered so hard her skull knocked against the tiles behind her. Her fingers were so badly wrinkled they looked like dried fruit. Her eyes burned, and her head throbbed from the inside out with every beat of her heart.

This was it, then. She was doomed. She couldn't change facts. Syrus, against all inclination of hormones and his sai, wouldn't touch her to save her. Unless they'd been stupendously lucky, there was still Syrus's old team to contend with and the family of the woman hidden in his mind. She didn't believe for a second that they'd give up their hunt for Syrus just because he'd made it to the Kiprinog ship. Once she and Jossa were on a ship with him, things would go right back to the way they'd been before. Those two riding each other into oblivion and Delfi having to siphon the excess. All that in the claustrophobic space of the escape ship.

Delfi looked at her hands, clenched around the soles of her feet. When she opened her fingers, they shook. Something yawned inside her, soft and slippery around the edges. It wanted to suck her in. Wanted to pull her down.

She was half tempted to let it. Give in, say goodbye to self-control, and let emptiness take her. It'd be easier than trying to reason her way around the gut-wrenching fear and absolute horror.

No. She couldn't give in. Couldn't let either of them know just how fragile she was. Jossa needed her to be a rock, or else who knew how many people could die? Syrus... She wouldn't give him the satisfaction. She'd find some dignity in all this. That was all there was to it.

Delfi clung to the wall of the shower as she got her feet under her and somehow managed to stand. Teetering more than a little, she made her way out of the tiny space. And promptly tripped over a towel on the floor.

Syrus's. The one he'd lost when—

She hiccupped down a sob and groped for her own towel. Thank the Ancestors, it was still hanging from the hook next to the stall door. Tipping her head over to dry her hair only made it hurt worse, so she scraped the unruly mass of out of the way and wrapped the cloth around her body with shaking fingers. It took three tries to get the *tukovoj* thing to stay put.

Why bother? she wondered. There's no one around to see you. You could wander the halls naked and none of them would be interested in you for *that*.

But she'd still be naked. Exposed. They'd *see* her. See the body of a woman unworthy. See and reject, and she would be thrice confirmed as—

Her mind shied away from the thought and tried to find Jossa down the bond. Still nothing.

She almost crumpled again. Keening, Delfi clutched at the towel hook and bent nearly over, trying not to think of what a blessed relief it was that Jossa couldn't pick up on the anguish of her sousi.

If Delfi didn't understand it herself, how in the universe could she make Joss realize? See? *Know?*

Another throb of her head warned her to stand upright, send the blood somewhere else. Get moving, she told herself. Jossa *will* be up eventually, and you need to get yourself straightened out before you have to control her too.

And Syrus.

Ancestors-blessed *Syrus*.

She barely heard the tap on the door at the front of the room. The second noise was louder. Sniffling, she took a better grip on her traitorous towel and shuffled down the narrow pathway between shower stalls to the crosswalk between the doors in either wall.

She did *not* look at the one leading to Syrus's bunk.

Assuming he'd gone back to it.

Maybe he'd changed his mind and gone to hers instead.

Her heart quailed a little at that.

::Delfi?:: Jossa's mental voice was a bit fuzzy. Muffled even. But it was there. ::Disfesa, what's wr—::

Delfi slammed her hand on the lockpad of the door. She got halfway through before the metal panels were even a quarter of the way open. Her towel gave up the fight to stay on her body and sagged around her waist. The man standing just inside the bunk yelped in surprise and backed away.

Delfi ignored him. Jossa. Jossa was awake. Jossa was here!

She skidded to a halt next to the glide-chair taking up most of the floor space and grabbed for Jossa with both hands and her mind. ::Joss! Joss!::

People shuffled and muttered around her. Delfi ignored them. Her sousi was alive. Ancestors bless!

Jossa lifted her head from the cushion built into the back of the chair. Her skin was chalky, her collarbones jutting, and the bags under her eyes big enough to make a cow jealous. "Del?"

Oh no. What was wrong? Medunits were supposed to heal! This looked more like she'd been locked in a box and starved! Delfi glanced around, saw Karakof, and lunged over Jossa's frail form to grab at his shirt. He dodged, hands up. "Easy," the man murmured. "Easy. I promise. She's ok."

Delfi snarled, opened her mouth, and remembered just in time not to speak aloud. Instead, she pointed at Jossa and made her best "What is this?" face.

Karakof looked behind her. Delfi turned. The man she'd nearly run over had picked her towel up off the floor and was holding it out, eyes trained on the ceiling.

Oh. *Oh.*

Delfi took the towel, stomped past the man to her bunk, and grabbed the pile of clothes she'd left there. No use wondering why she hadn't noticed losing the towel. Even as the cause of pain, Jossa would always somehow override any self-preservation instincts Delfi had left.

Delfi wondered how many holes that knowledge would put in her soul before she died. The thought gave her hands some extra force as she yanked the pants up her legs.

"Del?" Jossa murmured, reaching with trembling fingers to snag the shirt before Delfi could do more than pick it up. "Del, what's wrong?" Her voice was scratchy with disuse, but her presence in the mind bond strengthened by the second.

Delfi stared at her sister's too-thin fingers, then looked at the medic.

He shrugged, his attention on Jossa. "The medunit was a very good model. Best there is, in fact. I gather that she was placed in it very soon after being injured?"

Delfi made a face and finished pulling on the shirt. She had no idea.

"In any case, her injuries were extensive. Even given the quality of the unit, because of the fact that she was still healing from a prior injury, and because of where she was stabbed, it took longer for her to heal than originally anticipated."

Delfi froze as the mental image of uterine and status readouts she couldn't understand floated through the medic's mind before settling down below the calculations of heart rate and oh-two sats. She realized he was looking at a small screen built into the cuff of his sleeve. Jossa's vitals?

"We are hopeful that everything will continue healing well," the medic went on, oblivious to Delfi's scrutiny. "But you should have a local physician give her a thorough exam. She shouldn't move around much. Short walks. Nothing strenuous."

Something pulled on the hem of Delfi's shirt. She flinched away on instinct, then realized the tug came from Jossa. Her eyes were clearer now, though her hand still shook. "Del," Jossa wheezed. "What is—"

::Not now,:: Delfi snapped. She couldn't do it. She couldn't talk, not with Jossa like this.

Delfi squeezed her eyes shut. So much damage. So much pain. If only she hadn't broken back in that room on the shadow base. Hadn't lost control of the siphon on the bond. She should've done a better job protecting her sister instead of leaving them both wide open to Kizen's manipulation. No wonder Jossa thought she had to be the one doing the protecting.

At least there couldn't be any athletic sex for a while. That was a small blessing.

::Sex? Delfi, *what did he do?*::

Oh no.

Delfi yanked a double fistful of rage and indignation from Jossa and shoved them into the void before they could manifest as anything more than a stain on Jossa's cheeks. Then she slammed up every mental wall she could manage, narrowing the bond down to the thinnest of threads.

Jossa hissed and stiffened in pain.

The medic leaned over, frowning alternately at his sleeve and the woman on the glide-chair.

::Delfi! Answer me!:: Jossa's hand tightened on the shirt. Delfi resisted the urge to slap at her sister. She'd been exposed enough for one day. She wasn't going to act like a child on top of everything else.

Jossa seemed to get the hint, because she eased her grip. She did not, however, stop pounding on Delfi's mental barriers. Gritting her teeth, the younger woman tapped the distracted medic on the shoulder. He looked up from the readout on his cuff and blinked at her. She waved her free hand at Jossa and did her best to project "And then?" with her face.

Either he understood or he decided that Jossa was in no immediate danger. Pulling a small, hard-sided silplat pouch from his coat pocket, he held it out to Delfi. "These are her records. The data dump from the medunit and my notes. Give them to whichever physician looks at her when you arrive. Make sure you keep a copy for yourself. Regular visits, understand?"

Delfi didn't scoff, but she wanted to. Regular visits with a doctor? While running from bounty hunters? Karakof must have caught something on her face, because he leaned over the float and pressed the pouch into her palm, then wrapped both hands around the whole. "This is *important*. I know what you are. What you both are. If you don't—if she overexerts herself or lets her recovery slack in any way— she could find herself in a lot of trouble. A medunit can only do so much at once."

I may not worship at your altar, his mind said. *That doesn't mean I don't take my oaths seriously.*

Delfi frowned and looked at the pouch. The medic let go and backed up. "The kristaf-priest will be here soon to bring you back to your ship. We passed through the Barbican and into Gatekeeper territory." His mind shifted, but Delfi couldn't pinpoint what was wrong with his thoughts before he spoke again, words overlaid with images of heart monitors and medical data scrolling over a screen. "Remember, ma'am. Regular visits with a local doctor."

Then, before she could protest, he bowed himself out of the room.

"Delfi," Jossa snapped, pulling the pouch from her sister's hand and tossing it aside. Delfi watched as if through someone else's eyes as the older woman laced their fingers together and squeezed tight. "Del," Jossa said again, just as urgently. "What in the name of Ancestors is going on? Why are there images of Syrus naked bouncing around your brain?"

Delfi slammed her shields up, cursing herself for getting distracted enough to drop them. Fool! And fool again! Tearing her hands free of Jossa's, she turned on her heel, looking for an open bit of floor to pace on.

Jossa's chair blocked the walkway between the bunks. Getting around her to the opposite wall was out as well. That left the wall behind her and the door to the showers.

Delfi twitched. No. He might have come back. She wasn't going to risk the temptation to open the door and find out.

What would she do if he had? Scream at him in a language he didn't understand? Try to force the issue again? He'd refused her without Jossa there to distract him. Ancestors knew how he'd react to having his toy back in mostly working condition again.

The mind bond flooded with fury, blinding in its strength. "I'm going to kill him," Jossa ground out. "I warned him. I told him what would happen if he broke faith with me. We had a *deal!*" Her voice climbed in decibels and up the scale as she spoke, ending in a near shriek. "The second I was out of the picture. The second!"

Delfi felt Jossa's emotions boil down the bond linking their minds.

Felt them hit the shields she'd put up.

And found she didn't much care to let them in.

In fact, she herself didn't feel much of anything at all.

Interesting.

She watched Jossa rage, the blood flushing her sister's cheeks with life. The glide-chair wobbled as the Feel pounded the armrest and tried to rise to her feet, vowing ten kinds of bloody murder.

The rests that supported her feet gave way. Jossa stumbled, tripping forward on legs too weak to support her.

Delfi snagged her sister under the arms and shifted her momentum up and back so she landed in the chair once more, all on autopilot.

A distant part of her mind wondered that she'd had the strength to manage it.

The rest of her watched as Jossa thrashed her way upright like an insect flipped on its back.

Would she make it? What would happen if she got out of this room and over to the bunk where Syrus stayed? Attempted murder? Or, more likely, animal sex?

Reality hit Delfi's brain in a deluge of cold horror. No. She couldn't live through it again.

She *couldn't*.

::Shut up,:: she snarled through the bond, taking Jossa by the shoulders and pushing the older woman back into the chair. ::Shut. Up!::

Jossa froze, staring up at Delfi. "Del," she said. "I'm just trying to—"

::Protect me, I know.:: Delfi turned away, trying to resist the temptation to shake Jossa until her sister saw reason. ::I never asked for it.::

"De—"

::Ever!:: Delfi swung around to glare down at Jossa. ::That's *my* job. Mine! I'm the one who's supposed to keep us safe. Keep us sane! And yes—:: She threw her hands in the air as Jossa reached out. ::Yes, I know I failed! But you! You had no right! No right *at all* to take it on yourself to-to—:: Delfi spun and slammed a fist into the metal panel that formed the baseboard of the bunks. "Zo'li o'li shuyeks *kidda'yj* neh!" The words burst out of her mouth before she could stop them. ::Like a child, Jossa! I tried to stop you. Tried to tell you. Don't fuck him. Did you listen? No!::

Jossa stilled halfway out of the chair. "What was that?" Her voice, still husky from disuse and anger, still managed to be hard.

Delfi's hand throbbed. She punched the baseboard again, softer this time. The pain felt good. ::You heard me::

"You. Nearly. Died," Jossa ground out. "You were gang raped."

Delfi felt her back go rigid.

Jossa kept going. "You wouldn't leave the ship. You had panic attacks anytime a man even glanced your way! Who was left, Delfi? Who was left to pick up the pieces and take care of us? Of *course* I babied you. You *were* a—" She clapped her hands over her mouth and dropped back into the seat.

Delfi heard the words anyways. They echoed through the bond, ringing in the silence of the room.

Jossa was right. She had acted like a child. To her everlasting shame, she'd abandoned her duties twice over. Cowering in corners and fainting under the onslaught of all the outside minds crushing her thoughts beneath theirs. Nonfunctional. Useless.

But she'd picked herself back up and clawed her way free of the morass, and Jossa'd been too caught up in protecting her from Syrus to see it.

Syrus, the only man who *didn't* terrify her half out of her mind. Not till today. Short-tempered, violent Syrus. The only one who'd looked at her after the rape and seen a person. Not a broken toy, like Jossa. Not a possible toy, like so many who'd watched her in the bases and cities they'd passed through during their travels.

He saw an actual person.

Syrus, who'd already shepherded one shattered woman across the stars.

"Zhuzhu *jeha'o* o'li innipi nih," Delfi said, words rasping in her throat. She switched back to mental speech. It hurt too much to talk aloud. ::Never, except to—::

"He *just* touched you!" Jossa yelped, finishing the job of levering herself out of the chair. Delfi ground her bruised fist against the baseboard of the bunk, focusing on the pain. If she distracted herself, she wouldn't try to catch Jossa. Wouldn't keep her sister from tripping over her own feet. Wouldn't lose the battle against the sousi bond.

Ancestors knew she couldn't keep this up for long.

Jossa hit the wall with a gasp and a thud, turning her fall into a controlled lean. Rolling to one shoulder, she reached for Delfi's hand with shaking fingers. The anger in the bond ebbed, flowed into a rush tide of guilt, then surged to the fore again.

"Del, he had you pinned. Naked. Tell me how that's not touching you."

If only Jossa knew how much she sounded like Syrus right then.

Delfi shook her head and leaned away.

Jossa's face twisted, one lip curling in a sneer. "Tell me, Del. Tell me how he didn't hurt you. How he didn't bruise you or scare you or any other *odavek* excuse you want to come up with.

"Why, Del? Why would you defend him? After all he did to us? After what his people did to you?" The last words were barely understandable for the snarl in Jossa's voice. Her face flamed. The tendons in her neck strained. Delfi could practically hear teeth grinding.

Actually, those were her own teeth. No wonder she could hear them. Holding back the words that would destroy Jossa. Destroy *them*.

She searched her mind for different words. Words she could say in her head without having to open her mouth. Words just as true.

::He never came after me,:: Delfi said. She loaded the bond with images. Memories. Feelings. Heavily edited. Not the whole truth. The truth would only solidify Jossa's opinion of her little sister as a shattered doll. ::*Never*. Not in all the time we travelled together. And if you hadn't been so obsessed with *protecting* me from him instead of helping me *heal*, maybe you would have listened.

::I told you he was hiding something! That something was off about his story. And you blew me off!

::That night—Ancestors, the whole *month* before you made your deal with him? I was slipping into his bunk, trying to crawl inside his head to figure out what it was. Over and over, he hauled me back to my room. Like a disobedient child! Then, when I finally got the nerve to force my way in, you showed up!::

Jossa hissed and reared back, then scrabbled for purchase as she overbalanced.

Delfi leaned in. Jossa didn't get to escape yet. She'd dug this particular hole. She got to find the bottom for herself. ::And I didn't find what I was looking for. Not quite. But I found something better. You want know what he's kept locked up where no one could Feel or Hear it?::

Jossa just stared. Anger gone, shock ascendant, and horror a close second.

Delfi gave a mental shrug, shedding the emotions out of the bond, away from the sinkhole growing ever larger in her heart. ::He knows how a sousi can lose her partner and survive. Do you have any *idea* what I'd give to know that, what with how you treated me this past year?::

The universe. She'd have given the universe to know how to survive without being hitched by the soul to another person. To Jossa.

The fact that it was the least evil of the truths she could give did nothing to slow the surge of emptiness inside as the great, gaping hole in her soul turned itself inside out and swallowed her up, heart and all.

> Jossa

TWENTY-EIGHT--JOSSA

*One of the hallmarks of those who abandoned the new
colony systems for their own is the utter rejection of
anything and everything to do with sai. Be careful what
you say when you are there. Be even more careful of what
you think.*
  - Mistress of Sai to Uvlaku trainees

Jossa managed to aim her body at the chair she'd just vacated, but it
was a near thing. She couldn't be hearing this. Her ears must be
damaged. The medunit missed fixing them.

Delfi? Live without a sousi? Without *her*?

::Del?:: she whispered through the bond. The bond that still existed.
Had to exist, because otherwise she wouldn't be trying to string
thoughts together. She'd be screaming. Raving.

Lost.

The bond between their minds, their souls, didn't so much as
ripple. Instead there was a wall. Unforgiving and empty as the space
between stars. Black and gaping as the center of a Barbican.

Not lost. Abandoned.

Despair rose, choking off breath, sight, even thought. Jossa panted,
trying to claw her way back to some semblance of sanity, but she

couldn't find her way free of the emptiness. Couldn't drag herself free of the black hole that'd wrapped around her head.

For long moments, she sat clutching the arms of her chair. Her breath dragged in her throat and burned her lungs. Her eyes watered. Her heart fluttered unsteadily.

Delfi ignored her through it all, snatching up the discarded med records. Her face was a mask, white and smooth. Even her eyes were blank, flat blue and hooded.

Then, wonder of wonders, the wall cracked. Not enough. Not nearly enough to grant Jossa access to the refuge of her sister's mind. But it cracked. Before Jossa could quail at what she saw through the gap in Delfi's defenses, her sister spoke.

Not aloud, thank the Ancestors. There was still enough of the bond left for mental speech.

::You know the worst of it?:: Delfi's voice broke around the edges, driving splinters of pain before it. ::We're about to make it to the Gatekeepers. He promised to get us there. And to leave us alone. Freedom, Jossa. He promised freedom and safety from the Fleet. And Ancestor's Balls if he didn't try.::

Jossa found the strength to swallow. Hard.

Delfi leaned down to brace her fists on the armrests of the chair. Jossa wanted to reach up. Wanted to smooth the damp curls out of her sister's eyes. Wanted to pull her close and promise her—

What? What could she promise? Not protection. She'd failed her sister in so many ways. What in the universe could she offer Del to make her listen? To ease the pain?

Something struck her lightly on the forehead. Once. Twice. Three times. Jossa jumped and stared at up Delfi, who pulled her hand back and scowled. ::The hunters followed us,:: she said, her voice flat. ::All the way to the rendezvous. They'll get through the Barb, eventually. The nobles are after us too. We blew up their infirmary and injured a son of the House. On top of that, we're *sai*. They already tried to strong-arm the Kiprinog into denying us passage through the Barb.

::Guess what our best bet is for getting away?::

Jossa stared up at her sister, trying to focus. Instead, all she could hear was "don't want you" ringing with the finality of a death-priest's call.

"Neh!" Delfi waved her hand in front of Jossa's face again. "*Shynks neh! O'li uethga zo'li aksuks'yj nih. O'zo uethga Syrus aksuk'yj nih. Shkrokro nihneh? Nuh phenshuch a'azudi'e nih.*"

Stuck together. Not willing partners. Not sisters. Delfi was *stuck* with her. With a burden she didn't want.

The second half of the statement caught up with Jossa's misfiring brain. She nearly choked on the knowledge. They were stuck with *him* too. With Syrus. No escape. No relief. More days and weeks and months, maybe even *years*, of his company. Of his appetites.

He'd expect her to keep their bargain. There was no way he wouldn't. He'd rejected Delfi. That left only Jossa. She'd had the thin shield of protecting Delfi to guard her dignity. Stripped of that, what was left?

And yet, without him even being in the room, her body sang with need on a cellular level.

Derision burst through the mind bond in fireworks of fury. Delfi threw up her hands and barked something too fast for Jossa to parse, given how her brain had just tried to detach from her skull. The older woman rocked in her chair, clinging to the armrests for balance as she gasped for breath. ::Why?:: she wailed helplessly. ::Why?::

A knock on the door canceled the possibility of an answer.

As swiftly as Delfi'd lost her temper, she sucked it back in, taking Jossa's hopeless despair and rootless lust with it. The wall across the bond stayed in place, but Jossa could breathe again. Could *think* again.

Apparently, despite her distaste for her role as sousi, Delfi was not yet willing to abandon innocent bystanders to the full effects of Jossa's lack of control.

Although if it were Syrus on the other side of the door, Jossa would skewer him herself. Nothing Delfi could do would hold a candle to the pain Jossa wanted to inflict on him.

The door slid open before Delfi could respond to the promise Jossa'd left floating in the bond. It was not Syrus, but another man.

"Miss Delfi," he said, inclining his head at Delfi. His words, in the local trade tongue, were oddly accented. He looked at Jossa and nodded again. "Miss Jossalyn, I presume. It is a pleasure to make your acquaintance. I am Brother Markos. Has Miss Delfi filled you in on events while you were in the medunit?" The look on his face said that he clearly expected she *hadn't*. Jossa reached with her sai to see if his emotions offered any sort of reason for that expectation.

And found nothing.

::Del,:: she yelped in the mind bond. ::What happened to my sai?::

Panic swelled and ebbed, so fast she almost didn't recognize it. Delfi, still doing her job. Well, half of it. She didn't leave behind the grace as she would have before... before Syrus.

"Del?" she said aloud, carefully. It was odd, knowing that she was on the verge of panic but having the emotion ripped from her almost as it made itself known. When she looked up at her sister, she was met with flat blue eyes in an expressionless face.

No. The Delfi she'd known and loved no longer lived in that body.

Delfi bared her teeth slightly and turned away, shaking her head at Markos.

"Ah," he said, voice calm. "A pity. I'm afraid it will have to wait. I have urgent news, and we are too close to docking to afford time for a lengthy discussion. Once we have you settled at the monastery and quarantine is in place, I'm sure you will have time to fill in the details."

Quarantine? For what? How would they be able to escape the hunters if they were stuck in quarantine?

And what in the name of Ancestors was a monastery?

Jossa looked to Delfi, hoping for a clue. The younger woman ignored her, keeping her eyes fixed on Markos.

"I'm sorry," Jossa said, turning back to him. "I don't understand."

Something chimed in the ceiling. A male voice announced that they were five minutes from seal-lock with Duftorst Station.

Markos sighed. "If I may explain as we move? The crew will want to clean these quarters and start resupply for the trip back as soon as possible. We will be very much in the way if we remain.

His face showed no expression. His emotions were just as quiescent. But there was something in the way he held his body. A certain cant to his head that told Jossa his urgency had less to do with being underfoot of the crew and more to do with something else.

Delfi made the decision for her and stepped around behind Jossa's chair, took hold of the guidance handles, and started forward.

"Very well then," Markos said. As if he had entirely expected Delfi to try and run him over with a glide-chair. He stepped back and to the side, clearing the door, then took up station on Jossa's left side while Delfi finished maneuvering the chair into the hall and pulling the train of her dress out of the way before the door slid shut over it.

The medic who'd brought Jossa to the room had told her she could guide the chair in a limited fashion by shifting her weight, if she so desired. Jossa almost told Delfi to leave the chair be but decided discretion was the wiser course. Given Del's state of mind right now, she'd march right out of the ship and off to this monastery thing before Jossa even figured how to turn the first corner.

So she let Delfi push her down the hall, all the while trying to resist the urge to turn in her seat and beg her sister for a way to fix things between them.

The man next to them walked on, oblivious, as another round of announcements filtered through the overhead comms.

Once the voice was done telling all personnel to man their duty stations, Markos spoke. "Apologies for not explaining before now. I am a Brother in the Order of Kristoph," he told her. "We send liaisons out with the various ships and trading organizations who are sanctioned to bring people and goods through the Gates from the Empire into the Coalition."

"Gates?"

"You call them Barbicans."

Jossa frowned. "But we paid the Kiprinog for passage. They are..." She trailed off, unsure if she should tell this man that Syrus had contracted with people considered to be outlaws on the Imperial side of the Barbican.

Markos smiled thinly. "They are smugglers and, to the eyes of your priests, heretics fighting a war of attrition against the established religion."

Jossa jerked her head up to stare at Delfi. Heretics? Did she know? How could Syrus have gotten them involved with what amounted to rebels?

::There's a dumb question if I ever heard one,:: Delfi said, her voice flat.

Chastened, Jossa shrank back in the chair and returned her attention to Markos.

He kept talking. "We are well aware of what they are. We are also aware that, unmonitored, they would still try to slip through the Gate as it opened for traffic approved by the local nobility. Or they would bribe and threaten those who have legal cause to come through the Gates. By dealing with them directly, we cut short any delays that would occur as they are caught and are able to bring people and sometimes goods through that the Coalition may..." He frowned. Jossa felt for his emotions again, but either Delfi's constant suction was stunting her sai or the man was simply good at shielding.

"We do not wish the Imperials to know of everyone and everything leaving their space for ours," Markos finished. Then he shrugged. "I'm sure you can understand the implications of this."

She could. Very much so. And yet. "Given that," she said. "I still don't understand. Why us?"

"Because Syrus and I are very old friends," Markos answered. He glanced at Delfi. "Yes, young lady. I know his real name. And he has a long history of using means such as this to enter our territory. The Kiprinog must still submit a list of applicants to us before they bring their cargo through."

Jossa opened her mouth to ask another question, but he lifted a hand. "Anything more can be explained once you are settled. The quarantine is relatively short. Three weeks. That you have recently come out of a medunit makes things simpler. Once we are sure that you harbor no diseases or parasites and that you do not bring the taint of sai within our borders—"

Jossa was about to refute that last, indignantly too, when Delfi gave another mental yank. ::Take the hint, you fool,:: Delfi snapped.

Jossa shut her mouth.

"... you will be given assistance in either moving on or making a home in this system." Markos looked down at her again. *Now* she could see the warning in his eyes. Feel it in his voice. Delfi was right. She *had* been a fool. Too willing to take offense. Too willing to ignore the hidden meaning of the words and argue against the surface of them.

::Better,:: Delfi said shortly. ::Although—:: She cut herself off abruptly. Jossa turned to stare at her sister.

Delfi's eyes flickered with emotion, but with the barrier across the bond still in place, Jossa couldn't tell what her sister felt.

::Where's Syrus?:: Delfi asked. ::Why isn't he getting the speech same as us?:: She needed to find him, fast. They didn't have three weeks to sit around waiting for the bounty hunters to catch up. They might not even have three days. Who knew when the Kiprinog would make their next foray through the Barbican?

::Maybe because he's been here before?::

::They only let us off that escape ship because you were injured, and the medunit needed a boost. It was implied that we'd have to get back on the ship and debark that way. So. Why isn't he with us?::

"Miss?" Markos asked.

Jossa turned so she could look up at him. "Where's Syrus?"

He leaned back on his heels and waited till another member of the crew trotted past and around a corner. "Ah. Yes. Well, that was the thing I came to tell you, actually. Isk Kallura lis Kerute have reclaimed their escape pod. And him as well."

Delfi stopped abruptly. Jossa jolted forward in her chair. Alarm surged through the bond and retreated to Delfi with all the swiftness of a fire sucked into vacuum. Jossa gasped with the shock of it, clutching at the armrests as she groped blindly for a place to anchor her thoughts.

She found Markos. And the tiniest, slimmest sliver of regret. It showed only on his face, but it was enough to pull her out of the emotionless void Delfi'd left her in.

"Wha?" Jossa gasped. "Reclaimed?" She twisted in her seat to look at Delfi. The younger woman didn't even see her, eyes fixed on the Coalition man, pupils pinned and her face a mask of pain.

Pain? Why pain? Did she feel something for the nehkeh after all?

More importantly, what was this about reclaiming?

"Delfi," Jossa said. "What *happened* while I was out?"

"I'm afraid we don't have the time for that," Markos said gently as he moved to stand next to Delfi, one palm out in a gesture obviously intended to comfort. The young woman shied away from him. He dropped his hand and stepped back. "We have only a short window of time in which we may get off the ship. After that, the checkpoints will not reopen until the next emissary arrives for the trip back through the Gate."

Jossa blinked up at him, confused.

Delfi apparently decided to take him at his word, because she started pushing the chair again, knuckles white on the handles.

"But," Jossa said.

Markos fell into step beside them and shook his head at her. "I've told you all I can, miss. I—" He quieted as a crewman hurried past, intent on the screen in his hands. Once the man turned a corner at the next junction of hallways, their guide shook his head. "I have vows to honor, Miss. Ones that preclude me from explaining further. Once we have you settled, there may be more news."

There wouldn't be. He was trying to pacify her.

If it weren't for the fact that Delfi was *still* keeping up the steady siphon through the bond, barely allowing Jossa to know what she felt before the emotions vanished, it might not have worked.

As it was, logic won. Wincing as her muscles complained of the sudden use, Jossa sat straight in the chair again and dropped the line of questioning.

For now.

Their exit from the ship was a blur of flashing status lights, critical eyes, and impersonal questions. Jossa had an idea that Markos was making their journey from checkpoint to checkpoint smoother than it might have been, but she was too disoriented by the lack of emotion coming off anyone they encountered to pay much attention. In fact, it was starting to become difficult to keep her head straight on her neck.

Delfi stayed silent through it all, nodding or shaking her head as needed. She also kept up the steady pull of emotion through the bond, not giving outward indication that Jossa was anything other than particularly unwieldy baggage. Jossa felt like her eyes had been dimmed and her hearing dulled. Was this what normal people, people without sai, felt all the time? Blind to the inner workings of those around them?

She couldn't even tell if she herself was frustrated, depressed, or happy for the change. Delfi wasn't giving her a chance.

Finally, Markos shook hands with the last man in a black uniform, this one with warm brown skin and a white cloth wrapped around his head in an elaborate knot, and they were on their own in the corridor. Jossa propped her elbows on the armrests and shifted to ease the ache in her side. "Is that everything?" she asked once she'd caught her breath. Would they have to go through all that when they left? Getting ahead of the hunters was going to be hard enough as it was. She hoped

Delfi had a plan for escaping because so far, she couldn't see any gaps in security or chances to shake Markos's company.

"Yes," Markos replied. "Now we can get you settled." With a nod to Delfi and a gesture to follow him, he set off.

Down the hall they went, past gray-painted metal covered in symbols and glyphs she didn't understand. Around a corner, down another long hall and then another. People passed them by, men and women both, in variants of the uniform worn by the entry clerks. But nobody stopped to ask what they thought they were doing, and Markos kept walking with hardly a glance back.

Just when she thought they'd spend the rest of their lives in this warren, they turned a last corner and broke out into open air.

Delfi's grip on the bond wavered as she gasped. Jossa felt awe quiver its way through the link between her and her sister. Jossa agreed.

She'd been on more space stations, bases, and converted asteroids than she cared to remember. They came in all flavors, from narrow twisty stone passages sprayed with sealant and draped in wires, to gigantic wheels of metal and plasglass that left any astrophobic occupants clinging to the nearest wall for fear they'd fly off into vacuum.

But it had been a long time indeed since she'd been in a terraformed wheel. And that had been such a sad, pitiful effort in the face of the glory before her.

"The station is not meant to house many people," Markos said as Jossa's chair drifted to a stop next to him. "As it is only a waypoint, it is less... developed than some would expect."

Jossa stared at the forest and fields laid out below her, curving gently up to either side, and decided that the Empire could probably learn a thing or two about how to make a satellite habitable. Craning her neck, she saw the trees fade and give way to golden fields before the curve of the station hid the terrain from view. In the other direction, the trees changed slightly, climbed a rocky slope, and vanished into what looked like a small canyon.

Then she looked up. And was stunned all over again.

Buildings. At least, she thought they might be buildings. They hung from the inner surface of the station's hub like so many stalactites. Some sturdy and solid, some dangling like beads on a string. Very faintly, she could see walkways and guidewires strung among them. And so many lights. Hanging from every building, cord, and walkway hung lights. Warm like a sun, they lit the interior of the station as bright as day.

"Ancestors," Jossa whispered. Looking at Markos, she asked, "And at night?"

A smile, the first genuine expression she'd seen cross his face. "You shall see for yourself, yes?"

She nodded, then looked back at Delfi. Her sister stood, hands slack on the handles of the chair, and stared at the city hanging from the ceiling. Wonder filled both her eyes and the bond as a flush colored her cheeks. Jossa's heart turned in her chest. So there was something of her sister left in the shell Delfi'd become.

Without thinking, Jossa reached up to touch her fingers to Del's.

Just like that, the magic was gone. Delfi yanked away and slammed the barrier up across the mind bond. Jossa wheezed and clutched at the armrests, feeling tears well in her eyes. Tears of pain, though, not sadness. Delfi had sucked all the emotion back to her side of the bond.

"Speaking of night," Markos said as if nothing had happened. "It comes soon. We should get you to the monastery and settled so you can watch the show."

So soon. So little time left to find a way free of this man without harming him unduly. She hoped Delfi could come up with something. Not that they couldn't overpower him, but making enemies of the people giving them sanctuary was not the way to make a good impression or keep themselves alive long term.

They might just have to wait until he left them alone.

The man turned to the nearest wall and passed his hand over a small scan screen. A moment later, something chimed from a hidden speaker as the vertical surface split, revealing a tiny room. Markos stepped inside, and Delfi followed him. Jossa realized it wasn't a room at all. It was a lift, one wall made entirely of decorative metalwork so the occupants could watch as they were lowered to the forest.

If anything, it was more stunning on the ground level. Jossa stared around as they descended. There were birds. Birds! Fluttering and chirping between the branches. The air smelled like warm vegetation and dirt. An Ancestors-blessed *breeze* wafted through the air, shifting the leaves.

The lift opened onto a small open area surfaced in something dark. Then a shift from the chair to an enclosed flit, and even the gasping exhaustion pulling at Jossa's bones as she pried herself up and hobbled to the vehicle couldn't diminish the feeling welling inside her. Not even *Delfi* could make a dent in it.

They stayed low along the narrow road through the trees. There were occasional turnoffs, glimpses of distant structures through the shadowed trunks, and still more birds. Even insects, if that was what the creatures with wide, colorful wings were, fluttering around bushes covered in flowers.

"How?" she asked finally as the flit eased around another turn. She wasn't sure what question she was asking. How did they do it? How had they come up with it? How did they justify letting outsiders in?

"We've had a very long time to get it right," he replied, looking at her sideways.

Well, if legends about the Seps Coalition were true, no wonder.

Then they were there, and her heart stuttered again in amazement. Between one tree trunk and the next, a building appeared. No. Not a building. A wall. Made of stone? At least that was what it looked like. After what she'd seen so far, she wouldn't be surprised if it were so.

Under an arch and into another large, open space also covered in that dark substance. Jossa craned her neck to look as the flit settled into a parking slot. There was only one other vehicle like it in the row. A wheeled sled with long poles extending off one end and a number of small, round discs that she couldn't make heads or tails of sat further down the way. Small buildings lined the opposite side of the large courtyard. Directly across from the gate sat a building, square and squat. Patterned windows filled with colored plasglass made it feel somewhat less looming. It still dominated the courtyard.

This was what a monastery looked like?

Men moved in and out of the building. Some in long black coats, some in the uniform of the station, others in a random assortment of clothing styles. Some vanished into the sheds. Some walked along the building's walls and turned the corners. A few came their way.

"Remember," Markos said. "Here, there is no room for any other god but ours. If you are familiar with the talents of sai"—his eyes hardened—"they are not to be spoken of or displayed while here."

Jossa opened her mouth, and he cut her off. "Please, miss. I am only trying to help. For Syrus's sake." He unlatched the door of the flit and stepped out before she could come up with a coherent reply.

Good thing too, because Delfi's hold on the bond wavered again, her outrage rushing through to mix with Jossa's indignation. For a heartbeat, they were one again.

Then Delfi clamped down tighter than ever. The emotions vanished, leaving only a vague burning behind Jossa's eyes.

She rubbed her breastbone absently and sighed. "Well, better get this over with."

Delfi didn't answer. She simply slipped out and around the back of the flit, snagging the chair from the storage compartment as she went. Coming to a stop on Jossa's side of the vehicle, she punched the button for the door and then stood there, eyebrows raised as if to say "we don't have all day."

Jossa shook her head and started the arduous process of getting out of the flit. They might not have all day, but they did have the rest of their lives.

Unfortunately.

>>><<<

As it turned out, a monastery wasn't just a large stone building with a wall around it. The tour Markos's compatriots gave Jossa and Delfi wasn't extensive. Jossa suspected that was as much because they had things they'd rather not reveal to outsiders as it was in deference to her weakened state. She might have been angry about that, or even tried to prove that she could do more than she seemed capable of, but she didn't have the energy or heart to protest for now.

She listened with only half an ear as Markos outlined the basic precepts of his religion while he showed them around. Hopefully Delfi was paying more attention because, while Jossa couldn't feel the unease flickering in her chest, she knew it was there.

One last look at the stone-worked cross built into the far wall of a room Markos called a cha-pel and the multitude of flickering lights set in layered shelves below it, and she was very glad indeed to finally be shown to their quarters. Markos left them at the door as it slid open, bowing slightly as he told them to make themselves at home; someone would come with food shortly.

Then they were alone. For the first time all day, Jossa found that she couldn't simply sit and take it in. Couldn't be clinically observant. Couldn't even think of escape, although she knew they needed to come up with a plan.

For the first time since Delfi'd tightened the bond down to the barest of threads, Jossa started to really feel.

She found that she was hurt near unto death.

And furious as a raging beast.

>>><<<

"Really, Del? Shutting me out?" Jossa braced her hands on the armrests of her chair and tried to lever herself upright. "Of all the childish, self-centered..."

Delfi walked over to the small window in the far wall and stood, back straight and arms crossed. The bond quivered, but the barriers stayed put.

"You've always been such a hot-headed fool," Jossa muttered as she finally got her feet under her. She wobbled slightly but held. "Do you have any idea what I've sacrificed for you? What I've given up to keep you safe?"

Delfi's shoulders tightened. Jossa sent a lance of irritation towards her sister as she pounded a mental fist on the wall blocking her from her sister's mind. "Do you?"

No answer.

For some reason, the lack of response made Jossa that much angrier. Pampered, spoiled Delfi. Who'd never had to give herself up to keep them fed and alive. Who'd never had to let strange men paw all over her. Never let alien lusts and drives taint her mind and overtake her emotions, making her body respond to the animal grunts and thrusts in ways that gave her nightmares.

Never given up her dignity to a man who knew exactly how to use her sai for his own gains. Who knew how to stoke the unwelcome fire to an inferno that blotted out all rational thought.

Ancestors, what she'd give to have Rui here right now. Even Denz, to pull the asteroid out of her sister's achek and give her something else to think about.

Delfi snarled and whipped around, one hand raised. Jossa didn't so much duck under it as lose her balance just before it connected with her face.

That. Was. It.

Forget irritation. She lashed out, battering her sister through the bond. Sending emotion through the air in a channeled stream of plasma. "No." Fury choked Jossa's voice, scratching and clawing at her throat. "You don't get to tell me how bad you've had it. We were going to be free. *Free*, Del. I don't care if he was taking you back to your room that night. Tucking you in. Whatever you want to call it. I don't care if you provoked him."

Jossa took another step, adrenaline pulsing through her veins, moving her without the need for support. "He would have taken you and *then* where would you be? You'd barely started leaving the ship! You still flinched anytime a man looked at you for more than two seconds! He was threatening to harm you before you even came out of cryo sleep! Why would he care if you were awake? You think he had any consideration for what you went through?"

What I put you through with my failure?

Jossa locked the thought down before it could escape across the bond. Another step and she was able to grab Delfi by the shoulders. Her little sister stiffened, eyes blazing, teeth clenched. She brought her fists up between Jossa's arms, pushing out and away.

Jossa let her, dropping her hands and bringing them back around. This time she snagged Delfi by the wrists and held on tight. "You weren't baggage anymore, Del. You weren't some whimpering little girl who spent her days huddled in her bunk or crying in the shadows. You think he didn't *see* that? You think, for one second, that he'd pass up a chance at you?"

Delfi's lip curled. Something lanced through the rage armoring Jossa.

Scorn.

And pain.

Shocked, Jossa loosened her grip on Del's wrists. Her sister yanked free. Backing up one step, then two, she snarled aloud. "O'li zhuzhu i'rithaks keha'oks neh!?"

Jossa stared. What? Delfi *wanted* him?

"Well, I don't know what the fuck you just said, girl, but the bounty on your head makes a shit ton more sense now."

Jossa spun towards the new voice, lost her balance, and nearly fell.

Tarva bared white teeth in a rictus smile. Behind her in the door were three more members of her crew, each with a weapon raised.

Something flashed. Stung Jossa in the shoulder.

And then she knew no more.

TWENTY-NINE--DELFI

Yeah sure, you'll get the bond money back. Soon as you bring in the bounty.
  - clerk of Bounty Hunters Guild to unknown hunter

A smooth surface against bare skin. The low buzz of grav tethers nearly touching their anchors. The shift and rise of conversation somewhere nearby, but not close enough she could make out the words. The whole-body ache that cramped muscles and made her joints complain.

It took too long to find the will to move. When she tried to look up, it felt like trying to pick up a spaceship with only the strength in her neck. She couldn't leverage the rest of her body to help. The pain wouldn't allow it, nor the bands around her torso.

Finally she managed to get moving. Rolling and shifting her head along her shoulder, she achieved a precarious sort of balance. That done, she worked on prying her eyes open. That came only a little easier.

At first she thought her eyesight was damaged. Light hit the rods and cones of her retina, but the images wouldn't focus. Vague, humanish shapes shifted back and forth. The light around them was bluish and soft, cracking and sparking at the edges.

Then she realized her eyes were fine. She was just looking at a translucent phasewall.

Finally, *finally*, she remembered why she was bound hand and foot.

Ancestors behind, she'd kill them. She could kill herself for not trying to run before they got to the monastery. For even agreeing to leave the ship! For not checking sooner to see if anyone was following them. She knew better!

And what about her sai, failing to give them any warning? What good was it to be a Foreseer if it never worked when she really needed it?

Jossa.

Delfi clawed at the mind bond, worrying it like a feral cat might attack a length of string. No response.

Swallowing panic, she slewed her head around and breathed a sigh of relief. There. Jossa was there. Sitting on an odd stool with the base enclosed, tethered to the wall hand and foot.

But whole. Unconscious, which explained the eerie silence in the bond.

And naked from the waist down.

The sane part of Delfi's mind remembered that she was trying to break free of Jossa and the mind bond. To become her own person, independent of Jossa's constant need to smother. Away from the deep-seated obligation to regulate the Feel and all her myriad problems.

The sane part wasn't what shrieked in unholy terror. Her sanity wasn't more than a whisper against the fury and disgust Delfi felt when she realized the feel of cool metal on skin was that of a seat.

A seat with a hole in it.

Ancestors.

She thrashed, pulling at her bonds without plan or reason. Desperation numbed her brain. Her heart pounded in her ears. Again. Caught again. Pinned down. Stripped of any dignity. They had her again. They had her. Had her. Had—

More voices. This time muffled by the roaring in her ears. Their forms weren't blurred by the phasewall. They were dimmed by the black tunnel closing around her vision, narrowing the world to the tiniest pinprick of information.

Something struck her face. She tried to lash out with her hands and feet. Something yanked her limbs back before she got anywhere near her targets.

The band around her chest tightened. Her ribs creaked. She couldn't draw breath. Couldn't... couldn't breathe.

People pressed around her, invading her airspace. Contaminating it with shouts that should have been loud and the rustle of fabric on fabric that scraped harshly in her ears.

The pressure on her chest eased. Then her wrists flopped to her sides. Not free. But looser.

"Sedative... fucking... give," someone growled over her, the words fading in and out.

Someone else snapped back with a torrent of unintelligible foul language.

"Enough! You're making it worse." A woman's voice, clearer than the rest. Something touched Delfi's shoulder. She jerked back. Her head bounced off the wall behind her. Then the stranger forced her down and over, bending her in half at the waist. Strong fingers dug into Delfi's scalp and pushed her head down between her knees.

Fucking bitch. The words rang in Delfi's mind with bright clarity. *Is this all she's good for?*

But the hand holding Delfi's head down gentled. "Just breathe," the woman said in a soothing voice.

Surprised at the juxtaposition between audible and mental, Delfi obeyed.

First inhale.

Exhale.

Inhale.

About damn time, the woman thought, taking her hand from Delfi's head. The woman's mental voice fuzzed into nothingness.

Delfi had her breath now. So long as she kept her head down, she didn't have to look up. Didn't have to face these strangers and their judgements.

Ancestors, how she never wanted to do this again. Ancestors *please*, let her never break like this again.

She had a feeling her Ancestors didn't care one way or another. They'd bred and sold their offspring for too many years as a means to power. Dignity was the one thing their Progeny weren't allowed.

The bodies around her shifted. Someone, a man, told the woman to go get Tarva. The woman cursed and left. The sense of too many people in a tiny space eased. But only slightly.

Delfi dragged in another breath, tasted the stale tang of shipside air mixed with the sweat of her body, and tried to gauge who was left. She only knew of two women on Tarva's crew, including Tarva herself. The rest were men. Which two men held her now?

She didn't know how many people were on the crew, all told. Were either of these two the Crack? Probably not. They weren't usually at the forefront of action.

Denz glanced up from her memories and winked, then faded into the blur of the past. Her throat locked up. Her breathing stopped again. She fought to keep the tears in her eyes from falling free.

"Hey now." Someone grabbed her by the shoulder and pulled her upright. "What's this?"

Delfi stared up into the face of a man with sharp eyes and a narrow mouth and bit her lip as the traitorous tears tracked their way down her cheeks.

"Tears won't solve nothin' darlin'," the man said, eyebrows pulling together. "Best not try."

Well this is boring, the man growled to himself. The words ricocheted around Delfi's skull. *Why do they always think cryin'll save them?*

She hissed and straightened, grabbing at the hand on her shoulder. Pulling it to the side and back, she bent his fingers in the wrong direction. He barked in surprise, yanked free, and swung at her with his other fist. She ducked, felt it move her hair as it passed over her head, and shot both hands out in front of her.

They found his crotch just as the other man grabbed her by the shoulders and shoved her back against the wall.

The man she'd grabbed howled in pain and brought his palm down on her head in an open-handed slap. Stars burst in front of her eyes. Delfi let go, gasping and swaying. Faintly, she was aware of him coming back for another hit, but the second man stepped in, muscling his teammate back and away. "Not worth it, man. Not worth it. Need her in one piece. Leave off."

The first man snarled and growled but let his companion pull him away.

Delfi shook her head to clear it and watched as a man with a large beard and shaved head talked his teammate down. They were past the spot marking the shift from cell to main room, but they didn't bother to put the wall back up. The space outside the tiny cell was wide, surfaced on all sides in metal plating. There were a couple of tables in her line of sight, worn and dented. One had a chair pulled up next to it. Another was empty of seating that she could see.

Looking closer, she could tell that what she'd thought was the far wall wasn't a wall at all. It was another cell, empty. Why hadn't they split up her and Jossa? Easier to keep an eye on two in one cell? Or saving the space for Syrus?

If they left him alive long enough to see a cell to start with.

Not that any of that mattered right now. She should count the blessing of her Ancestors that she'd be able to talk to Jossa when her sister came to. Syrus's problems wouldn't become theirs unless these people managed to catch up to him.

"Tell Fiel and Tarva to get that sai booster shit over with and get in here," the bearded man said.

Delfi watched the man she'd had by the balls grumble and stand. She was more than a little satisfied to see him limp as he walked off.

But not satisfied enough to keep from turning wary eyes on the man who'd stayed behind. What would he do with this bit of alone time? Would he take advantage now?

"Relax," the man said, half sitting on the edge of the table and lacing his fingers together over his knee. "Get enough the easy way. Don't need to try and fuck a prisoner. Specially not one tied to a shitter. Ban, now…"

Delfi felt the blood drain from her face and then rush right back in, with interest. Crude. Low. Demeaning man!

And wasn't that a twist in her thoughts? She ought to be grateful. *Was* actually grateful that he wasn't desperate enough to take her, trapped as she was. The men of the Fleet certainly wouldn't have cared what position she was in.

Delfi clamped the thought down on reflex and glanced over at Jossa. She needn't have worried. Her sousi was still out, head lolling and body sagging against her restraints.

"Will say this," the man continued, either oblivious to or ignoring her lapse in attention. "Good job on blocking me out of the nav controls. Syrus knows code, but he doesn't know code like that. Where'd you learn to slip sideways around it?"

Delfi stared at him.

"Unless that was your sister's doing?" He jerked his chin at Jossa. "Either way, been a while since I had to work that hard to keep a tag on a target. Woulda thought you were a Crack 'f I hadn't heard you talking."

This time Delfi was ready for Denz to dance through her mind and back out again. She took a deep breath against the pain and set her jaw. Even if she could manage a single word in less than five minutes, she wasn't going to give this step-father's child the satisfaction of answers. He could speculate all he wanted. It wouldn't get him anywhere.

"Course, you might want to try making your 'they're coming to get us' prophecy a little sooner than you did." He frowned and tilted his head. "Although, you shouldn't have been able to pick up on us at all."

She hadn't. Not with her Hearing. Not with her Foreseeing. Not even through Jossa's Feeling. With the siphon she'd stuck on her sister, something should have come through. Because of the Null? Very likely.

The man shrugged and settled his weight more firmly on the table. "Don't matter now. You're coming with us to the world of trees that grow out of skulls. Whatever motherfucker runs that system is going to pay through the nose to get you back."

Delfi blinked at him. Trees and skulls. Why did that sound familiar? She couldn't place the sigil. Was it one of the noble Houses that ran the Border systems? Had she seen it in passing during that desperate first rush to get ahead of the Fleet?

Then she remembered. The infirmary. Jossa going catatonic at the mention of the sigil. But she still didn't know what it *meant*.

"Don't talk much, do you?"

Delfi refrained from rolling her eyes. Crack he may be, but this man's skills with code had obviously been acquired by sacrificing common sense and observation.

"You done teasing her yet?" asked a half-familiar voice. "Or are you going to talk her to death?"

The feeling of fabric wrapped around Delfi's mind strengthened until she felt as shrouded as a headless corpse waiting for cremation. Tarva walked into view and stopped next to the man on the table, crossing her arms as she looked Delfi over.

Delfi met the woman's eyes, then looked at her companions. She assumed the man must be Fieltar. The other was the woman who'd held her head down to her knees. Nadi, Delfi remembered.

"So, you two are set to bring us a fuck ton of money." Tarva leaned against the table next to Agadi and hooked her thumbs in the belt loops of her pants. "Syrus—"

Nadi growled under her breath and started pacing, flipping an activated knife from hand to hand. The others stopped to look at her, then turned back to Delfi. "Syrus said we oughta ask them for steady work. You know anything about that?"

Syrus? Sending these people after *more* work? Why in the universe would he help the people who'd hounded him across who knew how many light years of space?

One dark eyebrow arced up. Tarva leaned forward. "This ain't the time to keep quiet, girl. Tell me. Who wants you? How much money we out if we don't bring that fucker Syrus along with you?"

"Tarva!" Nadi spun to stare at the leader.

Tarva held up a hand but didn't look at her teammate. "He tell you why *we* want him, little girl?"

Delfi curled her lip.

Tarva sucked her teeth and shook her head. "Well, that figures. How long you been riding his exhaust, anyway?"

Delfi did her best to smooth her expression. She knew *why* he'd left the people in front of her. Their reasons for wanting him dead were fairly easy to deduce from there.

Tarva took two steps forward and crouched at the edge of the cell, bringing herself into alignment with Delfi's line of sight. "He even tell you what the Uvlaku are?"

Delfi couldn't help it. She raised an eyebrow. Hadn't they run a blood scan on her or Jossa? Even if they'd taken their prisoner's maruste at face value, they should have at least done that much. If they had, they'd know what she and her sister *really* were and...

Oh. Of course. These were nehkeh. Only one sort of maruste glyph meant much to them. Even if they could read the web of ownership and lineage that covered her back, how could she expect them to know that the kuchruog were ever anything but pleasure toys?

"Well, he shouldn't have. But that makes it simpler to—"

"How much simpler does it need to be?" Nadi snapped. "He left us to die. Hell, he blew the charges early and damn near crippled Ban for life." She flung a hand out in the direction of the narrow-mouthed man with the short hair. He caught her by the wrist and twisted her arm so he could lace his fingers with hers. She pulled against him but relented when he kept his grip. "He tried to kill us," she said, quieter now. "'F it weren't for—" She stopped when Tarva and the others hissed at her in unison.

"You know how Uvlaku units work?" Tarva asked after a moment, turning back to Delfi.

Short of knocking herself unconscious, she wasn't going to get out of listening to the lecture. Delfi shook her head.

"The Karukap takes nehkeh off the streets," Fieltar said. His voice lilted with an odd accent for a few words before settling back into featureless Common. "Young as they can. Trains them. Sends them out on the shit jobs the normal soldiers can't get caught doing." He lifted a shoulder. "Nothing a thousand armed forces haven't done in one form or another for thousands on thousands of years. The fun part is how they keep us in line."

With sai, she wanted to say. Senders and Feels, conditioning the recruited children from the moment they set foot in the training facilities to the moment they armed and armored up and went out to keep the peace between the systems. The practice was as old as the Empire itself.

Did they know that, though? Syrus must have. But it wasn't just done to the Uvlaku, and it wasn't supposed to be common knowledge. Knowing meant you could fight it. The value of an armed force that would never turn against its master was too great to hinge on something so unstable as a recruit's faith in the greater good.

"If we didn't come back from our missions, all of us together," Tarva said, "we got slapped with a No Travel mandate and turned into target practice for everyone from an isloste to planetary law enforcement. If we came back but one or two people didn't make it, we'd better have the skin off their backs as proof of death.

Well. That explained the kemvate on the shadow base. And Syrus's near obsession with disguising his identity.

"He blew us up. Literally. Took us *years* to make sure we were safe. Now the whole fucking Empire is crawling with military. Between them and the Svis Konanuog, we're losing the race to stay alive.

"Don't matter to us if we take him alive or dead. Prefer alive, so we can make him dead the long way." Tarva leaned forward. "You, though. We spent a fair bit getting ahold of you. You going to be worth it when we bring you to whatever jumped-up noble with delusions of grandeur wants you?"

Delfi shook her head. No, no she wouldn't be worth it. Neither would Jossa. Syrus or no Syrus, she was done managing Jossa's moods. Ancestor's balls, the best way to deal with whoever they got handed off to would be to just let Jossa have free rein.

Something in her cringed at that. A part she didn't want to examine.

Tarva must have seen it on her face and misread it. Shaking her head, she levered herself up to standing and held out a hand to Agadi. He handed her a screen. A couple taps and the tethers holding her shackled arms to the wall went all the way slack. The bands around her ankles fell away, then clanked as the tethers pulled them back to the anchors on the wall.

Delfi hunched over, folding her arms across her lap in a belated effort to hide her nakedness from the crew of nehkeh.

Agadi snorted. Nadi rolled her eyes. Only Fieltar refrained from making a comment or reacting. He kept his eyes on Tarva, who did something else with the screen, then handed it back to Agadi. "Get comfortable," she said, voice dry. "You've got the run of the cell. Do I need to tell you not to cross your tethers with hers?"

Delfi looked over and saw Jossa slumped on her toilet, hands hanging near her ankles. Glancing back at the room outside, she saw that Agadi and Nadi were both gone. It was just Tarva and her silent companion watching her through the reactivated phasewall.

"Be good now," Tarva said. "Can strap you right back on the toilet if you don't behave."

Then she stalked out of the room. Fieltar gave Delfi one last inscrutable look and followed.

Delfi waited a minute. Two. Then five. When she was sure they weren't coming back, she scrambled off the toilet, pulling frantically at her pants. That taken care of, trying not to listen to her too-loud breathing in the echoes of the room, she dropped to her knees next to Jossa and felt her neck for a pulse.

There. Faint, but steady.

The young woman sank back on her heels and breathed a sigh of relief.

They were alive. For now.

Sane. For now.

But would she have the strength to do what was needed when the time came?

> Syrus

THIRTY--SYRUS

The Karukap may have the monopoly on saiog now. So be it. Even one sai in the service of the House will be enough to change our fortunes.
- Kizrard Ejorum lis Azo af Azizate, to his nephew

He thought he remembered struggling. Fighting. Definitely not winning. It was all a blur of unintelligible commands, the rustle of cloth, and the thump of tactical boots on a metal surface. He thought he remembered trying to force a door open. A hatch? Something that'd stood in his way. Obviously he'd failed.

He definitely remembered not being able to breathe.

Syrus's head pounded in time with his heart, a steady *whump-whump* of pain that dug in behind his eyeballs and wrapped a vice around the base of his neck, squeezing the two areas together with all the inevitability of a ship venting air into space. The world spun around him. He couldn't get enough air. He was breathing, but he couldn't get enough air.

On the other hand, he'd just strung enough words together in his head that he probably hadn't suffered major brain damage.

That's debatable, Rissa muttered in a nonexistent voice.

Ok. He didn't have any *more* brain damage than before.

The air around him shifted. A presence came into range of his sai senses, bringing with it the scrape-pop of impatience and scorn. Syrus agreed with whoever it was. He was about done with drifting around in the fog of pain and very much willing to kick his own ass for letting himself get caught so easily.

How the fuck had they found him anyways?

And who were they?

The bundle of emotion moved behind him, then came around to stand in front of him. Syrus fought the weights on his eyelids, swallowing a groan as more pain stabbed through his head. Mother fuck. What the hell'd they hit him with?

"Enough dawdling," said a voice. Male. Not young. Not Almovak or Jirdis. None of his old crew either. Something about it sparked a memory deep in his brain, but the spark died when he tried to reach for it.

Syrus managed to roll his head on his shoulders. It felt heavy. Almost as if someone had crowned him in chains instead of the more usual skull plates. His eyelids fought him, but he finally got them open a crack and immediately wished he hadn't. Fucking sun seared his eyes and set fire to his brain.

Something hard and rounded tapped his cheek. Not gently, either. Syrus couldn't hide the groan, but at least his lips were mostly stuck shut, so it was muffled. He might have yelled in pain if he could manage it.

Another hard tap. This time to his sternum. Syrus grunted and doubled over. Or he tried to. He was brought up short by the fact that his hands were bound behind his back attached to who knew what. Smart people, tying him to a wall. Or whatever else it might be. Probably a wall. Not that he was in any shape to do much damage.

"I find that you are much less than promised." Another prod. More pain. "Where is the vaunted nehkeh endurance? Where is the legendary rage?"

Oh, he'd show the man rage all right. Just as soon as he got done reattaching his cognitive processes to the rest of his body. Syrus bit back another groan and managed to pry his eyes open all the way this time.

A man stood in front of him, looking down at him with bland eyes, a long wooden stick capped by silver metal in one hand. He was average height, broad shouldered, and maybe in his fifties, as the Imperial standard calendar assigned ages. Sharply arched eyebrows, a sardonic mouth, rich brown skin lined near the eyes, and close-cropped black hair showing a bit of gray here and there. His clothes were deep red trimmed in rusty orange and made entirely of organic-based materials. Not a stitch of synthsilk or synthcot to be seen. The cost of the outfit would feed a family in the poor quarters of Kallura lis Kerute Base for a month.

Somewhere, Syrus found the strength to curl his lip. He couldn't manage words just yet, though. His tongue was stuck to the roof of his mouth, and his throat had shriveled up like a raisin around his voice box.

The man raised an eyebrow and set the metal-shod tip of his rod against the floor. "It lives."

Syrus's monster stirred sluggishly in the back of his mind. Suddenly, he found he had energy after all. The growl that rumbled in his chest was perfectly audible.

"Now, now," the man said. "Behave. For one thing, there is quite a bit of expensive equipment attached to you, and I do not have the time to replace it."

Syrus growled and gave the shackles around his arms an experimental tug. Seemed liked standard grav tethers to him.

The man snorted. "Ancestors, they've given me an idiot." The cane came up again. Syrus tried to shy away, but he didn't have enough slack in his bonds. The weight still dogging his head wasn't helping either.

The cane struck him on the cheek, hard. He snapped at it out of reflex. The man whipped it around and brought it down right on the crown of Syrus's head. Gently this time.

Something smaller, sharper, pressed itself into the bone of his skull. Syrus groaned as pain lanced its way straight through his head, brain and all, and set his spine on fire.

"I have use for you, nehkeh," said the man. "If you pass the test I'm about to set you."

"No." Syrus forced the word out between gritted teeth. It was all he could manage through the pain. Even his rage couldn't dent it. Not with the monster staying hidden in his mind.

"You don't have a choice." The cane shifted, lifting, and Syrus braced himself for another tap.

It didn't come. The man placed the tip of the polished wood back on the ground and leaned on it. Syrus noticed the grip was carved in the shape of an abstracted sample tube chased in gold. Something in his thoughts clicked into place, realigning with reality.

The Kizrard Ejorum lis Azo af Azizate. Mother fucking cunt. It explained everything.

"Now, aside from the sensors attached to your head, there is a more immediate reason for you to abort the pointless struggle you are no doubt preparing to engage in. If you would look down?"

Syrus looked. A cluster of red dots lay on his chest, shifting as he breathed. Raising his head, he looked past the Kizrard and saw the turrets.

They were well hidden in the decorative stonework that surrounded the small courtyard he sat in. One over the small fountain that burbled water into a fluted basin. Another shaded by the wide fringed leaves of a tree in the corner. A third shielded by the huge flowers of the bush growing flat against its wall. The barrels aimed his direction were too narrow for plasma shot. Lasers then.

He snarled under his breath. "Markos." The fucking lying excuse for a holy man. They hadn't been kicking him off the fucking ship because of Delfi. He'd been set up. Mother fucking piece of shit!

"Who?" The Kizrard's emotions, which had been fuzzing around the edges, refocused. Curiosity drifted off him but carried no real concern. "If you are referring to the captain of the ship my son-in-law made to stop in order to retrieve you, then yes, I can see cause for being disgruntled." The cane moved, and Syrus tracked it with his eyes. "But when the final tally is made, nehkeh, you are the only one responsible for your capture."

The monster roared to life, tired of the games, tired of Syrus just sitting there *taking* the bullshit from this man. Caustic sludge flowed down Syrus's spine, spreading through his body like slow lava. He growled, yanking at the tethers that held him fast, pulling at the apparatus stuck to his head. Pain flared, chasing the monster out of his veins and leaving only a struggle for breath as his nervous system rose up in unified revolt. He sat, gasping and panting as he tried to find his way back to reality.

Rissa didn't emerge to help. She'd retreated.

By the time his vision cleared and he was able to do more than sag in the chair, the environment around him had changed. Sounds of vehicles grew in his ears. The low hum of a flit, the deeper hum of a heavy transport, and something he couldn't identify. His memories kept saying anti-personnel carrier, but that just didn't fit with the setting. Especially since, once he pried his eyes open again, he found himself sitting in the same courtyard as before.

The Kizrard wasn't alone anymore. A younger man had joined him. Dressed in the same colors but a shade or two paler than the older noble, the new man had a narrower face, a leaner build, and held his hands like they should have weapons in them rather than the screen he was holding out for the Kizrard to read.

Beyond the stranger was a small metal cart, on wheels instead of floating. Next to it, a woman wore the standard uniform of female medics, stiff gray skirt and paler gray shirt with the squared red cross of a medic not sworn to the priesthood. Someone else stood back there. Probably a woman, by the big poufs of material. Definitely a noble, given the fact that it too was natural fiber and not synthetic. And all but boiling with anticipation and anger. Perfect. Now people were coming to poke the captive nehkeh, like he was some animal about to do tricks. Fuckers.

He looked at the younger nobleman to give his brain something to do besides stew in its own juices and possibly let the monster nearly fry him from the inside out again.

There was something familiar about the man. Something trying to pound its way free of the wall created between himself and his critical thinking by the pain and whatever they'd used to knock him out. Syrus groped through his mind, trying to figure it out. Something to do with the Kiprinog. Research he'd done to make sure they were still the best contacts to reach out to when he'd come up with that idiotic plan to hide from the Fleet in the Seps Coalition.

Then the man stepped away from the Kizrard and turned so he could enter a few commands into the screen without elbowing the older noble. Syrus let out a bark of surprised laughter when he saw the younger man's face. "Appulu, of course. "

Both nobles snapped their heads up, identical frowns on their faces and identical feelings of indignation sizzling out to burn Syrus's exposed skin.

He laughed harder. There was no mistaking it. They were related. Father and son, maybe? No. He'd looked into the Kizrard. The man had only spawned daughters. Illegitimate son, maybe? Distantly possible. The old bastard had a nephew though, set to inherit. And the younger man was about the right age. It'd just taken a little to recognize him without all the junk he used to disguise himself when he went out as the Kiprinog's leader.

The cane caught Syrus under the chin and shoved his head up, nearly choking him in the process. "What, precisely, is so funny?" The Kizrard's voice was so icy it nearly froze the air around them.

Syrus leaned back so he could keep laughing without the can stabbing him in the throat. "Markos," he said. "Fucker wasn't the one who got me caught after all." He met the eyes of the younger noble. "Appulu. Did you know the whole time that they had me on board? Tell the captain to slow down just enough for Almovak and his bunch to catch up? Or did you find out when they kicked things up the chain to see if the Kiprinog could afford to piss off your House?"

For a moment, all the churning emotions around them stopped, leaving only the eerie flatness of stunned amazement ringing through Syrus's mental "ears" in near-perfect stereo.

Then rage blossomed out of the younger noble. The Kizrard erupted not a millisecond behind.

"Kiprinog? Appulu?" The older man reared back. He had to use his cane for its intended purpose, bracing himself against the weight of his derision as it threatened to send him over backwards. "You?"

The younger noble sneered and lifted a fist. "You *fikekoj* piece of odevek nehkeh," he growled at Syrus. "You think—"

"I know," Syrus snapped back, all amusement gone. Their emotions had lit the fire in him again, burning out the last of whatever drug they'd used to keep him under during transport. His monster lunged forward, and he had to haul it back before the unreasoning fury could take over and force him to rip his own spine out. "I didn't walk into that fucking arrangement blind. You should do a better job of scrubbing your image from the data feeds.

"Though I gotta say, the clothes..." He nodded at the man's fine outfit. "The face..." He jerked his chin at the clean-shaven face that looked about ready to explode. "You clean up good, after you been slumming." Syrus found a smile somewhere and fueled it with the rage that poured off the man by the bucketful. "But you didn't change enough. Synthskin can give you a new maruste for a little while, but it wears off. Especially with *your* sort of activity. And the minute you palm a lock, the truth is out."

The noble brought his raised fist down on Syrus's jaw, sinking all his weight into the blow. Pain took over again, stars bursting in Syrus's vision, nerves screaming as the array attached to his head shifted. He fought the monster down, although he didn't know how. All he knew was that if he let it loose, if he gave in to the urge to fight free of his bindings, there wouldn't be anything left of him but a mewling carcass scratching in the dust for the last of his sanity.

Where the fuck was Rissa? He couldn't do this on his own much longer.

No answer.

If he'd had anything left for it, he might have cried. Instead, he told himself that the reason his eyes were leaking was from the pain.

"Is this true?" The Kizrard wasn't giving off fury now. Syrus didn't have a word for what it felt like, the ice so cold it burned, the rawness of a wound healed wrong. He thought it felt like hate. But he couldn't tell if the Kizrard was talking to him or Appulu.

"My Lord Uncle! You would believe the word of a nehkeh over me?"

Syrus tried to laugh at the irony, but all he could manage was a sort of hoarse rasp. Fuck, but his head hurt.

"Excuse me," said a new voice, timid and female. "Honorific, the lead float is ready. The—" She paused. Sheer terror rammed its way up Syrus's nose to burst behind his eyes. She finished on a whisper. "The parade marshall is asking if you are coming? Your guests have arrived."

"Indeed." The Kizrard's voice was back to frosted now instead of bone chilling. "Thank you, Lesker. I will be there momentarily."

Light footsteps hurried away.

"You," the Kizrard snapped. "You will accompany me."

How the fuck were they going to manage that? Put the whole tether and EEG-rig on a smaller float and load him like so much cargo? And why? What possible fucking reason did they have for carting him around when it was simpler just to leave him here?

"My Lord Uncle! I am supposed—"

"You will stay where I can see you until such time as we have verified the validity of the accusations made against you." Some of that hate-filled cold leeched back into the air. "Do you understand me?"

Ah. That made more sense. Old bastard didn't want his heir running off to the arms of his followers.

"And you." The cane tip again, this time to the shoulder. Syrus let it push him upright and smiled at the Kizrard with all the bloody teeth he could manage. The older man grimaced. "You are going to either prove you are worth all the expense of retrieving you, or you will die." The cane moved, hovering over Syrus's head again. Syrus couldn't help it. He flinched.

The Kizrard smiled thinly. "This will tell me the truth. I hope you enjoy the Parade of Natural Sons. I know I will, no matter what you've done to try and mar the day. New life, celebration. The continuation of duty and the sense of fulfillment therein." He leaned down. Syrus fought the temptation to spit in the man's face. "You failed your duty once. Let us see if you can live up to the obligation this time, yes?"

He straightened and turned, bringing the cane down to brace himself for the walk. And froze. Surprise tore through the air. Syrus yanked his head around to see what else had gone wrong.

Fuck.

Fucking hell.

Shit, fuck, and all the other expletives he could think of. None of them covered this.

The big bundle of cloth that'd been mostly hidden behind Appulu was revealed in full now. And Syrus knew the woman that wore it.

Alrurisi.

Son of a bitch.

"Lady Alrurisi," the Kizrard said, "I had not expected to see you before the feast tonight."

Alrurisi sank into a low curtsy, one hand sweeping her skirts out and back, the other coming up to touch her heart in the salute of a subject to their noble. "My deepest apologies, Your Grace."

The Kizrard drew himself upright, barely leaning on his cane. Syrus couldn't see the man's face, but the disapproval radiating off him was all he needed. Alrurisi was dancing on thin ice with her liege lord. Did she realize it? She'd stayed away from politics when he'd lived in the lis Tova household. But twenty-eight years was a long time in which to learn. Syrus had a fair guess as to what had made her change her hands-off policy.

Oblivious of his train of thought, the two nobles continued their little drama. "Your son will be missing you," the Kizrard said. "You are very nearly late as it is."

Alrurisi sank lower. Syrus was a little surprised a woman of her age had that much bend in her.

He shook off the memories of Rissa and Okini complaining about nobles' fashion choices that commoners didn't need to put up with, returning to the present in time to catch the Kizrard's next comment. "Your family has had plenty of time to observe and ascertain the truth of his claims. I fail to see how any insights you glean could help your situation now."

Claims? Claims!? Fucking assholes. He'd never made any claims. Never done anything but trail after Rissa like some fucked-up lost puppy, hands bloodied and heart thinking it'd found a home at last. Look at what good had come of that.

Fucking claims.

Rissa kept silent. It was starting to worry him now, how completely she'd vanished from the corners of his mind.

"Please, milord." Syrus jerked his attention back to Alrurisi. Her words and tone were pleading. The emotions boiling off her were anything but. "My husband's poor judgement all but destroyed our House. Just a moment? Before this creature is ruined by his own lies?"

Oh, that was rich. That was fucking spectacular. She should have been apprenticed out as an actress. Head down, still holding that curtsy, not a tremor in her body from the strain. If he hadn't felt the simmering anger pooling around her feet in a growing puddle—if he didn't know what had gone on in that house in the years before he'd been sold—he'd almost believe the act.

But he did know. And he could Feel.

So he curled a lip and did his best to shove down the answering rage in his own heart. Otherwise, he'd try and wrap his hands around her throat and end up scrambling his brains in the process.

A young man in the red and rust trotted up, a screen clutched in one hand and a worried look on his face. He bent in a curt bow, then held the screen out to the Kizrard. "Milord. The parade is about to start. Your float..."

The Kizrard sighed and pinched the bridge of his nose. "I will be there momentarily." To Alrurisi, he said, "Very well. Although I will be very disappointed if the Float of the Mothers sets out for the parade without its brightest jewel." Turning to the medic standing behind the small cart, he said, "She has five minutes. After that, I expect the prisoner to have been dosed and the loading procedures started. Clear?"

The medic dipped her head. "Yes, milord."

The Kizrard harrumphed and stalked off, leaning on his cane only slightly, leaving a comet trail of impatience and disapproval in his wake.

Syrus waited until he was out of earshot before raising his head to meet Alrurisi's eyes. She stood tall now, back straight, face a mask of cold fury. The emotions she buffeted him with were *anything* but cold.

He managed a sneer. "Speaking of lies."

Her hand flashed. The right side of his face stung with pain.

Syrus snarled at her and lunged, catching himself just before the array welded to his skull started yanking on his brain. The monster stirred and woke. Two of the Kizrard's guards had stayed behind when their rard walked away. They stepped forward, hands dropping to the weapons at their hips.

Alrurisi held up a hand, and they stepped back looking unhappy.

"You," she said. Her voice cracking and shaking. But not with fear. No, this was anger. And under it, yawning like the gaping jaws of a behemoth, grief. "You ruined us. You ruined *her*. My *daughter*. You took her from her family. From me."

"I didn't fucking *sell* her to some backwater Edgeworld jumped-up rard who'd already beaten four of his wives to death!" Syrus roared back. "I didn't abandon her to die as something less than garbage."

No, his mind whispered, you just got there too late. Always too late. He ignored it.

"I spoke for you," she hissed. "Rissa brought you to the gates, proud as if she'd pulled a diamond out of a trash pile, and I *spoke* for you. And how did you repay that? How did you prove you were her sousi instead of an *astnuoj vifoggek* looking to taint our bloodlines with your foulness? You had her sneaking out. At all hours, no matter the day, no matter the duties she was abandoning. If it weren't for you—" The woman stopped, heat boiling off her as she clenched her hands into fists in the folds of her dress and visibly fought for words.

Syrus fought himself. He wanted to let the monster go. Tear free of his bonds and rage through the courtyard. They thought he was trash? A creature? He'd show her exactly what she'd had under her roof all those years. He'd show her what Rissa'd seen when she found him in that dusty little alley, a sticky puddle of blood turning the dirt at his feet to mud as his hands ached for another neck to wring.

He'd show them *all* exactly what they got when they tried to keep a nehkeh as a pet.

Some part of him, some small, sane part, reminded his monster that he wouldn't get two steps into the rampage. Breaking free would mean ripping the array off his head, and it already set his nerves screaming in pain at the slightest sudden movement. Who knew what the fuck they'd wired it to and what would happen if he pulled it free on his own?

"Where is my daughter now?" the noblewoman cried, breaking into Syrus's train of thought. The guards behind her twitched but stayed put. The nurse let off a shiver of anxiety that was drowned almost immediately by the emotions coming off Alrurisi. She reached into a fold of her skirt and pulled something out. Something pale that slid and folded over her hand like thick fabric.

It wasn't fabric.

Syrus stared at the leather as she shook it in his face. "Where is my daughter now?" she demanded, voice grating. "She is *gone*. Dead! We can't even make a proper death tablet for her because she was so mutilated by her association with you."

The shock faded, leaving the monster clawing at the chains Syrus had wrapped around it. Fucking Almovak. Fucking stupid piece of shit. Syrus wasn't sure if he'd meant that last for the noble rard or for himself. He should have grabbed the skin. He shouldn't have let Delfi drag him out of that room without getting it back.

He shouldn't have taken it off Rissa in the first place.

"How long?" Rissa's mother asked, still holding the pale, marred, leather under his nose. "How long has my daughter been dead?"

And the unspoken questions: Were you the one who skinned her? Could you even do *that* properly?

Syrus clenched his fists, feeling the shackles bite and pull at his wrists as he tried to wrestle the monster down long enough to form coherent words. He owed them this much, Rissa and her mother both. Alrurisi *had* spoken for him. Because of Rissa's mother, he'd had ten years that, if they weren't the best years of his life, they were better than anything but the brief time he and Rissa'd had before her husband caught up with them. He'd been wanted, at least by someone. He'd been... whole.

"Four years," he rasped, the words catching in his throat and sticking on his tongue.

"How?" Her voice was hard as compressed carbon, but the hand holding Rissa's skin still quivered.

He shook his head as the memories flooded his mind. An arm sticking out of a medunit, bending in all the wrong directions. Blood. So much blood. The echoes of her screams blending with his own as he beat Brander to bloody pulp.

He'd spent too long respecting the woman in front of him to destroy her memories of Rissa with that. She shouldn't have to carry them.

The skin in her hands would have to be enough.

"Was it her husband?"

Syrus unlocked his jaw, feeling muscles pull and strain. His monster didn't want to let go. "No."

"Milady," said the medic, stepping forward as Alrurisi reeled back. "You will have to leave now. It is time."

"Was it you?" The noblewoman ignored the medic, fingers whitening as she clutched the skin even harder.

"No." It was easier to speak this time.

"Milady."

Alrurisi twisted the tanned and softened skin of her daughter's back between her shaking hands, wringing it like a wet cloth. When she untwisted it and laid it against the front of her skirt, every glyph of Rissa's maruste, marred and broken as they were, was clear for Syrus to see. Then, with careful fingers, she folded the skin and tucked it into the hidden pocket of her skirt.

She didn't give any warning. Syrus couldn't shy away before she set fingers like two hot coals under his chin and jerked his face up so she could meet his eyes. "The Kizrard has plans for you, Syrus, nehkeh lis Tova af Mitachte. My husband cost him a sai. Two, in fact, with his machinations. His Grace was so close to making his claim on the throne." She spoke softly. Syrus doubted the medic could hear her. But her eyes were hard and her voice even harder. "He has decreed a test for you."

Syrus remembered that part. He had a fucking EEG stuck to his skull.

"In the interests of not rendering you useless, should you prove to actually possess sai, the medic will be injecting you with a paralytic meant to keep you from damaging yourself." She stepped sideways to stand next to him instead of in front of him, then leaned down and whispered in his ear, "I paid attention, all those years you spread your taint in my house.

"Here is *my* test for you, nehkeh. Prove you *aren't* sai. Stay in your cage. Or prove that you *are* and show everyone what a Savage really is."

Syrus froze, staring at the medic still standing next to the little cart. The women had an injector gun in one hand and an ampule of some clear fluid in the other. The guards were paying attention to the tableau before them, but they didn't show more than a general concern.

And then, so gently he wasn't sure how it even happened, Alrurisi's free hand found his and pressed something cool and hard between his fingers. She'd moved so she could hide what she was doing, he realized. The thing in his bound hands felt like a shackle key.

Mother fuck.

"Milady," the medic said, stepping forward with her loaded injector gun. "I must dose him now. And you will be late for the start of the parade."

"Yes," Alrurisi said, straightening and backing away from Syrus. The feeling of a bonfire roasting his skin subsided a bit, but not much. "I am off." To Syrus she said, "Do try not to fail milord's test. That is, unless you prefer being fed to the dogs."

He had no doubt she meant it literally.

Huge skirts floating around her in a puffy cloud, one hand over the place where the hidden pocket held Rissa's skin, the woman walked off. She didn't look back.

Syrus didn't have a chance to turn the key she'd left in his hands and bring it to bear on the shackles. The medic came forward, injector raised. "Do not struggle," she told him in a voice that oozed contempt. "The turrets will fire."

Right. Laser turrets. He'd forgotten.

She pressed the injector to his neck and put her thumb to the trigger pad. Pain blossomed, making his eyes water. Then she stepped back, set the injector on the cart, and tapped in an order on a small screen set in the cuff on her wrist.

The chair he was tied to rose in the air, then moved backwards. He tried to struggle, but his muscles responded sluggishly and he nearly dropped the key. Clutching it with the tips of his fingers, he breathed hard, fighting for consciousness as his monster raged. The chair. Platform? Whatever it was, it moved backwards. Syrus realized it was a cargo sled about the time the light started to dim and he saw the metal walls of a large troop transport in his peripheral vision.

No. Not troops. The noise was too uncontrolled for troops. They'd mentioned a parade. They were packing him up in the bowels of a fucking parade float like so much cargo.

And then he stopped moving. Darkness closed around him, though his eyes were wide open. He couldn't tell if he'd lost his sight to whatever the medic had stuck in him or if it was just that dark.

He didn't have time to figure it out, because as soon as the clanking of braces and clamps stopped and his little float finished merging with the larger one, the whole massive unit started moving again.

And he could Feel. First one person, then another as the float lurched into motion and prepared to wend its way past the masses of people who'd turned out for the holiday. An entire city full of people celebrating the birth of naturally conceived offspring.

The cacophony of sound was rivaled only by the deluge of varied emotions battering his mind as his monster howled in furious reply.

> Jossa

THIRTY-ONE--JOSSA

*The Stable half of a sousi bond is the anchor, the pivot.
Without her, the Unstable sai is useless.*
- Karukap Mistress of Sai to aides

There was an ancient phrase: Deafening silence. Jossa'd never understood it as a child. How could peace and quiet overwhelm your hearing? She'd spent her life among the women of the Churus lis Kuchruis. Among the girls being raised to make that House prettier with their beauty. Between the near-constant chatter and the low thrum of their emotions seeping through the expansion gaps in her crown, her world had never been silent.

It wasn't until later. Years and *years* later. That she'd come to understand what the phrase meant. Not until she'd been bonded to Delfi. Saved from the overwhelming flood of emotion, she'd realized that the surcease had its own dangers.

She hadn't *truly* understood the phrase until she'd woken up in Syrus's little infirmary aboard the Fleet flagship. Until she'd realized that Delfi hadn't woken with her. That her sister had slept on and no one, not even the chief medic of the Fleet, had known when she would wake.

Jossa hadn't needed a crown then to help her realize just how damaging silence could be. To be sure, they'd crowned her. She'd driven hundreds, maybe thousands, of Fleet personnel to their deaths without realizing what she was doing. But even before the crown, there'd been an emptiness. The aching silence in her mind where Delfi should have been.

Now it was a million times worse.

Because now... now she wasn't trying to cope with existence alone, waiting for Delfi to wake up. Praying that Delfi would wake up. *Now* she was locked in a tiny cell with her sister, and not a single thing she did could convince Delfi to break her silence. Not out loud. Not in the mind bond.

Not a single thing.

She'd tried. Oh, how she'd tried. She'd battered at Delfi's mental walls. Pleaded. Cried. Screamed until her head ached with the rebounding echoes. She'd let her anger spill over. Tried to swamp the bond with the agony that'd taken up residence in her heart. Delfi took only as much as was needed to keep the emotions from escaping their cell and infecting the people holding them captive. Nothing more. Nothing less.

Their captors were no help. Not that she'd expected any from them. Why think they would help? But in a small, very secret part of herself, she almost wished they'd make the conditions worse. Do something, anything, to force a break in Delfi's wall. And wasn't that the most appalling part of this whole affair? Here she was, wanting them to overload her with emotion. Hoping they'd threaten and torment her so that Delfi would *have* to do something.

But no. Once, one of them lowered the filter settings on the barrier keeping their cell separate from the rest of the ship. The man, Jossa thought she remembered his name being Banuo, explained the basics of living in the cell and promised they wouldn't be coming out until the final bounty was paid to the crew's accounts. Then he'd walked off, leaving her in no small amount of despair. All of it hers. Not a scrap of emotion from him.

Delfi could have deigned to explain things through the mind bond if she'd wished.

Instead, she'd sat there on her pallet through the entire speech, staring at the opposite wall like a life-sized poppet, not acknowledging anyone or anything around her.

By the second day, Jossa's small secret wish for a catalyst had grown into burning desire. Something. Anything. How could Delfi do this to her? How was she keeping it up? Didn't her sister understand how much it hurt? How much fear existed inside her that even the small surcease the mind bond granted might get taken away? Jossa's hands shook with it. The muscles of her neck had turned to rods of iron, waiting braced for the moment when Delfi stopped siphoning the maelstrom of emotions churning in Jossa's gut. Or the moment when one of the minor disagreements the crew engaged in—although she and her sister could not hear from inside the cell—got powerful enough to penetrate the muzzy haze that'd wrapped around Jossa's senses since the moment she'd woken up.

It'd taken her a full day to realize what that haze was. The Null woman. Tarva. Either she was actively cloaking her crew's psyches, or her passive field was just that strong. Jossa almost laughed when her too-slow brain remembered that bit of information about their captors. She wondered if Delfi realized it at all. Realized that she *didn't* have to keep the siphon going. Not even the tiny bit she was keeping up. Jossa could let herself run rampant in this ship, and their captors would hardly notice. For the first time since she'd first been consigned to a casket and cold storage all those many years ago, she was alone inside her head.

She'd thought the despair was bad. She'd thought she'd been brought as low as was possible.

She'd been wrong.

She barely noticed when the pull Delfi exerted on the mind bond increased. Hardly realized that someone held food to her lips thrice a day, forcing the edge of a silplat pouch past her teeth, squeezing liquid into her mouth. Hardly noticed when hands smaller and stronger than hers wrapped around her elbows, pulled her to her feet, and maneuvered her lax body under the shower spout in the far corner of their cell, soaping and rinsing them both in fits and starts as the lukewarm water turned on and off. She caught glimpses of the crew outside the cell either keeping watch, talking to each other, or ignoring their prisoners completely.

But the awareness of events around her percolated only slowly through the fog that muzzed her head. And it wasn't until one of them walked up to the barrier holding Jossa and Delfi separate from the rest of the ship that she noticed things had changed.

The woman, not Tarva, spoke. Her voice didn't penetrate the barrier, but for the first time something *did* penetrate the despair that'd wrapped Jossa's existence in numbing ice. It took her a moment to figure out what it was, and she needed to look at the woman's— Nadi's—face for clues in order to do so.

Then she realized. Scorn. It was scorn twisting the other woman's features, driving a knife into Jossa's mind.

But that was all she got before Delfi pulled any further insights away through the mind bond. Jossa wanted to scream. Wanted to slap her sister and demand that she give the feelings back. If she didn't want to be a sousi anymore, at least give them back. The awareness. The clues that Jossa had so long used to keep them both alive in the face of so many dangers.

But instead she sat there, shaking with a need she couldn't define, feeling her stomach twist and turn as she tried to remember why she wanted to live in the first place.

Until, too late, she realized that the churning of her gut had very little to do with her abandonment. That while the blank feeling in her head might be related to having more emotion than she was used to Delfi taking, the insistent pressure trying to squeeze her brain down to an atom wasn't a side effect.

At least not of emotional over-siphoning.

And then, before she'd taken the realization and parsed it out into a coherent thought, Delfi cried out and toppled sideways.

And every single thing Jossa hadn't felt for the past however many days came flooding back, slamming into her like a ship free falling out of orbit.

Ancestors. Oh, Ancestors! She was herself again! They—they were themselves again! A unit. A whole, instead of crippled and bleeding.

Delfi opened her mouth. A torrent of Imperial Common poured forth.

Oh. Oh no. Not again.

"Unwanted, undead. Unwanted prize a fine centerpiece makes. Spare the rod, spoil the tool. A closed mind wins no wars. Find a corner, find a hole. Shelter, frail child! Death is freed. He comes on bloody wings." Delfi gasped the last words out and then curled tighter in a ball, hugging her stomach.

No one. There was no one. Nadi was gone. Jossa couldn't see her. Didn't know where she went. They didn't have a receiver. Didn't have anyone to hear the translation.

Her gut twisted again. She retched, doubling over and falling from the pallet where she sat to the decking beneath. She landed badly. The pain in her shoulder was a distant thing compared to the acid in her gut. She fumbled, trying to sit up. Trying to find her balance. Trying to turn so she could see Delfi, who she could hear gasping behind her.

No one. No one to hear. No one to save them from themselves.

She gagged again and threw up a little clear liquid. Her fingers scrabbled for purchase against the smooth metal plates of the floor. She couldn't get her feet under her. Couldn't tell if she was standing on her head or curled up in a ball.

Words tried to form in her mouth but got stuck somewhere in her throat, blocking air. Blocking everything. She slipped on something liquid and cracked her cheek against something else that was much harder. Her stomach tried to rebel for the third time. She saw red.

Not a veil over her eyes. Not a metaphorical thing at all.

She saw red. On the deck beneath her. On her hand as she tried again to brace herself and skidded in a puddle of her own vomit.

And blood.

Why was there blood? Why did she taste acid and copper?

Someone—Delfi—yelped. Surprise shot down the bond between them before alarm and anger drowned it. Jossa felt her lips pull back in a snarl, but she couldn't hold the expression as her stomach folded in on itself.

"Hey!" The words were faint and far away, but she heard them. "What the fuck are you doing?"

Oh good, Jossa thought as yet more bloody bile tried to dribble out of her mouth. But the person had turned her face up. Gravity was stronger than whatever force propelled the emesis. She coughed and choked, then choked again as all the words of the translation tried to make their way out at once.

She hit the deck again, felt her head bounce, then cried out as something caught her hair and dragged her across the room. Weeping and gagging, Jossa hung limp as the woman, Nadi, pulled her up and turned her so she was somewhat aimed toward the gaping hole of the toilet.

Jossa gagged, managed to get the clot of vomit and blood into the bowl, then gasped as the stench of sterilizing chemicals nearly seared her nostrils and burned the lining of her throat. Nadi let her scramble back and away but kept hold of her hair. There was a shake—once, hard—and then the nehkeh woman pulled Jossa's head around, anger and disgust not blunted at all by the fact that it was hair, not skin, that she touched.

Jossa nearly cried in relief when she met the other woman's hard blue eyes. Finally.

She took a breath, ready to let the prophecy's translation pour forth. And stopped.

Delfi loomed behind Nadi, her face terrible and wild. Far more so than the nehkeh herself. Jossa cried, "No!" But she was too late. Delfi brought her raised arms, heavy with the weight of the shackles, down on Nadi's head.

A crunch. A spatter of blood, hot on Jossa's skin, and then they dropped. Jossa grunted as the dead weight of the other woman landed on her chest, shoving all the air out of her body. Then grunted again as Delfi hit the woman a second time, knocking her to the side and over.

Jossa's insides, already insulted enough for one day, tried to eject themselves entirely. She managed to turn her face to the side so the blood didn't choke her again, but it was a near thing. She could do nothing about the wet warmth spreading between her legs, nothing except close her eyes and whimper.

When she finally stopped retching, for now, and managed to take a breath, she looked up at Delfi. The words of the prophecy still held her for ransom of her sanity, so she forced the thought through the mind bond instead, praying her sister would see fit to answer. ::Why?::

And wonder of wonders, a reply. ::You can talk to a dead body as easy as a live one. Get on with it.::

It didn't matter that the walls came back, just as strong and impenetrable as before. It didn't matter that Delfi's face was spattered in blood and harder than compressed carbon. None of it mattered.

For one second. One glorious, heartbreaking second, Jossa hadn't been alone. Hadn't been abandoned.

And that was enough.

She turned her attention to the body lying across her midsection. Opened her mouth. And spoke.

Thirty-Two--Delfi

Never underestimate the desperate.
- unknown

Delfi strained against the tethers holding her to the wall of the little cell. Just a little further. Just a little...

She clung to the wall with one hand, bare feet braced against the corner where the deck met the vertical surface, and strained again. Jossa was better suited for this, being taller. But since she was having difficulty staying upright at the moment, Delfi was the only one left.

An inch. Another. She found the corner of a raised display screen and wedged her fingers in around it. Another inch. She managed to slide her leading foot forward just a little bit, praying that the blood that'd covered it was mostly dry. She'd already lost ground twice when she'd found new wet patches and skidded backwards because of it.

Her foot held. Her fingers trembled on the tiny lip of the screen. She wished it was the one she needed. But, smart people that they were, the bounty hunters had made sure the lock pad was out of easy reach of any enterprising—and lucky—prisoners.

What nobody had counted on was having to make an emergency check on one of those prisoners suddenly vomiting blood. Or the fact that it might happen while Tarva was out of range of whatever sai was in the cell.

Ancestors bless, Delfi thought as she fought for the next inch. The hand that wasn't clinging to the wall for dear life stretched out in front of her, hovering over the edge of the lock screen. Ancestors bless and Progeny thank. If Jossa weren't what she was. If the bounty hunter lying in a cooling heap on the deck had thought just a couple seconds ahead, Delfi wouldn't be spread-eagled over six feet of wall, trying to unlock their shackles and praying that she'd guessed the security measures correctly.

Nadi could have had the system pull up the slack in the tether between shackles and anchor. She could have stuck both Jossa and Delfi to the wall like museum pieces and waited until Jossa'd thrown up half her stomach. She should have.

She also should have been holding mental shields in place, to keep Jossa from being able to affect her like that. But either she was as bad at it as Syrus occasionally claimed to be or she'd gotten complacent with Tarva shielding her most of the time.

Another inch. Almost there. Don't touch the pad yet, you little idiot. Not until you can make full contact. No room to mess this up.

If she failed and the system didn't read the blood signature of the dead bounty hunter, she wouldn't get a second chance. She could go back and dip her hand in the puddle of blood again, sure. But the tethers would contract, pull her in, and not let her get anywhere near the locks again.

Museum pieces.

How appropriate.

Something pulled in her shoulder. Her hip bone grated, and she gained another half inch. So close.

Her leading foot quaked once in warning. Her knee started to give. Delfi lunged, found fresh purchase for her foot a little ways forward of where it'd been, lost contact with the little lip of screen housing she'd been clinging to with the one hand, and slapped her forward hand over the pad of the lock in front of her.

She caught sight of the long smear of blood she left on its surface before the tethers on her shackles claimed dominance once more. She hit the wall hard, sideways, and her shoulder and hip complained loudly before she lost her balance. Pulled by artificial gravity as relentless as the natural thing, she overbalanced and skidded backwards.

"Del! Del, are you ok?"

Delfi groaned and tilted her head back to look at Jossa. Her sister's worried face, chin crusted in blood and bile, peered at her from the ceiling. No. Well yes, the ceiling. But she was upside down. Or maybe Delfi was upside down? Her head was still ringing from the smack to the floor. She couldn't quite figure out which way was up for the moment.

::Del?:: Jossa's mental voice was hesitant. Scared. Delfi didn't need the bond to know that.

The tension pulling her wrists eased suddenly. Jossa's face wavered and tipped sideways with a surprised "Oh!" And they were free. Well. As free as they could manage while still being stuck together at the soul.

Delfi grunted and shook her hands out of the now-loose shackles around her wrists, then sat up with a groan. Jossa didn't know that her words had made it through to her sousi. At least, Delfi didn't think so. And she wasn't going to clue the older woman in. So, she kept her mouth shut and the bond narrowed, and siphoned off as much of Jossa's worry and fear as she could manage in between gasps for air.

"Delfi?" Jossa asked again.

Delfi waved a hand in acknowledgement and frowned. Was there anyone else on the ship? She'd assumed not, since nobody had come to check on them after the woman died. But she spread her sai through the vicinity anyways, just to check. Someone could have been sleeping. Or out of earshot. Or—But no. Not an internal mutter, not a half-known daydream, not even a complaint about the cost of fuel cells. Nothing but Jossa's insistent pushing down the bond.

Setting a portion of attention to keeping a mental ear open for returning bounty hunters, Delfi turned her attention to their physical surroundings.

What did they have to work with? Sleeping pallets, the inactivated shackles... The anchors were part of the wall, built into a housing that let them slide as needed, which was the only reason she'd been sure the key to releasing them had to be outside the cell. And the dead bounty hunter. Nadi's corpse was by far the most valuable thing in the room.

Or rather, the gear hanging from her vest, belt, and arms were the most valuable things.

Grunting again as her hip complained, Delfi turned over on her hands and knees and crawled over to the body. The puddle of blood was relatively easy to avoid, at least from this direction. She felt Jossa move around from the other side, and together they rifled through the various pockets and pouches in the woman's clothing.

In short order, they had a tidy pile of gear sitting on a clean corner of the pallet. Several knife hilts in various sizes. A stun baton, quiescent and not likely to activate without its owner's touch. Four metal rings with silplat cred slips hanging from them. Two had been in pockets, one was clipped to a thin belt under Nadi's waistband, and the last had been tucked inside her bra. A small metal file, a hand-sized screen, a data crystal, and other assorted odds and ends that ended up stuffed in pockets and forgotten. A screw. A bit of lint. And was that a rodent skull?

Delfi let Jossa sort the things into useful and non-useful piles. As her sister busied herself with that, Delfi lifted Nadi's left arm and examined the comm/data unit mounted in the wide band that covered her from wrist to elbow. It was tight. Too tight to slip over the hand. But there was a... Delfi hunted around with her fingers and found the catch at the elbow end of the cuff. It loosened, then flopped back. She caught it and held it up to examine.

It was inactive, obviously, flex-screens dark and unresponsive to touch. How paranoid were the bounty hunters? Paranoid enough to keep the data units slaved to the ship computer, logging any entry or use?

Nehkeh who'd abandoned their commitments to the Karukap, surviving over twenty years on the run as they hunted down bounties all over the Empire. Delfi set the cuff out of the way. Sure as faulty buffer panels fell off when you dropped through atmo, the thing was trapped. Best not to chance it at all.

Although if she could get into the main computers, maybe she could find something they could use.

"So what now?" Jossa's tired voice cut through Delfi's thoughts. It wasn't a question. Not really. More a statement on the fact that they were, yet again, running from a force more powerful and indomitable than a newborn star.

Delfi looked at her sister. Really looked at her for the first time in days. Jossa's skin was ashy. Her face drawn and lined, her eyes dull. Her hands were listless as they fidgeted with the small pile of useless and random junk.

Delfi clamped down on the surge of sympathy that rose in her chest and boiled towards the mind bond. No. She couldn't afford it. Couldn't let herself soften, no matter how small Jossa looked. How defeated. There was only room for one overly emotional weakling in this situation, and she couldn't let herself be overtaken. Not now. Not until they'd found their way free of this mess.

And not ever again either.

But "not ever" would come a lot sooner than she'd planned if they didn't get moving.

Scooping up the pile of knives, credit slips, and other useful things, Delfi split the loot between them. She kept one ring of credits for herself, all but one of the knives, and the small screen as well. Jossa took what remained without complaint, then grabbed the stun baton. Thank the Ancestors she wasn't battering her way across the mind bond, asking what Delfi was doing. This particular dance was familiar enough, even at years removed, that they didn't need to speak to get the work done.

Pushing her sai just a bit further and finding still emptiness around the ship, Delfi sighed. She'd have to open up to Jossa in order to extend her own range much further. Ancestors provide it didn't come to that.

Jossa hesitated when Delfi told her what they needed to look for, but nodded reluctantly and wobbled her way out of the cell. Delfi followed her out, stepping carefully to avoid the body and its puddle of blood. The main room was sparse, just the table and chairs and another cell on the opposite wall. She glanced at its lock pad for it but didn't bother to examine it closer. Why she and Jossa hadn't been split, she couldn't say. Maybe it had to do with being sai, and the hunters not wanting to deal with the headache of separating them.

If only they'd known.

Jossa whimpered. Delfi cringed. Nothing she could do about it now if the thought had slipped across the bond. Leaving her sister to work her shaky way up the low steps out of the room, Delfi headed out the opposite door and into the next.

That one proved to be a galley. One with all knives and assorted hole-making utensils safely stowed. A screen in the table there, by the faint line around the rim, but not what she needed.

A hall, lined with rooms she didn't bother checking. Internal doors all. Nothing that could be sealed against decompression with its own small airlock the way a bridge would.

She found a set of stairs and was just about to start down them when Jossa spoke along the mind bond, mental voice hesitant. ::Del, I have the bridge.::

Delfi headed back the way she'd come, pausing to dip her hand in the blood again.

The puddle was thickening, congealing around the loose strands of Nadi's blonde hair. The other bounty hunters would probably, probably be back before it started to smell. Maybe even with Syrus.

By then, she and Jossa would be long gone.

Shaking the memory of the prophecy from her mind, she headed down the next hall towards her sister.

The ship's computer answered to her bloody handprint easily enough, and she worked quickly while Jossa went back to the galley to look for supplies and maybe some fresh clothes.

She entered the code carefully, working around the logins where she could and giving the screens the old blood where she couldn't. She wasn't Denz, not in a thousand years, but she'd picked up enough from him and others that she ought to be able to get the ship running. Sometimes her ways of coming at code had surprised Syrus when he checked her work. Three hundred years of drift had closed some doors and opened others.

Apparently they hadn't opened the correct doors this time. Ancestors curse Agadi, she thought to herself, backing carefully out of the manual ignition sequences as she tried to keep her tear ducts from overflowing. She should have realized the defenses on his primary weapon would be nigh impenetrable considering how hard she and Syrus'd had to work to keep him out of the half-crippled escape ship.

But he hadn't locked access to the data networks quite as thoroughly.

::Del.:: Jossa again. Delfi lifted her hands from the screens and waited. Had Jossa felt something? Was there someone coming that she couldn't Hear yet? Punching her sai out to its furthest bounds, Delfi scoured the area around the ship. Nothing.

::I found a flit.:: Jossa's voice was hopeful, but sad too. And nervous.

Delfi resisted the urge to pass a mental hand over her sister's hair, gave another yank on the emotions coming over the bond, and turned back to her work. None of this mental wandering was getting her any closer to where they needed to be. Although the flit would help if she could disable any tracking on it.

Later. Find a place to run to first, then worry about how to get there.

A map finally lit up the screen. Local. Topographical. They were on an island. Probably a tropical port. Good. That meant spaceports, which this ship had obviously avoided. Someone had to be looking for passengers. The money they'd taken off Nadi would be enough to buy at least a pallet and water rights on something. They could make themselves useful later.

And not on their backs. Never again.

She found the spaceports on the map and made some careful adjustments to code to bring up the lists of vessels taking passengers.

Then she saw the name of the planet and the alert flash about a holiday in the upper corner of the screen. She froze.

::Delfi!:: Bare feet pounded an uneven rhythm down the hall and into the bridge. Delfi rocked as Jossa staggered and caught herself on the chair. Alarm and denial flooded the bond. Delfi pulled it in, wondering if she was taking on Jossa's feelings or adding to her own. Nobody would be going anywhere today.

Ancestors behind, how had they managed to land on a Ruse lis Esab, in the Ruse lis Net no less, on a High Feast Day?

Jossa looked at the screen and breathed a profane prayer to the Ancestors, then followed it up with a string of curses that would have made Syrus proud no matter the language.

Syrus. This was his fault. There were nobles after him. Of course they'd bring him back to their seat of power once he was caught.

She checked. Except this wasn't the seat of power for that particular family, may their Ancestors hide their faces. This was the seat of power for their liege lord. A Kizrard, no less.

Delfi scrubbed her hands over her eyes and tried to think. They had to find some place to hole up now that the promise of immediate evac was gone. They had the flit, if she could get it running and disable the tracker, and that was all. Could they find somewhere in the city to hide until tomorrow? Until the crews of the ships staggered their way back from the festivities and sobered up enough to fly?

Could she find a place to stash Jossa and go looking for a flight anyway? Take the risk that there might be one captain out there who despised the holiday as much as she did? Too risky. She couldn't split from her sister. Her sister was healed, according to the medics and the medunit she'd been stuffed into.

But big trauma like that didn't just go away. Just because the tissue was knitted together and infection burned away didn't mean the victim's body had great reserves left afterwards. It didn't mean she was up for taking care of herself, possibly even defending herself, on her own. Ancestors, she was having difficulty walking.

Not to mention that given the state their bond was in, parking Jossa in the middle of the city would probably make her overload and lose control of her sai before Delfi could rein her in.

Delfi stiffened as realization struck her. If she didn't open up the bond to her sister, Jossa would lose control. Yes. True.

That wasn't the only thing that would happen, though. There was the prophecy to consider.

Syrus didn't have anyone to siphon him. He didn't have the greatest control over his external shields either. Internal, yes. Trying to hear his thoughts when he shielded them was like trying to move a planet just by putting a metaphorical shoulder against it and pushing.

The prophecy.

She didn't just have to worry about Jossa's sai or the hunter's checking in. Or worse, returning. No.

She had to get them out of here before Syrus lost his mind and started butchering people in the streets. Because sure as ships fell down a gravity well, the nobles who'd caught him would lock down the city and cut the people's data feeds to keep news of the bloodshed from spreading. They were bringing a nehkeh, a known murderer, into a city on a High Feast Day and knowingly putting hundreds of lives in danger. A known murderer wanted by the military, at that.

It didn't matter how highly ranked they were. Other noble families would cut ties. Trade would dry up. If it came out that Syrus was sai, their allies would scatter like animals from a wildfire. It would be known that they tested a weapon, for that was what he was, on their own people. Who would they scruple to aim him at next?

She sat there for a minute or so, running calculations in her head. Some of it must have leaked through her shields because Jossa pressed against them tentatively and asked, ::Del?::

Delfi ignored her.

Was it smart?

Not in the least.

Should she do it?

Probably not.

Would it help her and Jossa in the long run?

Her heart stopped. Tears pricked her eyes. The panic nearly caught her again, but she forced it down, taking deep breaths and staring resolutely at the ridiculous centerpiece in the middle of the plaza until the stupidity of the display overtook the gut-wrenching agony of the future likelihood.

Yes. It might help her and Jossa in the long term, if she could pull it off. It would help them as a collective, if not herself individually. Because there was no doubt in her mind, none at all, that if she went through with this idiotic idea, Jossa would go right back to past behaviors, completely confident that she was doing the right thing.

Hard brown eyes looking into hers, telling her to brace herself; this was going to hurt.

A stab, as if to her heart.

And the blessed relief of discovering she could breathe again, if only a little better than before.

Delfi shut down the map on the screen, then wiped as much evidence as she could from the computer logs. Standing, feeling the drying blood pull and flake from her skin as she fisted her hands, she turned to Jossa. "Zo'li Syrus tsijach akkeks oksuks neh."

Jossa stared at her. Delfi pulled the shock and horror from her sister and stuffed it down where it could only hurt one of them. Then she crossed her arms and lifted her chin.

"Find him? Why?" Jossa croaked. "We got rid of him. He's not our problem anymore."

Mainly mine, Delfi thought to herself, but blocked the thought before it could slip into Jossa's head.

Her sister didn't notice. "Let the nobles have him. Let him fulfill the prophecy and draw their attention, and we can get away. We don't even have to try to make it to space right away. Planets are big."

Not as big as space. Especially not the seats of power, where every grain of sand was counted and every drop of water tracked as the Commons paid through the nose for the privilege of breathing fresh, unfiltered air. If they could get to him before he became the key player in the storm to come, maybe they could avert it. Get in, get him out, get him to help them off planet. He knew more ways to counter and avoid being caught than anyone she'd ever heard of.

Her memory tossed up the bounty hunters, as if she needed the warning.

Too bad the defenses on the ignitions were so strong. She'd have set the ship to self-destruct.

But now that they knew they were being hunted, they could do a better job of avoiding pursuit.

Right?

It was a horrible plan.

They'd survived on less.

"We could steal a ship, even!" Jossa kept going, oblivious to Delfi's train of thought. "Or bribe someone into—"

"Jeh!" Delfi stopped her hands half an inch from grabbing her sister's shoulders and shaking her till her head popped off. There'd be no bribing, no favors. And they'd have as much luck sneaking into a spaceport on Feast Day and taking off unnoticed as they would prancing into a festival naked.

Sighing, Delfi dropped her hands. "Jeh," she said again.

Then, before Jossa could come up with any more arguments, she stalked off the bridge and down the hall. They didn't have time to hem and haw. She could feel the countdown in her bones.

> Delfi

THIRTY-THREE--DELFI

Be grateful that most saiog in the nehkeh ranks are low-level Receivers. Can you imagine the chaos if one of them were a strong Projective?
-Military Mistress of Sai, to her aides

It wasn't as simple as just walking off the bridge with purpose and stubborn will. First, they needed some way to get out to wher-ever it was Syrus had ended up.

Delfi winced when Jossa tapped her on the shoulder, the buffet of impatience and irritation nearly swamping the narrowed mind bond. But she followed her sister's pointed finger and breathed a sigh of relief instead of growling like she wanted to. A flit hung from the ceiling with four empty brackets next to it.

The controls to lower it weren't bloodlocked, thank the Ancestors for small favors. While Jossa poked through the two compartments mounted on the back end, Delfi swung a leg over the front seat and looked for the ignition. That was locked to DNA. She growled as she climbed back down.

Jossa flinched. Pain seared the image of Syrus out of the bond. Delfi decided she didn't have the attention to spare for worrying about her sister's hurt feelings. Instead, she pulled the pain over, felt it slice at her psyche, and then shoved it down to the well at her center. Stupid Syrus. Stupid Jossa.

Stupid sai bond.

Another yank, to take care of the anguish that thought caused her sister, and then Delfi headed for the stairs, taking them two at a time and nearly running back to the body and its puddle of blood.

Back down the hall and thumping down the stairs, a chant of hurry, hurry, hurry running through her head in time to her steps. The flit answered to the smear of blood on the thumb-sized lock pad and Delfi stopped. She was still covered in blood. She couldn't work the controls like this.

::Here.:: Jossa's mental voice was almost hesitant. She couldn't have been too afraid of Delfi's reaction, though, because she kept insisting on using the bond to speak instead of her mouth.

Delfi turned and saw that her sister'd been doing more than random poking. Jossa held out a small bottle labeled "H2O2" with a pressure dot and a tiny nozzle. And a small rag, the sort mechanics might use to clean grease from their hands.

Frowning, Delfi leaned over to look at the rest of the stuff Jossa'd spread over the back seat of the machine. Three knife hilts, a cluster of spare power packs of the sort that went in guns, another little bottle that said "Sanitizer" in rough handwriting, a tube of lip color, a small gray plastic box with another bloodlock on it, a ring of credit slips, and two clear vacuum-sealed bags that seemed to hold folded cloth. She snorted. Everything a mobile bounty hunter needed.

Taking the little bottle from Jossa, she pointed at the vacuum-sealed bags with her chin. Jossa sighed and opened a bag as Delfi cleaned the blood off her hand. The cloth turned out to be clothes, two full sets. Delfi tossed the bloody rag aside and grabbed for the shirt and pants as Jossa laid them out over the back of the flit.

::Do we really have time?:: Jossa started to ask, but stopped when Delfi yanked her old, filthy shirt off and sent it after the rag. When she hesitated again, Delfi stopped undoing her own pants and grabbed at

Jossa's clothes, pulling the tattered hem of her shirt out so her sister could see the dried blood that stiffened the fabric.

Jossa didn't waste any more time arguing after that. While she was cleaning up and changing, Delfi went to work on the flit's nav system. It didn't take her long to find the tracker. Even less time to realize that the Crack had shielded it even tighter than the ignition sequence on the ship's engines. And pulling the hard wired unit would fry the machine entirely. Nothing for it. They'd have to find a place to switch vehicles.

In short order, they had the carrying compartments repacked and the main airlock doors open, and they were out into wet jungle heat, clinging tight to the flit with hands and arms and legs as Delfi turned its power up to full and aimed it for the canopy of tree limbs above. She just made it, the rear fins of the flit scraping over the metal of the ship beneath as she struggled to make it to open air without ending up a smear on the metal or a twisted wreck in the trees around them.

Jossa yelled in alarm as they popped into open air, corkscrewed once along both vertical and horizontal axes, and settled out on a straight-line course for the city they could see climbing the distant mountainside.

Delfi ignored her. The chrono on the control panel of the flit mocked her. The prophecy pounded in her ears, drowning out the wind as she guided the flit.

Faster, faster, faster.

She was trying to outrace doom.

>>><<<

They were about halfway to the outskirts of the city when Jossa grunted and clutched tighter at Delfi's sides. Half a second later, the emotions hit the bond. Not the low-level hum they'd both been feeling for the past ten minutes. This was wild, bright, and jagged with pain.

Delfi gasped as she pulled it across the bond, feeling it slice her mind to ribbons as she stuffed it down into the well at the core of her being. Ancestors bless, was that what she thought it was?

The scrape and thwap of leaves and branches hitting the under-side of the flit brought her back to herself. She wrestled the thing back to a safe altitude, checked to see that they hadn't damaged any-thing important, and shouted, "Appare'its a'appa'ih zoturyj nihba?" over her shoulder at Jossa. She really hoped it hadn't been what she thought it was.

Her sister shuddered once, twice, and shook her head. ::I think... I think it's Syrus.::

Delfi hated being proven right. Growling to herself, she cranked the speed up another notch or so and cracked the bond a little wider so she could pull more of that strange anger out of her sister before something truly catastrophic happened.

>>><<<

Fifteen minutes later, the jungle beneath the flit fell away and the first warning pings of a flight control flashed on the flit's control screen. Too high. Show proof of lineage or face immediate punish-ment.

Delfi nearly jabbed her thumb onto the lockpad. They wanted lineage? She'd give them lineage. There wasn't a person alive who was fit to breathe her air.

EMPs arming in three... two...

No. She was smarter than that. It was just the anger driving her. Not her anger, either. She pulled it back in and stuffed it into the abyss as she circled wide, dropping the flit to a lower altitude. It came up against roofs this time as the navigation grid over the city snapped the vehicle into place on the sky lanes. Glancing up, she saw that the jungle topped a sloping ridge she hadn't noticed and cut off abruptly when the ground dropped off in a short cliff. Then she was facing the city again.

A small sea of clay tile and rusted metal roofs over plaster in all the colors of a pastel rainbow, the ground level of the city spread out before them in a jumbled riot of mismatched color. Here and there she could see festival decorations tethered or tied to the corners of buildings.

The staggered shimmer of anti-grav lenses rose in a reversed cascade from buildings to sky, the pattern of it lost from this angle but undoubtedly there. A few flits and barges floated here and there, using the lenses to keep to both their allowed altitude and course. Many were also covered in decorations for the day.

"Is that a... that's a monstrosity." Jossa leaned over Delfi's back to peer at a particularly gruesome depiction of fertilization and the sexual differentiation of an embryo mashed together on a single barge.

Delfi tugged some of the disgust and horror over to her side of the bond. At least her sister'd said the words out loud.

She'd just started scanning the roofs ahead for a parking lot or rental sign when the speakers near her knees buzzed to life.

Interlude III

Degra op Lappuog, logs

3786.10.14.1737-

Access code TAU-23: Status update: No breach of hull. Portside cell wall lowered at 1525. Cargo bay doors open at 1608.

Access code TAU-23: Recording of main cabin accessed. Playing from 3786.10.14.1524:

Delfi: Unwanted, undead. Unwanted prize a fine centerpiece makes. Spare the rod, spoil the tool. A closed mind wins no wars. Find a corner, find a hole. Shelter, frail child! Death is freed. He comes on bloody wings.

Retching noises.

Nadi: Hey! What the fuck are you doing?

Sounds of struggle.

Retching noises.

Quiet.

Jossa: They didn't want Syrus in their home. But now they do. Because of what he is. They're going to put on a display. Discipline, to teach him who is in charge. Someone's drugged him. Something to open the sai so he can't keep it out, can't keep it in. Hide! He's going to kill you. Going to kill you all!

Access code TAU-23: Recording Stopped.

Comm traffic:

Tarva: Pull out of the slums. We have an idea of where he is.

Fieltar: Where to, boss?

Tarva: Agadi, get into the data feeds. See if you can find anything about public punishments slated for today.

Agadi: Yes, boss.

Tarva: Fiel, you and Ban start working your way through the edges of the city. See if your flits ping off one of ours.

Banuo: What's up, boss?

Tarva: The bitches got loose.

All:....

Banuo: And Nadi?

Tarva: We're on Protocol Anek now. Grid the city and report back.

Fieltar: Yes, boss.

Banuo: Fuck!

Agadi: Yes, boss.

End transmission, 3786.10.14.1741

Thirty-Four--Syrus

I'm going to kill them, you hear? Going to kill them all.
Make it stop. Make it stop!
  - overheard, Syrus to Rissa 3748.03.15

He really needed to stop underestimating the people who wanted him dead. Not that it would do much good, because he was pretty sure that this time it would actually stick.

Every twitch sent a fresh stab of agony through his body. He growled as the shocks ran their course and pooled behind his eyes, then snarled louder as even that small reaction set off a fresh wave of pain.

He breathed a string of curses as the float turned, shifting him to the side. He tried to adjust, entirely without thinking. The sensors and activators stuck to his body all lit up together, and his muscles seized and tingled for half a heartbeat before the array timed out and let him go.

This shit was going to get old fast.

Somewhere down in its hole, the monster tested the walls of its prison and found them easier to climb than usual. Syrus knew he should make sure the seal on its lid was locked down tight, but he couldn't find enough coherent thought to scrape together for the attempt. His subconscious kept wanting to pull on the shackles, adjust to the movements of the float, and twitch away from the unholy mess of wires wrapped around his arms. The array obligingly zapped and reset and zapped again. A white-hot scrawl of pain skittered through his nerves and turned his vision fuzzy.

Fuck on a stick.

When he had his breath back, he reached for his shields instead. He might be fucking useless with them most times, but every little bit helped. Every scrap of willpower he could pull together. Every grain of sand he could pile into a dam between himself and what he knew was coming. He'd need it all.

He had no business being surprised that his shields evaporated before he'd even laid mental *hands* on them. But he was. He expected the result when he tried again. Was only disappointed the third time. Resigned the fourth.

He didn't get another chance.

The float, wherever it was in the line of the parade, finally made its way out of the staging area and into the first part of the official route. He could tell because the emotions of the crowds went from a slowly rising background hum to a full-fledged waterfall.

He grunted and bowed his head under the deluge, then ground his teeth on a scream as the sensors responded to his movement by adding a fresh load of pain to the weight hammering his head.

Desperate, gasping, and then almost heaving as the emotions and agony blended into a seamless whole, he tried to find purchase for sanity as the flood nearly washed away his mind. Even the monster lost its grip on the wall of its pit. The caustic boil that signaled its presence receded.

They should have muzzled you, a dry voice said somewhere in his subconscious. *Or at least wired your jaw shut. Although I suppose they're counting on the forest they have growing all over this floating monstrosity to muffle whatever noise you make. And the crowds are making enough racket to cover whatever makes it past that.*

He hadn't realized he was screaming. Rissa's words gave him enough to latch onto that he could hear it. Some of the ringing in his ears actually came from his own voice ricocheting off the metal around him.

His heart stuttered in his chest, a wholly physical reaction this time, and then an invisible mule team kicked him in the ribs, one from the front and one from the back.

Holy shit.

The monster picked itself off the floor of its pit and tried the walls again. They were seamed and riddled with cracks, but not cragged enough to climb easily. Not yet. It started up again anyways.

Shhh. I'll deal with it. You worry about keeping what's outside... outside.

Through the twitches of nerves gone haywire, something about the arrangement seemed off. But he couldn't string one thought after another well enough to figure out what it was. Lacking a working plan of his own, he decided to give hers a try.

And almost. Almost it worked. At first.

He turned his mind outward, looking for something to orient to. The mass of wires attached to his body presented a first option, but he kept going. He already knew how it was set up and what it'd do. Even the defibrillator that'd just punched his heart back into rhythm.

Focusing on the rig would only keep him stuck in the loop of pain.

As if on cue, his fingers twitched. An answering jab of current shot down his arm. It was just about all he could do to keep his muscles slack and let it happen, but he managed. Maybe because he'd temporarily lost the strength to react beyond a hitch in his breathing.

It had better be temporary. He didn't plan on staying here forever.

So he looked further. As far as he could without moving more than his eyes.

He didn't find much.

No security cameras. He'd guessed wrong. The Kizrard must be counting on whatever readouts the equipment spat out on whatever screen it was all hooked up to. Well, he was getting a fuck ton of it then. The rig must be going as crazy as he was, all the signals it'd be getting.

Nothing else to see in the dark of the room. Two low red lights, probably to keep whoever came in here from tripping over whatever they usually stashed in this compartment. He almost laughed at that, then caught himself as the nodes stuck to his arms and legs gave a warning buzz.

Somewhere else in the float he could hear the movement of machinery and the low hum of anti-grav generators. But that wasn't what drew his attention.

No. It wasn't his attempt to find a focus that pulled his mind out of this room and out of the moorings that held his sanity together. It was the same thing that had overloaded him to start with. He'd only *thought* he was pushing back, with the help of a ghost too long dead to actually be any use.

The crowd.

Their emotions.

And all the shit that came with them.

They were so strong he could see them in his mind's eye, fed to him by the eyes of everyone else in range of his sai. The throngs of people along either side of the causeway. The showers of confetti. Handfuls of candy tossed wide to keep children out from under the low-flying barges. Gaggles of little boys toddling and trotting and walking along the parade route. Each one the pride of his family and treasure of his town, neighborhood, or even district. The Natural Born, conceived and carried to term without the intervention of the priests and their equipment. More, many more of them common born. A very few from the higher echelons of society. A precious one or two of the sector nobility.

Almovak was probably up on the first float with the Kizrard. Bastards, both of them. Behind them would be Alrurisi's float, the proud and revered mother capable of producing an egg without help, and carrying him to term to boot. Like a nav computer locking onto a destination, his sai swung round and found the noblewoman. Almost directly overhead. He felt the frustration and puzzled anger of the Kizrard as a scratchy blip against his mind and, yes, Almovak's wary concern. But Alrurisi was a beacon compared to the noblemen.

As soon as Syrus got a good look at her, he knew why. That wasn't just pride for what an accident of biology had managed. The emotion pouring out of her *felt* like the hard reverb he was familiar with. But its source was nothing like the other women he could feel up and down the length of the parade.

This pride was sourced in a molten ball of angry satisfaction, roiling and oozing in the woman's heart before filtering out through her veins and pores to lash him with whips of fire.

Gasping, trying not to move, he pulled together a few more scraps of self-control and looked deeper, trying to see why. He was caught. He was being tortured. The Kizrard had what he wanted. Almovak had fulfilled his obligations and probably saved the family from repercussions. And she herself...

Now he knew what she'd been doing behind the Kizrard while that fucking bastard had stood there and listened to himself talk. She'd replaced the paralytic with the psychotropic sai booster the Karukap used. Or one like it. The drug they used when one of their saiog didn't have the reach or strength for what needed to be done. The city wasn't a background hum grating on his nerves and rubbing the inside of his skull raw. Not anymore.

No. She'd forced his sai as wide open as Jossa's. Forced him to Feel *everything*. Every nuance. Every shift in mental state. Every. Little. Thing.

The monster in his mind surged halfway up its prison pit, howling a wordless war cry. When the electrical nodes finally stopped shocking his body and gave him half a second to sag in his restraints, Syrus found that he'd been screaming again. His throat was one raw wound. Every breath he tried to drag in burned against the abused flesh. Swallowing was out of the question. He felt a cough start to build in his chest and almost whimpered in anticipation of the pain the movement would cause.

Almost whimpered; but snarled instead. Warning zings from the array sent tingling fire down his arm. He bared his teeth. The monster didn't care if his voice was broken. It didn't care that he was hooked up to a fucking torture device. It didn't even care that he was locked in a storage compartment barely tall enough to stand and turn around in. It would get out. And then it'd climb this fucking float and tear that woman limb from limb, and then anyone else who got in their way. It would turn all the smug, self-satisfied pride she was radiating to its own purposes, fuel for the revenge she was so happy about, and it was going to lose its shit in the most bloody way possible.

Then the feelings swamped him again, called to his attention by the knowledge he'd just gleaned. The monster went down under the onslaught, back to the bottom of its pit. His artificially expanded sai scooped up the concentrated emotions of everyone in who knew how many miles and dumped it all on his head and Syrus forgot, for a moment, what Alrurisi'd done to him. Those closest hit hardest.

Nobles. *High* nobles.

Each and every one of them jumping up and down on his head, singly but somehow all at the same time too.

The thought gave his monster a bit of a boost as it pulled its caustic, hissing self back together in his mind and started climbing again.

Among those in closest proximity, there was none of the joy or pride that lay strung out like jewels on the line of the parade winding its slow way through the city. What he'd gotten before was a high-level view of the parade, probably as much a product of his imagination and memories as anything else. Now that his sai had pulled in some, he found the individual noble houses. Each marked by the family out front and the servants in the alleys. All showing the support required by the Kizrard. At least on the surface.

Under the surface though. *There* was the envy. The resentment. All mingling together into a saw-toothed blade that laid his mind open to the bone. Sharpest were the men, the rough scrape of their frustration like a cat's tongue in open wounds dealt by the crowd as a whole. The resulting mess of sensations set Syrus's teeth on edge. The monster climbed a little faster.

Why not *their* wives? the noblemen asked themselves and each other. Their sisters? Mothers? What use were the women at all? Going to the priests cost above and beyond the tithes that kept the clinics running. Why not do away with a living womb and get their heirs without ever bothering with a moody, expensive mouth to feed who couldn't be gotten rid of easily, if at all? What use were the laws against artificial wombs or genetic selection?

Syrus knew then that the parade had reached the base of the mountain. The pace would slow here. The parade would take its time displaying the wealth and resources and honor of those who remained. Rubbing the blessings of their Ancestors in the noses of the lower nobility and upper ranks of the commoners. Those who tried to breed themselves sai or into the ranks of the nobles.

Sons wouldn't do the job. Only daughters could marry up the ranks, unless extraordinary circumstances rendered the other heirs of a line invalid. But natural sons still gave status. And a daughter who was sibling to a natural son could be advertised as possibly having the same childbearing potential as her mother.

These lower-ranked nobility and the others who stood half a rung down on the social ladder, Syrus knew well. He'd stood behind them year after year in the af Mitachte's Northern Capitol, watching smaller versions of this parade crawl their way through the streets and on to the Feast plaza. Folks at this level of society didn't even think of *themselves* as people. Just breeding stock.

The air around him fairly simmered with the men's emotions. If he opened his eyes, he knew he'd be able to see the heat waves, even in the tiny compartment. Stupid fucks. Didn't they have anything better to do?

His monster thought it was a good thing they didn't. It boiled and bubbled, nearing the lip of its hole, sending the first runnels of caustic ooze to thread through his veins. Syrus bared his teeth at the feel of it, enduring the shock of the array while he tried to decide how hard to fight this time.

The monster didn't get far. True, the men might have the brightest, lightest burden. The women, they ran deeper. Duller. More painful. Why? Why not her? Why had *her* womb failed her? Why could *she* not live up to the hopes her parents and husband'd had for her? This one's husband rutted with the lowborn and brought back bastards for her to raise as her own. Another abased herself to the pseudo-priests in illegal clinics, banking on the promises that this concoction or that drug would waken her ovaries and bring about a pregnancy. That one was dull, beaten down physically and emotionally, because of her failures. Someone else mixed the gnaw of physical hunger with her emotions, sure that if she were prettier, her husband would do his duty and not leave *her* to run the risk of being caught breeding with the lowborn. Another was only on her feet because the man next to her held her tight, whispering words of promise and threat in her ear as the parade passed by.

And from each of them, guilt. Viscous, almost gluey. It oozed from every pore of every woman the float passed. Rooting in his mind, finding purchase on his sai where it slid from the celebrants riding the floats. He could almost hear their thoughts, could almost see the mental images playing behind their eyes. Hopes dashed. Conditional love lost. Futures bleak and wan with the washed-out images of children conceived by normal priest-assisted means, playing as if to taunt their mothers with their failure.

He'd felt it all before, though never this strong. It was impossible not to at least *sense* the undercurrent beneath the haze of manufactured happiness that blanketed the parade. It emanated. It radiated. It crept along the ground and floated among the shoulders of the crowds.

It tied the noble and highborn in knots and fed their jealousy, resentment, and anger on this, the happiest of feast days.

And it drove spikes in Syrus's mind and set down barbs in his memories.

It wasn't until he heard the moan that he realized he'd been fighting his restraints. The chain of electric shocks set off by his involuntary struggling stopped short of fibrillation, but only just. *He'd* stopped. Stuck in place by the weight of the guilt. Even his monster had slowed its climb. The caustic boil in his veins still simmered but had nowhere to go. All the extra space was taken up by the outside emotions.

And why shouldn't it be? some part of him said. Why the fuck should he bother, given what he'd done?

He'd tried to pretend she was a nuisance. That she was the bane of his existence, even though he was drawn to her side like magnets to a planetary pole. He'd told himself he was strong for surviving without her in the military training camps he'd been sold to. He'd lied to himself in so many ways.

And he'd known them to be lies even as he rooted them in his heart. It'd taken her terror, sent to him against all odds across billions and billions of miles of space, to make him face what a liar he'd been.

And somehow, though he had no idea why, she gave him the grace of her forgiveness. Somehow they'd managed to patch things up between them. And although he hadn't made it in time to save Okina, he *had* saved her. Had let her save him. Guarded her through nightmares of blood and pain. Fed her when she was too weak to do it herself.

It took losing her a second time to realize he hadn't just done it out of some warped sense of self-preservation. To realize he'd still been lying to himself. It took the frantic hours, days, and weeks of travel. Took sneaking through the Fleet ships to figure out that part of the reason he'd taken care of her was, yes, to keep himself sane. But it was mostly for her.

How much of a fucking idiot had he been to not realize he didn't have to fall back on his training to save her? If he'd clued in fast enough. If he'd thrown off the half-done conditioning the military'd forced on him with drugs and beatings and threats to *her* safety. If he'd just moved *faster*. Let his instincts take over just a little earlier.

She'd be alive.

His soul wouldn't have shattered into a million pieces.

He wouldn't have been so desperate to get her back that he built a semblance of her in his mind, the better to torture himself with.

They'd still be running. Still hiding. She wouldn't have the sort of life she deserved. But she'd be *alive* .

Something sliced through his consciousness, cutting the train of thought away at the root. Not the resentment of the noblemen or the envy of their women. Not even the despair of those past childbearing, who wouldn't have any more chances for success.

No. This was scorn. He knew this like he knew the feel of a weapon in his hand. He'd been raised on it. Fed it with every scrap of food he'd stolen, every shopkeeper's boot he'd dodged. Every step he'd taken in the family compound. It was the birthright of his blood. It had come at him from every direction in Navlad and Fleet society alike.

And just this once, it wasn't aimed his way.

The surprise of that realization was enough to cut through the weight of the guilt nearly flattening him where he sat. The pain of it spurred the monster back into motion.

The parade had reached the lower parts of the city. Here were the people who'd come to laugh. To jeer. To whisper behind their hands about the barren husks wrapped in fine fabrics and finer jewels. Here was where the women on top of the floats stopped radiating pride in an accomplishment and started putting out a different sort of pride. The sort that said, "I'm still better than you." And: "I have given birth to a son who *matters*— while you only whelp culls who will be sent off world before they reach adulthood because you must not be allowed to overrun the planet."

The people knew it. They took the offerings of candy the same way they'd take a bribe, so they wouldn't throw anything, such as rotten fruit or their extra children, back.

The sarcasm of the thought cut the guilt a bit further. The weight on Syrus's shoulders eased just a tiny bit. His head cleared enough that the pain could make itself known again.

Fucking wires. Fucking shackles on his arms. Fucking Kizrard, sending Almovak to chase him halfway across the Empire just so he could have another weapon in his pocket for the day he finally made that bid for the throne.

Syrus laughed at that, silently so the harness wouldn't go off again, and was rewarded with only the mildest warning buzz. What would happen, he wondered, if the idiot noble did a blood test on his new prize? How long would he wait to kill Syrus when he realized it wasn't just a freak nehkeh he'd wrapped up like a Feast Day present and stuffed in a box to Feel the entirety of a city?

Something about that last didn't make sense. Syrus tried to reason it out, but his mind was too fogged, too full of emotions to function properly. Oozing guilt ran in sluggish runnels, sticking and pooling in the dark spaces between conscious thought. Scorn slid through his awareness, leaving wads of clinging hatred in the torn gashes left by the highborns' collective envy and resentment. And something rose above it all, taking the bits here and the bits there. Absorbing. Converting. Turning into a bubbling amalgam that burned its own special knowledge into his veins.

He *did* deserve this. Alrurisi was right. But not because he'd ruined her family. Not because of what he was, nehkeh and worthless.

No. He'd failed to protect the one good thing that'd ever happened to him. He'd been too blind and stupid to protect her from her family, from the Kizrard's politics, from her husband.

From Brander and the Fleet.

The caustic mix in his veins surged again as he straightened, taking the pain from the harness's shocks and transmuting that too. He bared his teeth at the shackles on his wrists. At the wires draped over his head and shoulders. He had a modicum of slack in the tethers, probably so he'd have the chance to move and shock himself. The wires had some give in them, too. What wasn't there, he could make.

The nodes attached to his arms throbbed and tingled in warning. Then the ones on his legs. Some last scrap of his sanity pulled the monster back before it could fling itself into the maw of agony that waited for them. Not even he could count on surviving arrhythmia and reset and arrhythmia.

He wanted to wrap his hands around the Kizrard's neck and feel the bones crunch as he twisted. He wanted Almovak to watch Alrurisi die trying to pull her entrails from that monstrosity of a dress and stuff them back in her abdominal cavity.

He'd killed Rissa's husband, all those years ago.

Now, he had to live long enough to take care of the rest of the fuckers who'd screwed her over.

If he died after, fine.

But first.

His outer shields weren't even memories anymore. No matter. His life was pain. It always had been, and it always would be. The lashing of an entire city across his brain was nothing on what he'd felt, what he still felt, on realizing the broken body in the Fleet medunit was all that he had left of Rissa.

Slowly, in fits and starts, he built up his internal shields, setting them deeper than usual, penning in the monster's pit. He reinforced them with a promise. *Kill, kill them all. Kill the Kizrard. Kill Appulu.*

He had no idea if this would work, but it was the best he had. If he could close himself off. Shut himself down.

He planned his motions carefully. Bring his arms in from the armrests. Pull against the tether. He'd dropped the key Alrurisi'd given him. Not enough slack in anything to go looking for it. Not enough time. He couldn't hold the shields forever. Not with the entire city jumping up and down on his head.

Snag the node closest to his right hand. Drag the left over. Fold the little circular pad thing around the end of the wire and shove it into the lock point of the housing.

Someone nearby flared with anger. The monster ate the heat of it and used the extra burst of energy to fuel its next lunge for control. The array gave a warning zing.

Syrus set his jaw and *moved*. The folded-up end of the wire barely fit in the lock. He didn't know if he lost his shields or consciously dropped them as he finished jamming the thing into the narrow slot in the shackle's housing.

The wave of agony broke over his head.

Blood rushed in his ears. His heart pounded. Everything was on fire. At some point, he lost control of his voice and screamed.

The mule team kicked him in the ribs again.

And in the ringing quiet of the aftermath, he felt the shackle fall into his lap. Felt it roll down his legs and bounce off his boot.

The harness barely had a chance to give him another low zap before his free hand grabbed a fistful of wires and yanked. Teeth still bared in a feral grin, he turned his attention to the next cuff.

Thought they could hold him, did they?

The half-second of smug superiority cost him. The hateful mass of rage and grief shattered his internal shields like so much sugar glass. Syrus had the space between one heartbeat and the next to realize what'd happened. Then the monster swallowed him whole, and the only thing he could do was try to aim it at the right target. *Kill them all,* he told it as its jaws closed over his throat. *Get the Kizrard. Alrurisi. Almovak. Live long enough. Kill them all!*

> Delfi

THIRTY-FIVE--DELFI

At the end of the parade, the various floats go their
separate ways to serve as centerpieces for the public feasts
put on by local rulers. If there is more than one feast, the
rulers themselves rotate from year to year between
locations so all may be blessed by their presence.
   -"Guide to the High Holidays of the Empire," Lady
   Katar lis Apap aso Arul

"What are you doing?" Panic now, in the air and through the bond. All Jossa's, not a whiff of it from anyone around them. Not that anyone was nearby. They were all off at the various feasts scattered around the city.

Which was perfect, because Delfi'd spotted a lot full of flits with a rental notice painted on the exposed pavement, and she didn't need any witnesses. Thankfully, Jossa realized what was going on, although she breathed curses all the way to the ground.

Delfi kept hers between her teeth, too focused on trying not to crash while keeping up the steady flow of emotion through the bond. She was numb to the pain now. The slice and burn of the distant rage had already done all the damage it could. All she could do now was try to endure and keep it from taking control of their combined emotions.

They thumped and skidded to a stop at the end of a row of battered and scuffed flits. Five minutes later they lifted off again, lighter some of the credit slips but still carrying the knives and power packs. Now all she needed was a heading. Reaching back to tap Jossa on the knee, Delfi asked "A'atsijah?"

And just like that, the pain was back. Delfi grunted when it hit the bond but managed to keep her eyes open so she could see where Jossa was pointing.

Of course. Why not? They only had to cover the whole city, or just about, to get to it.

Delfi turned the flit again, ignoring the warning flashing across the screen as she popped it out of one sky lane and over to the guidance of another.

Faster, faster, faster.

>>><<<

By the time they were able to pinpoint the correct feast, she was fairly sure that even a Numb could feel the emotion Syrus was putting out. Ancestors, she was surprised people weren't in the streets, pointing at the localized storm cloud parked over the middle of the city.

Behind her, Jossa breathed harder, fingers clutching convulsively at Delfi's waist. And not out of nerves either.

"Joss," Delfi growled in irritation, letting a wealth of meaning sink into the word. Don't do that. Don't make me crash us. Just stop being *you* for ten minutes.

Further proof that her shields across the bond were holding. Instead of being hurt by that last, Jossa growled under her breath and gave her sister an extra-hard pinch. Delfi narrowly avoided flipping the vehicle over on the x-axis and dumping the other woman right there.

Once she got the wobbling under control, she took a deep breath and gave the bond an experimental tug. A fresh wave of pain ripped through her brain. Delfi bared her teeth in the face of it.

As she thought. It was getting harder and harder to separate her own frustration from what she picked up via Jossa's sai.

They needed to get to Syrus, and fast, before his cancerous rage overtook them entirely.

And then they were out of time for childish bickering, because the center of the emotional storm cloud was there, right in front of them. And below it was a funnel laying waste to everything in its path.

Delfi circled the flit in a wide arc around the plaza, trying to get a handle on what she was seeing. And feeling. And *Hearing*. This close, she could filter words out of the general background hum of the citizens' minds. Not many words. Just a throbbing mental chant of *Kill, kill them all. Kill the Kizrard. Kill Appulu.*

Apparently her guess was correct that even a Numb would feel the knot of boiling rage, hatred and, yes, that other one was grief. If she hadn't seen it with her own eyes, if she didn't know that her siphon on Jossa was still in place, she'd wonder if her sister were the one causing all the mess.

But she knew, and Jossa wasn't, and still, there it was. A roiling, teeming mass of people. Pushing, shoving, coming together and breaking apart like birds on the wind as they fought, found new targets, and fought some more. Tables overturned, chairs turned into weapons, and bodies everywhere.

One end of the plaza seemed slightly calmer than the rest, but only because someone had had the presence of mind to turn over the largest table and form a sort of barricade across one corner of the triangular space between buildings. A few bodies in uniform lay draped over the table. A few more knelt, aiming weapons at the crowd, picking off anyone who came too close. She thought she saw the crushed remains of a flit before the crowd flowed and obscured it again.

Just before she turned her head to be sure she wouldn't ram the flit into a wall, a man behind the barricade stood up, shaking a cane at one of his companions. When she glanced back down, satisfied she had room for another pass, the man was on the ground, a puddle of blood leaking from his neck as the person who'd been on the receiving end of the cane shake flung something over the table and towards the crowd.

They were too late. Syrus had lost his mind. The prophecy was already fulfilled, just not the way she'd expected. Somehow, although she'd never thought he had enough Projective sai to reach past his own skin, he'd taken the whole feast down with him.

She wanted to bang her head against something. Stupid, stupid, stupid. Why hadn't she thought of that? Why had she assumed she'd be rescuing a sane and emotionally stable man instead of the rabid beast? Stupid! If he'd been at all in his right mind, she wouldn't be looking for him tied up in the middle of a feast to begin with!

Behind her, Jossa hissed and bumped her head into Delfi's shoulder. Giving the bond another yank to be sure the siphon was working, Delfi tucked the sudden spurt of fury down with all the rest of her stored emotions. Ancestor's Balls, couldn't anything go right anymore? Now what should she do?

Cut their losses, load Jossa on the flit, and make their own way off the planet? Or try to find Syrus and see if she could talk him down?

Leaving would be smarter, on the surface of things. They still had some time. They could dump this flit and get another. Go to ground for the rest of the day. She could pray to the Ancestors that the bounty hunters wouldn't find her and Jossa. And she could pray some more that whatever the fallout of the mess down on the ground, she'd be able to find a ship that could take them off world.

Too much prayer for things to go right when the plan was already blown.

Delfi looked down and back along their flight path. There. On the opposite side of the plaza from the people hiding behind the barricade.

A float, white and fluffy and entirely out of place. It should have been in the center of the feast. Or behind whatever officials were using this plaza as their designated public appearance for the day. Not on its own.

Even odder, there were no guards. None living, at least. A loose ring of bodies in uniform lie around the float. The flits were probably all that remained of any aerial guards. And she'd bet all their stolen credits that several of the shattered windows in the surrounding buildings had once hidden snipers.

This was the best chance they'd get. She'd already all but reached the finish line. Better to risk the crossing than start all over.

"Gatsljeh neh," she told Jossa as the flit set down on the crushed shells that surfaced the alley.

"I'm not a dog, to stay when you command," Jossa groused. "And why did we set down at all? It's too la—"

"Bojeh!" Delfi rounded on her sister, jabbing a finger in Jossa's bony collarbone. She *wanted* to wring her sister's scrawny neck, not settle for childish prodding.

The rage again. She needed to get ahold of herself. The more time she wasted here, the smaller the window of escape before Tarva and her people discovered them.

She couldn't keep this up much longer.

Jossa ignored her. "He's going to get loose and kill you! We need to get out of here, not serve our heads to him on a platter. You aren't strong enough to take him! If you die, I..." Jossa trailed off. Her mind churned, the welter of panicked thoughts mixing with her anger to bludgeon at the barrier Delfi held across the bond.

Delfi pulled on the siphon and brought the emotions over, feeling tears wet her cheeks as they scraped and tore at her heart.

Jossa. Always Jossa. Why, Ancestors? Why them? Why was she tied, heart and soul, to a woman who couldn't see past the end of her nose? What was it about the bond that obliterated all rational thought? She couldn't even make an escape without automatically taking Jossa into account. Ancestors, she should have just taken off on her own the minute she had a flit. It might've killed her soul, but at least she'd be free.

::Del.:: Jossa's mind twisted in on itself. ::Del, please. Please Del. Don't do this. Please.::

Delfi sighed. Now she'd done it. Syrus broadcasting unending fury and Jossa leaking panic faster than the siphon could pull it across the bond. All about to go up in a city-wide explosion of violence because one stupid Foreseer with a minor sai for Hearing couldn't keep her thoughts to herself.

The history books would never even know whose fault it was.

Delfi yanked on the bond again, throwing it open to its widest point. Grabbing double handfuls of the anger and desperation welling within her sister, she set her mental feet and hauled, pulling the emotions through the bond in a tangled knot that threatened to plug the connection before it was halfway through. She hauled again, shuddering as it sliced through her consciousness on its way to the abyss.

Jossa's panic faded, leeching out of the air around them to flow down the bond and etch itself into Delfi's brain. The pain lasted only a breath. The relief and exaltation hit harder, making her head spin as Jossa turned into the connection like a flower to a sun. Then the fury, rolling over her mind like a tsunami, mindless and devastating.

And finally, as Delfi tried to get a grip on the overflow, to direct it towards the empty maw where her heart should have been, *then* came the devastated agony, a solar flare of betrayed hope. She couldn't shield against it. Not if she wanted to keep it from ricocheting back out into the riot on the other side of the float.

Or worse, to Syrus.

She'd just have to keep her head. Remember that however angry she was, the bulk of it wasn't hers. It *wasn't*.

Jossa went limp, hitting the ground with a crunch of shells and nary a whimper of pain. Delfi didn't whimper either. She was too busy gasping for air that her lungs could no longer process. Too busy trying to wrestle all the feelings into a manageable stream.

She might've been too late to avert the prophecy. She didn't have to make it worse.

"Eyruth," she whispered, hearing her voice crack. So very, very sorry.

Jossa stared back at her with unseeing eyes.

So long as she could keep Jossa down, Feeling only at the subconscious level, she might be able to do this.

Kill them. Kill them all. Get the Kizrard. Alrurisi. Almovak. Just live long enough. Kill them.

She could practically hear Syrus's voice in her ear now that the volume on Jossa's emotional speaker was lowered. Although the crowd on the other side of the float was as loud as ever.

Snag the node near the right hand. Drag the left over. Fold the little circular pad thing around the end of the wire and shove it into the lock point of the housing.

Delfi spun to stare at the float as Syrus's mental chant shifted. She'd just run out of time.Stumbling and slipping on the loose shells, she lunged towards the float.

A pause in the litany.

She hit the side of the monstrosity and found herself elbow deep in white flowers, cellulose streamers, and cheap tinsel sperm cells. There was a gap in the flowers, partially hidden but still visible. Frantically, she shoved her hands into the mess and found a lever. Manual override. Thank the Ancestors.

The chant started up again, more frantic than before. *Kill them all! Get the Kizrard. Alrurisi. Almovak. Live long enough. Kill them all!*

Delfi yanked, nearly brained herself as the hatch popped open, and fought her way through the streamers of cellulose and into the belly of the float.

Mad brown eyes met hers in the dim light.

Syrus snarled.

THIRTY-SIX--DELFI

We may never know all the things these women are capable of.
-observations, Professor Rusithe, New Hopks College of Medicine

Syrus lunged for her, teeth bared, but fell back when he hit the ends of the tethers anchored to his body. His head was the first to go, and it took Delfi a second to push past her surprise in order to see the mass of wires wrapped around his body.

The way he stiffened in the chair he was tied to did not speak well for his physical well-being. The groan forced out between clenched teeth sounded even worse.

Then, just as suddenly, he relaxed and sat slumped among the cords and wires, sweat pouring down his face as he panted for breath.

Kill them, kill them all. Just live long enough. Kill them.

Outside the float, the noise of the mob rose. Delfi winced and finished crawling into the compartment, pulling the door closed behind her. Hopefully, she could get Syrus free before the crowd spilled out of the feast area of the plaza.

Syrus's low growl filled the tiny space, echoing off the metal around them and grating in her ears. His mental chant didn't change, but she didn't really expect it to. More surprising was the fact that he hadn't tried to attack her again.

What had they hit him with? Electricity? Drugs?

Both, probably.

Delfi threw up a few more shields to filter his mantra out of her mind and tried to peer into the shadows around the fuming man. The safety lights set into the base of the walls didn't illuminate enough for her to see much. What to do? Even if she could get him loose, she couldn't control him. He didn't need weapons to kill her, and she was at a disadvantage in grappling range.

She was at a disadvantage no matter what the circumstance, given his state of mind.

Syrus shifted in the chair, stiffened, then shifted again. His foot struck something that rattled across the floor. She looked harder. Was that a shackle key?

No time to wonder how it got there. The bigger question was how could she get to it without getting her head kicked in?

"Syrus?"

He jerked and grunted but gave no answer.

Too late, she remembered that even if she tried to talk him down, he wouldn't understand her. Although the urge to curse in the nehkeh dialect told her that she was picking him up just fine.

Another problem. This close to him, her shields were buckling dangerously fast. Worry should have been her strongest emotion at the moment. But here she was, hovering on the edge of frustrated anger instead. He'd picked up the chant in his mind again, a rhythmic undertone to the high chorus of the mob outside.

Beneath her, the planet rotated, implacable.

She needed to do something. And soon.

Slowly, carefully, she built up her shields again. She couldn't afford to rush this. She was running out of time, but she would run out of life expectancy if she did this wrong. Finally, when she was sure she'd put as much of a barrier between herself and Syrus as she could, she settled her weight over the balls of her feet. This would have to be quick.

Above her, Syrus twitched and growled again.

Lost her. Lost her. Need to get out of here. Didn't deserve her. My fault. Next arm. Didn't deserve her. Kill them all...

At least she hadn't made him worse.

She lunged, reaching for the key. Syrus barked something she didn't understand and kicked out. One foot caught her on the shoulder, twisting her to the side. She landed hard, scrabbled with one hand for the metal rod of the key, and found it just as his foot came back down to drive his heel into her collarbone. She caught most of the blow on the arm she'd left free. Bone bruise, at least. But not a broken collarbone, so she'd take it.

He didn't try to kick her again. He couldn't. His whole body was locked up. Something ground audibly. His teeth.

Right. Can't save him if he can't move.

She pulled herself to her feet, doing her best not to touch him. She managed, mostly. Bracing one hand on the armrest of the chair, she squinted at the mess of wires wrapped around the man's limbs.

Kill you, kill you. Bitch! Get out of this and kill you all.

"Gatsykk oli sujeks neh!" Delfi snarled at him without thinking. Then panicked as the sense of her own words penetrated the red haze starting to film her eyes.

The chant cut off abruptly.

Delfi paused her frantic reinforcing of her shields. Ancestors. Did he recognize her?

The current let him go. He groaned but didn't try to sit up.

Now, before he recovered enough to attack again.

One handful. Two. Legs cleared of wires and sensor pads.

She got one more bundle of wires off his arm before she ran out of time. Between one second and the next she found herself halfway across his lap, her wrist caught in one massive hand as he pulled and twisted. Delfi froze, feeling him staring at her back. That wasn't a human gaze. That was pure animal, a predator considering where best to attack.

Images of Rissa, long dead, scraped at the edges of her consciousness. As a child of eight or nine, with enormous eyes and dark hair, standing in a dusty street, another young girl hovering at the edges of her vision. As she and the girl laughed in a garden. As a young woman, sitting crumpled in the tangled limbs of her sousi, covered in blood and bruised from head to toe. Rissa laughing in sunlight, wearing a smile he hadn't seen in years.

A bloody arm hanging out of a Fleet medunit.

She knew that medunit. Knew that room. She'd woken up in it, just over a year ago. She'd thought she'd lost Jossa in that room.

Normally the images and words she saw came entire of themselves. No emotion. No greater clues as to the significance or intent.

Not these.

Rage, despair, grief, and guilt slammed into her, a maelstrom of feeling she could barely sort into its component parts. Distracted by the onslaught, she missed the hand reaching for her throat.

"Get the fuck out of my head." Syrus's snarl echoed dimly through her ears, the sense of his words lagging behind the sound.

She wanted to tell him to make her, but she couldn't get her voice to work. Couldn't draw in air. Couldn't force it through her larynx. His hands burned the skin from her body where he touched her. Her legs, draped awkwardly over his, were roasting.

Her shields melted faster than she could reinforce them, crumbling under a planet's worth of pent-up emotion.

Blackness crept in around the edges of her vision. She wasn't in the tiny compartment of the float anymore. She was pinned. Immobile beneath unwelcome weight. Real weight. Psychological. Physical pain laid over with the knowledge that she'd lost control and failed her sister and they were all going to die because of it.

Because she'd been too blind, too distracted, to see the truth.

The band around her throat tightened. She felt cartilage crunch and grate. Terror froze her heart.

No. Not again. She wouldn't let it happen again!

Fingers crooked into claws, she lashed out, found purchase, and dug in.

Syrus roared and reared back but didn't let go. Her head snapped back and forth as he shook her.

And her brain, stupid and slow as it was, finally clued into the fact that her hands were free.

Free. Not shackled and stuck to the floor.

This wasn't the room on the shadow base.

Suddenly she was furious. All outside the flood of rage battering the last of her shields, she wanted to make this man—this animal—*hurt*. She could have left him here. Should have! But she'd taken a chance that he'd be worth saving, and here she was. Getting the life choked out of her. Hovering in that liminal space where her sanity always failed her, turning her back into the panicked, frantic *child* that couldn't even look at a man without remembering what *this one* had saved her from.

She couldn't breathe. Couldn't force the air in or out.

She'd be no better than him in a moment. Just a mindless, drooling beast, pissing itself in a corner because she didn't have the guts to stand on her own.

The hand around her throat wasn't going anywhere. She couldn't escape that. But she still had her brain, in the few seconds left to her. She'd make him feel every bit of what he put her through. He'd been jumping up and down on her head for a *year* now.

Time to return the favor.

She reached for the pit. For the gaping hole that sat where her soul should be. The maw that swallowed all and gave nothing back.

It would now.

She made it just as her last shield fell. As the onslaught of guiltangerdespairhopelessness overtook her mind completely. Rissa, young and faithful, grown and battered, dead and mutilated, followed the Seer over the edge.

And the snarling man just behind.

THIRTY-SEVEN--SYRUS

*Build for yourself a home in your sai. Visualize it, and you
will always have a place to retreat to when the outer world
overwhelms.*
    -Chataf Kuchru isk Churus lis Kuchruis, to Jossa

He'd had the chance to look at her soul once before, back in the early
months of their race through the Empire. He'd forgotten the exact
details of the events. But he remembered thinking that if Jossa was a
flood, then Delfi was the deep ocean.

If only he'd known how wrong he was.

She wasn't an ocean. What lived inside her was so much bigger.
Vast as space itself. A black hole sucked in light, warping everything
around it, including time. A Barbican was a black hole harnessed for
human use.

This. This was...

"It's not what I planned."

Syrus turned to look at the young woman floating next to him in
the immense kaleidoscope of stars and colors. She was thin. Wan. A
figure of light and fire, dimmed in some way he couldn't understand.
He simply knew she was less than she could be.

He looked down at himself, curious. If a being could be made of slag and half-cooled rock, he'd fit the description. No clothes, he noticed. Neither of them. Yet they weren't exposed.

Ignorant of his eyes on her, Delfi gestured at the vastness before them. "You've been dumping emotion on my head ever since I woke up in that infirmary. Jossa's been doing it since I was six. There should be *something* here."

Stars in every direction. Nebulae that moved and shifted in real time.

This wasn't nothing.

"But it's not what I was looking for, either." She looked up at him, eyes disturbingly human in a face made of shadows and light and little of substance. There was anguish in those eyes. A hopelessness he knew all too well.

Without thinking, he reached for her.

She flinched away, drifting faster than he would've thought possible given she didn't have anything to push off of.

He sighed and dropped his hand. Figured. "What were you going to do with it?"

Her lips weren't red here. They were wrinkled. Puckered in as if she hadn't had water for so long she'd started shriveling in on herself. She still quirked them up at the corners. "I was going to dump it on *your* head."

He doubled over laughing. Little flakes of rock cracked and floated around him. Once he got the first round of hilarity over with, he brushed them out of his line of sight so he could get a better look at her. "That's a stupid idea."

She fiddled with her fingers and looked away. A star coalesced, burned, and blew up somewhere in the middle distance. The wave of energy would hit them soon. Would it push them back?

"If I'm going to die," she said softly. "Might as well do something I've wanted to for..." She trailed off and shrugged.

Syrus drifted closer. "Die?"

She didn't float away again. Instead she touched her throat. A shadow lay there. A dimness in the light beneath her skin. "You're suffocating me."

He jerked backwards and found himself half a mile away before he realized he'd moved. "Say what now?"

He didn't think she heard him. Too far away. And he was still moving. How the hell did he stop?

"You don't." She appeared next to him and poked him in the arm. He spun once, twice. Corkscrewing through space. Then she caught up to him again and matched his rotation. "You don't because you can't. You're stuck. I'm dying." She laughed, a disturbingly young sound. "And I'm entitled to use my last breath to do idiotic things like try to overload your brain with the agony of my existence."

Now he knew why she looked dim. Less than whole. Growling in frustration as the supernova of the dead star crossed his line of sight for the umpteenth time, he grabbed for her. It was hard. By now, her light was so dim she was more a blackness blocking out stars than she was internal light.

His hand landed on her throat, right over the shadow that banded it. "That's a stupid way to go out."

Her teeth flashed behind blackened and withered lips. "Then stop me."

>>><<<

Syrus knew he was too late. It was in the pallor of her skin. The slack way she slumped in his lap, held up only by his grip on her neck. But most of all, it was the lack of emotion. No anger. No fear. No determination.

He remembered feeling them as separate from the maelstrom inside his mind. She'd flared so bright he'd thought the only way he could save himself from the backwash of her self-immolation was to extinguish her entirely. Get rid of the obstacle she presented so he could go back to fighting free of the chair and getting on with his plan.

Kill everyone he could reach.

Live long enough to take out Rissa's family before he went down in a storm of plasma bolts.

Well, he'd killed the first person in reach.

And he didn't have any rage left to fuel the rest. Guilt, yes. Grief in spades. But he'd lost the fury somewhere in that galaxy she called a soul.

It wasn't until he felt the flutter that he realized he'd been rubbing his thumb over her carotid. He stopped and looked, as if he could tell with his eyes that his sense of touch wasn't lying to him.

Flutter.

Holy shit, she was still alive.

Carefully, he scooted her a bit closer. Her jaw dropped open at his touch. This was all wrong, but he couldn't move the one hand very far, and he couldn't even remember if they'd shackled his legs too. He'd have to do this with her upright and pray to.... whoever.... that she wasn't too far gone.

Flutter.

Weak. But there.

"What is it with you and me needing to fix your breathing," he muttered. Then he took a deep breath, eased her closer, and sealed his mouth over hers.

When he'd used up all his air, he pulled back and checked her pulse again. Still there.

Deep breath. Hold her head right, keep her airway open. Exhale into her mouth. Check the pulse.

And again.

She blew it all back at him on the third try, coughing and hacking before mewling in pain as she reached for her throat. He shifted her away so she wouldn't get her arms tangled in his. And so he could catch his breath.

They both choked and gasped a bit before things evened out. He recovered first, of course. He hadn't been the one nearly dead.

"Dump it all on my head, huh?" He tipped his chin towards her. "Looks like you took it all instead."

Her mouth, lips red now instead of pale and wrinkled, twisted. "More's the pity."

He blinked. He'd heard the words all right. She was still speaking He'la. But the understanding came to him whole, instead of the delayed and piecemeal fragments he'd learned here and there in the past year.

She frowned at him, confusion rippling under his hands. "What?"

He laughed and patted her cheek with his free hand. "Think you gave me the wrong thing." He held up a finger before she could snap her teeth at him. He could see her plan clear as day in her eyes. "Just don't go expecting me to translate for you if a Seeing hits."

She blinked. Her eyes went glassy and blank. He grunted as horror mixed with the stinging wind of surprise nearly flattened him where he sat. But she was back before he could do anything more than brace for the pain of landing.

"She's still there," the young woman whispered. "Still," she patted a hand on her sternum, "stuck there."

"Good." He let go of her neck and started hunting for a loose wire. "I've already had one sousi living in my head. Botched that all to hell and gone. Don't need another one." He eyed her. "Or two, to go messing life up any more than it is."

This time her surprise was like a hammer to the skull. She reeled back, almost fell off his lap, and scrabbled at his arms to keep herself in place. "You *what*?" she all but screeched, nearly losing her balance again as she waved her hands in the air. Apparently, the charades were here to stay.

Syrus gasped for breath as he tried to keep from headbutting her in the chest dumping her off his lap. "Son of a bitch, woman," he snarled.

She grabbed his jaw, hauling his face up so she could meet his eyes. "Just how many extra-super-special things *are* you?"

He pulled free and went back to hunting for a wire so he could short the other locks. His head was still ringing, but stars'd stopped popping in front of his eyes. And for a wonder, the beast inside stayed quiet. Distant even.

No time to wonder about that right now. Although... He peered at the young woman still sputtering and fuming, hands propped on her hips as she shifted her balance to stay seated. "How the fuck didn't you figure it out?" he asked her. "You spent weeks trying to dig through my head. You actually broke in, twice!" Although this last time probably didn't count, given they'd ended up in her mindscape instead of his.

She huffed and slid off his lap to crouch by his feet. "First, I didn't consider that you might be some variant of the Star Women. Only one in a thousand *women* saiog ever find a sousi. Why in Ancestors' names would I think *you* had? You kept seeing two women in your memories. Why wouldn't I think they were sousi to each other?"

Syrus snorted at the comparison to the mythological winged women and kept pawing at the bundles of wires hanging off the rig, trying to pull one free of the mass without zapping himself on all the loose ends. "That was Rissa's maid. They were almost like sisters"

Delfi glared up at him.

"Almost," he growled. "Non-saiog can be close too." He finally found a free end he could grab. "She died keeping Rissa alive." He shunted those memories aside as he tried to pull enough wire free of the mess to reach his other shackle.

Delfi ignored him as she knelt and stuck her head past his knee, reaching for something deep in the shadows. "In any case," she continued in a muffled voice, "I only dug around in your head to see if you'd murder us in our sleep."

"I told Jossa I'd get you to the Gatekeepers," he replied. "What the fuck are you doing down there?"

Low heat lashed his legs in warning. "Looking for the key. Don't kick me in the head again," she snapped, then went back to her explanation. "When I actually got in..." She paused. "I wasn't thinking straight enough to go looking for details."

Syrus frowned. The odd overlay of He'la and translation would take some getting used to. Easier to focus on that, though, than the acid etch of fear she'd left all over his legs.

Right. Because she'd been terrified out of her mind in the shower. *He'd* been the one scaring her. Syrus gritted his teeth and swallowed down the growl. He deserved whatever she dished out for that, well-intentioned or not.

Apparently, her sucking the monster into the metaphysical universe in her soul did not mean she could handle the knowledge of how vulnerable she was, even sitting on top of him.

He was about to tell her that feeling might never go away when she popped up to her knees, a blast of joy rippling out to punch him in the gut. She had the key in one hand.

She grinned at him. "Found it."

He pointed at his shackled arm. "Get it off then."

As she went to work on the lock, he started pulling the sensor pads off his head with the other hand, carefully because of how small the space was and how close she was. Fucking thing. How much of all that had the sensor picked up?

She finished before he did. He swatted her hands away when she made as if to help him. "Let me take care of it."

Then something occurred to him. He frowned at her. "What the fuck were you thinking, coming after me? You're supposed to be safe with the Gatekeepers."

Safe, away from him and the trouble he caused. Safe, under the care of Markos. Too bad he wasn't likely to get his hands on the Kizrard's nephew. There was one bastard who needed killing, that was for sure.

She didn't get a chance to answer him. Footsteps crunched over the ground somewhere nearby. Someone, male, spoke quietly. Someone else answered. "My lord, the mob."

"Does not preclude you from the duty of guarding this float." The voice was clearer now.

Delfi's eyes went wide. She yanked a knife hilt out of a slim pocket of her pants. Where the hell had she gotten that?

And where was Jossa?

And what was that about a mob?

Delfi looked at him, eyes huge. But that wasn't fear weltering off her; it was frustration leavened with a heavy dose of impotent rage, attacking his skin like biting insects made of fire.

He growled.

"Check the compartment and make sure the beast is still in there. Then lock it up. He'll keep until we get this mess sorted out." Now he recognized the voice. Appulu.

Delfi ducked low, making herself as small as possible. The door behind her swung open. A man in the Kizrard's livery stuck his head in.

Syrus bared his teeth at the man.

The guard took a second too long to realize that Syrus was no longer chained. Syrus lunged forward over Delfi and bowled right into the guard.

The man went over backwards with a shout of surprise. Fear etched patterns in Syrus's hands. He ignored the sensation and held tighter. Together, he and the guard fell out of the tiny cell in the middle of the float. Syrus pulled a fist back, letting the momentum of the fall drive it forward as they hit the ground. He caught the guard right in the jaw. It crunched and slipped sideways.

"Shoot him!" Appulu yelled.

Syrus was already moving. He threw himself to the side, away from the first wild shot, and lunged in under one man's arm. Grab, twist, and punch with the butt of the short-barreled gun. The guard went down. Syrus could smell overheated dirt behind him. Shit. Plasma. What moron put plasma weapons in the middle of a city?

A question for later. Syrus shied to the side again, away from the next round of fire, and came up on one knee, weapon raised.

There was no one to shoot.

Delfi stood over the body of Appulu, knife in one hand, her face and clothes spattered with blood. She didn't look at Syrus. She was staring off to the right.

Where Tarva and Agadi waited, tranq guns aimed.

Syrus turned, not out of hope but to confirm what he already knew.

Fieltar and Banuo were there. Also armed.

Before he could do much more than wonder where Nadi was, he heard the puff of air, felt a prick on his arm, and the world went fuzzy as it slid sideways.

"Got you, you son of a bitch," Tarva muttered.

His last conscious thought was that Quinn wouldn't appreciate having a warlord who'd been taken out by something as simple as a tranq dart.

> Syrus

EPILOGUE--SYRUS

Some say the Seps left us before we could cast them out for nonconformity. Others say we forced them to leave, and they cut us off in retaliation. But what's done is done.
They are Separate, and ever they strive to stay.
-unknown, Imperial Records 1029.11.20

Cold metal touched his shoulder, his cheek, and his ear. Light came next, bright blurs of gray in various shades. He tried to bring his hands up to rub the grit from his vision and found himself weighted down. Heavily weighted down.

Teeth clenched against the dizziness and nausea churning his stomach, Syrus got his hands under him, pushed off, and rolled onto his back. The surface beneath him gave a solid thud as his head made contact. Ow.

Cursing to himself, he tried seeing again. Still gray blurs, but slightly more in focus. His eyes still felt like someone'd dumped sand on his face.

"Fuck," he muttered.

"Wakey wakey," a woman said, her voice oozing cheer. "You overslept."

That wasn't Rissa. For one thing, he heard the voice with his ears. For another, she'd *never* been that cheerful of a morning.

Grunting as his neck complained about the movement, he turned his head towards the voice.

Tarva crouched on the other side of a translucent phasewall, her hands over her knees and a wicked smile on her face. He knew that smile. Someone was about to get gutted.

Probably him.

"Urg," he told her, then went back to looking at the ceiling. Dammit. Couldn't he catch a fucking break?

As least he understood why he felt like someone'd wrapped his head in cloth and beaten him senseless. Her sai, swamping his.

"Hey, lazy. Pay attention. You're ruining my fun."

He turned his head to look at Tarva.

She gave him a sharp smile. "Hope you enjoy the trip. It's going to be a short one. I'd like to make things longer for you, but we actually got paying cargo." She jerked a thumb over her shoulder. Syrus levered himself up on his elbows to see what she was pointing at.

In the middle of the cabin, Agadi and Fieltar were working at a table, which probably doubled as a screen based on how they touched and tapped at its surface. Past them, Banuo stood with his arms crossed, glaring at another translucent wall. A long strand of red hair curled across the floor near the man's boot.

Syrus looked at Tarva. "What happened to chaining us to a shitter so we didn't make a mess? Used to be your favorite thing."

She'd enjoyed making the people they caught and held for the military as unnerved as possible. If it were possible, her hatred of Navlad society ran deeper even than his.

She shrugged. "You ain't been out that long. Plus, you know how it works. And so do they, so there ain't much point."

Ah. That explained how Delfi had ended up on planet. Which meant Jossa probably hadn't been far away. He'd felt her, or thought he felt her, when Delfi'd done whatever the fuck it was she'd done to pull him out of his funk.

Also explained why Delfi'd been in such a hurry. She'd been trying to get him loose before Tarva and her crew showed up.

Well, the little Foreseer'd given it a first-class effort. If he hadn't been so much hassle to deal with, she probably would've managed it too.

He frowned. "Where's Nadi?"

Tarva's smile turned sour. "Your girls were a bit more than we expected. That's on me. Should've seen it coming, given the little redhead managed to zap Fiel with a fucking fibrillatory pad back in that Guest House. They pulled their prophecy bullshit and got Nadi to open the wall, then splattered her brains all over the inside of the cell." Her eyes sharpened. "They won't get a chance like that again."

No, but not for the reason she thought. He had his suspicions about how their prophecies worked, but as long as Tarva was holding her Null field over the ship, there wouldn't be any DEW systems operating out of Del's mind.

At the table, something pinged. Tarva twisted on the balls of her feet, watching with Syrus as Fieltar opened whatever it was on the surface of the table before him.

"Well?" Tarva asked when he didn't do anything.

Fiel frowned, bright green eyes narrowing as he looked up at her. "We're being recalled."

"What do you mean recalled? By who? If it's the buyer, tell them they can't recall us—we're already meeting them." Tarva stood and walked over to her second-in-command. Syrus gathered his arms under his body and levered himself into a half-sitting position.

"We're being recalled," Fiel said again, and slid the message across the table to Tarva.

She read it, shoulders a solid line of denial.

Agadi sat up slowly, closing out whatever he'd been working on. "Boss?" he asked.

"I won't," Tarva hissed. "I won't! We finally got him! Twenty-two fucking years, Fiel! Twenty-two years! And they want me to—? No! I won't do it!" She yanked the gun from her thigh holster and aimed it at Fiel.

On the far side of the room, Banuo got out of the line of fire.

Agadi rose to his feet, one hand on his weapons belt, eyes darting between Fiel and Tarva.

What the fuck?

"It's too late," Fiel said in a calm voice. "I already sent the acknowledgement. The course overrides are being locked into navigation right now. It's completely automated. And there's no failsafe. Shoot me. Kill me." He shrugged, hands out. "Won't matter."

"But we just fucking got him! He betrayed you too! He left you to die there in that factory, and I had to drag you out!"

Holy shit. She was actually shaking. Syrus got to his knees and used the wall to pull himself upright. Nobody noticed.

"I'm not Navlad," Fiel said. "I'm not even nehkeh. You've known this as long as you've known me."

It was true. His parents had left the Seps Coalition, run afoul of the Navlad government, and Fiel had wound up stuffed into the Uvlaku training program for the sole reason of his lack of nanites.

Syrus suddenly understood what was going on.

Tarva did too. "This whole time? This whole time you were—" She trailed off, sputtering. Banuo slipped up next to her, his own gun drawn. Agadi pushed away from the table. They'd wait, because they were her men, to see which way she'd jump before they followed her over a cliff.

They were loyal like that.

The way Fiel apparently wasn't.

Syrus leaned a shoulder against the wall of his cell, crossed his arms, and let a slow smile cross his face. "Looks like you got played, Tar. How'd they manage to wrap the noose around your neck?"

She spun to glare at him. "How much did you pay them? Where did you even get the money?"

He lifted a shoulder. "No money. Guess they just want me for me." Let the bitch sort that one out. He didn't know if Markos'd had anything to do with this, but he wouldn't be surprised.

He'd bet every nanite in his body that some high-level bureaucrat in what passed for the Seps government had decided they wanted Syrus in their territory. Markos had as much as said it back on the ship. They might hold themselves apart from the Empire, but they sure as fuck didn't ignore what happened in it.

And here he was. The blood of emperors flowed through his veins. He kept company with concubines bonded to that lineage. And, unbeknownst to any of the high-handed pricks on the Seps Council, he also had intel on the Svis Konanuog to trade. He'd have to keep that one in reserve as long as possible. Didn't want them thinking they had him entirely under control. Eventually he'd be able to leverage it into an escape of some sort.

So, it wasn't what he'd originally planned, but it beat the shit out of letting Tarva and her crew torture him. Or Quinn getting the girls back. Two sai, and Syrus had been dumb enough to hand the bastard exactly what he needed in order to control them.

It'd taken a while. And he'd done it the long way around. But it looked like he and the girls were going to make it to their destination after all.

He'd call it a win.

>>>><<<<

Thank you for reading! Reviews are an author's lifeblood. Good, bad, or indifferent, I'd love it if you'd leave a review!

If you'd like to read more in the world of Devour the Stars sign up for my newsletter at: https://www.artseklektos.com/ml-landingpage/ and get a free short story

HE'LA

A note on He'la pronunciation:

He'la is a syllabic language. Vowels are short, unless doubled, in which case they are given the long pronunciation. There are no silent Es or long vowels if only one consonant stands between them (which I attempted to show with the spelling of the words). I, for example. Mostly it is pronounced "ih". If it is seen as "ii", then it is pronounced "ee". Apostrophes have been added here and there, to indicate glottal stops or separate vowels where the form of the word means they'd otherwise be doubled. Go'o, for example, as seen below, would be "Go-oh"

A'appa'ih
> What?

Appare'its a'appa'ih zoturyj nihba?
> What the hell is that?

A'asheh zhuzhu ii'wehrich ritha nihba
> Ask him who wants him dead.

Bojeh
> Maybe it's not!

Eyruth

I'm sorry

Jeh
No.

Keh
Yes

Keha'oks nihba?
What is it?

Kiddach
Childish.

Neh!
Hey!

O'li zhuzhu i'rithaks keha'oks neh!?
What makes you think I didn't want him to?

O'zo.
We

Sheh
How?

Skaeksyj
Fuck

Shweshe'o. Sheh'o weshor jehokshuks nih. Jeh kiprinog nih. Nishbudo'yj nihba?
Professionals. Didn't know their employer. Connected to the cartels maybe? Not the Kiprinog.

Shynks neh! O'li uethga zo'li aksuks'yj nih. O'zo uethga Syrus ak-suk'yj nih. Shkrokro nihneh? Nuh phenshuch a'azudi'e nih.
This is important. We're stuck with each other and with him until we shake the hunters. Do you understand?

R Coots

Uppalith
    Ancestors

Uppalijaoth, nashe
    Holy Ancestors, she—

Zhuzhu jeha'o o'li innipi nih.
    He never touched me.

Zo'li o'li shuyeks kidda'yj neh!
    You treat me like a child!

Zo'li Syrus tsijach akkeks oksuks neh.
    I need to you to help me find Syrus.

Zoturyj nakekks neh! O'li jegah zo'li ra'eh zudieh sekkidl o'li lu ya'eo je'luhkoks neh!
    Fucking hell. I take my mind off you two for a second!

HIGH NAVLAD

A note on Navlad pronunciation

Like He'la, High Navlad is syllabic. Vowels are sounded out individually, even when they are next to each other. U, and O are usually given long sounds. E and A are short. If I is seen at the end of the word, it sounds like "ee", otherwise it is short.

Achek
> Ass

Adafek
> asshole

Ajiri
> Agriculture, designation for Earth-like planets where people can live without artificial life support.

Anek
> Bad test/ordeal

Asjokochek
> Breeding cunt

Astnuoj vifoggek
> Guttersnipe; literally, one who lives in the trash

R Coots

Bajbar
An animal genetically engineered to serve as underground guard for owners. Created using mostly badger and brown bear DNA.

Bittek
Bitch, literally: [morally] unclean dog

Chataf Kuchru
Head concubine literally: Guardian concubine

Dedaf-Priest
Death-priest

Degra op Lappuog
Dance of Birds

Disfesa
Sweetheart, literally: good heart/focus of attention

Fikkek
Fuck, Literally: [morally] unclean, illegitimate sex (likely to result in an unclean child)

Fikkek achek
Fucking asshole

Fikkekoj/Fickektoj
Verb of fikkek/past tense

Fuerrus
Highest Lord

isk Churusimpir lis Kuchrog lis isk Fuerrus
The imperial house of concubines of the emperor, Literally: The Imperial house of concubines belonging to [worshipful] Emperor

isk Churus lis Kuchruis
House of Concubines

isk Detriog lis Osagil
    The Battles of Osagil

Isloste
    Quadrant Commander

Kafe
    Coffee/caffeine

isk Kallura lis Kerute
    House of Guardian Strength

Karukap
    Military; Literally: strong allies.

Kiprinog
    Those of Kiprius

Kizrard Ejorum lis Azo af Azizate
    Sector Lord Ejorum of the Blood Born

Kovavek
    Commerce, designation for planets requiring life support systems before they can be settled. Usually used for gathering and processing of various resources.

Kristaf
    Christian

Kuchruogi
    Concubines, literally: Emperor's [legitimate for childbearing] mistresses

Lis Apap aso Arul
    Of rabbit and wolf

lis Tova af Mitachte
    House of the Thorn Moon

Marus-Priest
Blood-priest

Marusteog
Plural form of maruste

Maruste
Marks on back projected by nanites in blood, showing lineage, place of origin, trade, marriage, children, and any other pertinent information; Literally: Blood rank.

Nehkeh
subhuman, bestial, [untameable] savage

Obijaf lis Ralchuroj
Death tablet; literally: Tablet of Remembering

Odavek
Shit

Panris op Akuev
Lake of Many Blessings

Rard
Honorific/title to denote or address nobility

Rardog
Plural of Rard

Ruse lis Esab
Capitol of the solar system

Ruse lis Net
Capitol of the planet

Skatasi op Essi
Star Sister

Skolm lis dasal
　　Skin of the back

Svis Konanuog
　　Star Eaters; Literally: Those who consume stars.

Tarard Jirdis
　　Sub-Lord Jirdis

Tukov
　　Damn

Tukovoj skat
　　Damned girl, literally: torturing female

Uvlaklu
　　Military division, literally: Ghosts, undead

Vers fikekoj
　　Universe be fucked

About the Author

R Coots has been telling stories since the days of imaginary friends. Not serious until a two-week power outage meant that a pencil and paper were the only forms of entertainment, there have been several detours along the roads of comics, animation, and finally the written word. Aided by two neurotic dogs, a murderous cat, and a very down-to-earth husband, she exorcises the imaginary people in her head by means of art and writing, getting them out on paper so she can share them with the world.

Feel free to stop by my site for more on this universe, including art, blog posts, and the occasional bit of character silliness: https://www.artseklektos.com

www.ingramcontent.com/pod-product-compliance
Lightning Source LLC
Chambersburg PA
CBHW030849030726
47495CB00005B/1437